A Woman of Spirit

Also by Margaret Dickinson

Plough the Furrow
Sow the Seed
Reap the Harvest
The Miller's Daughter
Chaff Upon the Wind
The Fisher Lass
The Tulip Girl
The River Folk
Tangled Threads
Twisted Strands
Red Sky in the Morning
Without Sin
Pauper's Gold
Wish Me Luck
Sing As We Go
Suffragette Girl
Sons and Daughters
Forgive and Forget
Jenny's War
The Clippie Girls
Fairfield Hall
Welcome Home
The Buffer Girls
Daughters of Courage
The Poppy Girls
The Brooklands Girls
The Spitfire Sisters
Secrets at Bletchley Park
Wartime Friends
The Poacher's Daughter
A Mother's Sorrow
No Greater Love

Margaret Dickinson, a *Sunday Times* top ten bestseller, was born and brought up in Lincolnshire, where she lived for most of her life. She has written novels based not only in Lincolnshire but also in Nottinghamshire, Derbyshire, South Yorkshire and Leicestershire, where she now lives and where *A Woman of Spirit* is set.

Margaret Dickinson

A Woman of Spirit

MACMILLAN

First published 2026 by Macmillan
an imprint of Pan Macmillan
The Smithson, 6 Briset Street, London EC1M 5NR
EU representative: Macmillan Publishers Ireland Ltd, 1st Floor,
The Liffey Trust Centre, 117–126 Sheriff Street Upper,
Dublin 1, D01 YC43
Associated companies throughout the world

ISBN 978-1-0350-7686-4

Copyright © Margaret Dickinson 2026

The right of Margaret Dickinson to be identified as the
author of this work has been asserted in accordance
with the Copyright, Designs and Patents Act 1988.

All rights reserved. No part of this publication may be reproduced,
stored in a retrieval system, or transmitted, in any form, or by any means (including,
without limitation, electronic, mechanical, photocopying, recording or otherwise)
without the prior written permission of the publisher.

Pan Macmillan does not have any control over, or any responsibility for,
any author or third party websites (including, without limitation, URLs,
emails and QR codes) referred to in or on this book.

1 3 5 7 9 8 6 4 2

A CIP catalogue record for this book is available from the British Library.

Typeset in Sabon by Palimpsest Book Production Ltd, Falkirk, Stirlingshire
Printed and bound in the UK using 100% Renewable Electricity by CPI Group (UK) Ltd

This book is sold subject to the condition that it shall not, by way of
trade or otherwise, be lent, hired out, or otherwise circulated without
the publisher's prior consent in any form of binding or cover other than
that in which it is published and without a similar condition including this
condition being imposed on the subsequent purchaser. The publisher does not
authorize the use or reproduction of any part of this book in any manner
for the purpose of training artificial intelligence technologies or systems.
The publisher expressly reserves this book from the Text and Data Mining
exception in accordance with Article 4(3) of the European Union
Digital Single Market Directive 2019/790.

Visit **www.panmacmillan.com** to read more about all our books
and to buy them.

*Remembering the family members
we have loved and lost this year
Una, Betty, Trevor and Les*

Always in our thoughts

One

Leicestershire, June 1912

'They're following us again.'

Queenie tossed her blonde curls and swayed her hips. ''Course they are. Don't keep looking round, Moll. They'll think we're interested.'

Molly giggled. 'Well, aren't we? I reckon the way you're walking is sending that message very clearly. But if your mam catches you swinging your hips like that, you'll be in for a good hiding.'

'I'll mind she doesn't,' Queenie retorted.

'What? Give you a hiding?'

'No. Catch me.' She paused and then added in a whisper, 'By the way, Harry's mine, so keep your hands off.'

Molly and Queenie, born within a month of each other, had been best friends from the time they could toddle. They'd lived on the same terraced street in Loughborough since birth, and their mothers were friends. Molly's parents, the Wyngates, had moved into their house on their marriage. They already had a son, William, by the time the Palmers moved in four doors down.

'Welcome to the street,' Mabel Wyngate had greeted

the newcomer the first time she had met her. 'I see you're expecting like me.' She'd nodded towards the mound beneath Ethel Palmer's coat.

Ethel had beamed. 'I'm seven months gone. You?'

'The same,' Mabel had laughed.

'This is my first,' Ethel had confided and then glanced down at the little boy clinging to his mother's hand. 'How old's your young 'un?'

'Just turned two. He's a handful now. I can't chase after him like I used to, but my hubby's very good when he's at home. He takes him to the park whenever he can.'

'That's nice. My Jack wants a boy, but I'd like a girl that I'll be able to dress in pretty clothes . . .'

Over the months that followed, the two women became friends, especially when their babies – both girls – were born. Their husbands were already acquainted, for they worked at the same place in the town, the bellfoundry of John Taylor and Company, and also went to the same pub on a Saturday night. Over time, they too became friends.

The Spencer brothers lived two streets away and were well known in the neighbourhood. Harry, the elder by two years, was, even as a young boy, startlingly handsome. He had shiny black hair and dark brown eyes full of mischief. The girls in the neighbourhood vied with one another to walk out with him, or even just to talk to him in the street. Harry never took advantage of his popularity, although he was quite proud of his reputation as a lovable rogue. He was their mother's favourite and she made no secret of the fact. Aware of this, their father, a quiet, serious man, deliberately concentrated his attention on Ben, the younger brother, in an effort to even up the scales. Ben was like his father in character and in looks, with light brown hair and hazel eyes. Ben was a kind young man, and everyone said he was 'such a nice boy' but that he lacked the spark of his brother.

'That Harry,' they all said with an indulgent smile. 'He's a lovable rogue. But watch your daughters with him when he gets older. That's all I'd say.'

Molly and Queenie had known the brothers from the day they'd started at the local school. Boys and girls were separated in the classroom, so they only encountered each other on the way to and from school. Then, it had been pigtail-pulling or pelting the little girls with snowballs in winter. When he left school, Harry found work at The Brush Electrical Engineering Company Limited, where his father, Luke, also worked. Two years later, Ben had followed in his brother's footsteps.

The two girls, who were the same age as Ben, left school at that time too. Molly found work in a local hosiery factory, learning to be a stocking machinist. But Ethel, Queenie's mother, had higher aspirations for her daughter – her only child. It was she who found work for Queenie in a draper's shop in the centre of town.

'Such a refined atmosphere,' Ethel had told Mabel. 'She'll meet a better class of people working there. She'll be serving the ladies of quality who come in to choose fabrics to take to their dressmaker.' Ethel had sighed. 'How lovely it must be to be able to have your outfits made by a dressmaker.'

'Mr Gilmore's got a dressmaker who works in the back of his shop, hasn't he? I think her name's Miss Parkinson. Perhaps, when Queenie's been there a while, she could ask her to make something up for you,' Mabel had said, tongue-in-cheek, deliberately feeding her friend's aspirations.

The two women remained friends, but Mabel was aware of Ethel's ambitions. Jack Palmer had worked his way up to become a foreman at the bellfoundry and was well-liked by all the men under his supervision. Mabel was surprised the Palmers still lived in the same terraced house, but she supposed that even a foreman's wages wouldn't stretch far enough for them to move, especially considering the amount Ethel must spend on Queenie. The young girl seemed to have a new dress every few months.

Ethel's eyes had glinted at the thought of having a dress made especially for her. 'Maybe,' she'd murmured.

'Walk a bit slower, Moll,' Queenie said now. 'So they can catch up.'

'Oh Queenie, you'll get us into such trouble. My mam'll go mad . . .'

'Then don't tell her.'

'I won't have to,' Molly retorted. 'Someone'll see us with the lads. You know what gossips they are in our street.'

The girls often saw the Spencer brothers when they were all on their way to and from work. They met up a short distance from their own homes. In the early morning it was a rush not to be late, but in the evening, there was time for chat and even a little flirting.

'Ay up, you two. How's the prettiest girls in the neighbourhood, then?'

Queenie simpered and tilted her head to one side coquettishly but Molly hung her head. She was quite aware that she was not as pretty as her friend, nor as well-dressed. It was no use wearing fancy clothes to work in a factory, but Queenie could dress smartly. Indeed, it was almost a requisite for working in a drapery. Today, they were both wearing their working clothes, but there was still a sharp contrast between the two. Queenie wore a smart navy-blue costume with a ruffle of lace at her throat, while Molly's plain skirt and blouse were made from a coarse, grey material.

With her soft brown hair, dark eyes, smooth unblemished skin and regular features, Molly was by no means ugly, but, nevertheless, she faded into insignificance at the side of Queenie. With blonde curls and bright blue eyes, a perfectly shaped mouth and white, even teeth, everyone turned twice to look at Queenie Palmer. At sixteen, both girls now had a young woman's shapeliness – a fact that did not go unnoticed by the local lads, and especially the Spencer boys.

Harry, with his hands in his pockets, sauntered down the street beside Queenie. Ben fell into step with Molly.

'If you're not doin' owt on Sunday afternoon,' Harry asked, 'would you like to come for a walk in Queen's Park?' Before Queenie could reply, he added, 'Molly can come an' all. Ben'll look after her, won't you, Ben?'

Ben, towering above Molly, smiled down at her and said gallantly, "'Course. Be my pleasure.' But inside he was fuming. He liked Molly – she was a nice girl – but it was Queenie who disturbed his dreams. It was Queenie with whom he wanted to walk in the park. He sighed inwardly. As always, his brother had first pick. Harry had the first choice of everything. Their mam saw to that. Strangely, up until this moment, Ben had never felt resentment. He'd always been devoted to his elder brother and, as a youngster, had trotted happily in Harry's wake, following his lead in all things. The only unfairness had been when they both got into trouble: it was Ben who got the blame, never Harry. But even then, Ben hadn't minded. At least, not until this moment. Now he couldn't help feeling jealous as he saw Queenie daringly tuck her hand through Harry's arm as they walked a little ahead.

'I'm sorry,' Molly murmured at his side. 'You've no need to take me walking in the park, Ben.' With an unusual spark of boldness, she added, 'We don't have to do everything they tell us, you know.'

Ben laughed wryly. 'Don't we? I reckon we've both been doing it since we were kids.'

'We're sixteen now. It's high time we stood on our own two feet.'

'And you're going to do that, are you, Molly? Stand up to Queenie?'

Molly shrugged her shoulders. 'Probably not,' she said honestly with a wry smile, 'but you can.'

His eyes narrowed as he watched the couple in front of them, their heads bent together. 'Queenie's mam won't let her go to the park on Sunday without you, now will she?'

'No, but, like I say, there's no need for you to come. I can play the chaperone from a distance.'

'Not much fun for you, though, is it?'

If he only knew! It would break her heart to see Queenie flirting with Harry and him smiling in the way Molly wished he would look at her.

'Well – no – but . . .' She pulled in a deep breath as, trying to turn her thoughts away from her own broken dreams, she added bravely, 'Look, Ben, I can see it's Queenie you like. I can see it in your eyes every time you look at her. So why are you letting him . . .?'

'Do I have any choice?' Ben said bitterly. 'It's obvious that she likes him, not me.'

Molly sighed. She couldn't deny that. 'So, we're both getting hurt, are we?' she whispered.

Now she felt his gaze full on her, but she couldn't meet his eyes. 'Oh Molly, no. You don't mean – you can't mean – that you . . .?'

Molly squared her shoulders and forced a weak grin. ''Fraid so. We're a couple of drips, aren't we?'

Ben said nothing and for a while they walked on in silence.

'So,' he said at last, 'what are we going to do about Sunday?'

'I'll go with her,' Molly said. 'But, like I said, there's no need for you . . .'

'I'd like to, Molly. Honest. I do like you, but—'

'But not in the same way you like Queenie.'

'Well . . .' he said slowly, reluctant to admit the

truth, and yet he found he couldn't lie to her. He did like Molly – he liked her a lot – but, as she rightly said, not in the same way he hankered after Queenie. 'Look,' he added with sudden certainty. 'Let's you and me be friends, eh? Proper friends that can tell each other everything.'

It was unheard of in their world. Boys and girls played together as youngsters but, once they hit young adulthood, all that changed. Then, if a boy and a girl were seen talking or walking together, friends and family at once assumed they were courting. Both sets of parents would assess if they were 'suitable' for each other and the teasing among their peers would begin.

Molly giggled, her mood lightening. 'There'll be gossip.'

'I don't care if you don't.'

She glanced up at him. She liked the way a curl of his light brown hair flopped over his forehead. His eyes were kind and a lopsided grin crinkled the corners of his mouth. She sighed inwardly. She really liked him – but not in the same way she liked Harry. Ben couldn't make her heart flutter and her knees feel weak every time she saw him, but, if she were friends with Ben, then she would see Harry more often. And Ben too could see Queenie.

She didn't stop to think what heartache that might bring to both her and Ben.

Two

'You're not going strolling in the park with a lad on your own, Queenie Palmer, so you can forget it.'

'I won't be, Mam. Molly and Ben are coming.'

Ethel Palmer, a thin, wiry and energetic little woman, was slightly reassured. But only a little. 'Look me in the eyes, Queenie, and repeat that.'

Queenie returned her mother's gaze steadily. 'I promise me an' Harry won't be alone.'

'You'll stay together? The four of you?'

'Yes, Mam.' Queenie's gaze never wavered.

Her father, sitting in his chair in front of the kitchen range, dropped his newspaper. 'Aw, let her go, Ethel, me duck. Lasses need a bit of fun now and again. They work hard all week.'

'I know that, Jack, but it won't be you who has to face the gossip in the street if she comes home with a belly full, will it? You spoil her.' It was not often that Ethel used crude language – the language she'd been brought up around and had tried so hard to leave behind. It was only when she got angry that her resolve wavered and words from her childhood came out without being filtered.

Jack, a rotund, good-natured man with thinning hair, retreated behind his newspaper, muttering.

'Aye, mebbe I do, but she's the only one I've got to spoil.'

Luckily for Jack, Ethel, a little deaf in one ear, did not hear. It was a sorrow for both of them that they had not been blessed with more children and a subject that was rarely spoken about. But Queenie heard what her father had said and hid her smile. She was glad she was an only child. She liked being the centre of her father's attention, and even though Ethel was strict, Queenie could usually get what she wanted. Her mother never realized when she was being manipulated.

Ethel gave a little grunt and then nodded. 'All right then, but just mind you keep your promise.'

It was the greatest fear in Ethel's life that Queenie should 'get herself into trouble'. She would rather face poverty and hardship, even illness and death, than the shame of an unmarried, pregnant daughter.

It was a warm, sunny afternoon when Queenie knocked on the door of the Wyngates' home. The terraced houses they lived in were built in much the same way. The front door opened straight from the street into the parlour, which was used only on Sundays, Christmas and Easter. Through that was a tiny hallway where the stairs led up on the left-hand side – or right-hand side, depending on which house you were in – and beyond that the kitchen and then a small scullery. Upstairs there were three bedrooms, though one, where Molly slept, was only very small. Across the backyard was a wash-house and the privy. Bath night was on a Friday, in a tin bath in front of the range in the kitchen.

The men of the house went first and Molly – the last for a dip – usually found the water almost cold and covered with soapy scum.

"Lo, Aunty Mabel. Is Molly ready?'

'My, you look bonny.' Mabel Wyngate's broad smile lit up her face and made her brown eyes twinkle. She was round in build and, in Queenie's mind, resembled a cottage loaf. The vision was enhanced by the untidy bun of mousey hair on the top of her head. She was warm and welcoming to any visitor who knocked on her door, especially to the Palmers.

'Aye, she's ready. Been ready an' waiting this past hour.' She turned away slightly to shout over her shoulder. 'Molly – Queenie's here.'

Molly appeared behind her mother and Mabel moved aside. 'Now, you two, don't be late. I want you home before dark. Yer dads won't be too happy if they have to come looking for you, an' it'd be the last time they'd let you go.'

'Yes, Mam,' Molly said meekly and Queenie gave her a winning smile.

As the girls hurried down the street, Queenie said, 'My mam's made me promise that we'll all stay together. The four of us.'

'Mam didn't exactly say that, but I think that's what she'd expect too.'

'That's what we'll do today, but when Mam's got used to the idea of us walking out every Sunday afternoon and stops actually saying it,' Queenie went on, planning ahead, 'then we'll pair off. You'd like that, wouldn't you? To be on your own with Ben?'

No, I wouldn't, Molly wanted to shout. It's Harry

I want to be with. But of course she did nothing of the sort. Instead, she shrugged and said, 'We'd have to be careful. If your mam found out you'd deliberately disobeyed her, you'd be in real trouble. Let's see how it goes for a bit, eh?'

Queenie pulled a face, but deep down she knew Molly was right.

The brothers were waiting near the park gates. The four of them strolled through the park among the other youngsters, several of whom they knew: classmates from their school days and colleagues from their current places of work. There were one or two who lived on the same streets.

'Oho, trust the Spencer boys to get the pick of the bunch.' Tom Mayberry, who lived opposite the Spencers, walked jauntily towards them, sporting his Sunday best. 'Put a good word in with Queenie for us, Harry.'

Harry grinned and put his arm possessively around Queenie's shoulders. 'Not likely, Tom. You find your own girl.'

Tom guffawed loudly. 'Not much chance when you and your brother have got the best two in the neighbourhood.' He turned his attention to Queenie. 'Got any more pretty friends?'

Queenie tossed her blonde curls and her blue eyes sparkled. 'I'll see what I can do for you, Tom.'

The young man's face sobered suddenly as he added in a low voice, 'You want to watch yourself with Harry Spencer. He's a bit of a lad, y'know. Different girl every week, so they say. You'd be safer with Ben.' He nodded behind them towards where Ben and Molly were walking. 'Molly's got the right idea.'

Harry was frowning. 'What would you know about it, Tom Mayberry? You've never been able to get yourself a girl. They've all got more sense.' Harry's arm fell away from Queenie's shoulders as he stepped closer to Tom and seemed about to square up to him.

'Now, now, you two' – Ben hurried forward – 'you're not in the playground.'

For a brief moment Harry and Tom glared at each other and then Tom laughed again. 'He's right, y'know, Harry. We were always getting into a fight, you and me, weren't we?'

Harry stared at him for a few seconds, toe to toe, but then suddenly he too relaxed, smiled and stepped back. He landed a gentle, playful punch on Tom's shoulder. 'You're right, mate, and, if I remember right, I always won.'

'Most of the time, I grant you, but not always. There was one time when I sent you home with a bloody nose and your mam came marching across the street to our house to have a go at my mam.'

Harry threw back his head and laughed, the merry sound bouncing on the breeze. 'I remember that. Our mam's never one to let anyone touch her boys.'

Tom wasn't smiling now. He cast a quick glance at Ben – almost an apology – as he muttered, 'Aye, and especially you, Harry.'

There was a pause while the two young men eyeballed each other, then Tom laughed again, breaking the tension, and raised his cap saucily. 'I'll bid you good afternoon, gentlemen. Ladies.'

The four friends watched him go, swaggering with his hands in his pockets and whistling a cheerful tune.

Queenie put her arm through Harry's. 'He's a drip.'

'I could think of a stronger word, but I'm not one to use bad language in front of ladies.'

'Tom's all right,' Ben put in swiftly. 'He doesn't have an easy life with his mam being a widow. You should know that, Harry. He's always been the butt of people's jokes right from our schooldays. It's high time everyone was nicer to him.'

Harry pulled a comical face and then grinned. 'Aye, mebbe you're right, Ben. He's not a bad lad, but he's a bit of a mummy's boy, isn't he?'

'Hardly surprising. He's all she's got.'

Molly glanced up at Ben. How caring he is, she thought, sticking up for Tom even against his own brother.

'What's happening over there?' Queenie said as she caught sight of a small gathering beneath the trees. A woman, dressed in a white gown and wearing a green hat with a purple feather, was standing on a chair speaking to a group of women clustered around her. Above her head was a banner strung between two poles, held aloft by two women. VOTES FOR WOMEN was printed in bold lettering on the banner.

'Oh, it's them ridiculous suffragettes,' Harry said scathingly. 'Come on, we don't want to get involved with them. We hear enough about that at home from our mam.'

'Well, I want to know.' Queenie pulled her arm from Harry's. 'Come on, Moll. Let's have a listen to what they're saying.'

A Woman of Spirit

'Queenie, I don't think we should,' Molly said tentatively. 'What would your mam say?'

'My mam's not here.' She turned and glared at Molly. 'And you're not going to tell her, are you?'

'No, of course not, but—'

'Then come on.' Queenie turned away and began to march across the grass towards the women.

'I'd better go with her,' Molly said apologetically to Ben.

The two brothers were left staring after the girls.

'That's that, then,' Harry muttered. 'I'm not going to be seen with a load of mad women. I'm off home.'

'But I thought you wanted to be with Queenie?'

Harry shrugged. 'It seems she's got more important things to do with her Sunday afternoon. You coming?'

Ben stared after the two girls, who had now reached the small crowd of women. Although he couldn't hear what was being said, Ben could see the woman addressing the crowd, gesticulating and turning from side to side as she delivered her message.

'We shouldn't leave the girls on their own,' he murmured. 'Besides, I wouldn't mind hearing what she's got to say. It might help us to understand a bit more what Mam's always going on about.'

Harry made a derogatory sound. 'You're on your own, then, mate. I'm off. See you later.'

Ben crossed the grass to stand behind the two girls just in time to hear the speaker say, 'Now, ladies, are you with us?'

With one voice – including Queenie and Molly – they shouted back, 'Yes, we're with you.'

The speaker stepped down and began to hand out

leaflets. She was soon engulfed by several women clustering around her, eager to speak to her personally.

'We ought to go,' Ben said.

'Not yet, Ben,' Queenie said. 'I want to know how we join.'

'Join what?'

'The suffragette movement, of course. I've heard about it, but I didn't know we'd got anything going on here.'

'Oh, Queenie, I wouldn't . . .'

Queenie whipped round and glared at him, her chin jutting out ominously. 'You wouldn't what, Ben Spencer?'

'G-get involved.' Ben stuttered a little in the face of her disapproval. 'Your mam—'

'My – mam – is – not – here,' Queenie said, emphasizing every word. 'And if either of you tell her, I'll never speak to you again.'

Ben and Molly exchanged a glance and knew themselves beaten. Suddenly, Queenie's mood switched. She smiled winningly up at Ben and put her arm through his. 'Oh, come on, Ben. See it from our point of view, eh? You fellas have got it all. It's a man's world. But we live in it too. We should have the right to say what government should rule us. We should have a woman in Parliament.'

Ben laughed. 'That'll never happen.'

'Don't you be so sure. With people like Mrs Pankhurst, we'll get the vote one day, you'll see. But she needs all us women to support her.'

'Are you going to join the marches, then?'

'I might,' Queenie said boldly.

A Woman of Spirit

'Not if your mam hears about it, you won't.'

Queenie pulled a face. 'I'll worry about that when it happens. In the meantime . . .' She looked behind her, but the crowd had now dispersed. 'Oh bother, you've made me miss getting a chance to have a word with the speaker.'

'I think they come here most weekends,' Ben said, trying to get back into Queenie's good books.

'*Do* they? Thanks for that, Ben. Come on, then, we'd best go home, seeing as Harry's gone off in a huff.' She pulled on Ben's arm, turning him round. They began to walk back the way they had come. Now she was looking up at him, smiling and laughing, almost flirting. For a moment, Molly stood staring after them. Although Queenie was her dearest friend, for a brief moment she felt a stab of envy.

Why did the girl get her own way in everything?

Three

'So, did you have a nice time, love?' Mabel Wyngate asked.

'Yes thanks, Mam.'

The older woman's smile widened. 'So which of the Spencer boys have you set your cap at, then?'

Still smarting a little at the ease with which Queenie seemed able to capture the attention of anyone she chose, Molly said, 'Neither of them, really. What chance do I have against Queenie?'

'Aw, don't put yourself down, love. You're a pretty girl too.'

Molly sighed. 'But I can't hold a candle to her, now can I? Let's be honest. The boys hardly look at me when she's around.'

Mabel was silent for a moment as she regarded her daughter solemnly. 'It's just as important to be a nice, kind and truthful girl. You're certainly that. Sometimes, I'm not quite sure about Queenie. I think she's got a devious streak in her. Just be careful she doesn't – well – *use* you in some way to get what she wants.'

Molly stared at her. 'But you're friends with Queenie's mam. Aunty Ethel is your best friend.'

'I know that. We've been friends ever since they

came to live here, just before you two girls were born, but that doesn't mean I'm blind to her faults – or her daughter's.' Now she was smiling again as she said softly, 'And you can tell me anything, you know. Mothers and daughters always share secrets. Things you can't tell anyone else, not even your best friend. And certainly not a man. Your dad is a good man – the best – and a wonderful father, but men don't understand the emotions a young girl goes through as she's growing up.'

'I don't think Queenie would confide in her mam,' Molly said slowly.

Mabel gave an unladylike snort of laughter. 'Now that is one of Ethel's faults I'm well aware of. Much as I like her, there's no softness about her. She's hard as nails. All she really cares about is what the neighbours think and having the cleanest front doorstep in the street.' She chuckled. 'You know as well as I do she's first out on a Friday morning to donkey-stone her step before she goes into town to shop for the weekend.'

All the housewives on their street followed the same pattern of housework. Washday was on a Monday, when all the women would be in their wash-houses in the backyards, coppers boiling and dolly pegs pounding the clothes in the tubs. The air would be alive with laughter as the women called to one another over the fences between them. Then the wet washing would be pegged on a clothesline strung across the yard to dry. Tuesday was ironing day; Wednesday cleaning the house from top to bottom; Thursday was baking day and Friday whitening the front doorstep and then shopping in the town, though there were additional trips to get the bargains on market days.

'So,' Mabel said, 'you still haven't answered my question. Which of the Spencer boys do you like the best?'

Molly hesitated and then decided she needed to have someone she could tell. Queenie was not the one, and there was no one else among her peers to whom she was close enough to confide such secrets. She took a deep breath. 'I like Ben. We're friends, but it's Harry I really like.' She shrugged. 'You know what I mean.'

Her mother did indeed know. 'Aw love, I can see why, but it's a shame it's not Ben who's your favourite. He's a nice lad but Harry's a bit of a one for the girls. He'd break your heart.'

Molly lifted her chin. 'Aye, mebbe he would, but it's not me he likes. It's Queenie and – and she likes him. So, there you have it, Mam.'

'To be honest, love, I don't quite know how to advise you on this one. See, there was never anyone else but your dad for me and, luckily, he felt the same about me. We began walking out – in secret, mind – from when we were fifteen. I never had another boyfriend.'

Molly smiled. She witnessed her parents' love for each other every day and was thankful for it. She and her brother knew how fortunate they were. They often heard from their peers of turbulent home lives. Even Queenie's parents bickered at one another and, although Queenie had everything that she wanted materially, Molly was astute enough to know that a happy, settled home life was far preferable to possessions. She felt too – though she never said anything – that Queenie's parents vied with one another to spoil their only child and win her affection. Molly was sensible enough to realize that you couldn't buy love. She loved her parents unconditionally, not because of the presents they gave her. She had the sneaking suspicion that Queenie played her parents against one another to get what she wanted.

Mabel broke into her thoughts. 'What's going on in that head of yours?' she asked softly. 'Because I can see there's something.'

'I was just thinking, Mam, how unlucky Queenie is to be an only child.'

Mabel blinked. 'Unlucky? You surprise me. She gets all sorts of things that we can't afford to give you and your brother. Mind you, it is a bit easier now that you and William are both working.'

Molly pulled a face. 'We don't give you much for our keep though, do we?'

'You don't earn much yet, love, either of you. William's doing well with his training at the foundry and you at the hosiery factory, but you're both still learning. You can't expect to earn much yet.' She paused and then asked, 'What did you mean about Queenie being unlucky?'

'I – I can't explain it really, just a feeling that despite all the things she has, she's not all that happy.'

'Her mam's very strict with her, I'll give you that. She doesn't seem to trust her.' She eyed Molly as she added, 'Not like I trust you. Just don't let her lead you into doing things that you know aren't right.'

'I won't, Mam, I promise.'

They didn't see the brothers that week.

'I don't think Harry liked you running off to listen to that suffragette woman,' Molly said after work on the Friday night.

Queenie tossed her curls. 'If that's true, then he's not worth bothering about.' Her eyes shone. 'I did it to try Harry out – to see if he'd hang around and wait for us.'

'But he didn't.'

'No,' Queenie pulled a face, 'he didn't.' She was thoughtful as she murmured, 'I'll have to think of another way to make him jealous. Maybe if I flirt with Ben . . .'

'Oh Queenie, that would be so unfair on Ben.'

Queenie grinned. 'Because he likes me an' all, you mean?'

Molly gaped at her friend. So, Queenie had guessed what Ben's feelings for her were. Now Queenie was laughing out loud. 'Oh Moll, you're so naive. You should know by the way a boy looks at you if he fancies you.'

'Maybe I don't know because they don't look at me in that way,' Molly was stung to retort.

'Oh Moll,' Queenie said at once, contrite, 'don't let you and me fall out over a fella. None of them are worth it. We're best friends. We're Forever Friends. Don't let anyone else spoil that.'

A Woman of Spirit

'Mam says that once you get a boyfriend, you lose your girlfriends,' Molly said.

'Well, that's not going to happen to us.' Queenie linked her arm through Molly's as they walked towards home. 'Look, were you actually interested in what that suffragette had to say?'

'Yes, I was. We only caught the end of her speech but I thought some of the things we did hear were right; that women should have a greater say in how the country is run.'

'Then we'll go to the park again on Sunday afternoon and see if she's there.'

'Oh, I don't know . . .' Molly began.

'Go on, Moll. We're not doing any harm. It's high time we started learning about real life for ourselves and not just following whatever our parents tell us. We're sixteen. We've been working women for four years. We're old enough to get married now and start having babies.'

'Is that what you want?'

'Yes. Especially if it's to Harry Spencer. Isn't that what you want too?'

Oh Queenie, Molly thought. If only you knew. Aloud she said, 'Yes, but not yet. I want to *live* a little. See a bit of the world, maybe. *Do* something with my life before I become tied to the kitchen sink.'

'But isn't that what girls are expected to do? Get married, look after their husbands and have a family. "A woman's place is in the home", isn't it? That's what my dad always says. And my mam, too, if I'm honest, even though at the moment it seems the last thing she wants me to do is to get involved with a lad. She's terrified of me "letting them go too far", as she puts it.'

'Marriage and babies is all right for our mams and their mams before them, but not for us, Queenie. And what about those women who don't get married? The ones who are spinsters the whole of their lives—' She paused, thinking that she might well be one of them. Perhaps she would never find a man to love her. 'There's a big, wide world out there, but we're not allowed to be a part of it just because we're girls. Well, the suffragettes are trying to change that. I've been reading the leaflets they handed out last week. They think women should have the same rights as men. Be able to do the same jobs as men, if they want to, and have equal pay.'

Queenie laughed. 'That'll never happen. You couldn't have women working as miners, now could you?'

'They used to in times gone by. And children. Didn't you listen in history lessons?'

'So, what do *you* want, Moll?'

'I want to be treated as an equal with men, and that's what these suffragettes want. So, yes, we'll go again on Sunday.'

'My word, Molly Wyngate, you are coming out of your shell all of a sudden.'

Molly merely smiled but did not say any more. Deep inside her she knew that, in listening to the speaker in the park and reading the leaflet, she had found a new strength that she didn't know she had. Not until this moment.

*

A Woman of Spirit

When the girls went to the park the following Sunday afternoon, there was still no sign of the Spencer brothers. Molly didn't know whether to be pleased or sorry. Pleased because she wouldn't have the heartache of watching Queenie flirting with Harry, but sorry because it meant she wouldn't see him for herself either. And, strange though it seemed, she had enjoyed Ben's company too. He was someone she instinctively knew she could trust. But now, she told herself sternly, she had something else to focus on, instead of mooning after a boy she couldn't have.

'Look,' Molly gripped Queenie's arm as they entered the park, 'just look at all the women and girls heading towards where that speaker was last week. Come on, let's hurry . . .'

As they arrived beneath the trees at one side of the park, the woman they had seen the previous week was climbing onto a chair to face the gathering in front of her. They were a mixed bunch, Molly thought, as she glanced around her. The oldest there was probably a grandmother, the youngest a little girl of about ten clinging to her mother's hand.

'Thank you for coming today,' the woman standing on the chair began. 'It is encouraging to see so many of you. We all share a common cause, that of equal rights for women. We want the vote alongside our menfolk. Women who own property have to pay taxes just like men. Why should they not be able to vote – just like the men – for the Members of Parliament and ministers who set those very taxes?'

'What about women who don't own property?

We're not all wealthy,' someone from the crowd shouted.

The suffragette responded at once. 'But we're all affected by the laws of the land which the politicians make – we have to obey them – so we should have a say in choosing those who make the laws.'

'But they're all men in Parliament. They're never going to listen to the likes of us. They're never going to listen to *women*.'

'Members of Parliament are supposed to listen to their constituents, to carry their wishes and, yes, sometimes their grievances, to the House. And we're their constituents just the same as our husbands, fathers and brothers are, aren't we? And we believe that if women had the vote, Members of Parliament would treat matters affecting women more seriously.'

'My brother doesn't get the vote yet because he's not a householder,' a voice from the back spoke up. 'Not all men get it yet either.'

'You're right and that's unfair too,' the speaker agreed at once. 'Everyone over a certain age – *everyone,* men and women – should have the right to vote. So, I ask you, are you with us?'

'Yes!' came the chorus from all those listening to her.

Four

As the meeting broke up and the women and girls began to disperse to their own homes, Queenie and Molly walked back towards the park gates.

'So, what do you think?' Queenie said. 'Shall we join the local branch of the Women's Social and Political Union?'

'Are they the ones that are militant? That – that go around smashing windows and chaining themselves to railings? Because I don't fancy doing that.'

'If you want something in this life, Moll, you've got to go out and get it, not sit and wait for it to come to you, because it won't. I do agree with her in that.'

Molly laughed. 'You've changed your tune. The other day you were all for getting married and having babies. Now, suddenly, you're wanting to rule the world. Make up your mind what you want.'

Suddenly, Queenie grabbed Molly's arm. 'Look! Look who's over there.'

Molly glanced up to see the Spencer brothers standing just inside the park gates.

'They're waiting for us,' Queenie said.

'I wouldn't bet on it,' Molly said. 'Harry went off in a right bad mood last week and we haven't seen them since.'

Queenie's smile widened. 'You don't want to let a lad think you're too keen on him.'

'I don't understand.'

Queenie sighed excessively. 'If you're a bit offhand with them, it keeps them interested.'

'Does it? So, you think that's what Harry's doing to you?'

'Oh no, Moll. It's what I'm doing to him. It's for the lads to do the chasing, not us.'

Molly giggled. 'Oh, so all that swinging your hips and walking slowly so they could catch us up, isn't chasing them?'

''Course it isn't. Just' – Queenie waved her hand in the air – 'helping them on a bit. Anyway, let's see if it's us they're waiting for.'

'I bet it isn't. You had your chance, Queenie. Harry isn't used to being deserted.'

Queenie tossed her curls. 'That's his look out, then. There're plenty more fish in the sea.'

Yes, Molly thought, there are, but they're not like Harry Spencer.

As they neared the brothers, Harry called out, 'Hello, girls. Been to your meeting?'

'What's it to you if we have?' Queenie retorted, but she was smiling as she said it.

'Because you missed spending the afternoon with the two handsomest boys in the town.'

'Full of yourself, aren't you?' But she fell into step beside Harry as they left the park and turned in the direction of their street. Molly, glancing up at Ben, who towered over her by a good six inches, walked beside him.

'Are you really interested in this suffragette nonsense or are you just following Queenie?' Ben asked.

His remark stung. She didn't want anyone – least of all Ben – to think that she just followed Queenie's lead, that she didn't have a mind of her own and yet, that's perhaps what it looked like to others. And deep inside her, a little voice prodded at her conscience. Yes, you do follow her in everything. You always have done.

She pulled in a deep breath and said carefully, 'I'd like to know what they stand for and what they're trying to achieve before I make a firm commitment, but I certainly don't want to get involved in any militant stuff.'

'Just be careful, Molly, that's all I'm saying. Queenie can be hot-headed. I wouldn't like to see you get into trouble because of her.'

'I thought you – *liked* Queenie.' The emphasis on the word let him know that she was well aware of his true feelings for her friend.

Ben smiled ruefully. 'I do, but it doesn't make me blind to her faults.' He paused and then asked, 'So, was the meeting interesting?'

'Yes, it was.' She went on to tell him much of what the speaker had said, ending, 'Basically what she said was that all those who have to obey the law should have a say in choosing those who make the laws. And women especially should have the right to voice their opinion on such matters that apply to the home or to children. But I don't suppose you'd agree with any of it, being a man.'

He walked in silence for several moments before saying slowly, 'Actually, I do understand. Our mam has a lot of sympathy with what the "Votes for Women" brigade are saying.'

'Really?' Molly was surprised. She didn't know Mrs Spencer well – only by sight – but it had never crossed her mind that someone who was from the same streets as her own family would be interested in such a progressive movement. Her own mother certainly wasn't and she doubted if Queenie's mam would be either. Then she remembered what Harry had said a while back about the brothers hearing about 'the ridiculous suffragettes' at home.

'Has she been to their meetings, then?' she asked.

Ben nodded. 'Not here, not in the park, but she's been to one or two in the town hall. If you want to know more about them, why don't you come round to our house? I'm sure Mam would be happy to talk to you about it.'

'I'll ask Queenie. See what she thinks.'

'Oh, I didn't mean—' Ben began and then stopped in embarrassment, but Molly was quick on the uptake.

'You don't want me to bring Queenie?'

'It's just—' He sighed. 'Oh, I suppose it'll be all right. It's just that Mam has high hopes for Harry. She thinks he can work his way up in the factory and that if he gets involved with a girl . . .'

Molly chuckled. 'She doesn't know her son very well, then, does she? Harry will *always* be involved with a girl.'

Ben had the good grace to grin sheepishly. 'I suppose you're right. I'm glad you can see him for what he really is, Molly. That way, perhaps you won't get so hurt.'

'Oh, I know exactly where I stand with Harry. Right at the back of the queue.'

'Don't say that. You're a lovely girl.'

'And you're a lovely bloke,' she said, smiling up at him and impulsively hooking her arm through his. 'But we both know where we stand, now don't we? So come on, what more do you know about the suffragettes?'

'Not much. I haven't taken a lot of notice, to be honest.'

'What does your dad think of your mam being involved? Does he mind?'

Ben wrinkled his forehead. 'No, actually, he's all in favour of it. He reckons women get a raw deal a lot of the time. He doesn't agree with a woman being expected to wait on a man hand and foot and obey his every whim.'

'Would you ask your mam if I can go round to see her some time? I won't bring Queenie.'

'All right, but I don't think she'd mind you just calling round.'

Molly shook her head. 'It's only polite to ask her first. My mam's big on politeness.'

Ben grinned down at her. 'D'you know something, Molly Wyngate? You're a very nice girl.'

Molly blushed. It was a lovely compliment – just not quite the one she would have liked to hear, or from the person she'd have liked to have heard it from. But it would do.

On the Thursday evening when they met up after work to walk the last few streets towards their home, Queenie said, 'Can you do me a favour, Moll? Go to our house and tell my mam I've got to work late. Miss Parkinson – you know, the woman who works as a dressmaker behind the shop – is making me a dress and I've got to go back for a fitting. Mr Gilmore won't let her do it during opening hours. Harry's asked me to go out with him on Saturday night but Mam doesn't know that, so don't you go telling your mam or she might tell mine. So, are you waiting for Ben on the corner as usual?'

Molly's heart plummeted. 'Oh – er – yes – all right.'

Queenie squeezed Molly's arm. 'Thanks. You're a pal. See you tomorrow.'

Queenie hurried away, waving to Ben, who was already standing on the corner. Molly stared after her friend. Harry had asked Queenie to go out with him. That must mean they were courting. Her footsteps slowed and her head was bent as she reached Ben.

'You all right, Molly? You look as if you've lost a sixpence and found a farthing.'

Although there was a lump in her throat, she managed not to let the tears fall. When she told him about Queenie and his brother, for a moment, Ben's face too turned bleak. He sighed. 'Oh well, I suppose it was to be expected. Ne'er mind, Molly. Look, why don't you come round now to see me mam and talk to her about the suffragettes? She said it'd be all right if you came any night after work on your way home. Harry's working late, so he won't be there.'

'Well, I would, but I'm in me working clothes. I look a mess.'

Ben smiled. 'No, you don't. You look perfectly fine. Besides, me mam admires girls who work hard. Your working clothes are a badge of achievement to her, and they don't get as dirty as ours do.'

'All right, then. I suppose it'd be a good idea to go now. At least there's no Queenie tonight.'

'Where's she gone? I saw her rushing off.'

'Back to work. The dressmaker there is making a new dress for . . . for Saturday.'

'Ah,' he said, understanding at once. 'Come on, then. Let's hope Mam's got the kettle on.'

'Come away in, me duck,' Harriet Spencer called out when Ben ushered Molly in through the back door. 'And sit yourself down. Ben tells me you want to hear all about the suffragettes.'

'We've seen a speaker in the park, Mrs Spencer, and I'd really like to know a bit more about them.'

'Very sensible, I call that,' Harriet said as she set a cup of tea and a plate with two biscuits on it in front of Molly. The girl didn't know Harriet Spencer well, though of course she'd seen her many times over the years. Now, close to, Molly could see that it was from his mother that Harry got his good looks. Her abundant black hair was swept back from her face. Strands of grey were just appearing at her temples but she was still a fine-looking woman, tall and straight-backed.

'Right, I'll leave you to it,' Ben said, 'and get out of my mucky clothes. See you later, Molly.'

When the door leading further into the house closed, Harriet asked bluntly, 'Are you and Ben courting?'

Molly shook her head. 'No, Mrs Spencer, but we're really good friends.'

Harriet looked sceptical. 'I'm not sure that can work between a boy and a girl. That "liking" might become a bit more than that on one side or the other, and then someone's going to get hurt.'

Molly decided to be honest without telling her the whole truth. 'We like each other very much but not in a romantic way. We just want to be friends, that's all.'

'Ah well, we'll see how it goes, eh? Now then, let me tell you about what the suffragettes are aiming to do . . .'

Five

For the next hour, Harriet explained what the movement hoped to achieve.

'Early in the 1800s, women had few rights. They depended on their menfolk and, if they were not fortunate enough to have a good and caring husband, then there was little they could do. They had no independence, few rights to education or work and even less legal protection. It was a man's world, Molly, and it still is in many ways.

'In the mid-1800s, various societies were set up throughout the country, but towards the end of the century, a lady called Millicent Fawcett brought all these separate societies together with the formation of the NUWSS – the National Union of Women's Suffrage Societies. They were called suffragists. Their aim was peaceful protest by writing letters to politicians, putting up posters, organizing petitions and making speeches. They got a certain amount of publicity, it's true, and their membership grew. But for some women the progress was too slow. They weren't getting any attention from Parliament and they felt more action was needed.'

'What sort of action?'

'Something that would make people sit up and take notice. Mrs Pankhurst . . .'

'I've heard of her,' Molly said.

Harriet nodded and then continued. 'She set up an alternative society, the WSPU – the Women's Social and Political Union. Their motto is "Deeds not Words". That's the society we have here. Two years ago, she spoke at two meetings in the town hall here. She told us that none of the political parties would help, so we have to find a way to make them. Members of the Liberal Party had promised to give them the vote but had failed to fulfil that promise. I heard her speak and was so impressed I joined the local branch there and then.'

Molly's eyes widened almost as if she knew what was coming next. 'What – what *deeds* do they do?'

'All sorts.' Harriet smiled, knowing she was going to shock her young listener. 'Chaining themselves to the railings outside Buckingham Palace, for one thing.'

'Did Queen Victoria agree with what they were trying to do?'

'Strangely, no. I've always thought that odd. She was a woman with power and yet couldn't see that ordinary women wanted a say in determining their own lives.' Harriet shrugged. 'And of course, since her passing, we've had two kings.'

'What else?'

'They burned down the homes of MPs and also churches.'

'No!' Molly gasped. 'Was anyone hurt?'

'No, they always avoided causing harm to people. They just attacked property. They smashed shop windows in the main streets. All to attract interest in their cause.'

Molly was quiet for a moment before saying softly, 'But was it the right sort of attention?'

Harriet regarded her young visitor. Though Molly had not been educated beyond the age of twelve or so, already Harriet could see that, at sixteen, she was intelligent and thoughtful.

'Perhaps not,' Harriet had to acquiesce. 'Women who commit acts of violence can be arrested and even imprisoned now. A few have gone on hunger strike and have been forcibly fed. I understand that's a very unpleasant experience.' She paused before asking, 'Have I put you off the idea of joining us?'

Molly shook her head. 'No – you haven't, but I must be honest with you, Mrs Spencer, I wouldn't want to take part in any militant action. I'd do anything else to help the cause – but not that.'

'I can understand that. I think the members of our branch would respect that too.'

They had been talking for almost an hour when Molly got up. 'I'd better be going. Mam will wonder where I've got to.'

'Is your mother interested in the movement too?'

'I don't know, Mrs Spencer. I haven't really talked to her about it much.'

'Well, you do that. If you decide to come to our meetings regularly, she ought to know. I'd want to know what my daughter was up to, if I had one.'

'I will. Mam and me are very close. I can talk to her about anything.'

'That's nice. I suppose, having two lads, I miss having a girl to talk to, but, of course, I wouldn't swap them for the world.'

Molly delivered the message to Queenie's mother, blushing a little as she told the lie. It was the first one she could ever remember having to tell either of their mothers and she didn't like it. When she reached home, Mabel Wyngate said, 'There you are. I wondered where you'd got to. I was beginning to get a bit worried.'

'I've been round to see Mrs Spencer.' There was no use in lying to her mother about this. Their street's grapevine was very active and even seemed to extend to several streets beyond their own. Besides, she'd told quite enough lies for one day.

Mabel raised her eyebrows. 'I didn't know you knew her that well.'

'I don't. Well – I didn't. Ben fixed it up for me to go round one night after work. She's a member of the WSPU and I wanted to know more about it.'

'What's that, dear?'

'It's the Women's Social and Political Union. The suffragettes. Me and Queenie have seen them twice now at meetings in the park.'

Mabel stared at her for a moment while she came to a decision. She was debating inwardly whether to encourage her daughter to become interested in such matters. She sighed inwardly. Molly was growing up fast. She was sixteen, almost seventeen, a working woman and contributing a portion of her weekly wage to the household. She deserved to be taken seriously, and Mabel was acutely aware that if she dismissed this matter as being a lot of foolishness, then Molly would stop confiding in her. More than anything, Mabel wanted the good relationship she had with her daughter to continue.

'You've listened to one of their speakers?'

Molly nodded.

'And Queenie?'

'Yes, it was her that wanted to hear what was being said at first. Then Ben told me that his mam was involved, so I thought it was a good idea to talk to her.'

'Did Queenie go as well?'

'No – she – she . . .' Molly hesitated and glanced away. 'She had to go back to work.' She didn't want to lie to her own mother, but she knew that if she told her about Queenie going out with Harry on Saturday, Mabel would feel honour bound to tell her friend Ethel. And Queenie did not want her mother to know.

Until this moment, the friendship between the two girls had been straightforward, with very few arguments or fallings out over the years. But now it looked as if things could get very tricky.

'You didn't tell your mam about me and Harry going out, did you?'

'No, of course not.'

'Well, mind you don't.' Queenie paused and then added, with a note of accusation in her tone, 'But you did tell her about us listening to the suffragette in the park, didn't you, because she's told my mam that?'

Molly lifted her chin, trying to give herself a little confidence in facing Queenie. 'Yes. I didn't think that would matter. Anyone could have seen us there. In fact . . .' She went on to tell her friend about her visit to see Harriet Spencer and what she had found out about the suffragettes.

Queenie's eyes were glistening with excitement. 'Harry's mam's actually a member?'

'Yes, she said she joined about two years ago after she'd heard Mrs Pankhurst speak. Now she goes to their meetings in the town hall.'

'Then we're going to go too.'

'You can't do that without your mam finding out, because I think mine's interested in going with me if I go.'

Queenie chewed her lower lip. 'Mm, you've got a point there.'

'Maybe it would be best if you were honest with your mam about our interest in the suffragettes,' Molly said. For once, it was Molly who was being rather crafty. 'At least it might keep her from asking questions about you and Harry.'

'Does Mrs Spencer know about us? Me an' Harry, I mean.'

'I've no idea. You weren't mentioned.'

Queenie seemed a little piqued. She liked to think she was always the centre of people's interest. After a little more thought, she said, 'I'll sound Mam out tonight.'

'Mrs Spencer said there's a meeting in the town hall next Monday night.'

A Woman of Spirit

'Right. We'll go.'

'My mam'll probably want to go too.'

Queenie shrugged. 'That's all right. Mam probably won't mind me going if Aunty Mabel will be with us.'

'Oh no, Queenie, I don't want you getting mixed up with that lot. You'll stay at home.'

'But Mam, Aunty Mabel's going with us. I only want to find out what it's all about. Why don't you come along too?'

Ethel shook her head. 'I don't want anything to do with it. Women should know their place. Politics, voting and suchlike is for men.'

'Why?' Queenie was emboldened to ask. 'Even if we never get the chance to vote, why shouldn't we be able to understand about how laws are made and why? We have to abide by them.'

'Of course we do. Why do you think it's in the marriage ceremony that we promise to "love, honour and obey" our husbands?'

Queenie stared at her mother. 'You don't obey Dad. You always have the last word.'

Ethel wriggled her shoulders. 'A wife and mother looks after the home and brings up the children. That's her domain and most of the time a husband will agree with what she says about such matters,' she said, skirting round Queenie's statement. 'But the man is the head of the household and decides all the important things. He's the breadwinner.'

'Then I'll ask Dad what he thinks.'

'Very well, ask him, but I shall let him know I don't approve.'

'But you'll abide by what he says?' Queenie persisted. For once, Ethel knew herself beaten.

'Aye, I will, but I'll only agree to you going if Mabel is with you both.'

When tea was finished and Jack Palmer was seated in his favourite armchair by the fire in the range, packing his pipe with tobacco, Queenie came and sat on the hearth rug at his feet.

'Dad . . .' she began.

Jack chuckled, a deep rumbling sound. 'I know that tone of voice. There's something you want, isn't there? What is it this time?'

'Aunty Mabel and Molly are going to a meeting of the suffragettes in the town hall and I'd like to go with them. I really want to know what these women are trying to do.'

'What does your mam say?'

Queenie hesitated, but she knew there was no point in lying to her father. No doubt her parents would discuss it later and she'd be found out quite easily.

'She's not keen for me to go, but I have promised her that I will go with Aunty Mabel and Molly.'

Jack was thoughtful for a few moments before saying slowly, 'Well, if you keep your promise, I can't see the harm in it. I'd quite like to know what all the fuss is about myself, but I wouldn't be seen dead at one of their meetings. So' – he smiled down at her – 'you can go, but I'll want to know all about it when you get home.'

Queenie jumped up and planted a kiss on her father's cheek. She would keep this promise, she told herself. But she was not telling either of her parents about the proposed trip into town on Saturday night with Harry. She had told her mother that she was going out with Molly that evening. Now, all she had to do was convince Molly to cover for her.

Six

'I don't like it, Queenie,' Molly said. 'If they find out, they'll never trust either of us again. They'll never let us go anywhere. We'll become like – like prisoners.'

'Oh Moll, why do you always have to look on the dark side?' Queenie was thoughtful for a moment before saying, 'Tell you what, why don't we ask Ben if he'd like to come? Then you and him can go off on your own, and me and Harry can be on our own.'

'Where exactly are you going?'

'Don't know. Harry said it was a surprise.'

'Oh, I don't know. What if our parents find out . . .'

'They won't if we're careful. Look, I'll talk to Harry when we meet them after work tomorrow night. See what he thinks.'

'All right,' Molly agreed reluctantly, but she wasn't happy. She could see all this ending in tears.

As the four of them walked home from work the following evening, they paired off as usual, Harry and Queenie walking a little ahead. Queenie was talking animatedly, although Molly and Ben could not hear what was being said.

'She's going on a bit about something, isn't she?' Ben said.

Molly sighed. 'I told you about her and Harry going out together on Saturday night, but she hasn't told her parents. She wants me to cover for her – say that we're out together.'

Ben glanced at her. 'And you don't like that idea?'

'No, I don't. Once we start being deceitful, there'll be no end to it. And if we're found out . . .'

'Would her parents mind her walking out with Harry?'

'I don't think her mam wants her courting at all yet. She's so afraid of her getting into trouble.' Molly blushed a little and then added, 'You know what I mean?'

'Yeah, I do,' Ben said absently, his gaze on the two figures walking ahead of them. 'She'd be safer with me,' he murmured. 'I'd never hurt any girl like that.'

They walked in silence for a few minutes until Ben asked, 'So, what's she telling Harry?'

'She wants him to persuade you to take me, then we can go as a foursome. We can pair off, she says, once we get to wherever we're going.'

'And where's that?'

Molly shrugged. 'I haven't the faintest idea.'

'What do you want to do?'

'I'd like to know what it is Harry has in mind first.'

'Right. Let's catch them up and sort all this out.'

Coming up behind Harry and Queenie, Ben laughed and said, 'So, where is it we're all off to on Saturday night, then?'

Harry and Queenie turned round, a surprised look

on their faces. They glanced at each other and then Harry said, 'You up for it, then?'

'We might be – if we knew what it was.'

'I thought I'd treat Queenie with a trip to The Loughborough Hippodrome.'

Ben turned to Molly. 'Would you like that?'

'Actually, I would. Very much. I've never been to the theatre. But are the seats very expensive?'

'Don't you worry about that. It'll be our treat,' Harry said swiftly. 'We earn good money. It's a pity if we can't treat our girls once in a while.'

So it was arranged that they'd all go together on the Saturday night. Even Ethel had no objection when she heard but, a little shrewder than Queenie would have liked, her mother said, 'No pairing off, mind, and going your separate ways. You stay together.'

Arriving at the theatre, the two girls stared around them in awe.

'Isn't it wonderful?' Molly breathed. 'Where are we sitting?'

'Up there. In the circle,' Harry said. 'Come on, I'll lead the way.'

'My word, you're pushing the boat out, aren't you?'

'Only the best for our girls, Ben.'

They sat a few rows away from one another, but in the darkness, they couldn't see each other.

'Isn't that Tom Mayberry who lives on your street?' Molly whispered to Ben.

'Looks like him. He's with his mam. That's definitely Mrs Mayberry sitting next to him.'

'Hasn't he got a girlfriend?'

A Woman of Spirit

'Who? Tom? Nah. Not for the want of trying, I might say, but the lasses don't exactly fall at his feet.'

'Not like they do at Harry's,' Molly said without rancour. Wasn't she one of the many who would willingly do just that? 'Or yours, for that matter. I've seen the way some of the girls from our factory look at you when we're walking home together after work.'

'Really?' Ben said casually. 'I can't say I'd noticed.' But the tone of his voice told Molly that he wasn't quite as ignorant of girls' interest as he liked to make out. She wondered why he wasn't walking out with one of them. Of course, she reminded herself with a sigh, he was still holding a torch for Queenie, but it was obvious now to Molly that Harry and Queenie were courting. Surely he must know that too.

As the lights dimmed, all conversation stopped as they watched the show. There were singers, dancers, comedians, jugglers and magicians.

'Well, it's certainly what the advert says,' Ben said later as they walked out into the evening air. 'It was certainly a "variety".'

'It was all wonderful,' Molly said. 'Thank you so much for bringing me, Ben. I've loved every minute. I'll have so much to tell Mam.'

It was a lovely evening as the two young men walked the girls back to their respective front doors.

'So are you going to the park tomorrow to listen to the suffragettes?' Ben asked Molly.

'Not tomorrow. Your mam told me that there's a

meeting in the town hall on Monday evening and we're going to go to that. My mam's coming too.'

Ben nodded. 'You'll probably see our mam there, then. I'd better be off. Goodnight, Molly. It was a lovely evening. We must do it again sometime.'

Molly watched him disappear into the dusk, whistling jauntily. She sighed as she turned towards the alleyway leading between the houses to her own backyard. If only both she and Ben could have fallen for each other, instead of hankering after two people who were definitely out of their reach. How much simpler life would be.

There were a surprising number of women of all ages at the meeting when Molly, her mother and Queenie stepped into the large room. Ethel was still resolutely having nothing to do with it.

'My Jack wouldn't approve,' she'd said primly when Mabel had suggested that she should join them. 'A woman's place is in the home. We've always believed that and we've no reason to change our minds.'

'But Queenie says her dad's letting her come with us? Is that right, because I wouldn't want to be doing anything either you or Jack didn't approve of?'

'He's said he wants Queenie to find out for herself. I think he hopes she'll find out it's all a lot of nonsense and soon lose interest.' Ethel sniffed. 'It's certainly what I'm hoping.'

'Mm,' Mabel murmured. She wasn't too sure. 'We shall see. Molly seems very caught up in it. That's why I'm going myself, just to make sure I know what she's getting involved in.'

Ethel nodded. 'You do right, Mabel. I'll come round in the morning when I've done my ironing and you can tell me all about it.'

'Well, well,' Mabel said, gazing around her. 'I would never have believed there was so much interest. Not in our town. There must be forty or more women here.'

'There's Mrs Spencer over there,' Molly said, spotting Harriet in the second row from the front. 'Shall we go and join her?'

'Oh, I don't think so. I don't know her very well. Besides, she might be with her friends.'

'I'll just go and say "hello" to her, then,' Molly said. 'It'd be rude of me not to speak to her after she was so kind. You wait here.' But when Molly approached her and spoke to her, Harriet turned and waved them forward.

'Come and sit with me. You must be Molly's mother. I recognize you.'

'I'm very pleased to meet you, Mrs Spencer,' Mabel said as she sat down beside her. 'Thank you for inviting us to join you.'

'And I'm Queenie Palmer.' Queenie stood in front of Harriet and held out her hand. 'You're Harry's mam, aren't you?'

Harriet looked up at Queenie as she took the outstretched hand. She'd heard the rumours about the girl who was supposed to be 'the prettiest girl in the neighbourhood'. She was indeed lovely. Harriet had heard the gossip about her two sons meeting both Queenie and Molly in the park on Sunday afternoons. She also knew about their recent trip to the theatre together. There wasn't much about her two boys that escaped Harriet's notice. But she kept the information to herself. They were both grown men now. In Harriet's book, if boys did a man's work, then they deserved to be called 'men'. Even Ben, who was only sixteen – tall, broad-shouldered and strong – could pass for the age of eighteen at least.

The woman in charge of the meeting banged on the table with a gavel to bring the gathering to order.

'My name is Mrs Forster. Miss Anstruther can't be with us tonight. She has a meeting in Leicester and she has asked me to step into her shoes.' Mrs Forster smiled as she added, 'But only for tonight. I wouldn't want to usurp the place of one of the founders of this branch.' A titter rippled around the room.

'I see we have one or two new faces among us tonight,' she said, her gaze resting on Mabel and the two girls, 'so I will just briefly set out what our aims are and why.'

Molly listened carefully. It was much the same as Harriet Spencer had already told her, but it was new information to both her mother and Queenie.

'As you know, we follow Mrs Pankhurst's leadership, but I realize that some of you are not comfortable with militant acts and, at this branch, we are lenient about that. But please remember, we are in a kind of war. When men go to war, they kill people. We don't want to do that, so we damage property where people will feel it, but we do not endanger lives. However, as long as you are prepared to join our marches, to hand out leaflets and to promote our aims in any way you can – perhaps even to make speeches – then we welcome you as members.'

Seven

'So,' Harriet said as the four women took the same route back to their respective homes, 'what did you think of it, Mrs Wyngate?'

'I found it very interesting and I am in favour of women having the right to vote, but . . .' She hesitated, not wanting to offend the woman she'd only just met properly.

'Go on.'

Mabel sighed. 'I'm not happy about militant action. I don't condone violence.'

'I understand your feelings, but if that is the only way we can get the authorities and the public to take us seriously' – Mabel noticed at once that Harriet used the word 'we' – 'then surely it's justified.'

'Aren't there other, more peaceful, ways? Protest marches, talking to our local MP, writing to the press, demonstrations outside Parliament. That sort of thing.'

Harriet nodded. 'All that – and more – has been tried for years by Millicent Fawcett's group, but to no avail. We – that's Mrs Pankhurst's followers – have been forced to take drastic action to get ourselves noticed.'

'I'd like to support you and the movement, but I

won't get involved in any violence. Nor will Molly, and I'm sure Ethel – Mrs Palmer – won't want Queenie to either.'

Walking behind the two older women, Queenie and Molly exchanged a glance and Queenie pulled a face.

'I can appreciate that,' Harriet said, 'and I respect your opinion, especially where the two girls are concerned.' She paused and then added, 'What about your husband? We get a lot of problems from husbands not supporting their wives in this, but, on the other hand, we have many who do agree with our efforts. I am fortunate that my Luke is a supporter,' she added with a smile. 'But he refuses to attend our meetings.'

'My husband, Ron, and my son, William, will be very interested to hear what has been said tonight,' Mabel said.

'My dad will be too,' Queenie piped up. 'It's only because of him, really, that I was allowed to come tonight. Mam wasn't in favour of it.'

'Then you must be sure to tell them both all about it,' Harriet said over her shoulder. 'Perhaps next time your mother will come with you, Queenie.'

Behind her back Queenie pulled another face and muttered, 'I doubt it.'

Both Ron and William were waiting to hear all that Mabel and Molly had learned. They listened quietly, without interruption, but they did exchange a glance now and then.

'So, the Loughborough group – a branch of the

WSPU – are the militant wing, are they?' Ron said when at last Mabel and Molly fell silent.

'Yes,' Molly said. 'But there is another group who don't believe in any violent acts. The NUWSS – headed by Millicent Fawcett. They try to achieve what they want by peaceful methods, such as lobbying MPs to get debates in Parliament.'

'Couldn't you join them?' Ron asked. 'I'm not happy about you getting involved in any trouble. You could get arrested, you know.'

Before either Mabel or Molly could reply, William, who had been silent until now, suddenly burst out, 'I'm not happy about any of it. It's not fitting for women to be parading through the streets carrying banners. I've seen them. Their place should be at home, looking after their husbands and families. I'd be ashamed if you, Mam, or you, Molly, did anything like that.'

Mabel and Molly stared at him, for the moment utterly lost for words.

It was Ron who spoke up first. 'Now, wait a minute, son. You've no right to speak to your mother like that.'

'Then why don't you put your foot down?' William said heatedly. 'You're the head of the household.'

'Your mother and I work as a team. We have always discussed things and decided matters together. There is no "head of the household" who controls the other.'

'You control us.'

'That's different. You and Molly are our children and need guidance to become responsible adults and good citizens.'

'And you think marching through the streets waving banners, damaging property, holding rowdy meetings and making a spectacle of themselves in public is acting like responsible adults or good citizens? It's not – it's not womanly.'

Without answering his question directly, Ron said, 'So you don't think women should have the vote, then?'

William laughed scathingly. 'What do women know about politics? Would they even know what they're voting for? None of us learn it in school, and I don't see Mam or Molly reading the newspapers avidly to educate themselves in such matters.'

'What about women who have to pay taxes?' Ron began, but it was Molly, who, finding her voice at last, interrupted.

'That's what the speaker said at the meeting. If a woman has to pay taxes, then she should have a say in making the laws.'

'You're talking about the upper classes,' William argued. 'Intelligent and educated women, who own land or property. That's not you. That's not working-class women.'

Molly bristled. 'Oh, so you think we're not intelligent? Just because we're women and not born into the upper classes? That we can't listen to both sides of an argument and form our own opinions?'

'I think you're being swept along on a tide of flag-waving excitement. These speakers want to brainwash you, just so that you'll join them and swell their numbers. They don't care about you and your little lives. They're in it for their own glory. But they're wrong. Women will never be as good as men or as intelligent. Besides, you can't have it all ways. If you want to be equal to men, then all chivalry goes out the window. No more "women and children first". What if you had been on the *Titanic* when it sank in April? Would you have been prepared to go down with the ship like the men did?'

Molly stared at her brother as if she no longer knew him. She glanced at their mother and saw the same bewildered look in her eyes.

Mabel was shaking her head sadly as she said, 'I never knew that that is how you view me and your sister. That, as women, all we're good for is to keep house. To wash, iron, clean and cook, and make life comfortable for you men.'

'We go out and earn the money,' William persisted. 'That's the way it should be. Men are the breadwinners.'

'And we're supposed to be your servants, are we? Your sister goes out to work and contributes to the household, and let me tell you, working in a factory for a young lass isn't easy. And I should know because I did it for several years before I married your father.'

'But once she gets married, she'll have a home of her own and a husband to care for and maybe a family too. She'll never be a property owner or a landowner, now will she? Why on earth would she ever need to be able to vote?'

'And what if, for some reason, she never gets married? Who's going to "look after her", as you say? Her father won't be here for ever.' Mabel folded her arms across her ample bosom and, with a belligerent tone, asked, 'So are *you* going to support your sister for the rest of her life?'

'No, I am not. I'll have a wife and family of my own one day. Besides, she's got a job.'

'Aye, she has, but do you really think a lass working in a factory could afford to pay rent on a house for herself?'

William was beginning to lose the argument and he knew it. It made him angry. 'Then she'd better find some poor sod to marry her, hadn't she?' With that, he turned away and left the kitchen, stamping upstairs to his bedroom.

There was silence in the room for several minutes until Mabel said with a sigh, 'I've never seen him like that. I didn't know he felt so strongly about the women's suffrage movement.'

'Aye well' – Ron tapped his pipe on the side of the fireplace – 'there's been a lot of talk at work about the women's marches and so on. Some of the fellas support the idea of women having the vote, but there are a lot who don't. He'll have listened to them.'

'So, what do you think?'

'I think,' Ron said slowly, 'all women should have the right to vote if they want but, like I said before, I don't hold with the violence.'

'To be honest,' Mabel said, 'neither do I, but if no one will listen to peaceful methods, then what are they to do?'

Ron heaved himself out of his armchair. 'You've got me there, love, I have to admit. But now, I'm off to me bed.'

'I'll be up in a minute. Molly, you should go up too. Goodnight, love.'

Bidding her parents goodnight, Molly climbed the stairs, but sleep was elusive. The meeting had inspired her and had given her a lot to think about. And William's heated opposition had motivated her even more. He'd always been a good brother and they'd got on well throughout childhood. He'd always protected her and kept her safe, but was that because he thought that was his role in life: to protect the weaker sex, and not through love for his sister? She had seen a different side to William's nature tonight.

She wondered, also, how Queenie was feeling. She couldn't wait to meet up with her the following morning.

News of the meeting had had much the same reception in the Palmers' household as it had in the Wyngate home, only this time it was Ethel who echoed William's sentiments, while Queenie's father, Jack – just as his friend Ron had done – listened with interest.

'You're to have nothing to do with any of it, Queenie.' Ethel raised her voice. 'Do you hear me?'

Queenie opened her mouth to argue, but seeing her mother's face, thought better of it.

'Do you hear me?' Ethel shouted again.

Queenie was on the point of retorting, *I could hardly miss it, when I can feel your spittle on my face*, but again she bit her tongue and instead said meekly, 'Yes, Mam.' She stole a glance at her father, but he was studiously avoiding her gaze.

Alone in her room, Queenie – like Molly – lay

awake until the early hours, but their thoughts were somewhat different.

Molly was thinking of all the things she could do if she joined the suffragettes, while Queenie was planning how she could even attend the meetings without her mother finding out. Now there would be two matters on which she was deceiving Ethel – the suffragettes and her romance with Harry – but then another devious idea slipped into her mind. In the darkness, Queenie smiled as she realized how she could use the meetings to her advantage.

Eight

'So, who exactly are you walking out with, Queenie?' Harry asked. 'Me – or my mother?'

Queenie laughed and tucked her arm through his as they walked home after work. 'Don't be daft, Harry. You, of course.'

'But you went to one of those stupid suffragette meetings with her when you could have been out with me.'

'No – I didn't. What I mean is, yes, I did go to the meeting, but it wasn't instead of being with you. It's very difficult for us to meet. You know that. I can only wangle it if Moll's willing to meet up with Ben too.'

'And isn't she? I thought she and Ben are – well, you know – courting like us.'

Queenie felt a thrill run through her. There, he'd actually said it. They – she and Harry – were courting. She wasn't going to disillusion Harry about her friend and his brother, but she guessed Molly's heart lay elsewhere. While she was certain she didn't have anything to fear as far as Harry was concerned, she wasn't going to take that risk. You just never knew with boys. If he knew how Molly felt about him, well, it was very flattering, wasn't it?

'I've had an idea. If Molly starts going to these meetings regularly, I'll pretend to go with her and then slip away to meet you. How would that be, eh?'

Harry shrugged. 'All right, if it works. But I thought your mother was dead set against you going to their meetings?'

'Oh, I'll get round her somehow.'

'But how will I know when that's happening?'

'We meet each other most nights to walk home from work, now don't we? Besides, if your mam says she's going to a meeting, maybe Moll will be going too. I'll set off with her and then come and meet you.'

'It's a bit hit and miss. Look, Queenie, I like you. I like you a lot, but I'm not hanging around waiting for you like some lovesick donkey.'

Queenie giggled. 'Have you ever seen a lovesick donkey?'

Harry had the grace to laugh. 'Not really, but I hear they're very companionable creatures. Always like to have a mate.'

'Let's give my plan a try, shall we?' Queenie said, trying to steer him away from the habits in a donkey's world and back to one in which she was far more interested. 'If it doesn't work, we'll think of something else.'

They walked in silence for a while until Harry said, 'Mam goes to meetings on a Monday evening when they have them. She leaves our house about seven after we've all eaten. There's one next Monday. I'll wait at the top of our road. If you're not there by a quarter past seven, I'll know you're not coming.'

Queenie squeezed his arm. 'There's one thing,' she said. 'At least my mam's not likely to decide to go.'

Molly sat down towards the back of the hall and glanced about her, hoping there was no one who would recognize her. But it was a vain hope; there were several women there she knew from their streets. She was feeling very uncomfortable on her own and she was very disappointed in her friend. Everything had started so well. Queenie had come round to her home to call for her as they'd agreed. It had taken Queenie a long time to persuade her mother to let her go to the meeting. At first Ethel had been adamant that her daughter should have no involvement with the suffragettes. It had only been because Jack had taken Queenie's side.

'We've got to let her have a bit of freedom, Ethel,' he'd said. 'And at least she's not going out with some lad. And Mabel will be with them.'

But Mabel was not. When Queenie had arrived at the house, Mabel had said, 'Now, you two, I'm not coming tonight, but I want you to promise me that you'll stay together, and no making any commitments to join in marches or anything like that.'

'We won't, Mam.'

'Of course not, Aunty Mabel,' Queenie had said, smiling winningly.

They'd set off together up the street, but when they reached the corner, Queenie had gripped her arm. 'Look, Moll, I'm not coming tonight either. I'm meeting Harry. Now, you're my best friend, aren't you? You'll cover for me, won't you? I'll come to the town hall at nine o'clock, so we can walk home together and you can tell me all about it.' Queenie had squeezed her arm and given her a quick peck on the cheek. Then she'd hurried off without even waiting for Molly to answer. Molly had watched her go, shocked and anxious. She'd seen Queenie reach the end of the road two streets away and a tall figure emerge from the shadows. Harry Spencer.

'You're using me, Queenie Palmer,' Molly muttered to herself. 'And don't think I'm daft enough not to see it.' She marched on alone, righteous anger in every step, but when she reached the hall and mingled with the other women, she began to calm down a bit and look forward to the meeting. She sat patiently now, waiting for the meeting to begin.

'Hello, Molly. On your own tonight?'

Molly jumped and looked up. It was the last person she wanted to see. She smiled thinly. 'Hello, Mrs Spencer. Yes – er – yes, I am.'

'Can we sit with you, then? This is my friend, who lives opposite us. Mrs Mayberry. You probably know her son Tom.'

Molly recognized the same woman she had seen with Tom at the Hippodrome. 'Oh, yes, yes, I do. We were at school together.'

'Yes, you would have been. He's the same age as our Ben. Alice, this is Molly Wyngate. She lives two streets away. Same street as Queenie. Now, you must know Queenie.' She gave a wry laugh. 'Everybody has heard of Queenie Palmer.'

'Nice to meet you, me duck,' Alice said as Molly moved along to make room for the two women to sit beside her.

'And you, Mrs Mayberry,' Molly murmured.

Further conversation was impossible as the meeting was brought to order. Molly breathed a sigh of relief. She was so afraid of being asked awkward questions about Queenie. But before long she became engrossed in what the speakers were saying. She listened intently, caught up in their enthusiasm, their cause, their fight for the right for women to have a say in political matters.

The meeting broke up just before nine o'clock and Molly, together with Harriet and Alice, walked out into the July evening. She glanced about her to see if Queenie was hovering in the shadows.

'We'll see you to the end of your street, Molly. You'll be all right from there, won't you?'

'I'll be fine, Mrs Spencer, thank you.'

'You're welcome to come round to ours any time you like if you want to talk about the movement,' Harriet said.

'Thank you. I will.' It might be a chance for her to bump into Harry, she thought, as her heart gave a little leap. Then she sighed. What was the use anyway? He was courting Queenie now and it sounded as if it was getting serious. She wondered how much his mother knew.

At the end of the street where Molly lived, Harriet said, 'Goodnight, then, me duck. Maybe we'll see you at the next meeting.'

'I – yes, I think you will.' Molly had been inspired by the passion of the speakers. If she couldn't have the man she loved and if she was about to lose the companionship of her best friend too, then she would immerse herself in the cause. It was high time she struck out on her own and became independent of Queenie's influence. Part of her was disappointed. Queenie had been her closest friend for years. They'd 'lived in each other's pockets', as her mam always said. But now they were growing up and, just as Mabel had warned her, when boyfriends came on the scene, things altered. But another part of her was excited. She could do things on her own now, if she wanted. She could make new friends. No longer would she have to trail in Queenie's wake.

Molly had walked about half the distance between the end of the street and her home when she heard the sound of running footsteps behind her and a voice calling softly, 'Moll, Moll, wait for me.'

With a sigh, Molly stopped and waited for Queenie to catch up.

'I was waiting outside the hall, but then I saw you with Harry's mam and another woman.'

'That was Tom's mam, Mrs Mayberry.'

'Is she interested in the suffragettes, then?'

'Mrs Spencer brought her along just to see for herself, I think.'

'So, you'd better tell me what happened, so I can tell my mam.'

'I'll tell you about it tonight, but I'm not going to play the scapegoat for you every week. Besides,' Molly added with a wicked grin, 'how do you know I'm going to tell you the truth? I might decide to drop you right in it.'

Queenie laughed and tucked her arm through Molly's. 'No, you wouldn't. You wouldn't do that to your best friend. There isn't a mean bone in your body, Moll.'

It was a compliment, Molly supposed, but right at this moment she was not sure she agreed with Queenie. She did, in fact, feel a little mean towards her friend. Then she sighed. No, she couldn't do it. Queenie was right. She couldn't be that unkind.

'There were two speakers tonight. One was the woman who helped set up this branch, a Miss Anstruther, and the other was a visitor. I think she was from Leicester.'

'So, what did they say?'

'Much the same as we've heard before, both at the last meeting and in the park, but tonight they told us about a march they're organizing.'

'When? Where? Can we go?'

'I don't think our mams will let us.'

'They don't need to know.'

Molly gasped. 'Queenie, we can't hide something like that. Someone who knows us is bound to see us. You know what our street is like for gossip.'

Queenie pulled a face. 'Perhaps you're right.' She paused and then added, 'Are you telling your mam about wanting to join the march?'

Molly giggled. 'I'm hoping she might want to come along.'

Nine

'You can't possibly be serious, Mam,' William was almost shouting in frustration. 'Dad, it's time you put a stop to all this nonsense.'

Ron sighed but continued to pack his pipe calmly, which only infuriated his son even more.

'Dad . . .?'

'I have no intention of ordering your mother to stop doing whatever she wants – or Molly, for that matter.' He chuckled. 'I'm not sure I could even if I wanted to. Besides, I'm quite interested in what these women are trying to achieve, although I shan't be going to the meetings or joining the marches.'

William stared at his father for several moments before saying, 'I bet Uncle Jack's not in favour, is he?'

Ron shrugged. 'I really don't know, but I plan to ask him when we meet on Saturday night for our usual pint.'

'Then I'm coming with you. I want to hear what he says for myself.'

'It's a free country, lad,' Ron murmured, 'and the pub's a public place.'

He put his pipe in his mouth, leaned back and closed his eyes. The conversation was at an end.

*

'Hello, William.' Jack Palmer held out his hand. 'Good to see you. I'm surprised though. I didn't think the company of three old fellas like us would be your choice on a Saturday night.' He nodded towards Luke Spencer to include him. 'I thought you'd be out with your mates or' – he winked – 'with a girlfriend.'

William grinned and shook hands in greeting. 'Good to see you, Uncle Jack. And you, Mr Spencer. Normally, I would be. Out with the lads, I mean. I don't have a girlfriend. Not yet, anyway, and to be honest, if they're all going to get caught up in this suffragette business, I doubt I will.'

Jack laughed. 'Not in favour of women getting the vote, then?'

'No, I am not. Are you?'

Jack considered this for a moment before saying slowly, 'Well, I can't see why they *shouldn't* have it.'

'But women aren't as well-educated or even as intelligent as men. I read somewhere that a woman's brain isn't as big as a man's.'

There was a spluttering sound as Luke seemed to choke on his beer. He gave William a quizzical glance, but decided – for the moment – to hold his tongue.

'Ah now there, William, I'd have to disagree with you,' Jack said. 'Ethel is every bit as intelligent as me, and probably better educated. I never did very well at school. All I wanted was to be old enough to get out into the world and earn money.'

'But – but you have the vote, don't you?'

'Only because it's my name on the rent book and I'm classed as a householder. But, I'll say this, William, I might not have had much book learning, but I do pride myself that I have a lot of common sense, and the only time I do a bit of reading is when there's a general election coming up and I have to decide who to vote for. And then, I listen to our local candidates and try to decide who might best serve our community in Parliament.'

William was silent for a moment while he digested what this man, whom he'd known for as long as he could remember, had said. He admired Jack Palmer, who'd worked his way up to the position of foreman at the bellfoundry where his father Ron, and he, also worked. That didn't happen without good cause. Jack trod the difficult path between the bosses and the workers. It was testament to him that he was respected by both sides. Whenever there was a dispute, Jack was the one to whom they all listened. Jack was the one who sorted it out.

'But *all* women, Uncle Jack? Even girls like your Queenie and our Molly? I mean, *I'm* not even allowed to vote yet.'

'No, but that will come. Eventually, the vote will be extended to all men and, I suspect, in due course to women too. But it'll undoubtedly come in stages.'

'How do you mean?'

'Well, first of all it'll be for women who own property and pay taxes.'

William shrugged. 'Well, I suppose I can see the fairness in that, but they'll be well-bred women. Women from the upper classes and well-educated too. They'd understand what they were voting for.' He laughed sarcastically. 'If she was given the vote, I can imagine our Molly voting for the best-looking candidate, can't you, Dad?'

But his father was not smiling. 'I think you do your sister an injustice, William. At least she's taking the trouble to find out what the suffragettes are all about and what their actual goals are, which is more than you're doing.'

William stared at his father for a long moment before saying bitterly, 'So, you're taking her side?'

Ron sighed. 'I don't want there to be any "sides" in this, son. We're family. You should look out for your sister.'

'That's exactly what I'm trying to do. I don't want to see her get arrested and thrown into jail.'

Ron winced. 'Oh, I don't think it would come to that.'

William took a deep breath and tried to keep his voice calm. 'If she goes on their marches, the next stage will be to join in their militant acts, and then what? There're a lot of folk in this town who wouldn't agree with that. Molly would be ostracized. She might even lose her job.'

The older men exchanged a glance. 'He has a point there, Ron,' Jack said quietly.

William turned towards Jack. 'What about your Queenie? She goes with Molly to the meetings, doesn't she?'

'So I understand, but I thought Mabel usually went with them.' He glanced at Ron for confirmation.

'She certainly went to one. She was full of it when she got home, but she didn't go to this week's meeting. The two girls went on their own.'

'I'm not sure Ethel knows that.'

'They'll have been all right if they stayed together, Jack.'

'Mebbe so, but Ethel likes to know exactly what her daughter is up to every minute of the day.'

'Where's Queenie?' Jack asked as soon as he got home.

'Round at Molly's.' Ethel glanced at the clock on the mantelpiece. She should be home any minute. It's almost ten.'

'Right,' Jack said, sitting down in his chair by the range. 'I want a word when she gets in.'

Ethel frowned. 'Nothing wrong, is there?'

'Not that I know of, love. But I've found out that Mabel didn't go to the suffragettes' meeting this week. Ron thought the two girls had gone on their own.'

Ethel was thoughtful for a moment. 'I wouldn't mind that, as long as they stayed together and didn't join up to anything.'

They waited together until they heard Queenie's footsteps in the alleyway and then the rattle of the back door.

'Hello, love. Had a nice time at Molly's?' Jack asked affably.

Queenie blinked. Tonight she could answer truthfully, because she had been with Molly all evening. She'd hoped to have been able to see Harry, but he'd told her the previous evening when they'd met on the way home from work that he was going out with his mates tonight.

She'd pouted and said coyly, 'Wouldn't you rather be with me?'

'Of course,' he'd said gallantly, but she could tell

he was lying. Like all the young men she knew, he still wanted time with his male friends and expected his girlfriend to be understanding. Surprisingly, Queenie had said nothing. She was determined to hang on to the best-looking young man in the neighbourhood, but once she was surer of him then she would not be so accommodating.

She'd forced a smile and, tucking her arm through his, had murmured, 'That's all right. I'll just go round to Moll's.'

'We'll meet you both in the park on Sunday afternoon,' Harry had said to pacify her.

'We'll be there,' she'd said, but now as she stood facing her parents, she wondered if she'd be able to keep that promise.

It was Ethel who spoke first. 'Did you go to the suffragette meeting this week without Mabel?'

'Yes, Mam, but we were fine.'

'So, just you and Molly went together?'

Now, she had to lie deliberately. 'Yes, Mam.'

Her knees were quaking, but Queenie managed to return her mother's gaze steadily.

'So what did the speakers have to say?' Jack asked mildly, but Queenie knew there was a good reason for his question. He was testing her.

She rattled off everything that Molly had told her, ending, 'They're planning a march. A peaceful demonstration. Just a walk through the town. Moll and me would like to go. She's going to ask her mam to go with us.'

'Ah, now I'm not sure about that. I'll talk to Mabel. When is it to take place?'

A Woman of Spirit

Queenie wrinkled her forehead as if trying to remember. She felt a ripple of fear. Molly hadn't told her any date. 'I – er – can't remember what they said. I'll ask Moll if she can.'

'No matter,' Ethel said. 'I'll ask Mabel. Molly will no doubt have told her.'

Queenie hardly slept that night and, as they walked to the park together the following afternoon, she told her friend what had happened. 'Moll, I think we might be in trouble.'

'*You* might be, you mean. I haven't done anything.'

'Yes, you have. You've lied to your mam about us going to the meeting together.'

'No, I haven't, because she never asked. She just saw us setting off together and arriving back home. Then she asked me what was said at the meeting and I told her. You've not been mentioned. So, no, I haven't told any lies.'

'Not yet,' Queenie said ominously. 'But my mam's going to ask your mam about this march that's being organized. I couldn't remember if you told me a date.'

'I didn't because it's not been fixed yet.'

'Phew, that's a relief. We might get away with it, then.'

'You'll get found out, Queenie, eventually, because too many people know us. I told you Tom's mam came on Monday when you skived off to see Harry.'

'I don't think my mam knows her.'

'Maybe it'd be better if you at least came into the meeting at the start.'

'Wouldn't that be worse if I was seen there and then went missing?'

'You could come back near the end. I mean, the meeting lasts over two hours usually. You'd still have a good hour with Harry in the middle. I don't think people would notice you weren't there for part of the time.'

'I'll think about it. I'll see what Harry thinks. Oh, there they both are, waiting at the gate. I'll see you later. Meet us back here at four o'clock, will you?'

'Queenie, I don't think you should—'

But Queenie had gone, picking up her skirt and running towards Harry. Molly followed more slowly and by the time she reached Ben, the other two had disappeared.

'Where've they gone?' she asked.

Ben grinned. 'Hello, Ben. Nice to see you. Are you well?' he teased.

She smiled apologetically. 'Sorry, Ben. It's just that Queenie's playing me up a bit at the moment. I think she's going to get us both into a lot of trouble.'

'Meeting Harry when you're both supposed to be at the suffragette meetings, you mean?'

'Oh, you know about that?'

'Of course I do.'

Molly sighed.

'Don't worry. Harry won't tell on you and neither will I.'

'It's not you and Harry I'm worried about. It's other people. She just doesn't seem to realize that a lot of people around here know us and several of them attend the meetings. Mrs Mayberry for one. She was there this week.'

'Ah, now you might be right to worry there. If she's anything like her son, then she loves a bit of gossip.'

'Oh dear,' Molly said, looking even more worried.

Ben took her hand and tucked it through his arm. 'Come on, Molly. Let's forget about them and enjoy our afternoon. It's a lovely sunny day.' He paused and glanced down at her. 'Do you want to go and listen to the suffragette speaker? I'm sure there'll be one there as usual.'

Molly smiled up at him. 'Not today, Ben. I don't want to subject you to that when you've given up your Sunday afternoon so that Harry and Queenie can be together.'

They walked on slowly.

'We're a couple of idiots really, aren't we?' he laughed wryly.

'Doing this for them, you mean, when really—'

'We'd like to be with them ourselves,' Ben finished for her.

She laughed with him and suddenly found that the pain of thinking of Harry and Queenie together didn't feel quite so sharp.

After a few moments, Ben said seriously, 'You do know that they're going to get found out, don't you?'

Molly nodded. 'Yes, I do, and I'm going to be in trouble too for – what do they call it?'

'Aiding and abetting.'

'Yes, that's it. I'll never be trusted again either.'

'Could you confide in your mam?'

'Not about this, no. It would put her in a very awkward position. She'd feel she had to tell Queenie's mam. They've been friends for years – ever since we were born.'

Ben wrinkled his brow thoughtfully. 'Yes, then I

can see you have a problem. I'm sorry, but other than that, I can't think what you could do, short of telling Queenie it has to stop.'

They strolled on a little further until Ben said, 'Why doesn't Queenie tell her parents about walking out with Harry? I know what you said before and I understand it, but to my mind, the more you try to stop someone doing something, the more likely they are to do it in secret. Surely, if it was all in the open and Harry could visit Queenie's home, her parents could keep a better eye on her, but this way . . .'

'They know that we meet up with you every Sunday afternoon, but they think we all stay together. And they don't know about the nights she pretends she's attending the suffragette meetings when she's actually meeting Harry.'

'So, what are you going to do?'

Molly groaned. 'Oh Ben, I don't know. I really don't.'

'Well, let's forget about it for this afternoon. Let's go over to the bandstand. I heard the band are giving a promenade concert in aid of the local hospital.'

Molly sighed. 'That's a good idea,' she said, as she heard the music drifting across the park towards them. 'It might help take our minds off other things, if only for a while.'

Ten

The decision was taken out of Molly's hands as she had feared it might. And yet, when it happened, part of her couldn't help feeling relieved.

On two occasions when there was a meeting of the WSPU, Queenie managed to slip away from the hall but return just before the end to join Molly to walk home. The third time, however, Queenie called at Molly's home as usual with the pretence of attending. As they were about to set out together, Mabel suddenly said, 'I've decided to come with you tonight. I want to hear about this march they're planning. I had a chat with Ethel today, and although she doesn't want to go herself, she wants me to find out what it's all about before you two go getting yourselves involved any deeper. So, just wait a minute while I get my hat and coat.'

Queenie, with panic in her eyes, whispered, 'What are we going to do?'

Molly shrugged. 'Nothing we can do. Harry'll just have to realize you can't make it tonight.'

'I don't think—' Queenie began, but Mabel appeared at that moment and all conversation had to stop. As they reached the end of their street, Queenie cast a quick glance to her left, but Harry was not waiting on the corner as she'd expected him to be. Instead, ahead of them, she was surprised to see him walking along with his mother on one side and Mrs Mayberry on the other. When they reached the town hall, he greeted her casually.

'Hello there, Queenie – Molly. I thought I'd escort these two ladies to the hall. Ah, hello, Mrs Wyngate. What a gathering they're going to have. Something special happening tonight, is there?'

'There's a very good speaker coming from Leicester,' Mabel said. 'I thought I'd come along and hear what she has to say, and find out more about this march through the town they're planning.'

'I'll leave you to it, then. I'll come back about nine, Mam, to walk you and Mrs Mayberry back home.'

The three women and the two girls entered the hall. As they settled themselves in the seats near the back, Alice Mayberry leaned across and said, 'Not sneaking out tonight to meet Harry, then, Queenie?'

Molly heard Queenie's sharp intake of breath and saw her own mother stiffen. But Mabel did not rise to the remark. Instead she kept her gaze fixed firmly ahead of her on the stage. Molly groaned inwardly. There would be plenty of questions later for both the girls.

As he had promised, Harry was waiting outside when they all left the hall, but Queenie had no chance to speak to him privately. As they walked home, Mabel did not speak and when they reached the Wyngates' door, she carried on further down the street. All she said was, 'I think we'd better get this sorted out with your mother, don't you, Queenie?'

A Woman of Spirit

The three of them walked down the alleyway between the terraced houses – the 'jitty' as they called it – and in through the back door of the Palmers' house. Queenie led them into the kitchen, where her parents were sitting on either side of the hearth in front of the range.

Ethel looked up in surprise and then anxiety crossed her features. 'Is something wrong?'

Jack was struggling out of his deep armchair. 'Hello, Mabel. Here, sit down. You too, Molly, love. Pull a chair out from the table. Queenie, make us a cup of tea, there's a good girl. Now, what brings you here so late?'

'I think it's Queenie you need to ask.' Mabel took the seat and looked across at Ethel. 'Harriet Spencer and Alice Mayberry – you know her by sight, I think – were both at the meeting tonight. The Mayberrys live across the street from the Spencers. Alice's boy, Tom, is the same age as our girls.'

Ethel's eyes were darting from her friend, Mabel, to her own daughter and back again. She was beginning to feel very uncomfortable. Queenie's cheeks were suspiciously pink and she scuttled away into the scullery before she could be asked any questions.

'Go on, Mabel,' Ethel said quietly.

'Let me start at the beginning. When Queenie arrived at our house to call for Molly, I decided to go with them. I'd heard that there was a particularly good speaker on this evening, and I also wanted to find out more about this proposed march before we agree to our girls joining it.'

Ethel nodded, but did not speak.

'When we got near the hall, we saw Harry Spencer. He'd accompanied his mother and Mrs Mayberry and said he'd come back for them at nine. Well, we all went inside – apart from Harry, that is – and sat together. And then, just before the proceedings started, Alice Mayberry leaned across in front of me and Molly and said to Queenie, "Not sneaking out tonight to meet Harry, then, Queenie?" Those were her exact words. But then the meeting started and I didn't have a chance to ask her – or Queenie – what she meant. Then, during the evening, I thought it'd be better if I came here to tell you. It's not my place to question your daughter, even though you and me are good friends. I don't want anything to ever spoil our friendship, Ethel.'

'No,' Ethel said firmly. 'Neither do I.' She glanced at Molly. 'I expect you know what's going on, but it wouldn't be fair of me to ask you.' She raised her voice. 'Queenie, come back in here, will you?'

'I'm just making tea, Mam,' Queenie's voice drifted in from the scullery.

'Very well, but be quick about it.'

The four people in the room waited in silence until Queenie carried in a tea-tray and set it on the table. As she handed the cups around, Molly noticed that her friend's hands were shaking.

In a surprisingly even voice, Ethel said, 'Sit down beside Molly.'

'I . . .' Queenie began, but then, realizing there was no escape, she did as her mother told her.

'Now, have you been seeing Harry Spencer?'

'We – me and Molly – meet him and Ben on a Sunday. You know that.'

Molly glanced down. Her heart was beating faster. She knew that at any minute she was going to be dragged into the questioning.

'And do you stay together – the four of you – like we told you to?'

There was silence in the room as if everyone was holding their breath. Molly certainly was.

In a low voice, Ethel added, 'The truth, Queenie, because I will find out.' Molly kept her head down, but she felt Queenie glance at her as she said, 'We – er – we walk in pairs. A bit separately, you know. But – but we're not far away from each other.'

'Molly? Is that true?' It was Mabel asking now – her own mother, to whom she had never lied in her life. She took a deep breath.

'Like Queenie says, we are all together in the park, but walking separately.'

'But can you still *see* each other? All the time?' Ethel persisted. 'The park's a big place.'

Now the two girls glanced at each other.

'Not – not all the time, perhaps, no, but we know where the other pair is,' Queenie faltered.

'So,' Ethel said, 'you have broken your promise to me – to us. And what's this about what happened tonight? What did Mrs Mayberry mean when she asked if you were sneaking out to meet Harry? Was that both of you or just you, Queenie?'

Now the colour flooded Queenie's face and her mother had her answer.

'I see,' Ethel said, tight-lipped. 'I don't know what you think, Mabel, but I think we should stop them meeting the Spencer brothers completely, and they mustn't be allowed to go to the suffragette meetings without one of us going too.'

Before Mabel could open her mouth, Jack said, 'Now, Ethel, love, you know I don't normally interfere in such matters concerning Queenie, but have you realized that you can't stop them meeting the lads entirely? They can see them on their way to and from work. I'm sure they already meet up then.' He turned towards the two girls. 'Don't you?'

Both Queenie and Molly nodded.

'Are either of you actually courting Harry or Ben?' he asked.

'Me and Harry are,' Queenie said. 'Ben and Molly are just friends. They – they come with us so that we can meet, like you said.'

Ethel sniffed. 'Well, that doesn't seem to be working, does it? If you don't stay together in the park and Queenie is sneaking out of the meetings to see Harry. She's on her own with him then, isn't she?'

'Why don't you let Harry see Queenie openly, Ethel?' Jack said. 'Have him round here? That way we can keep an eye on things.'

'She's only sixteen, Jack. She's far too young to even think of getting serious with anyone.'

Jack was staring at his wife. Then a slow smile spread across his face as he added quietly, 'I seem to remember we met on your seventeenth birthday and started courting then.'

Ethel appeared lost for words for a moment, so Jack turned to Mabel. 'What about you and Ron? When did you meet and start walking out together?'

A Woman of Spirit

Mabel wriggled her shoulders uncomfortably. 'Well, Ron's a couple of years older than me.'

'How old were *you*, Mabel, because it seems to be the girls we're bothered about?'

Mabel glared at him but was obliged to answer. 'Fifteen,' she whispered.

There was silence in the room before Ethel gave a sigh. 'Well, Mabel, it seems Jack's played a trump card on their behalf, but' – she wagged her forefinger in her husband's face – 'if either of these girls gets themselves into trouble, it'll be on your head, Jack Palmer.'

'Oh, don't get me wrong, Ethel, love. We need to keep an eye on things and know exactly where they are and what they're up to, but it seems to me that by being too heavy-handed we invite deception.'

'But *Harry Spencer*? Now he's a bit of a lad.' Ethel was still not ready to capitulate fully. 'Got a bit of a reputation with the girls, hasn't he? I was hoping she'd do a bit better for herself than a factory worker.'

Jack glanced at her and raised his eyebrows. He, after all, was a factory worker, even though he had worked his way up to a respected position.

Jack now turned to Molly. 'Are you and Ben really just friends, like Queenie says, or is there more to it?'

Molly shook her head. 'No, it was always so that Queenie and Harry could meet.' The words felt like they were choking her, but she managed to stay steady. 'Ben and I were just – useful.'

Jack nodded. 'Right, then.' He turned back towards

Ethel. 'So, love, what do you think? Shall we let Queenie invite Harry round and we'll have it all out in the open? No more skulking about and lying to us or making poor Molly play gooseberry.'

Ethel was thoughtful for a moment. 'As long as she sticks to the rules we set. You see, Queenie, it doesn't do to try to deceive us. We'll always find out one way or another. There's always someone around here who's going to tell on you.'

As they met up after work the following day, Queenie and Harry walked a little ahead.

'She seems to have a lot to tell him today,' Ben remarked as he watched Queenie talking animatedly to his brother. 'Has something happened?'

With a sigh, Molly explained, ending with, 'So, there's no need for you and me to meet in the park anymore on a Sunday.'

'Oh – right. So her parents are going to allow her to walk out with Harry, are they?'

Molly nodded. 'I'm surprised, actually, because her mother has been so adamant in keeping her – sheltered, I suppose you'd call it.'

'What about you? Are you going to be allowed to have a boyfriend, then?'

Molly pulled a wry face. 'They're not exactly queuing up at my door, now are they?'

'Oh, Molly, you're a lovely girl. Never forget that.'

'You're so nice, Ben.' Impulsively she put her arm through his. 'If only we could have fallen for each other, instead of longing for – what's the word – the unobtainable.'

'There's someone out there for you, Molly. I know there is.'

'And for you too, Ben.'

The meetings in the park with Ben came to an end, but Molly still went there most Sundays to listen to the speakers.

She was becoming increasingly fascinated by the Votes for Women campaign, and now that Queenie had all but abandoned her, she could devote more of her spare time to finding out about the movement. It was something to concentrate on and to help her try to bury her heartache.

'It's always the way, love,' Mabel said. 'When girls get boyfriends, their friendships with other girls usually fade.'

Molly nodded, unable to speak. She didn't know which hurt her the most: Queenie deserting her, or the fact that it was Harry her friend was courting. The two girls had been friends since babyhood. They had done everything together, to the exclusion of other friendships which might have developed. But now, Queenie had changed. All her time was centred on Harry and Molly hardly saw her any more. Even walking to and from work together had altered. Queenie left home a little earlier each day to see Harry on her way to work and then, in the evening, he waited for her to finish work at the drapery.

And as for Queenie's interest in the suffragette meetings – that had stopped altogether, now they were no longer 'useful' to her.

Eleven

The proposed march, which seemed to have taken a long time to organize, took place in mid-September.

'We're not taking part this time,' Mabel told her husband one evening. 'We're just going to watch and see what happens.'

Mabel attended the meetings more often now, though whether it was because she was genuinely becoming interested or whether it was to keep an eye on her daughter, Molly wasn't sure. But the girl herself was becoming deeply involved and wanted to play a greater part.

So, on the day of the march, Mabel and Molly were standing on the pavement watching the group of women walk through the town.

'This is a larger gathering than just our members,' Mabel said.

'Oh yes. Miss Anstruther told us a week or two ago that she was asking the Leicester group to join the march.'

'Anstruther? I know that name,' Mabel murmured, but Molly wasn't listening. She was waving her flag. 'Don't they all look smart?'

The marching women were all wearing white dresses, huge purple hats, and a large sash, with purple, white and green stripes, across one shoulder and fixed at the waist on the opposite side.

Mabel touched Molly's arm. 'They're all wearing the same colours. Is there a reason?'

'Yes, they're the suffragette colours. Those three colours are on flags, banners, pamphlets – oh, anything to do with the suffragettes.'

'But why? What's their meaning?'

'Miss Anstruther explained it. White is for purity, purple is for loyalty and green is for hope. She said all the marchers must wear a white dress with purple and green trimmings. A hat in those two colours is the easiest thing to wear.'

Slowly, Mabel said, 'Is that why you haven't asked to march with them today? Because you haven't got the right clothes?'

Molly hesitated. She didn't want to hurt her mother's feelings. Mabel managed extraordinarily well on the housekeeping money, but there was nothing left for fancy clothes and Molly was sensitive enough not to ask. Not like Queenie, she thought, with an unusual spark of bitterness. She would have had the outfit in a heartbeat.

Molly, without answering her mother's question directly, said, 'I wanted to see what happened first, Mam, before asking you if I could take part.'

Mabel was not deceived, and decided that she would scour the stalls in the market to see if she could find something suitable for Molly. She was a good girl who contributed to the household expenses and never asked for much for herself.

'Anstruther?' Mabel muttered again. 'I know that

name. I know I do, but from where?' And then she began to smile. Of course, she knew the name and knew it well. How could she have forgotten?

The line of women marched past, carrying a banner with VOTES FOR WOMEN printed in large lettering. The crowd cheered and jeered in equal measure, but there were no skirmishes. As the demonstrators passed, Mabel turned away.

'Right, we'd best get home. Your dad and William will be wanting their tea.'

Molly smiled to herself. Old habits die hard, she thought, remembering the saying. Even though her mother was showing an interest in women being given more rights, Mabel still couldn't shake off her role of devoted wife and mother.

One cold October Monday evening, having listened to the speaker, Molly stood up at the end of the meeting to return home when she felt a hand touch her arm. It was Miss Anstruther, who had been one of the founding members of the town's branch of the WSPU. Moments earlier, she had been addressing the gathering from the stage, her voice carrying across the large room.

'Even today,' Miss Anstruther had begun her speech, 'not all men can vote. The third Reform Act of 1884 gave the vote to about two thirds of the adult *male* population in this country. You will notice I emphasize the word "male" because women were, and are, still not included. Now, the organization known as the National Union of Women's Suffrage Societies, led by Mrs Millicent Fawcett, is indeed a worthy group. They were formed in 1897 into a federation made up of various earlier groups, which have been campaigning since the 1860s. But their methods are peaceful and they abide by the law. They are the suffragists who hold garden parties and 'at home' meetings. They write letters to anyone in the upper echelons of society who they think can and will help them and they lobby MPs. They go on marches carrying banners and distributing leaflets, but these are always peaceful demonstrations. But in over forty years, I ask you, where has this got us?'

There was a brief murmuring around the hall.

'Nowhere,' a voice said from the back of the room and there was a ripple of nervous laughter.

'Precisely,' Miss Anstruther said. 'And so about nine years ago, Mrs Pankhurst decided to form the Women's Social and Political Union with its motto "Deeds not Words". She and her suffra*gettes*, as we are now called, are quite prepared to take action that will certainly get us noticed. We are prepared to damage property to bring attention to our cause, but never to endanger life. I am now saying "us" because I am proud to be one of Mrs Pankhurst's followers, but I have to warn you that our somewhat militant actions can result in arrest, court appearances and maybe even prison. And' – her tone became even more serious – 'a term in prison is no picnic. Several of our most ardent supporters when imprisoned have gone on hunger strike. They are then force-fed. This is most unpleasant and painful to withstand.' She fell silent for a moment and her head drooped. Those watching were under no illusion that Miss Anstruther herself had at some point experienced this barbaric treatment. But then she lifted her head with a defiant look on her face and her voice was strong and purposeful again. 'We are fighting for the vote for all men and women. We are fighting for the equality of rights and opportunities between the sexes, and these will not be rectified until women have an equal say in the laws of this land. We have to obey the law, so why should we not have a say in deciding which Members of Parliament should make those laws?'

'Do you think women will ever become MPs – will enter Parliament?' someone interrupted.

Miss Anstruther turned her attention to the woman who had spoken. A smile lit up her face. 'I do indeed. If the day comes – *when* the day comes – I would certainly be willing to stand as a candidate in a parliamentary election.'

'I'd vote for you, miss,' the same voice said and Miss Anstruther inclined her head. 'Thank you. I am gratified to think that I will secure at least one vote.'

A ripple of laughter ran through the room and the meeting ended in a far more light-hearted atmosphere.

'Excuse me . . .' Miss Anstruther's voice as she touched Molly's arm was gentle and soft, nothing like the strident tone with which she delivered her speeches. She was holding a sheaf of papers in her hand. 'I have seen you at several of our meetings. I wonder if you would be willing to pop these leaflets through the letterboxes down your street?'

For a moment, Molly hesitated, then she smiled. What harm could it do? She would deliver them after dark and no one would see who had put the paper through their door. She wouldn't, on this occasion, even tell her mother.

'Of course.' She smiled brightly. 'I'd be glad to.'

She managed to get to her bedroom without Mabel seeing what she was carrying. After supper, she retired to her room at the normal time, but she did not undress and get into bed. She blew out the candle and sat near her window overlooking the backyard. She heard her parents and William mount the stairs and go into their bedrooms. After an hour, when she felt confident that they would all be asleep, she crept downstairs, remembering to miss the fourth step from the bottom, which creaked loudly, and let herself quietly out of the back door. Tiptoeing down the alleyway, she emerged into the street and glanced both ways. There was no one about. The hardworking people in her neighbourhood, all early risers, were in their beds. It didn't take her long to push a leaflet through each letterbox, being careful not to make it rattle and disturb anyone. If there was no letterbox, she pushed it under the door, but it wasn't until she reached the safety of her own bedroom again that she breathed easily.

The excitement of her clandestine activity made sleep a long time coming, so that, the following morning, she found it hard to rouse herself and go to work.

'Whatever's the matter with you this morning?' Queenie asked. She'd risen early to see Harry briefly, but now she was waiting on the corner until Molly appeared. 'You look awful. Are you sickening for something, 'cos if you are, don't get near me.'

'I don't think so,' Molly said, trying to stifle a yawn and failing. 'I didn't sleep much last night. Look, can you keep a secret?'

Queenie laughed wryly. 'I can, but whatever it is, it'll get out soon enough. It always does.' She paused and then added with a smirk, 'Got yourself a fella, have you?'

'No, nothing like that. It's just . . .'

'Go on. I won't tell, Moll. You know that. I know you were in a very awkward situation when they found out about me and Harry. I don't blame you for that.'

Molly wasn't sure she believed Queenie. Their friendship had altered since Queenie now spent so much time with Harry, but as Mabel had said, this was bound to happen. Queenie's spare time that had once been spent with Molly was now commandeered by her boyfriend. It was the way things happened.

'I went to a suffragette meeting last night . . .'

'You're getting very involved with them, aren't you? Can't say I'm that interested now. I hope you know what you're doing. Go on.'

'I was asked to deliver leaflets down our street, so I did.'

'Oh, so that was where it came from. Mam found it this morning.'

'I did it after dark. I – didn't want anyone to see me.'

'Why not?'

'Because I know what William would say.'

Queenie laughed. 'You shouldn't worry about your brother. As long as your mam and dad are all right about it, you should just do it. If you really believe in their cause, you shouldn't be ashamed of doing whatever you can to help them.'

Molly nodded. 'You're right. I will.' She paused and then added, 'Are you really not interested anymore?'

'In a way, but I've got better things to do with my time now.'

Her words and the smug smile with which they were delivered were like a knife through Molly's heart.

'Do you think you could do one or two more streets in your area?' Miss Anstruther asked Molly after the next meeting. 'Just the neighbouring ones.'

Molly, expecting this request, had already given the matter serious thought. She had even spoken to her mother about it, admitting her night-time delivery of leaflets.

Mabel had wrinkled her brow. She had become very interested in the Votes for Women campaign herself and didn't want to stop her daughter being involved in a minor way. Although her husband seemed relaxed about it all, there was still William to consider. She didn't want her family, who had always been so close, falling out. It would result in unpleasant tensions within the household.

'I can't see any harm in it, but perhaps it would be better not to tell William. You say you did it the first time after dark?'

Molly nodded.

'Well, stick to that, then. Once the darker nights come, it'll be easier for you. Perhaps a Saturday night would be the best time. William will be out with his friends and there's no work the next day. You can have a bit of a lie-in, as long as you're up in time to go to morning service as usual.'

'Thanks, Mam. That's a good idea.'

On the Saturday evenings when she was required to deliver leaflets, Molly waited until William had left the house before venturing out.

'Where's our Molly going?' Ron asked casually on the second occasion she left the house to carry out her task. 'Got a young man, has she?'

Mabel laid aside her darning. 'She's delivering leaflets in our neighbourhood for the suffragettes. You don't mind, do you?'

Ron was thoughtful for a moment before saying slowly, 'I don't, no, but William won't approve.'

'No, I know. That's why she goes out on a Saturday evening and waits for him to leave first.'

'He'll find out eventually, though, love. And he'll be out to cause trouble for her, because he's determined to stop her belonging to their organization if he can.'

Twelve

'I'm sorry, Molly, love, but I'm not letting you go. You've not stopped sneezing since you got home from work and you're shivering, aren't you?' Mabel laid the back of her hand against Molly's forehead. 'I think you've got a temperature.'

'But it's the fair, Mam. We always go.'

The annual fair that visited the town every November had arrived, and it had long been the custom for the Wyngates and the Palmers to go together on the Saturday evening.

'I know, love, and I'm sorry, but you're really not well enough. If you're not a lot better by Monday, you won't be going to work either. Your dad and William can go to the fair. I'll stay at home with you.'

'No, Mam. Don't do that. I'll be fine. There's no need for you to miss it—' Molly sneezed. 'I know how much you enjoy going.'

'I'll get your dad to win you something on the hoop-la if he can.'

Molly smiled weakly. She swayed a little. 'I've got an awful headache . . .'

'Right, up to bed with you, my girl. I'll bring you a hot drink before we leave.'

Molly's cold worsened and she developed a hacking cough, which kept her off work for a full week.

'It was a shame you missed the fair,' Queenie said when they met on the morning Molly was fit enough to return to work. 'We had a great time. We went on all the rides and saw all the sideshows.' She glanced at Molly, adding archly, 'Poor old Ben looked a bit lost, though, wandering around on his own. I even saw him with Tom Mayberry once.' She pulled a face. 'He must have been desperate for company. I'm sure he was missing you. Ne'er mind. You can make up for it when the fair comes again next year.'

Mabel had been saving hard for Christmas ever since the previous year. Things were easier now, of course, with both William and Molly working and contributing. All the food was already organized. Plum puddings had been made several months earlier and she had been busy baking batches of mince pies. The turkey, which had now become a popular Christmas dinner, was on order at the local butcher's and she would get her vegetables last minute in the market. Mabel loved the Christmas preparations and this year she was keeping an exciting secret. She had planned a special surprise for Molly and could hardly wait for her to open the gift on Christmas morning.

The purchase of a Christmas tree had always been Ron's task and he brought home a bushy four-foot one during the week before the celebrations.

'That's a lovely tree,' Mabel said admiringly as she helped Ron to plant it in a large pot. 'I've unearthed all the decorations, but I'm under strict instructions from Molly not to start without her.'

'Queenie usually comes to help, doesn't she, and then Molly goes to help with theirs?'

Mabel pulled a face. 'I doubt Queenie will be coming this year. She's far too preoccupied with Harry now.'

Ron glanced at her. 'Still going strong, then, is it? The romance?'

'As far as I know.'

'They must be toeing the line, then, else Ethel would have put a stop to it before now.'

'That's true enough, Ron, but it's our Molly I feel for. Queenie was the only friend she had really. They lived in each other's pockets, so now Molly hasn't any other friends to turn to.'

'Isn't she making friends at the suffragette meetings?'

'There aren't any girls of her age. Everyone's older than her.'

'What about where she works? There'll be a lot there the same age as she is, surely. Hasn't she made any friends there?'

'True, but they've all got their own friends. You know what I mean. Friendships made when Molly wasn't – what shall I call it – available, because she was so tied up with Queenie.'

'Ah, I see what you mean. Now, Mabel, love, have I got this tree straight? Molly will soon complain if I've got it leaning to one side.'

Mabel stood back. 'It looks perfect to me.'

Between them they carried it into the house, giggling

like two youngsters as they wriggled through the doorways and into the front room.

Ron straightened up and eased his back. He glanced around. 'I can see you've been dusting and polishing ready for the big day. Are Ethel and Jack coming to us on Boxing Day as usual?'

'Yes, and we're to go to them on New Year's Eve as we always do.'

'What about the young ones?'

'I expect William will be out with his mates, but I don't really know about Molly because Queenie will no doubt be with Harry.'

'So is there really nothing between our Molly and Ben?'

Mabel shrugged. 'She's adamant there isn't.' She did not break Molly's confidence that it was with Harry where her daughter's heart lay.

'Shame, really,' Ron murmured. 'He's a nice lad. I'd've been very happy if Molly was walking out with him.'

As if to refute Mabel's declaration, a knock came at their front door on the Friday evening before Christmas. Mabel opened it to find Ben pulling his cap from his head and saying, 'Good evening, Mrs Wyngate. I hope I'm not disturbing you . . .'

'Of course not, Ben. Come in.'

'Is Molly at home?'

'She is. She's upstairs. I'll call her.'

'Well, perhaps it would be better if I tell you first what I've come about.'

'Come through, then.'

As Ben followed Mabel through the front room,

he couldn't stop himself saying, 'Oh what a lovely tree, and so beautifully decorated.'

'Mainly Molly's handiwork,' Mabel said artfully.

He stood a moment gazing at the tree, murmuring, 'Well, she's done a grand job.'

'Hello, Ben. Sit yourself down,' Ron greeted him as Ben followed Mabel into the kitchen. 'What brings you here?'

'I just came to ask Molly if she'd like a trip to the pantomime in Leicester on Boxing Day. Of course, she might have other plans, but—'

'I'm sure she'd love it,' Mabel said. 'I'll call her down.'

Moments later, Molly came into the kitchen. ''Lo, Ben.'

Ben stood up. 'I just came to ask if you'd like to go to see *Aladdin* at the Leicester Palace with me. There's a special matinee on Boxing Day and there's a trip been organized from here. Harry managed to get four tickets. What d'you say?'

Molly's eyes shone. 'Oh, I'd love that. Thank you for asking me, Ben. Harry and Queenie are going, I take it?'

Ben nodded. His face clouded for a moment. 'You – you don't mind that, do you?'

'Of course not.'

'It'll be a lovely trip out for the four of you,' Mabel said, tactfully hiding her disappointment that it was not Ben asking Molly out on his own.

'We'll take good care of them both, Mrs Wyngate. I promise.'

Mabel smiled widely at him, 'I know you will, Ben.'

*

When Christmas morning came, it was Mabel who was like a child. She had been up early to put the turkey in the range oven. Breakfast was already laid out and now she couldn't wait any longer.

'Come on, you lazy lot,' she called up the stairs. 'It's present-opening time.'

A few minutes later, the other three trooped downstairs. Ron was fully dressed, but both William and Molly were still in their nightwear and rubbing their eyes sleepily.

Mabel laughed. 'Not like the old days, is it, Ron, when they were nippers? They were always up before us to see what Father Christmas had left for them.'

'About half-past four one year, I remember,' Ron said, grinning at the memory.

'Now, Ron. You start.'

Ron smiled and picked up the package with his name on it. 'My usual baccy,' he said and then added, 'I hope.'

Mabel chuckled. 'Well, I hardly dare change the habit of a lifetime. Now you, William.'

His gift was a thick, warm scarf knitted in secret by Mabel.

'That's lovely, Mam. It'll keep me cosy on cold winter mornings on the way to work. Thanks.' He kissed his mother's cheek and then turned to his sister. 'Now you, Molly. It looks like you have a big present this year. Let's be seeing it, then.'

Molly unwrapped the parcel and unfolded a long white dress with a lace blouse top.

'Oh Mam, it's beautiful,' she breathed.

'It's not new, I'm afraid,' Mabel said hurriedly. 'I

found it on a market stall but it's washed up lovely, though I say it myself. And' – she added, as she pushed another parcel towards Molly – 'there's something else to go with it.'

Molly opened it to find a wide-brimmed green hat decorated with purple and white ribbons.

'Mam – what the hell do you think you're doing?' William burst out.

The hat trembled in Molly's hands as she turned to look at her brother. His face was almost the colour of the purple ribbons on the hat.

'William!' came Ron's unusually stern voice. 'I'll not have you speak to your mother in that way. Apologize this minute.'

'Oh, so it's all right for Molly to go parading through the streets making a fool of herself, is it?' He turned to face Mabel. 'Mam, she'll get caught up in trouble if you let her go on like this. She's getting swept along in a tide of – of misplaced patriotic fervour.'

'Oh my word,' Mabel said, her lips tight. 'Them's big words for you, son. Swallowed a dictionary, have yer?' Mabel prided herself on having continued her education herself, long after leaving school at twelve, by reading and listening and trying to iron out the dialect in her speech. But when she was angry – as she was now – she slipped back into the ways of her childhood.

'I'm not staying here to listen to this,' William said, turning away abruptly. 'I'll get dressed and go out. I'll leave you to it.'

Despite her irritation, Mabel's motherly instincts rose to the fore. 'You haven't had your breakfast . . .'

'You can throw it in the fire for all I care. I'm not staying here – and I won't be back for dinner either.'

He stamped up the stairs and only a few minutes later was back down, fully dressed and heading for the back door. He pulled it open, stepped out and slammed it so hard behind him that it shook on its hinges.

'Where's he going to go? Where's he going to get his dinner?' Mabel asked of no one in particular.

'Don't worry about him, love. He'll be all right, and we're not going to let him spoil the day.'

But it was a vain hope on Ron's part. William's rage hung in the air and robbed them all of their appetite for Mabel's carefully prepared Christmas dinner.

'I never stopped to think,' she murmured late in the evening as the three of them sat by the range. William had still not returned home. 'I should have realized. I should have thought he wouldn't like it.'

'William doesn't rule this house, Mabel, love,' Ron said. 'Not while I'm still here anyway. There's nothing wrong with Molly being involved with the suffragettes. She's far too sensible to get caught up in any violence, aren't you, love?'

'Yes, Dad. I promise you I won't do anything you wouldn't approve of. I'd still like to deliver leaflets, if that's all right with you.'

Ron sighed. 'It is, yes, but just be prepared for William finding out, because he will. I'm sure of it.'

Thirteen

Despite Christmas Day being spoilt in the Wyngates' home, the trip to the pantomime the following day was a great success. Everyone joined in the atmosphere of a traditional pantomime, shouting back at the performers and cheering in all the right places. Back home, Harry and Ben were invited to spend the evening at the Wyngates'. Queenie's parents were already there, as had been the tradition between the two families for some years. The two girls excitedly regaled the older members of the families with the sights and sounds of the show they'd seen, and some of the gaiety that had gone out of the celebrations for the Wyngates was restored.

It was two weeks after the New Year that William found out about Molly delivering leaflets on behalf of the suffragettes. He was playing darts in the public house closest to his home, where he and his friends met every Saturday night.

'Hello there, William,' a voice said and he looked round to see Tom Mayberry grinning at him from a nearby table. Ben Spencer was with him but there was no sign of Harry. Of course, William reminded himself, Harry would be out with Queenie. He felt a moment's empathy for his sister who had lost, if not Queenie's friendship, then her companionship. But at once, their recent spat sprang to mind and he hardened his heart.

'Evening, Tom – Ben,' William said, as he stepped up to the oche. He was taking aim when Tom said, 'Not out helping your sister deliver her leaflets, then?'

The dart went haywire and missed the board completely. Slowly, William turned to look down at Tom. 'What are you talking about?' he asked bluntly.

'Your Molly goes out most Saturday nights. I've seen her pushing suffragette leaflets through everyone's door. I know it's true, because we got one. My mam read every word. She's quite interested in their cause. She goes to the meetings with Ben's mam sometimes, doesn't she, Ben?'

William's jaw tightened as he threw his darts onto the nearest table with a clatter. 'Sorry, lads, I've got to go.'

He blundered between the tables as Tom shouted after him. 'Hey, William, you haven't finished your beer . . .'

But William wasn't listening or, if he did hear, he paid no attention. He flung open the door of the bar and stepped into the cold night air. He glanced up and down the street.

'Where might she be?' he muttered. He set off at a run to the end of the road and turned into the next one. The street lighting illuminated the road in patches and a pale glow shone from most of the windows.

A Woman of Spirit

There were few people about and certainly, by this time, no children playing outdoors. He could see no one, so he went on to the next street. About halfway down, he saw a figure moving between the houses, stopping at each door and bending to push something through a letterbox or under the door. Even from this distance and in the darkness, he could recognize his sister.

William stiffened. So it was true. He walked swiftly towards her, anger in every stride. He was so enraged by the time he reached her that he grabbed her roughly by the arm. Startled and afraid, Molly screamed and tried to pull free.

William held her fast. 'What do you think you're doing?' he hissed close to her face.

'Oh William,' Molly almost fainted with relief, 'it's you.'

'Of course it's me. Who did you think it was?'

'I – I thought I was being attacked.'

'You're lucky you haven't been. There's a lot of folk around here who won't take kindly to having such rubbish shoved through their letterboxes.' He gripped her arm even tighter. 'You're coming home with me.'

'Let go! You're hurting me.'

'I'll hurt you if you carry on.' He gave her arm another vicious nip. Molly winced but said nothing. 'Do Mam and Dad know about this?'

Now she clamped her lips together to stop herself from answering him.

'Well, I'll soon find out, won't I?'

Reaching home, they clattered down the alleyway

and through the back door. William thrust her ahead of him so that she almost fell into the kitchen.

'Oh Molly . . .' Mabel was halfway up out of her chair before she saw William following his sister into the room. 'What . . .?'

'Did you know about this?' William thundered. 'I found her two streets away, shoving this – this garbage into folks' houses.' With a swift movement, he grabbed the rest of the leaflets out of her hands and flung them into the fire.

'That's where they ought to be.' He turned towards Ron, who was still sitting in his chair, calmly smoking his pipe.

'Dad, you really ought to put a stop to this. We'll be having bricks thrown through our window next. I thought her dressing up in their – their regalia was bad enough, but *this* . . .'

'Calm down, son. Sit down and let's discuss this properly. Molly, go and make us all a cup of cocoa.'

Reluctantly, William sat down, but he was still frowning.

When Molly had handed round the mugs with a shaking hand, William said again, 'You really ought to stop her going to these meetings, Dad. She'll get involved in all sorts of things if you don't.'

'What exactly have you got against women trying to get the vote?'

'In theory, nothing, but in practice, are women really intelligent enough to be given it? I mean, not all men have it yet, do they?'

Ron agreed. 'No, they don't. At the present time, only just over half of the male population have the right to vote. They have to be over twenty-one and a householder. So, William, do you agree with the way things are at the moment?'

'I think *all* men over the age of twenty-one should have the vote, but I just can't see the point of all women having it. I mean, a lot of girls can't even read and write.'

'A lot of men can't either,' Ron said mildly.

William looked at him in surprise.

'Your mother and I have always thought education was a great privilege,' Ron went on. 'We encouraged both of you to work hard at school for as long as you were able to attend. We couldn't, I'm afraid, afford for you to go on to higher education but, William, believe me, if we could have, then we would have wanted you *both* to have continued. Education is never wasted. Not even,' he added with a slight smile, 'on girls.'

'But – all they do is get married and keep house.'

'Maybe, if that's their choice. But think about this. They're the ones who give their children – the next generation – their grounding in learning. And what about girls who never marry for one reason or another? Don't they have the right to be able to earn a good living for themselves? Or are they to be forever dependent on their fathers, or' – he said pointedly – 'on their brothers?'

William glanced at his sister. 'Molly will get married. She's not *that* bad-looking. I know at the side of Queenie—'

Now Ron sat up straighter in his chair and prodded the stem of his pipe towards his son. 'Don't you ever – *ever* – compare your sister with that little madam. Our Molly is worth ten of her. A fine friend she's turned out to be. As soon as she finds herself a young man, Molly's cast aside. Queenie was forever on our doorstep but, now, we hardly see hide nor hair of her. Don't think that just because I'm a man I don't know what goes on in my own household.'

'I didn't mean—'

'Well, what did you mean? Spit it out, 'cos we'd all like to hear.'

William glanced at his sister. 'Sorry, Molly, I didn't mean to be unkind. I'm very fond of you and I just don't want you getting into bother. These women seem hell-bent on creating trouble. Delivering leaflets is just the start of what they might ask or even *expect* you to do.'

Ron, calming down a little now, leaned back in his chair. 'I do agree with you there, William. I don't want you getting involved in acts of violence, Molly, love. I've made that quite clear before, though I don't see that pushing a few leaflets through doors can do any harm. But anything more than that, then William's right.'

Molly had remained silent, but now she asked in a small voice, 'So, can I still go to their meetings?'

Before either Ron or William could answer, Mabel said in a determined voice, 'Yes, you can, because I will come with you.'

Fourteen

'Well, well, well. Betsy Anstruther, as I live and breathe. I never expected to see you as a stalwart of the suffragette movement. Such a quiet little mouse you were when I knew you. Wouldn't say "boo" to the proverbial goose.'

Mabel was smiling at Betsy while Molly gaped at the pair of them.

'Mabel Platt. Fancy seeing you here.' She held out both her hands in greeting.

'It's Wyngate now,' Mabel said, taking the woman's hands. 'This is my daughter, Molly. But I believe you've already met.'

'We have indeed.'

Betsy Anstruther was tall and thin with angular features, a sharp-pointed nose and piercing, perceptive blue eyes. She was dressed in a high-necked white blouse with leg-of-mutton sleeves. An ankle-length purple skirt, flecked with green, and a straw hat decorated with purple, green and white ribbons left no one in any doubt as to her allegiance to the suffragettes.

'I have a confession to make, Miss Anstruther,' Molly began in a small voice. 'I – er – lost some of the leaflets you gave me to deliver. Only about a dozen.'

'Not to worry, my dear,' Betsy said cheerfully. 'There are plenty more where they came from.'

'She's not telling you the whole story, Miss Anstruther,' Mabel said. 'Out of a sense of loyalty, I expect.'

'Oh please, call me Betsy, Mabel dear. We've known each other a long time. Surely you and I don't need to be so formal? So, what happened? Oh dear . . .' The woman's face was suddenly anxious. 'You didn't get attacked, did you?'

'No – no, nothing like that,' Mabel said hurriedly. 'It was her brother. I'm sorry to say he is vehemently opposed to your organization and is desperate to stop Molly having anything to do with it.'

Betsy sighed. 'I see. A lot of men are, I'm afraid. What about your husband?'

'He's quite relaxed about it and doesn't mind Molly coming to the meetings or handing out leaflets, but he is adamant she should not get involved in any militant action.'

Betsy nodded. 'I can understand that. She is only young yet, anyway. What about you, Mabel?'

'I'd like to help, so if you can accept us both on those terms . . .'

'Of course we can. There are so many other ways you can be a valued member. Not everyone has to take part in actions, although we do expect you to support us. We're part of Mrs Pankhurst's organization, but there is another group who are opposed to any form of violence. They're the National Union of Women's Suffrage Societies set up by Millicent Garrett Fawcett – the constitutionalists. We were part of that but we split away from them a few years ago when they wouldn't agree to more militant action. Perhaps you'd prefer to join them.'

'No, no, we'll stick with you, just so long as you don't expect us to take part in any – well – physical activities.'

'You'd be willing to take part in a peaceful march, though, wouldn't you?'

'Oh yes.'

'I'm glad. Now, come along and I'll find you a seat near the front. We have an excellent speaker tonight . . .'

Molly listened, entranced by the passion of the young woman, who she thought couldn't be much older than she was.

'It's not only ourselves we're fighting for. We firmly believe that all men, whatever their circumstances, should have the right to vote. If they are good enough to fight for our country in a time of war – to lay down their lives – then they're good enough to have a say in the laws that we all have to follow, or at the very least they should be able to have a say in choosing those who make the laws in Parliament.'

It was a lively meeting and Molly and her mother listened closely to everything said.

As they walked home, Molly said, 'Surely William would agree with what the speaker said tonight.'

Mabel sighed. 'I really don't know, Molly. I feel I don't know my son at the moment, but I do think your father would agree with her. And that's all that matters.'

'So, tell me about Miss Anstruther. How do you know her?'

'Betsy comes from a well-to-do family.' Mabel laughed, the sound loud in the night air. 'She's one of the women who William would agree to having the vote.'

'But how do *you* know her?'

'My mother used to do cleaning jobs to earn a little extra money and she worked for the Anstruthers. When I wasn't at school, she used to take me with her. Betsy was the same age as me and very shy then, but she was kind to me. We played together outside while my mother was working in the house. They had beautiful gardens. Betsy had a tree house which I loved. And if it was bad weather, we were allowed to play indoors in the playroom. I had some lovely times there,' Mabel ended wistfully.

'So what happened? Why did you lose touch?'

'My mother gave up her cleaning jobs when she became ill and there was no reason' – she smiled – 'no *excuse* for me to visit their house anymore.'

'Well, she certainly hasn't forgotten you either.'

Mabel felt a warm glow creep through her. 'No,' she said softly, 'she hasn't, has she?'

Molly began to read everything she could find about the suffragette movement, its beliefs and aims. She never missed a meeting and even on the occasions when her mother didn't go, she went alone. She also joined the town's public library and devoured the newspapers and any printed literature she could find about them. In the privacy of her own bedroom, she began to dream of being bold enough to stand up in front of a gathering and speak as persuasively as the other women she heard. Seeing the young girl's interest, Betsy Anstruther gave her copies of the suffragettes' publication, *Votes for Women*, which Molly took home and smuggled into her bedroom. She hesitated to show these even to her mother. She still wasn't quite sure how devoted Mabel was to the cause.

In quiet moments alone, Molly began to draft a speech that one day she might be able to deliver. In the meantime, she could always dream . . .

At least, she thought, it was taking her mind off hopeless dreams of Harry Spencer.

Life in the Wyngate household continued with its normal routine, but there was an unsettled feeling now. There was no longer the easy camaraderie between brother and sister. Ron seemed able to ignore the underlying feeling of tension, but Mabel could not. She didn't like the members of her family falling out with one another. 'Why don't you come along to one of the meetings, William? See for yourself what it's all about,' Mabel suggested over tea one evening, when the atmosphere around the table was particularly strained.

'I wouldn't be seen dead at one of their meetings.'

'There are a few men who go occasionally. You wouldn't be the only one there,' Mabel persisted, but William shook his head firmly.

'Queenie said she might come with us tomorrow night,' Molly said. 'Harry wants a night out with the lads, she said.'

William smirked. 'Oh, getting tired of her girly prattle already, is he? I never thought that would last very long. He's not a one-girl sort of chap.' Molly kept her head lowered as William added, 'I'll try and meet up with him in the pub. I like old Harry. And Ben,' he added, almost as an afterthought.

Poor Ben, Molly thought. He was always the afterthought, just like she was. A spark of rebellion ignited somewhere deep within her. Miss Anstruther was a single lady, who had made a life for herself without being dependent on a man. Perhaps . . .

'Mam,' she said suddenly, 'Miss Anstruther – what do you know about her life now? I mean, does she still live with family?'

Mabel wrinkled her forehead thoughtfully. 'As far as I know, yes. She's never married. She did live with her parents, but I don't know if either of them is still alive. I hadn't run into her for years. By now, perhaps, she's a woman who owns property and no doubt pays taxes. She was an only child and will have inherited everything her father left. If he has died, that is. He was a clever businessman and they had a big house.'

Molly forbore to ask why the woman had never married; she thought she already knew the answer. Betsy Anstruther, a strong and determined woman and obviously carving out a life for herself, was no beauty.

'Does she work?'

'I wouldn't think so. She'd have no need, but I remember her as quite a clever girl. Of course, she had a governess, and later a tutor, I believe.'

Molly said nothing. So, she thought, a girl doesn't have to be married to live an interesting and fulfilling life. But then, she reminded herself, my circumstances are not quite the same as Miss Anstruther's. I will always have to work for my own living.

For the next few weeks, Molly continued to attend the meetings. Several times she saw Harriet Spencer and her friend, Alice Mayberry, there too. Sometimes Mabel accompanied her, but often Molly just went on her own. And then came the day when Betsy asked her if she would like to speak at a meeting in the park one Sunday afternoon in May.

'Me?' Molly said in alarm. 'Oh, I couldn't.' Although she had secretly been dreaming of this in private and had jotted down some ideas, she didn't yet feel ready to do it.

'Yes, you could. Speaking is a way you could help, and especially in reaching out to the younger women and girls. Do say you'll at least give it some thought.'

Two weeks later, Molly found herself standing on a chair under a tree in the park. She was trembling from head to toe, but she was anxious not to let her new friends down, especially Miss Anstruther. Mabel was standing at the back alongside Harriet Spencer. Beside her was Ben. Whatever was he doing here? How had he heard that she planned to speak today? Then she realized. Queenie, in whom she had confided, would have told Harry, and he must have told Ben.

She took a deep breath. 'My name is Molly Wyngate. I am seventeen and I live and work here in this town. Whatever happens, I know I won't get the vote for several years, but I – and my generation –

are the future. A future where we should have the same rights as men. And if that's what we want, it's a future we have to fight for. We have to obey the same laws as men, so why should we not be allowed to have some say in the making of those laws, especially those that affect women themselves, children and the home? At the very least, we should have a say in the choosing of those who do make them.'

'Going to stand for Parliament, are you, me duck?' a man's voice shouted from the back.

Though her heart was beating fast and her knees were trembling with nerves, she forced a laugh. 'No, I don't think I'm clever enough to do that, but I do think I should have a say in who represents this constituency in Parliament.' Boldly, she turned the tables on the heckler. 'Do you have the vote, sir?'

'No, no, I don't.'

'But would you like it?'

'I – hadn't thought about it really. But, yes, I suppose I would.'

'You see,' Molly went on, feeling she was winning him over, 'our movement is not just about fighting for women to have the vote, but for all men too, whatever their station in life.'

Molly didn't see the missile flying towards her until the rotten egg hit her forehead and splattered down her face. It was swiftly followed by three squashed tomatoes, which hit her in the chest, staining her white blouse.

Betsy was beside her in an instant and Mabel thrust her way through the crowd to reach her. They were swiftly followed by Ben and Harriet, concern showing on both their faces.

'Oh Molly,' Betsy said, 'I didn't mean for that to happen. Are you all right?'

Though initially startled, Molly smiled and raised her arm triumphantly. 'A few rotten eggs and tomatoes won't stop us. You'll need to do better than that.'

'Go home, you silly girl, and learn to keep house. That's all you're good for,' another male voice called out. There was a low murmuring and then raucous laughter broke out and Molly knew some crude remark must have been made, but at least it hadn't been shouted out loud. As she stepped down from the chair, Molly had one last thing to say. 'I'll be back next week.'

Fifteen

'Come on, Molly, love. Let's go home and get you cleaned up, though what your dad will have to say about this, I don't know,' Mabel added worriedly, fearful now that they would lose Ron's tacit support. William's reaction, if he got to hear about it, would be bad enough, but if Ron decided to stop Molly's involvement with the WSPU, there wouldn't be much even his wife could do.

Luckily, neither Ron nor William were at home.

'Thank goodness for that,' Mabel muttered. 'Get those clothes off and I'll put them in the wash-house to soak, though I'm not sure we'll get the stains out. What a shame. You look so pretty in the white dress.'

'Did you see who threw them?' Molly said.

'Some lads at the back threw the tomatoes, but the egg came from the man who was so rude.'

'The second man who called out?'

'Yes.'

'You're not going to tell Dad, are you? He'll stop me going.'

Mabel sighed. 'I don't like being anything less than honest with your dad, but no, I won't tell him. But if he finds out, then I won't be able to deny it. I'll never lie to your dad, you know that.'

Molly said nothing, but hurried to change into fresh clothing before either her father or William came home.

Three days later, William arrived home after work with a grim look on his face.

'So, you got a rotten egg thrown at you on Sunday, did you, Molly?'

'Eh? What's that?' Ron asked.

'At the meeting in the park she went to,' William said. 'She stood up on a chair in the park and made a speech. A seventeen-year-old girl daring to stand up and tell folks what they should do. You've got some gall, Molly.' He pointed at her forehead. 'Is that what that bruise is? Is that where it hit you?'

'Is this true, Molly?' Ron asked.

Before she could answer, William said, ''Course it's true. Ben told me. He was there.'

Ron turned towards his wife. 'But you were there, Mabel? Why didn't you stop her?'

Mabel put down the dish of vegetables she'd carried to the table and turned to face her husband. 'Because I'm proud of her, that's why. Proud that she's standing up for the rights of women. Proud that she's got the guts to stand up there and address a crowd. She's got more spirit than I've got, or ever will have, and that's the truth.'

For a long moment, Ron stared at his wife and then – to the surprise of them all – he began to smile. 'D'you know summat, Mabel, love, so am I. I'm proud of her too.'

William gaped at his father. 'Dad, you're not serious.

You can't be. We'll be the laughing stock of the street – probably the whole neighbourhood.'

Ron touched his daughter's shoulder. 'All I'm bothered about is you staying safe, and that's why I don't want you getting involved in their more – violent activities. But I don't reckon a few mouldy tomatoes will hurt you.'

'What if it's a brick next time?' William muttered ominously, and then stormed out of the house.

When the back door had slammed behind his son, Ron said, 'I just don't want you to get hurt, Molly, that's all. I've been talking to some of the lads in the pub on a Saturday night and they have very mixed views. Some are – like William – dead set against it. Some don't care one way or the other, as long as their meals are always on the table, their clothes washed and their bed warm at night . . .'

'Ron . . .' Mabel said warningly, but Ron only smiled and carried on, 'However, there are a few who think that the women have a point.'

At last Molly spoke, asking softly, 'And who do you agree with, Dad?'

'Oh, the last lot. Like you said in your speech, Molly, it's not just about politics and having the vote, is it? It's all sorts of other things where women should have more say.'

'How do you know what I said in my speech?'

'And how do you know about the tomatoes?' Mabel put in. 'William only mentioned the rotten egg.'

Now Ron looked suddenly sheepish. 'Because I was there. I wore me scarf, pulled me cap down low and stood right at the back so you wouldn't see me. But I wanted to see for meself just what you're getting involved in, Molly. I need to be sure you're safe.'

'Oh Dad,' Molly put her arms round her father, 'thank you. You don't know what it means to me to have your support.'

'Just stay safe, Molly, love, that's all I ask, and' – he added with a chuckle – 'don't tell your brother I went to the gathering, will you? I'd never hear the end of it.'

'Oh!' Molly said, startled to see who had answered her knock at the Spencer house on the Friday evening of the same week. 'Harry! I didn't think you'd be here.'

She felt the colour rising in her cheeks and hoped he wouldn't notice.

Harry chuckled, a low infectious sound, and his smile crinkled his eyes, which shone with mischief. 'Not trying to avoid me, Molly, are you?'

Molly felt her blush deepen. 'N-no, of course not. It's your mother I came to see.'

He laughed again, louder this time. 'Suffragette business, I presume. Come in . . .' He held the door wider and then ushered her into the kitchen. 'She should be back in a minute.'

Molly took a seat near the range and tried to stop the wild beating of her heart at his nearness.

'So, how've you been? I miss seeing you in the park on a Sunday afternoon, though I did hear there was a bit of a party went on last week when you stood up to speak. I wish I'd been there to see it.'

This was no way to stop the somersaults her heart seemed to be doing inside her chest. She shrugged, trying to act nonchalant. 'There's no need for me and Ben to chaperone you now that you have the Palmers' blessing to – to walk out with Queenie.' It still hurt every time she uttered the words.

Now Harry let out a bark of wry laughter. 'Her old man's all right, but her mam's a bit of a tartar, isn't she? Always wants to know where we're going, and who with, and Queenie has to be in by nine-thirty every night on the dot.'

Molly put her head on one side and regarded him solemnly. 'It's very different being the mother of a daughter to being the mother of sons.'

His smile faded. 'I would never hurt a girl,' he said softly. 'I might play the flirt – the Casanova – but I would never, ever get a girl into trouble. I know I've got a reputation as "a bit of a lad", but my mother – in fact, both our parents – have drilled it into me and Ben since the time we could understand the facts of life that we must never, ever bring shame on any girl.'

She stared at him. 'Then, Harry Spencer, you and your brother are very unusual young men. From what I hear from the other girls, it's all boys want and it's up to the girl to say "no".'

Harry shook his head and said firmly, 'Not with me and Ben, it isn't. And if ever you're troubled by a lad, you just let me know and I'll sort him out.'

Molly felt a warm glow spread through her as they stared at one another for several moments. She cleared her throat nervously and asked, 'So, why are you at home? I thought you'd be out with Queenie this evening.'

Harry frowned. 'She said she was busy tonight. I thought she must be spending time with you.'

'I hardly see her these days, but' – she shrugged – 'my mam says that's natural, now she has a boyfriend.'

'So, what is she doing?'

'I really have no idea.'

'You – you don't think she's seeing someone else, do you?'

'Good Heavens, no,' Molly said quickly. 'Why ever would she do that when she's got you?' The words were out of her mouth before she thought to stop them.

Feeling embarrassed at almost revealing her own feelings, she got up. 'Doesn't look as if your mam's coming back any time soon. Tell her I called, but it's nothing urgent. Just – just about the next meeting of the WSPU.'

Harry stood up too. 'I'll tell her you came round.' As he opened the back door and she passed close to him, he looked down at her and murmured, 'It's been nice to see you, Molly.'

She glanced up at him and for a brief moment, their eyes were locked in a gaze. 'Bye, Harry,' she said, her voice wavering a little.

Her heart was still beating a little faster than normal all the way home.

*

'Queenie,' Molly began, her tone a little hard when they happened to meet the following day. 'Just what do you think you're playing at?'

'Me? What do you mean?' Queenie's eyes widened innocently.

'Oh, come off it, you know exactly what I mean. You're playing fast and loose with Harry, aren't you?'

'Why would I do that?'

'To keep him "keen", as you put it.'

'So what if I am?'

'You'll lose him if you're not careful.'

'No, I won't. Harry's besotted with me.'

It was a shaft through Molly's heart, but she didn't let it show. Instead, she continued to frown. 'I went round to see his mam last night and he was at home. He had no idea where you were. He – he even asked me if you were seeing someone else.'

'Did he now?' Queenie said softly, with a satisfied smirk. 'Look, Moll, what's sauce for the gander is sauce for the goose. He wants a night out with his pals now and again, so why shouldn't I?'

'But you weren't with me . . .' Molly began and then added, 'Ah, I see. It's me you want to keep *keen* as well, is it?'

Queenie crossed the space between them and put her arms round Molly. 'Oh Moll, don't ever think that. We're best friends for ever, you and me. Nothing will ever come between us. You know that.'

For a moment, Molly stood stiffly in her friend's embrace. She wasn't so sure. Their lives were already taking different paths. But their years of friendship went deep. She relaxed and hugged Queenie in return.

'Just be careful with him, that's all I'm saying, if – if you're really serious about him. I don't think Harry Spencer's the sort to wait around if he gets the feeling you're two-timing him.'

'Oh, I wouldn't do that, Moll.'

Molly smiled thinly. Once again, she wasn't so sure she believed Queenie.

'Anyway,' Queenie said, pulling back now. 'I'm coming to the next suffragette meeting. I want to hear you speak. Evidently, Harry's mam is getting even more involved with the WSPU.'

'Yes, she's often there now.'

'And' – Queenie smiled – 'Harry reckons she's not against becoming involved in militant actions.'

Molly blinked. 'Really? I didn't know that.'

'Mind you, Harry and Ben aren't for it and neither is their dad, but it seems' – she laughed – 'Mrs Spencer has a mind of her own already without being a suffragette. There's not a lot they can do if they want their clothes washed and meals on the table. You know, Moll, women already have the upper hand if they'd only think about it.'

Molly pulled a face. 'That's only if they've got decent husbands. What about those who knock their wives about? We know that happens.'

'You're right, of course, and they're the women who really ought to join the suffragette movement.'

'But sadly, they're the very ones who wouldn't be able to. Their husbands wouldn't let them.'

'No, I know,' Queenie said quietly. 'You know, Moll, we're very lucky, you and me, to have such good parents. I know I moan about my mam being so strict but, deep down, I know it's only because she cares.' She broke off and smiled. 'We're getting awfully serious, aren't we? Now, tell me, when's the next meeting, because I'm coming.'

'It's a week on Monday at the town hall.'

'I'll be there.'

Sixteen

'Oh Moll, you were fantastic!' Queenie hugged her as the meeting broke up. 'I never knew you had it in you. You've always been so shy.'

Queenie had been sitting with Mabel and Harriet Spencer. Alice Mayberry had also joined them this evening.

Molly blushed as Betsy Anstruther arrived beside them. 'Well done, Molly. You should be very proud of her, Mabel.'

'Oh, I am.'

'It's so good to have a younger member able to speak so forcefully. Now, are you going to introduce me to your friends? Mrs Spencer, of course, I already know . . .'

'This is my friend, Queenie, and this is Mrs Mayberry, who lives across the road from Mrs Spencer.'

'Ah yes. I have seen you here before, Mrs Mayberry.' Betsy shook hands with her and then added, 'So what do you think of our efforts? Are you going to join our fight alongside Mabel?'

The women glanced at each other.

'I've already joined,' Alice Mayberry said, 'along with Harriet, but I have to say we're not too keen on carrying out militant actions.'

Betsy smiled. 'Not even setting fire to a pillar box? Minor things like that?'

Mabel and Alice glanced at each other and then, in unison, shook their heads.

'You could still get arrested for that, couldn't you?' Mabel said.

'If you were caught, I expect so, but there are so many other ways you can help.'

'Then, as long as it's non-violent,' Alice said, 'you can sign us up in any way you think we can be useful.'

As they walked back home together, a little band of suffragettes, Queenie said, 'Is that what they do? Set fire to pillar boxes?'

'Yes,' Harriet said. 'Or pour ink into them so that all the mail is ruined. It's just to get a reaction. It's not against a person or a building. Can't do a lot of harm.'

'Except for the people who lose their letters,' Mabel murmured.

'It's just to create annoyance more than anything – and to get a piece in the local press to highlight their cause.'

Does it have the right effect, though? Mabel wondered. Maybe it irritates people and loses support rather than gaining it. But, wisely, she kept these thoughts to herself.

The following week, there was a piece in a national newspaper about pillar boxes in London which had had red and black ink poured into them, spoiling the mail by obliterating addresses and soaking through the contents.

When Molly emerged from her work at the hosiery

factory on the following Monday evening, two policemen were waiting.

'Miss Wyngate?' one of the officers approached her as she passed by them.

Startled, Molly stopped. 'Yes?'

'Miss Molly Wyngate?'

'Yes. Is – is something wrong?'

'We'll have to ask you to come with us, miss, to the police station.'

'Why . . .?' Molly began as the constable took her arm in a firm grip.

'You'll find out when we get there. My sergeant wants a word.'

They walked through the streets, the constable making no effort to hide the fact that Molly was in some sort of trouble with the law. Her workmates, walking home, stared after them and nudged each other, whispering together.

'What d'you think she's done?' Molly heard someone say as they passed close by.

'She's one of them suffragettes. Been up to no good, I bet.'

Molly felt her face burn with embarrassment.

At the station, she was put in a small room with a table and two chairs.

'Sergeant Davis will be with you shortly,' the constable who had frog-marched her through the town said.

Then the door clanged shut and she was alone. It was then that Molly began to tremble.

*

The sergeant who entered the room about half an hour later was rotund with a balding pate. He sat down opposite Molly and regarded her sternly.

'Miss Molly Wyngate?'

Molly nodded.

'We have received an anonymous report that you were seen damaging a pillar box on Ashby Road in the early hours of Saturday morning.'

Molly gaped at him, her mouth falling open. 'No, no,' she managed to say at last, her voice cracking. 'I didn't go out at all on Friday evening, and certainly not in the middle of the night.'

'You belong to the local branch of the WSPU, don't you?'

'Yes, I do.'

'They're the militant lot, aren't they?'

'They are, yes, but I made it plain from the outset that I would not take part in any militant action. I only joined them when that was clearly understood and accepted. I do speak at meetings and I have delivered leaflets to people's houses. I'm willing to join a *peaceful* march, to carry a banner and wear their colours, but that's all.'

Molly was surprising herself. Only weeks earlier, before she had found the confidence to stand up in front of a crowd and speak to them, she would have been a quivering wreck when faced by an unsmiling policeman and questioned in the harsh and frightening surroundings of the cell-like interviewing room. But now that she knew what she was being accused of and knew herself to be totally innocent, her fear fell away.

A Woman of Spirit

Sergeant Davis raised his eyebrows. 'Then how, do you suppose, did someone see you tipping black ink into that pillar box in the dead of night?'

'I have no idea, Sergeant Davis, but I assure you it wasn't me. In the darkness they must have been mistaken.'

'Mm.' He was thoughtful, before heaving himself out of his chair and saying, 'Show me your hands.'

Molly spread out her hands for him to inspect.

'Stand up so that I can look at your clothes. Are these your workday clothes?'

'Yes, sir,' Molly said meekly, anxious not to antagonize the man any more. She did as he asked.

'Well, no sign of ink stains, I grant you. My superior suggested that the miscreant might have ink on their hands or on their clothing.' He paused for a moment as if thinking, then said, 'I will escort you to your home and ask your parents to verify that you were indeed at home all that night. But first, I must arrange for you to have your fingerprints taken.'

Molly stared at him. She'd never heard of this. Seeing her puzzled expression, Sergeant Davis said, 'My superior is very keen on all modern inventions to do with catching criminals. We have found a fingerprint on the pillar box in question, in black ink. Now, if I take yours and it matches, then I'm afraid you could be in serious trouble.'

'How – how will you know it's mine? It could be anybody's.'

'Ah, now that's where this new invention is so clever. It seems that everybody's fingerprint is unique.

No one in the world has exactly the same fingerprint as you.'

'Really?'

'Yes, really. Difficult to believe, though, isn't it? Out of all the millions of people in the world, no two are identical.'

When the sergeant had taken her fingerprints, Molly looked down at her hands. 'Now I have got ink on my hands. It looks as if I *am* guilty.'

'That's all right,' Sergeant Davis said. 'I can vouch for you that you had no ink on your hands before I took the prints. In fact, I've written that down. Besides, it should scrub off. Now, we'd best get you home and see if your parents can vouch that you were indeed at home all night.'

Molly did not reply. It would be a little silly, she was thinking, to ask her family such a question. All the family had been in bed the whole night. How could any one of them say with certainty what another had been doing? She could easily have crept out into the darkness – just as she had done when delivering leaflets – and not one of them would have known. Molly said nothing but followed the sergeant out of the station and towards her own home. Leading him down the alleyway, she took him in through the back door and into the kitchen. Her parents and William were already sitting at the table as Mabel was in the act of serving up the tea: warmed-up vegetables for the two men, and bread and butter for herself and Molly.

'Mam, Dad, this is Sergeant Davis. He's had a report that I was seen in the middle of the night on Friday damaging a pillar box.'

A Woman of Spirit

She glanced quickly at her brother who, she was very afraid, might speak out. But, although he looked thunderous, William remained silent.

Ron rose slowly from his seat and turned to face the sergeant. 'I think you've been misinformed, sergeant, but please come in and sit down and we will sort this out. Mabel, love, put my tea back in the oven to keep warm and pour the sergeant a cup of tea. Please sit down, Sergeant Davis.'

'I'll stand, if you don't mind, sir, but I won't say no to a cuppa.'

Ron shrugged. 'Very well. So, what is it you wish to see us about?'

'Can you vouch for your daughter being at home the whole of Friday night?'

Ron met the sergeant's gaze squarely. 'No, to be honest, I can't. We were all in our beds and asleep, but what I can tell you, sergeant, is that my daughter is an honest and truthful girl. If she has told you she did not do it, then she didn't.'

'Ah well, sir, I'm afraid that's not quite good enough. We have a witness who said they saw her.'

'And who is this witness?'

Now it was the sergeant who seemed ill at ease. He shuffled his feet and glanced away from Ron's steady stare.

'You told me that it was an anonymous report,' Molly said.

'Well, yes, it was. It was a note pushed through our police station letterbox.'

'Then,' Ron said, catching on quickly, 'you don't actually know who left the note.'

'No, sir, but a letterbox was damaged that night. Black ink was poured into it and all the letters ruined.'

'So what happens now, if you have no one who will come forward to identify the miscreant in person?'

The sergeant straightened his shoulders. 'We have to take this matter seriously, so I shall caution Miss Wyngate that if we receive any more such complaints it will not go so easily for her the next time.'

Ron shook his head disbelievingly. 'The next time? There hasn't been a first time.'

'Not that I can prove, sir, no, but why would anyone accuse your daughter of something like this if they weren't sure it was her?'

'I can't answer you that, sergeant, any more than you can say who made this report in the first place.'

When at last the sergeant left, William burst out, 'Didn't I tell you that this would lead to trouble? But you wouldn't listen to me. Molly, you should stop your involvement with the suffragettes at once. Dad – you should forbid her to go to any more of their meetings. They're filling her head with nonsense. She should know her place. She's a *girl*.' The final word he spat out in contempt.

'Calm down, William. Mabel, love, I'll have my tea now.'

'Of course, Ron. Sit down and I'll get it.'

'There, you see.' William threw out his arm towards Mabel but his gaze was on his sister. 'See what a good wife and mother she is?'

Molly sat down suddenly as her legs gave way beneath her. Although she had stood up to the questioning bravely, the whole episode had been a nasty shock. She looked at her father with tear-filled eyes. 'I – I didn't do it, Dad. I swear I didn't.'

Ron regarded her steadily for a moment and then said, 'I believe you, Molly. Now, let's all sit down and have our tea.'

'I – I don't think I can eat anything.'

'Guilty conscience,' William muttered as he sat down and began to tuck into the plate of food Mabel had put in front of him.

'Now, that's enough, William,' Ron said firmly. 'Have you ever known your sister to lie about anything?'

'No, Dad, I haven't, but she's changed since she's become involved with – that lot. I don't know her anymore.'

'She's growing up, that's all. She's developing a mind of her own.'

'She shouldn't have a mind of her own, as you put it. She should obey you and her husband' – he glanced at Molly, his tone scathing as he added – 'if she can find one.'

No more was said as the family ate, though Molly only nibbled at her bread and butter. When they had finished, William pushed back his chair. 'I'm going out for an hour, Mam. I'll see if I can pick up any gossip about this.'

'Not a word to anyone about Molly having been questioned,' Ron said. 'You hear me, William?'

For a moment, William glared at his father as if he intended to defy him. Then he thought better of it and nodded curtly. When he'd left the house, Molly said again in a quiet voice, 'I really didn't do it, Dad. I have joined the local branch of the WSPU, as you know, but I told Miss Anstruther that I would never do anything militant. I don't mind making speeches or delivering leaflets, marching or holding a banner, but nothing else. I swear to you.'

'I believe you, Molly,' Ron said as he rose from the table and moved to his chair by the range. 'But you need to be careful now. There's someone out there who wants to get you into trouble with the law.'

Mabel spoke up for the first time. 'I'll come with you to the meetings, but I can't spare the time to go everywhere with you. Like your dad says, you'll just have to be very careful.'

Seventeen

The following morning, Queenie was waiting outside Molly's house to walk part of the way with her to their places of work.

'What's this about a policeman bringing you home last night, Moll? Half the street's talking about it. You in trouble?'

'Someone put a note through the police station letterbox saying that they'd seen me damaging a pillar box on Ashby Road in the middle of the night on Friday.'

'And did you?'

'Of course I didn't,' Molly said hotly, shocked that her friend could even think that of her.

'So – are you going to stop going to the suffragette meetings?'

Molly lifted her chin resolutely. 'No, I am not. I'll just have to be more careful, that's all.'

Queenie linked her arm through Molly's. 'That's the spirit.'

Molly glanced down at her friend's legs. 'Is that a new skirt? I don't think I've seen that one before.'

Queenie laughed. 'Not very observant, are you, Moll? I wore it yesterday. Miss Parkinson made it for me.'

'It's very nice, but I thought Mr Gilmore liked all his staff to wear navy so that it looks like a uniform. That skirt is green.'

'He does, but I'll explain to him and ask Miss Parkinson to make me a new one in blue.'

'What happened to your usual skirt, then?'

'Oh,' Queenie said airily, 'I spilt something on it and the stain wouldn't come out, so I had to throw it away.'

'That's a shame. It was a nice skirt . . .'

'Ah, here we are,' Queenie said as they reached the corner where they had to part company. 'See you after work. Be good.'

As she had promised, Mabel accompanied Molly to the next meeting of the suffragettes. As they entered the room, Betsy Anstruther hurried forward, holding out both her hands to Molly. 'Oh my dear girl, I am so sorry to hear that you were arrested. Was it so very dreadful?'

'I wasn't arrested, Miss Anstruther, just questioned. They had no firm evidence.'

Betsy beamed. 'How very clever of you!'

'But I didn't do it. I told you I won't carry out anything like that and I meant it.'

Betsy's face fell and she glanced between mother and daughter, a slightly disappointed look on her face. 'Oh – oh, I see. When I heard about it, I thought perhaps you'd changed your mind.'

'No,' Molly said firmly. 'I'll come to the meetings. I'll make speeches, if you want me to. I'll even march with you and carry banners, as long as they remain peaceful demonstrations, but I will *not* damage property.'

'Very well,' Betsy said. 'There's still a lot you can do to further the cause. Come along and take your seat. We're about to start.'

Mabel and Molly sat beside Harriet Spencer and Alice Mayberry.

'Are you all right, Molly?' Harriet asked, leaning forwards. 'We heard about your little escapade.'

'We thought you might have,' Mabel said dryly. 'The thing is, Mrs Spencer, Molly didn't do what she's been accused of.'

'Oh. Oh, I see. Never mind. We'd have been proud of you if you had done it, though. Alice and I have decided to take part in a few militant actions – just minor ones – so long as they don't hurt anyone.'

'Don't you see, we've got to get ourselves noticed,' Alice put in. 'The passive way doesn't seem to be working.'

Mabel sighed. 'I take your point. I really do, but . . .'

At that moment, Betsy called the meeting to order. The rest of the evening was taken up with organizing a peaceful march through the town the following Saturday afternoon. When volunteers were asked for to carry a huge banner with VOTES FOR WOMEN on it, Mabel put her hand up.

'Me and Molly will do that. We want to be seen to be doing something, but don't ask us to set fire to anything, will you?'

There was a ripple of nervous laughter through the room and Betsy, on the platform, smiled. 'Thank you, Mrs Wyngate, and no, we won't ask you to do that.'

More plans were made, the meeting came to an end and the three women and Molly walked towards their homes together.

The following Saturday dawned bright and clear and Mabel and Molly set out soon after an early lunch.

'You haven't said anything to William, have you, Molly?'

'Not likely.'

'I expect he'll get to hear about it and that we were involved.'

'Dad doesn't seem to mind. Are you frightened of William, Mam?'

'No – no – not exactly. I just don't like there being arguments and quarrels within the family, that's all. Ah, there's Mrs Spencer and Mrs Mayberry. Let's join up with them. It looks as if they've got a banner.'

'Were we supposed to make one?'

'I don't think so. Nobody asked us to.'

'We made this at home,' Harriet said as they met up. 'Miss Anstruther was organizing the one for you two to carry. We'll be at the front of the march and you two will be at the back. Is that all right?'

'Whatever you say.'

Several women, all dressed in the suffragette colours, apart from Mabel, who had not yet had time to source a white dress and colourful hat for herself, assembled at the town hall. They were formed into lines by Betsy. Mabel and Molly took their place at the back and held up the two poles with the banner declaring VOTES FOR WOMEN strung between them. Now, as the march moved off, they saw that the market place was lined with more women and several men.

'Go home and do the washing,' a gruff voice shouted from among the onlookers.

'I don't wash on Saturdays,' Mabel shouted back. 'Washday's on a Monday and I'll be doing it as usual, never fear.'

At the other end of the banner they were carrying between them, Molly giggled nervously. 'Oh Mam . . .'

The women marched the length of the market place to the sound of cheering from the women and ribald remarks from the men. Then into neighbouring streets until they came back to the town hall where they'd started. By this time, several of the marchers' dresses were stained with rotten tomatoes and stinking eggs. As they reached the main doors where their peaceful march was due to end, there was movement among the watching crowd and half a dozen men surged forward, grabbing at the banners to throw them to the ground and stamp on them. One stocky black-haired man seized Molly round the waist and lifted her off her feet.

'Want to make a spectacle of yourself, do you, me duck?' the ruffian shouted in Molly's ear. 'We can help you do that. Let's find a nice dark alley . . .'

Molly screamed and struggled but his grasp was firm as he carried her easily towards the side of the market place. Molly kicked his shins and tried to free herself, but he only laughed and gripped her more tightly.

Just as he was about to drag her into a dark alleyway, a voice Molly recognized spoke. 'Put her down this minute, Cyril Hinds, else it'll be the worse for you.'

The man's grasp loosened and he dropped her to the ground. 'Harry, mate. I didn't know she was one of your fancy pieces.'

'Watch your tongue, an' all,' Harry thundered, and then another voice chipped in. 'Or you'll have the two of us to contend with.'

The man was grinning uneasily now. 'Oh, *both* the Spencer boys. Well, well, I didn't know you were supporters of these mad women.'

'Careful, Cyril,' Ben said. 'Our mam's one of these "mad women". We came here to keep an eye on her, but Molly's our friend so you can keep yer filthy hands off her, an' all.'

The man, whose name Molly now knew was Cyril, put up his hands defensively and began to back away. 'No harm done, lads. Just a bit of fun.'

'Fun, you call it, do you? Trying to drag a young lass into a dark alley? Doesn't look like fun to us, does it, Harry?' Ben said grimly.

'No, it docsn't. You all right, Molly?'

'Yes, thanks, Harry,' she said shakily.

As Cyril scuttled away, Harry said, 'I'll stay with Molly, Ben. You go and see if Mam's all right.'

'She was at the head of the march,' Molly said, 'carrying the other banner.'

Harry grinned. 'Yeah, I know. We've been watching.'

At that moment, Mabel elbowed her way through the crowd, her face creased with fear. 'You all right, Molly?'

'Thanks to Harry and Ben I am. It was a bit scary there for a few minutes.'

'I saw it happening but I couldn't get through the crowd to you quick enough.' She glanced up at Harry. 'Thank goodness you were close by.'

Harry nodded and smiled. 'It seems you ladies need a couple of bodyguards even on a peaceful march.'

'It's just these idiots who don't seem to understand what we're trying to do. We'd best get home now, Molly, love. Your dad will be wanting his tea. Never let it be said that I neglect my family for the cause.'

'Will you both be all right?' Harry asked, but his gaze was on Molly's face as he said it. For a brief moment, as she looked up into his eyes, the rest of the world seemed to fade away. There were no crowds around them, no shouting and cat-calling, no raucous laughter or jeering. There was just Harry and her, enveloped in an oasis of calm. Harry reached out and touched her cheek gently. 'I don't want to see you get hurt,' he murmured so that only Molly heard his words.

'We'll be fine, Harry,' Mabel said briskly, breaking their reverie. 'And thank you again.'

When they reached their street, they could see Queenie waiting outside her front door. She was dressed in her Sunday best, but her arms were folded and she was tapping her foot impatiently. As Mabel and Molly reached their own house, she walked to meet them.

'Harry was supposed to come round this afternoon. I don't suppose you've seen him, have you?'

Mabel and Molly glanced at each other before Mabel said, 'As a matter of fact we have. He was at the march. Him and Ben. They were there to keep an eye on their mam. Lucky for us they were.'

Queenie frowned. 'Why?'

'Me and Molly were carrying a banner at the back of the march, and when we got back to the market place where it ended, a rough-looking fella got hold of Molly and tried to pull her into an alley. Harry and Ben rescued her. Anyway, I must get on,' Mabel said and moved away down the jitty towards her own back door.

'Oh, how very chivalrous,' Queenie said, her tone heavy with sarcasm, when Mabel was out of earshot. 'He was supposed to be with me, not rescuing damsels in distress.' She glared at Molly. 'It's your own fault, Moll. If you will get so involved with these people, you'll get yourself into real trouble one of these days. Pouring ink into a pillar box was bad enough, but demonstrating in the streets, that's something else. It's not – it's not ladylike.'

'I thought you supported the suffragette movement?'

'There are other ways for a girl to get what she wants,' Queenie said smugly. She leaned closer to Molly. 'And don't think you're going to steal my boyfriend from under my nose, Molly Wyngate, else you an' me are going to fall out.'

Molly turned away and hurried after her mother. About halfway down the passageway, she stopped as a thought struck her. She stood a few moments, thinking, and then moved on slowly into the backyard and then into the house. Mabel was already bustling about the kitchen preparing tea.

'Get the plates from the dresser, Molly, love, there's a good girl.'

Molly washed her hands in the scullery and helped her mother set the table. When everything was ready, Mabel breathed a sigh of relief. 'Your dad's been very good about me getting involved with the suffragettes, but I still don't want to give him any chance to moan.' She flopped into a chair at the side of the hearth and leaned back. 'Those banners are quite heavy, aren't they? I'm fair worn out.'

'Mam,' Molly said slowly. 'There wasn't anything in any of the local newspapers about – about the pillar box incident, was there?'

'Not that I saw. Why?'

'And you haven't said anything to Aunty Ethel about it, have you? About me being questioned by the police or anything?'

'No, I haven't.'

'Maybe William's said something in the pub and it's got back,' Molly murmured.

'What's got back and who to? Molly, you're talking in riddles. What are you on about?'

'Just now – after you came in to start the tea – Queenie said that if I go on as I am, I'll get into real trouble. "Pouring ink into a pillar box was bad enough," she said, "but demonstrating in the streets, that's something else".' Molly met her mother's gaze. 'Mam, I've never mentioned to her that the damage done to the pillar box was by ink being poured into it.'

For a moment, Mabel stared at her, then she gave

a short laugh. 'Harry will have told her. His mother knew all about it.' She paused and then added, a little uncertainly now, 'Didn't she?'

'She knew about damage being done to a pillar box, because she said as much at the meeting.'

Mabel nodded her agreement. 'Yes, I heard her.'

'But not . . .' Molly went on, 'about the ink.'

Mabel was still puzzled. 'I don't understand.'

'Everyone around here knows that I've been accused of damaging a pillar box but not exactly how I'm supposed to have done it. But Queenie knew and I've not told her. And there's another thing. The day after I'd been questioned by the police, I noticed that she was wearing a different skirt. A new one I hadn't seen before. She said she'd spilt something on the one she usually wears to work, that the stain wouldn't come out and she'd had to throw the skirt away.'

'Throw it away?' For a moment, Mabel was scandalized at the thought of such waste. Then her mind came back to what Molly was saying. 'And that was just a couple of days after the pillar box incident?'

Molly nodded.

'So, you mean – you mean, how did she know it was ink that had been used?'

'Exactly.'

Mabel stared at her and then shook her head. 'Oh no, Molly, love. Queenie wouldn't do that. She's your best friend.'

'Well, I thought so too, but she's just sort of – sort of threatened me. She warned me off Harry.' Molly shrugged and sighed. 'As if I could steal him from her anyway.'

A Woman of Spirit

'I've told you before, Molly, love, don't put yourself down.'

'Anyway, it seems she's not so interested in the suffragette movement now.' Molly smiled wryly.

'Well, love, maybe it's for the best. Like I told you before, once a girl gets a boyfriend . . .'

But in the darkness and solitude of her bed that night, Molly relived that special moment when Harry had touched her cheek and gazed into her eyes. For one brief instant, Molly could dream that he really cared about her.

Eighteen

Molly hurried back from work, not even waiting to meet Queenie on their usual corner to walk home together.

'Mam!' She burst into the kitchen waving a newspaper she had picked up at work. 'Have you heard about this?'

'Depends what it is, love,' Mabel said calmly.

'It's about a suffragette called Emily Davison. She ran out in front of the horses at a race at Epsom. The King's horse knocked her down. She's gravely ill.'

'Let me see.'

Mabel sank down into a chair, her preparations for the family's evening meal forgotten.

'Oh my goodness,' she murmured at last. 'Why ever did she do that?'

'To draw attention to the suffragettes' demands, but the tone of the newspaper isn't very supportive.'

'No, it certainly isn't.'

A few days later, the newspaper which Molly brought home reported that Emily Davison had died, even though an operation had brought temporary relief.

'There's to be a big funeral – a suffragette funeral –

for her in London. I wonder if anyone from here will go?' Mabel mused.

'We'll hear at the next meeting,' Molly said.

The news of Emily Wilding Davison's death shocked the world. At the next meeting, Betsy stood to address the gathering.

'I shall be attending Miss Davison's funeral in London. Is there anyone else who would like to go with me?'

Mabel glanced at Molly. 'I wish we could go, but I don't think they'd be sympathetic at your place of work.'

Molly shook her head. 'No, they wouldn't.'

Harriet and Alice were sitting in front of them and Mabel saw them glance at each other. 'We could go,' she heard Alice whisper. 'I've never been to London. Would your old man mind?'

Harriet laughed as she stuck up her hand. 'Two chances,' she muttered. Then she raised her voice to say, 'Me and Alice will go with you, Miss Anstruther, if you'll have us?'

Betsy smiled. 'I'd be glad to have your company. We can stay two nights and—'

'Oh, I don't know if we could . . .' Harriet began, thinking the trip was suddenly sounding expensive.

Betsy waved her hand and smiled. 'The branch's funds will cover all our expenses.'

Harriet relaxed then, and began to look forward to their trip, even though it was for a sad occasion.

'We shall want to hear all about it when you come back,' someone said. 'Did you know that when she was in hospital, some of her colleagues draped the screens around her bed with the suffragette colours? And they say there were bouquets of flowers delivered to the hospital for her.'

'I just hope she knew before she died.'

On their return from London, Miss Anstruther called a special meeting of the WSPU members and invited as many of her loyal followers as she could squeeze into the dining room of her home.

'It's a few years since I was here, Betsy,' Mabel said as she glanced around her. 'It hasn't changed much, I have to say.'

Betsy laughed. 'I fear it is not quite as spotless as when your dear mother worked here, Mabel. Please, sit down if you can find a chair. You too, Molly.'

'I'll stand, Miss Anstruther, so that Mrs Spencer or Mrs Mayberry may have a seat.'

Betsy smiled her approval. 'We'll find a seat for both of them.'

When they were all settled, Betsy began. 'Please make your contributions whenever you want to, Mrs Spencer and Mrs Mayberry. I am sure I shall forget a few details that everyone would like to hear.' Harriet and Alice nodded, and Betsy continued. 'Miss Davison had been brought from Epsom to Victoria in London, and the procession we witnessed was from there to St George's Church in Bloomsbury.'

'Is that where they had the service?'

'Yes, and then she was taken to King's Cross.'

'Why?' someone asked. 'Wasn't she buried in London?'

'Oh no,' Harriet said. 'She was being taken to Morpeth in Northumberland for interment in the family plot.'

'I've been told that the WSPU organized her funeral procession,' Betsy went on, 'and that five thousand suffragettes and their supporters followed the coffin.'

'The streets were lined the whole way,' Harriet said. 'There must have been fifty thousand there.'

'A woman in white carrying a cross led the way,' Alice added, 'followed by several girls dressed in white and carrying laurel wreaths.'

'There were a lot wearing black too,' Betsy went on. 'And I noticed there were others carrying bouquets of purple irises and red peonies. And there were bands playing.'

'I didn't like the scuffle that occurred when there were a few young men who waved their hats and cheered. Very disrespectful, I thought it,' Harriet said.

'It was only a very few. Most people there, even if they hadn't agreed with her beliefs, still wanted to pay their respects.'

Molly dipped her head. She had the uncomfortable feeling that had William been present, he might well have been one of the young men cheering.

'Was Mrs Pankhurst there? Did you see her?'

'No,' Betsy said, anger lacing her tone. 'She'd been arrested as she was setting out for the funeral.'

'No!' There was a murmuring around the room. 'That's dreadful.'

'The carriage in which she should have travelled

remained empty but still followed the coffin,' Betsy said. 'To make a point, I suppose.'

'Someone told me, though I don't know if it's true,' Harriet remarked, 'that there was a wreath on the coffin that said, "She died for women".'

There was a silence in the room for several moments before someone said softly, 'Well, she did, didn't she?'

'I've heard since,' Betsy went on, 'that there was another procession in Morpeth made up of suffragettes from the north of the country. She'll never be forgotten, will she?'

'No, we'll make sure of that.'

In the Wyngate household, William was as scathing as ever. 'I don't wish to speak ill of the dead, but it was rather foolhardy to rush in among horses thundering down the course. What was she hoping to achieve? Was she hoping to become a martyr to the cause? Because that's what she is now.'

'No one knows for certain, but it's all very sad,' Mabel said. 'Betsy is convinced she was just trying to pin one of our flags onto the king's horse. There were tickets in her possession – including a train ticket home – that suggests she had no intention of dying that day.'

'Well,' Ron said quietly, 'whatever her motive was, it's certainly raised awareness of the suffragettes' movement, but whether that's in a good way or not, I'm not sure.'

'I suppose,' Molly said slowly, 'if a woman is prepared to endanger her life, she must have cared passionately about it.'

'I just hope you won't do anything as daft as that, Molly, else I'll wash my hands of you completely.'

'I thought you already had, William,' his sister retorted.

A week later, Sergeant Davis knocked on the front door of the Wyngate house. Up and down the street curtains twitched and one or two women came out of their houses to stand staring brazenly, their arms folded across their chests.

'Bit of excitement when a uniformed officer visits,' one said. 'Don't want to miss it.'

'It'll be their lass again, up to her tricks with them suffragettes.'

'Good morning, Sergeant Davis,' Mabel said politely when she opened the door. 'Please come in.' She glanced up and down the street. 'I see you already have an audience.'

'Aye, nothing like the sight of my uniform to bring the nosey parkers out, eh, missus?'

Sergeant Davis removed his helmet and stepped inside. He accepted a cup of tea and sat down at the kitchen table.

'Molly at work, is she?'

'She is.'

'There was a bit of trouble last night. A pillar box was set on fire.'

Mabel poured her own cup of tea and then sat down opposite him.

She sighed. 'So, every time there's "a bit of trouble" you're going to come knocking at our door, are you?'

The sergeant had the grace to look a little sheepish. 'Not necessarily. It'll rather depend on what it is.'

Mabel was thoughtful for a few moments, but then she came to a decision. She was determined to treat the officer with respect, almost friendliness. There was no point in getting on the wrong side of the law for the sake of it. And, you never knew, one day she might need his help.

'Molly arrived home from work at the usual time last night. About six-thirty. She didn't go out again at all, although her friend, Queenie, called round here briefly. That was just after nine, because I remember thinking it was a bit late for a visit.' She shrugged. 'But then the girls have been friends since they could walk, so they're used to trotting in and out of each other's houses whenever they feel like it. She only stayed about half an hour last night. We all go to bed at about ten in this house. We're early risers for everyone to get to work on time, you see.'

'And who is this Queenie?'

'Queenie Palmer. She lives with her parents four doors down from here.'

'And does she work at the same place as Molly?'

Mabel gave a wry smile. 'Oh no. Not grand enough for our Queenie. She works at a draper's in town. Nice job for a lass, though, I have to admit.'

'And they've been friends since they were little, you say?'

Mabel nodded. 'They were inseparable until recently.'

'So, what's happened recently?'

'Queenie's got a boyfriend.'

'Ah,' Sergeant Davis said knowingly. 'And who is he? Someone local?'

'Harry Spencer. Lives two streets away.'

'Ah yes, I know the Spencer brothers. Good lads, they are. Never been in trouble. Not with us, anyway. And is that why Molly got interested in the suffragette cause, because her friend's time is occupied elsewhere now?'

Mabel frowned thoughtfully. 'Not – really. Queenie seemed interested in them too at first, but when her parents decided to allow her to meet Harry openly – well, like you say, her time's taken up with him now.'

'Has Molly got a boyfriend?'

Mabel shook her head. She didn't want to give away Molly's deepest secrets. Carefully, she said, 'She's friendly with Ben, Harry's brother, but they're not walking out.'

There was silence between them for a few moments until the sergeant said, 'So, you're sure Molly didn't go out again last night.'

'Positive.'

'You haven't asked me anything about the incident. Where it was or what time.'

'I don't need to. I know Molly wasn't involved.'

'It was on Ashby Road again. Same pillar box, only this time it was set on fire at about half past ten. Unfortunately, no one saw anything.'

'We all went up to bed at the normal time and I heard her moving about her room for about twenty minutes. There is no way she could have left the house and got up to Ashby Road by half past.' Mabel leaned towards the officer. 'Let's get something straight between us, shall we, Sergeant Davis? Yes, me and Molly do belong to the local branch of the WSPU and, yes, they're the militant lot, but we told them from the start that we will not take part in any acts of violence. We'll attend their meetings, we'll deliver leaflets, we'll march peacefully and we'll carry placards and banners, but we will do nothing to harm people or property. And if you want to verify that, ask Miss Anstruther. I'm sure you know her.'

Sergeant Davis laughed wryly. 'Oh, indeed I do. I've had cause to arrest her twice.'

'I don't suppose you have any sympathy with the Votes for Women campaign, do you?'

'As a matter of fact, I do. My wife is a strong supporter, but of course she can't get involved in any of their activities. It could end my career. Well,' he added, heaving himself out of the chair, 'I must be on my way. I'm satisfied Molly had nothing to do with last night's episode, but mind you keep an eye on her, Mrs Wyngate. I respect what she's doing, but I can't turn a blind eye if she breaks the law.'

'I understand that, Sergeant Davis. And Molly does too.'

The officer picked up his helmet and moved towards the back door, but Mabel said hurriedly, 'Oh, please go out the front way, sergeant. It's bad luck to leave a house by a different door.'

He chuckled. 'Right you are, missus. I'll face the curtain twitchers then.'

Ten minutes after the policeman had left the street, Ethel let herself in by Mabel's back door.

'Your lass in bother again, is she?'

'No,' Mabel said. 'She wouldn't have been last time either, if some busybody hadn't put an anonymous note through the police station's door.'

'I think it would be best if our girls weren't out quite so late. Queenie was far too late getting home last night, but I knew she was only round here, so I didn't worry.'

'I'll make sure she doesn't stay here too late. What time would you like her home, Ethel?'

'Oh, just before ten is fine, but it was a lot later than that last night.'

Mabel clamped her lips together. Queenie had left their house at half past nine. Maybe the girl had met up with Harry. She didn't want to get Queenie into trouble, but if it happened again, she would have to say something.

Nineteen

The appalling death of one of their most prominent members spurred the suffragettes on even more, and the Loughborough branch of the WSPU was no exception. The members were determined to continue their fight for enfranchisement. However, they were no longer entitled to use the premises at the town hall following a vote by the councillors. Meetings would now be held in the market place or a local church facility. 'At Home' events would be held in a local school room, and, for smaller gatherings, at Miss Anstruther's home, which she prepared by clearing the dining room completely of furniture and setting out rows of chairs.

'What do you think, Mabel?' Betsy said. 'I can accommodate forty or fifty, not exactly comfortably, I must admit, but I don't think the ladies will mind.'

Mabel chuckled. 'It'll be cosy, to say the least, but most of our members should be able to fit in.'

'Thank goodness my parents decided to buy a large house with spacious grounds too. I'm hoping to have a garden party in August to raise funds for our branch.'

'I'd be glad to help with that. Let me know what me and Molly can do.'

'Bake cakes,' Betsy said promptly. 'And man a stall on the day. Could you and Molly do that together? I plan to hold it on a Sunday afternoon, so she wouldn't be at work.' She paused and then added, 'Do you think your husband would be willing to lend a hand? Harriet's already roped hers in.'

'I can only ask. But there's one thing I do know. My son certainly won't help.'

Mabel had been right.

'Don't get involved, Dad,' William said when he heard about Miss Anstruther's proposal to hold a garden party. 'You'd be stupid if you do.'

'Thank you, William,' Ron said sharply. 'I can make up my own mind.'

But William was not about to be silenced. 'What will the chaps at the foundry say if you get the name of being tied up with these mad women?'

Ron lowered the newspaper he was reading and regarded his son over the top of his spectacles. 'It doesn't seem to bother Luke Spencer. He told us he gets a bit of teasing at The Brush, but he just smiles and shrugs it off. I think his reply is usually, "If it keeps the missus happy" and no one has an answer to that.' He glanced across the hearth towards Mabel, who was sitting quietly with her darning. He winked as he added, 'We all want to do that.'

'What about Uncle Jack? I bet he's not involved. He's got his reputation as a foreman to uphold. He'd lose credibility.'

Ron shook his newspaper. 'I don't think he has to decide, does he? Ethel's not involved.'

'No, she isn't,' Mabel said. 'Nor is Queenie now.

But I have the feeling that Jack wouldn't stop her if she was.'

William made a growling sound in his throat. 'Well, all I hope is that it pours with rain on the day and you all get soaked to the skin. I'll wish you goodnight. I'm off to bed.'

The garden party was a huge success and, despite William's curse, the weather was glorious. All the members of the local WSPU branch were there, many of them having contributed in some way, and several husbands – more than Betsy had expected – came to set up stalls and organize games for the children.

At first, many of the mothers tried to restrain their lively offspring from stampeding about Miss Anstruther's grounds, but then Betsy said, 'Oh, let them run wild, they can't hurt anything and if they do, it's a garden. Things will grow again. As long as they don't injure themselves, that's all I ask.'

When one enterprising boy spied the tree house in the branches of the oak at the end of the garden and began to climb up to reach it, Betsy commandeered three fathers to stand beneath the branches as other children began queuing to climb up too.

'I think my father wanted a boy,' she told the three men, 'but he was sadly disappointed. Mind you, I was a bit of a tomboy and had many happy hours hidden away up there where no one could find me. Keep an eye on them, Mr Spencer, I don't want any broken limbs today. Now, Ben, would you like . . .'

Betsy had a job for everyone. Molly had been

A Woman of Spirit

surprised to see both Ben and Harry turn up to the event.

'We're here to support our mam,' Harry told her with a laugh. 'Don't get any ideas that we're about to join the crusade, will you?'

'I thought you'd be out with Queenie.'

'I told her what I was doing today and asked her to come along, but she declined, so I've come on my own.'

'That was brave of you.'

He stared at her for a moment as if he didn't understand.

Molly laughed. 'To refuse Queenie.'

Harry frowned. 'Oh, I'm no pushover, Molly. I'm quite aware that she doesn't like it when I have a night out with my mates, but I refuse to give up my other friends to suit her. She either takes me as I am, or not at all.'

Molly couldn't quell the sudden stab of glee that swept through her. So, she thought, Queenie doesn't have it all her own way, like she'd have me believe. To hear her talk, anyone would think her boyfriend was putty in her hands. Harry was smiling again as he said, 'I bet you're not so possessive with our Ben, now are you?'

Molly shrugged. 'He's not my boyfriend, as I keep telling everyone.' Daringly – and something she would not have done only a few months ago – she added, 'But maybe if *you* were mine, I wouldn't want to let you out of my sight either. Anyway, I must go and take over from my mam on the cake stall. Tell you what, if you come round at the end of the day and there are any cakes left, I'll let you have them for half price.'

Harry threw back his head and laughed. 'Oh, favouritism, is it?'

'Of course,' she said, with a coy glance at him as she turned to walk away. Her heart was thudding in her chest as she marvelled at the way she had been able to flirt with Harry. Belonging to the suffragettes had certainly given quiet little Molly Wyngate some spirit, she acknowledged to herself.

At the next meeting of the branch, held in her home, Betsy Anstruther opened the proceedings by saying, 'I expect most of you have heard of the Women's Tax Resistance League?' She paused as she glanced around the room and then added, 'Ah, I see that many of you have not. It's a group of ladies who normally have to pay income tax, but who have adopted the motto "No vote, no tax". I have decided not to pay my income tax this year, so I may well be arrested.'

'Oh, how brave of you, Miss Anstruther. I'd join you if I could, but I don't pay taxes.'

'We'll come and visit you,' someone said in a jocular tone. 'If you're locked up.'

But Betsy wasn't laughing.

Betsy Anstruther was not arrested for refusing to pay her taxes, but items from her home were sold at auction in the street outside her home by the Income Tax Collector. After the sale was concluded, Betsy mounted an upturned box and addressed those there. 'I hope I have established a precedent,' she said. 'I

A Woman of Spirit

hope that next year any woman who pays taxes will refuse to do so.'

Harriet, standing beside Mabel, murmured, 'I admire her spirit, but she'll lose all her possessions piece by piece if she's not careful.'

Mabel nudged her and leaned closer to Harriet to whisper, 'I'm not sure she will. See that woman at the side there . . .'

Harriet turned to look. 'The one with the huge hat in our colours?'

'Yes. Her. That's one of Betsy's friends. I thought she looked familiar but I couldn't place her, and now I remember. She's altered a bit, of course, but she was one of Betsy's friends years ago. She used to come to the house. I met her a few times.'

'What about her?'

'She's bought all Betsy's belongings that have just been sold.'

Harriet turned to stare at Mabel. 'You mean it's a put-up job? That woman's bought them and is going to give them back to her?'

Mabel chuckled. 'Either that or she's bought them on Betsy's behalf.'

'So, Betsy – Miss Anstruther – has bought back her own belongings?'

Mabel shrugged. 'She can afford it. She can stand by her decree "No vote, no tax" and yet still not lose her things.'

'She's just done it to make a point,' Harriet said in admiration. 'How clever.' She paused and then added slowly, 'But I think we'd better keep these thoughts to ourselves, Mabel.'

'Absolutely. We've no proof that's what's happening. It's only because I recognize the woman who's bought the things.'

The two women smiled at each other, sharing the secret.

One Tuesday evening towards the end of October, Sergeant Davis knocked on the front door of the Wyngates' home once more. This time he had a young constable with him. Word travelled down the street almost before Mabel had opened the door. Neighbours appeared outside their doors and leaned out of their windows.

'Now what's she done?' they called to one another.

This time all the Wyngate family were at home, just finishing their tea.

As the two policemen followed Mabel into the kitchen, Ron and William glanced up with a frown, but Molly smiled at the sergeant.

'Hello, Sergeant Davis. What am I supposed to have done now?'

But Sergeant Davis wasn't smiling. 'This is a serious matter, Miss Wyngate, and I have orders to take you to the station for questioning. But first' – he turned to Ron – 'my constable and I must search these premises for evidence.'

'What "evidence"?' Ron asked at once, standing up.

'At the present time I am not at liberty to divulge that information, sir,' the sergeant said stiffly. He turned to the constable. 'You start down here, Perkins, and don't forget the backyard, the wash-house and so on. You know what we're looking for?'

The constable nodded. 'Yes, sarge. I'll call you if I find anything of interest.'

Sergeant Davis turned back to Molly. 'Now, Miss Wyngate, if you'd be so good as to show me your bedroom . . .'

'Dad, are they allowed to do this?' William burst out.

Ron shrugged. 'No point in resisting, son. They'll do it eventually, and to try to stop them would only make us look guilty.'

'Us? Don't you include me in any of this.' He turned angry eyes on his sister. 'If you've done anything to bring disgrace to this family, I'll never have anything to do with you again. You can starve in the gutter for all I care.' He turned to face the sergeant. 'You don't need me for anything, I hope? If not, I'm going out.'

'Not at the moment, sir, no, but we may need to talk to you at some point, depending on how our investigations proceed.'

William turned away. Over his shoulder he said, 'I'll see you later, Mam.'

Mabel said nothing but watched him go with worried eyes. This visit from the police seemed to be far more serious than the two previous occasions.

Sergeant Davis followed Molly up the narrow staircase with Mabel close on his heels. She was not going to allow him to be alone upstairs with her young daughter, whatever position of authority he believed himself to be in. They stood together in the doorway while the sergeant prowled around Molly's room. He opened her wardrobe and sniffed the clothing there, holding each garment up to his nose. Mabel and Molly glanced at each other, mystified by his strange action. He rummaged in the drawers of the chest and flung back the bedclothes, once again sniffing at the blankets.

'What exactly are you searching for, Sergeant Davis? Maybe we can help you.'

Without answering, he tipped up the feather mattress and drew out a handful of the suffragette leaflets which Molly had hidden there, away from William's prying eyes.

'Have you any copies of the publication called *The Suffragette* in your possession?'

'Not at the moment, no,' Molly said. 'I usually read them when I visit Mrs Spencer or Miss Anstruther. I don't bring them home very often because my brother would destroy them and they need to be passed around all the members of our local branch. Occasionally, I bring old copies home for my mother to see, but there's nothing here now.'

The sergeant's only reply was a grunt as he let the mattress fall back into place. He glanced around the room again, as if making sure he hadn't missed anything in his search. 'Right,' he said at last. 'We'll go back downstairs and see what my constable has found.' His gaze bored into Molly. 'You'll need to come with us and you may have to stay overnight, as it's getting late now.'

Back downstairs in the kitchen the constable was already waiting.

'Anything, Perkins?'

'No, sir. They've obviously been washing clothes

recently.' He glanced up at the airer pulled high up to the ceiling and gestured towards the clothes hanging on it, the result of Mabel's day of ironing.

'I wash on a Monday and iron on Tuesdays,' Mabel snapped. 'Like everyone around here. This week has been no different. If only you'd tell us what this is all about . . .'

'All in good time, Mrs Wyngate.' He turned back to Constable Perkins. 'Any paraffin? Matches?'

Perkins nodded. 'Yes, a half-full can of paraffin and three boxes of matches.'

'Anything else?'

'Not that I could find, sarge.'

The sergeant glanced upwards towards the lamp hanging from the ceiling, the one that Ron brought down on its pulley every evening to light.

'And no lingering smell of smoke?'

'No, sarge.'

'Smoke?' Ron, who had remained silent for the most part, burst out. 'What on earth are you talking about? I just wish you'd tell us the reason for all this.'

'All in good time, sir,' Sergeant Davis repeated. 'Now, Miss Wyngate, are you ready to come with us?'

Molly raised her chin and said steadily, 'Yes, Sergeant Davis.'

'I'm coming with you,' Ron said.

'You won't be able to be with her while she's being interviewed. She'll be quite safe with us, sir. I give you my word.'

'I'm not questioning that, sergeant, but I'd just like

to come to the station at least. Just – just to be with her and give her my support.'

Despite the gravity of the situation, Molly smiled at her father. She was filled with love and gratitude. She knew she'd done nothing wrong, but to have his unswerving belief in her meant the world.

Twenty

They marched along the street, with a policeman on either side of Molly. At least they haven't handcuffed me, she thought. Ron followed behind them, keeping his gaze upon the ground and ignoring the onlookers, but Molly walked with her head held high.

As the sergeant had warned them, when they reached the station, Molly was ushered into the small room where she had been questioned before. Ron was left sitting in the reception area of the station.

Sergeant Davis sat down opposite her. Constable Perkins sat beside him, his pencil poised to take notes.

'Were you at home all night on Saturday, Miss Wyngate?'

'I was, Sergeant Davis.'

'You didn't go out at all?'

'No,' Molly said, a little sadly. Before Queenie had started courting Harry, Saturday evenings had been fun. The two girls had always been together once Queenie had finished work at the drapery. They'd wander into the centre of the town to window shop or go to the park to see if there was a band playing. But now, all that had ended. Queenie was with Harry on Saturday evenings.

'Can you prove that you were at home all night?'

'Can you prove *you* were at home all night?' Molly snapped, her patience wearing thin.

'Now, now, Miss Wyngate, that attitude won't help. You've been a good lass so far whenever I've questioned you. Don't spoil it now.'

'I'm sorry, sergeant. I didn't mean to be disrespectful, but you haven't even told me why I'm being questioned.'

Ignoring her veiled request for more information, the sergeant continued, 'Have you attended suffragette meetings recently?'

'Yes, last week, but there isn't one this week.'

'Do you know why not?'

'No, sergeant. We don't have them every week. I think there will be one next week.'

'Do you know where that is to be held?'

'At Miss Anstruther's house, unless she can find a hall available somewhere.'

The sergeant leaned his elbows on the desk and clasped his hands in front of him. He leaned forward slightly towards her. 'Miss Wyngate, a serious incident took place on Saturday night in which we think you might have been involved.'

Molly shook her head. 'Whatever it was, Sergeant Davis, I was not there. I was at home all night, fast asleep in my bed, and I did not take part in any kind of incident.'

'Mm.' Sergeant Davis frowned. 'Perhaps a night in a cell will encourage you to tell us the truth.'

'I am telling you the truth, sergeant.'

'Then perhaps you know who carried out the

atrocity. If you do, then you must tell us the name or names of those who perpetrated this crime.'

'I don't know of any "crime" being planned. I still deliver leaflets around our neighbourhood, but I don't think that's against the law, is it? A *peaceful* march through the town is being organized for the beginning of December and I intend to take part in that, probably with my mother. We shall make our own banner this time and carry it between us. But other than that, I don't know about anything else being arranged.'

'So, you say you know nothing about Red House being set on fire on Saturday night?'

Molly's eyes widened and she stared at him in horror. When she found her voice she managed to say, 'No, I most definitely do not. I don't agree with any violent action. You know that, Sergeant Davis.'

'So you tell me,' he said tightly.

There was silence in the room until Molly dared to ask, 'Was anyone hurt?'

'Thankfully, no. The property has been unoccupied for some time. A fact that is well-known.'

'Not to me. I don't even know where Red House is.'

'It's on Burton Walks.'

Despite the gravity of her situation, Molly laughed. 'Burton Walks? I've only ever walked down there once in my life, just to look at the grand houses. And that was when I was little. Mam took me.'

Sergeant Davis straightened up and Constable Perkins closed his notebook. 'That will be all for now, Miss Wyngate, but you will be required to spend the night here. I shall need to consult with my superior about our findings and he won't be in until tomorrow morning. Perkins, make sure she has something to eat and drink before you lock her up for the night.'

As she stood up, Molly asked politely, 'May I ask you something, sergeant?'

He frowned but said, 'Go on.'

'Am I the only one being questioned each time there's an incident that might have been carried out by a suffragette?'

'We are pursuing several lines of inquiry, quite a few of which are with local suffragettes. So no, Miss Wyngate, you are not the only one.'

'That's all right then,' Molly said as she followed the constable.

Ron arrived home just before ten o'clock. William had returned home and was waiting with Mabel, his eyes still burning with fury.

'Well, have they charged her with something? Anything?'

Ron sat down heavily in his chair. His face was grey with tiredness and anxiety.

'No, but she's being kept overnight. Sergeant Davis must consult with his superior in the morning.'

'What's she done?' William asked harshly.

Ron looked at him. 'Why are you so ready to believe the worst of your sister?'

'Because she's caught up with – with these *women*.'

'So am I, William,' Mabel said.

'I know and I don't approve of that either, but at least you won't do anything illegal.'

'Nor will Molly,' Mabel said stoutly.

'I'd better take the day off work tomorrow . . .'

Ron began, but Mabel shook her head. 'No, you go to work as normal, Ron. I'll go to the police station in the morning to bring her home.'

'*If* they release her,' William said and earned himself a glare from both his parents.

Since there was no evidence to link Molly to the incident, she was released without charge the following morning.

'I'd better go straight to work, Mam,' she said, as they came out of the station into the cool of the October morning. 'I'm late already but I think my supervisor will understand.' Despite her ordeal, Molly was still able to smile. 'She belongs to the suffragettes too.'

Rumours were rife at the foundry but it wasn't until Friday's local paper that they learned more details. Ron summarized the piece as the family sat down together after tea.

'It says here that the chap who keeps an eye on the place for the owner went in on Sunday morning and found that a fire had been started on the staircase by saturating it with paraffin . . .'

'Ah, so that was why that constable was searching for paraffin and matches,' Mabel said. 'Go on, Ron.'

'Luckily the fire must have burned itself out because only four or five of the bottom steps were charred.'

'So why do they think it was started by a suffragette?'

'Because,' Ron went on slowly as he continued to read, 'there was a copy of that paper that Molly brings home now and again, *The Suffragette,* and also some leaflets referring to Emily Davison. It also says that none of the neighbours noticed anything amiss, which is strange because there must have been a good deal of smoke.'

'Ah, so *that* was why he was sniffing her clothes and bedding,' Mabel said. 'I thought it was a bit odd.'

'If the house was empty,' Molly said slowly, 'how did they know it was done on Saturday night? Because that's the only night he asked me about.'

'The caretaker chappie goes in every day and everything was all right on the Saturday evening, but he found the damage on the Sunday morning.'

Mabel sighed. 'It'll have set some of the locals against us now. The suffragettes, I mean.'

'You should both stop going to their meetings and taking part in their marches, Mam,' William said.

'We shall do no such thing, William,' Mabel said. 'Molly, we'll finish making that banner and be ready to join the march at the beginning of December, as we've planned.'

Twenty-one

It had long been the tradition for the two families – the Wyngates and the Palmers – to visit the annual street fair together, which came to the town during November.

'Why don't we join forces with the Spencers?' Mabel suggested to Ethel. 'Queenie will be with Harry, I'm sure, and Ben would be good company for Molly.'

'I thought William usually took his sister on the rides?'

Mabel pulled a face. 'He used to, but he's hardly speaking to her these days and he said last night that he's going with his pals this year. Molly will be on her own and it's not the same, is it?'

'Well, I don't mind, and I don't expect Jack will either.'

So, early in the evening of the Saturday, the three families met in the market place where merry fairground organ music filled the air. Rides and stalls spilled out into the nearby streets, which thronged with people. At once, Queenie clung to Harry's arm and pulled him away.

'Be home by ten, Queenie,' Ethel called after them.

Harry turned and waved. 'I'll make sure she is, Mrs Palmer.'

'He's a nice lad, your son, Mrs Spencer,' Ethel said. 'I'll be honest with you, I wasn't too sure about him when they started walking out together, but I see now that the reputation he had for chasing the girls wasn't deserved.'

Harriet laughed aloud. 'He's a good-looking lad, even though I say it myself. You can't blame the girls for buzzing around him like bees around a honeypot.' She would have liked to have added, your lass is a pretty girl, they go well together, but something held her back. She hadn't got to know Queenie very well yet, and though they made a handsome couple, Harriet needed to know that the girl's nature was what she wanted in a daughter-in-law.

She glanced at Molly. She had got to know her well through the girl's interest in the suffragette movement and liked her enormously. Although they denied it, she really hoped that something would grow between Molly and Ben.

Ben put his mouth close to Molly's ear. 'What do you want to go on first?'

'The gallopers,' she said at once.

'Come on, then. It looks as if Harry and Queenie are heading that way.' He turned back to Mabel and Ron. 'I'll look after her, Mrs Wyngate.'

Mabel nodded. 'Off you go, then. Have fun.'

After the four of them had ridden the gallopers twice, Ben asked, 'Where to now?'

'The cake walk,' Molly said promptly.

'And then the racing motors.' Harry grinned. 'We'll beat you two hollow.'

A Woman of Spirit

When they had ridden most of the rides and visited several of the stalls, Queenie pulled on Harry's arm. 'Look over there. It's a boxing booth. Are you going to have a go?'

'What, me get my handsome face bashed in? No thanks.'

Queenie's face fell. 'Oh, Harry, I didn't think you were a coward.'

Harry frowned and muttered, 'I'm not, but have you seen the size of the chap I'd be up against? If it's the same one as last year, he's built like a—'

'Harry!' Ben said warningly, as if he had realized what his brother might be going to say.

'Let's at least go and have a look,' Queenie encouraged. 'It might be someone you could beat easily.' She squeezed his upper arm. 'Just feel those muscles.'

Harry allowed himself to be pulled towards the crowd gathered around the boxing ring raised above the ground. As they drew closer, with Ben and Molly following them, he said, 'It's the same one they've been bringing for the past two years. I haven't seen anyone beat him yet. Big Billy, they call him.'

Queenie pouted. '*Cowardy, cowardy custard . . .*' she began to sing.

'All right, then. I'll show you.' Harry pulled his arm from hers and began to push his way through the throng.

'Harry—' Ben tried to catch hold of him but missed. 'Don't be an idiot. It's bare-knuckle fighting. He'll half kill you. Queenie, stop him.'

But Queenie was watching Harry approach the

ring and climb into it, her lips parted in a smile and her eyes shining. 'There, I knew he was brave.'

'That's not bravery,' Ben muttered. 'It's stupidity.' He pushed his way through the crowd to reach his brother. But he was too late. The promotor had seen Harry and had led him to the centre of the ring. To withdraw now would make Harry look foolish. Ben knew there were already several of their workmates in the crowd and, at the very front, thumping the air with his fist, was Tom Mayberry.

'Go on, Harry, mate. Give him what for.'

Ben pushed his way to stand next to Tom and say through gritted teeth, 'Shut up, Tom. Don't encourage the silly beggar.'

Startled, Tom looked round. 'Oh, sorry, Ben. I thought he'd volunteered.'

'Not exactly. Queenie's shamed him into having a go, but you know what he' – he nodded at the huge, vicious-looking man standing in the far corner of the ring, waiting for his next opponent, or victim – 'will do to him. We've seen him in action before.'

Big Billy was a fearsome sight as he glowered across the ring at Harry. Wearing tight, knee-length trousers and soft-soled boots, he was stripped to the waist, muscles bulging from his arms and shoulders.

'Then let's get Harry out of there.' Tom took a step forward, as if to climb into the ring himself to rescue his neighbour.

'Too late,' Ben said, putting a restraining hand on Tom's arm. 'We'd humiliate him now.'

The voices around them were getting excited,

cheering on one of their own from the safety of the watching crowd.

'Come on, Harry. Let him have it.'

'He'll rearrange that handsome face of yours.'

'At least it might give the rest of us a chance with the girls.'

Nervous laughter rippled around the crowd. They all knew what Big Billy could do to an opponent.

Harry had stripped to the waist and stepped into the ring. The promoter, who was also acting as the referee, drew the two combatants together to speak to them, but no one in the baying crowd could hear what was said.

Then he stepped away as Harry and Big Billy moved into the centre of the ring. Someone in the far corner clanged a bell and Billy shot out his right fist, straight into Harry's face. Harry tottered backwards but didn't fall. He moved forward and landed a punch on the big man's chin, but the blow seemed like the tickle of a feather compared with Billy's blows, which now came thick and fast until Harry was knocked to the floor, blood streaming from his nose. He was trying to pull himself up when Ben grabbed Tom's arm and said, 'Come on. We're getting him out of there.'

They climbed into the ring.

'Ah,' the promotor waved his arms, 'two more gallant opponents who want to try their luck . . .'

Ben and Tom ignored him and went straight to Harry. Between them they lifted him to his feet and dragged him to the side of the ring.

'Let me . . .' Harry began to protest weakly just as

Luke Spencer, Ron and Jack arrived. Willing hands reached out to help.

'Where's Mam?' Ben asked. 'She'll go mad if she sees him in this state.'

'Going round the stalls with Mrs Wyngate and Mrs Palmer, thank goodness,' Luke said. 'Let's get him cleaned up, if we can, before she sees him.'

'You'll not be able to hide his black eye or cut lip,' Ben muttered. 'I should have stopped him.'

Between them, they half dragged, half carried Harry to a small tent which seemed to offer first aid. Queenie and Molly followed them.

'I see it's placed quite near the boxing booth,' Luke said wryly. 'Probably deliberately. Whatever possessed him to have a go at Big Billy? We all know what a brute he is.'

Ben was grim-faced but he said nothing. He wasn't about to tell tales on Queenie, but he knew exactly who was to blame. The man at the first-aid tent managed to stop the nosebleed and clean Harry up a bit.

'But he'll have a right shiner in the morning,' he laughed. 'Now, can you take him home?' He nodded behind them where another man, helped by his friends, was being brought to him. 'Looks like I've got another customer. Oh dear, this one looks like he has lost two front teeth . . .'

When they met up with the women, Harriet shook her head in disbelief. 'I thought you'd got more sense, Harry Spencer. Showing off in front of your girlfriend, were you? Let's get you home and cleaned up properly. At least it looks as if no lasting damage has been done.' She shrugged and smiled ruefully at the other two women. 'Lads, eh? Always in some scrape or other. Come on, Luke – Ben – let's go.'

As they all parted company, Ben said, 'Thanks for your help, Tom. I couldn't have managed him on my own.'

Tom gave him a quick nod and disappeared into the crowd. Then, taking her elbow and pulling her to one side, Ben said, 'Queenie, you shouldn't have done that. Harry's courageous, but that was just stupid to go up against Big Billy. I hope you're pleased with yourself.' With that, he turned away and followed the rest of his family.

As the Palmers and the Wyngates walked home together, Molly said in a low voice, 'Why on earth did you do it, Queenie? He could have been seriously hurt.'

'Well, he wasn't, was he? Just a few bruises, but at least he proved he's no coward.'

'He'll look a sight for a few days. His nose will be swollen and his left eye's half shut now.'

'Then I won't be walking out with him until he's back to his handsome self, now will I? I don't want to be seen with a man whose face looks like a gargoyle.'

Molly's jaw dropped and the words were out of her mouth before she thought to stop them. 'How can you be so callous?'

Queenie shrugged. 'He was brave to take Big Billy on, I agree, but he shouldn't have let himself get battered like that.'

'I don't think he had a lot of choice. You saw the

size of the man. Who, around here, could stand up to him?'

Now even Queenie didn't have an answer.

Twenty-two

'Let's hope there are no ruffians in the crowd like there was last time,' Mabel said as she and Molly joined the other suffragettes in the market place. Molly was wearing her white dress but she was forced to wear a coat over it on this cold December day. She and Mabel were wearing hats with purple, white and green ribbons and feathers.

'Are Harry and Ben here, do you think?' Molly chuckled. 'My knights in shining armour.'

The unpleasantness over the fire at the Red House had faded now. There had been no further visits from Sergeant Davis or his colleagues, but Mabel and Molly were wary. They didn't want to be involved in any militant action, or even thought to have taken part.

'At the slightest sign of trouble, Molly, that sergeant'll be at our door again,' Mabel said. 'So just watch yourself today. Let's get somewhere where we can see Harriet, because, if they're here, her lads will be keeping an eye on her.'

But to everyone's relief the march passed off quietly and Mabel and Molly returned home unscathed. Mabel hid the banner in her wash-house.

'Best if William doesn't see it,' she muttered as she began to prepare tea for her family. 'He'd probably destroy it.'

Christmas was once again celebrated with the Palmers, though Queenie was missing most of the time. There were no invitations to the theatre or a trip into Leicester to the pantomime this year. Molly wondered why, but then she answered her own question. Things must be getting serious now between Queenie and Harry and no doubt they wanted to spend every spare minute together. They no longer needed chaperoning.

The realization brought Molly fresh heartache, so, as the New Year dawned, she threw herself even more into supporting the local suffragette movement, spending a lot of her spare time writing speeches, which she hoped would inspire younger women like herself to join. Even on bitterly cold winter Sundays, she still stood on a chair in the park and delivered her message to anyone who would listen. Molly's life evolved into a pattern. She worked hard at the hosiery factory during the week and immersed herself in working just as hard for the movement in her spare time, but she missed the companionship of someone of her own age.

She missed Queenie, but Queenie had changed and perhaps, if Molly were honest enough to admit it, so had she.

For many years, Jack Palmer and Ron Wyngate had met up in their local pub every Saturday night. Since Queenie had been walking out with Harry, this had been extended to include Harry and Ben's father, Luke Spencer. The three men got on very well and had become firm friends. Sometimes, William would join and them and, occasionally, Ben. But never Harry.

'They've had the snow bad further north,' Luke said in the middle of January. ''Specially in Scotland, so my paper says. Let's hope it doesn't spread down here. I don't fancy walking to work knee-deep in snow.'

His companions laughed. Their conversations usually began with the weather and then turned to anecdotes about their work or their respective families. By March, the snow had turned to rain and the country suffered one of the wettest months on record.

'There's been flooding, they reckon, in the east of England,' Ron said.

'It'll soon be summer,' Jack said hopefully. 'Maybe we'll get a good one to make up for it.'

But as they sat together one Saturday night at the beginning of July, the three men were in a sombre mood. The weather was no longer the most important topic of conversation.

'What do you reckon to the news of the assassination of that archduke and his wife in Sarajevo?' Jack began.

'I don't like the sound of it at all,' Luke said. 'He was the heir to the throne of Austria-Hungary, you know. One of the chaps at work reckons all it needs is a spark like this assassination to trigger a full-scale war.'

'In the Balkans, you mean?'

'Partly, yes. Evidently, so he reckoned, it's all about

the Serbians wanting to increase their power by breaking up the Austro-Hungarian Empire. Can't say I understand it all myself.'

Ron laughed. 'It's a bit above my head, if I'm honest. International politics has never interested me. I have enough of a job to follow what's going on in this country.'

'At least you have the vote,' Luke said. 'But your wife doesn't.'

'Aye, an' that's the bugbear at the moment, isn't it?' Jack said. 'I know I'm lucky in that Ethel doesn't seem to want to get involved in all that.'

'Harriet's quite fanatical about it.'

'Mabel only goes to the suffragette meetings really to make sure Molly doesn't get carried away and involved in anything dangerous. Every time there's a spot of bother somewhere, we get a visit from the police now.' Ron chuckled. 'Mind you, it gives the neighbours something to gossip about. Keeps 'em happy.'

'Queenie seemed quite keen on joining them a while back,' Jack said. 'But then she lost interest when Harry came on the scene.'

'You and Ethel happy about her courting our Harry, Jack?'

'Aye, he's a good lad, Luke, I can see that. And they're sticking to the rules we set out. Well, more or less. She's been a bit late home once or twice but only at the weekend, so we've not come down too hard on her.'

'I'll have a quiet word with him,' Luke promised.

The three fell silent for a moment.

'This business in Serbia then. If it did escalate into

war, you don't think we could get dragged into it, do you?' Ron said, looking at Luke, who seemed to have a better understanding than either he or Jack had. 'I mean, what's it got to do with us?'

'Nothing really, but it's all to do with alliances between various countries that have been in place for a number of years.'

Jack frowned, trying to grasp what was really above his head. He was good at his job – very good – and well-respected as foreman by all those in his charge, but when it came to anything outside the bellfoundry walls or his home life, he was the first to admit he was a bit lost. 'Tell us a bit more, Luke. I'd like to understand if I could.'

Luke wrinkled his forehead and was thoughtful for a moment before beginning slowly, 'I've been talking to this chap at work, Matthew Connolly. He's quite a well-educated man and studies history for his own . . .' Luke paused and smiled, 'amusement, I suppose you'd call it. I think he comes from quite a good family but had some sort of fall-out with them. It seems to me – and please don't take this as gospel, because it's only what I've picked up from him and the newspapers. Press coverage about anything is, after all, only what the editors or the journalists themselves think. But, from what I've heard and read, it's all to do with politics and the national pride of the main European countries. They all want power.'

'Who are we talking about here?' Jack asked. 'Germany and France, I presume.'

'And no doubt us,' Ron said with a grim smile. 'We always seem to have to stick our nose in.'

'Matthew thinks – and this is only his opinion, mind you – that Bismarck was a good Chancellor in Germany. During his time, although there was animosity between them and France, he formed peace treaties with almost all the other European nations to try to avoid war, although he did want Germany to be one of the major powers.'

'Sounds reasonable, I suppose,' Jack said. 'So what went wrong?'

'Kaiser Wilhelm the Second,' Luke said bluntly. 'He wanted to extend Germany's power in Europe. He fell out with Russia but forged an alliance with Austria-Hungary.'

'Ah, so this is where Austria-Hungary comes into it, is it?' Ron said.

'Yes, and they've had trouble with Serbia for quite some time.'

'So,' Jack said slowly, beginning to understand a little, 'you think that this assassination by a Serbian could ignite a war, and if it does, Germany will be on Austria-Hungary's side.'

'You'd think Germany and France, being close neighbours, would try to get along, wouldn't you?' Jack said.

'Not always the case though, is it?' Ron said. 'Not even in our own streets. Some neighbours are at loggerheads with each other half the time.'

'Trouble is, these countries are not always truthful with each other,' Luke went on. 'Just like neighbours,' he added with a grim smile. 'Matthew said that back in the 1880s, I think it was, Germany made a pact with Austria-Hungary and Italy agreeing to help each other if any of them were attacked by France. But then, and this is why I say they're not always honest, a few years later, Italy made a *secret* alliance with France that they would not aid Germany. France made an alliance with Russia and then, a few years later, with us, forming a triple alliance.'

'So let me get this straight,' Ron said, counting the countries on his fingers. 'On one side you've got Germany, Austria-Hungary and Italy, and on the other France, Russia and Britain.'

'That's right.'

'But,' Jack commented, 'you've got a secret understanding between Italy and France as well.'

Luke nodded. 'Complicated, isn't it?'

The three men were silent for several minutes, digesting what had been discussed.

'But why?' Ron spread his hands helplessly. 'Why do they want these pacts? Why does one country want to invade another?'

'Imperialism,' Luke said.

'Eh?'

'Countries like France and us have, over many years, created empires throughout the world and become very wealthy.'

'You could have fooled me,' Ron muttered. 'It doesn't feel like it when I'm struggling to find the rent or buy Molly some new shoes.'

The other two nodded their agreement. Although they all worked hard and were in comparatively well-paid jobs, life was still difficult at times.

'I suppose other countries, like Russia and Germany, are, well, jealous and want to create their own empires.'

'So it's all to do with power and wealth, then?' Jack said.

'I understand everything you've told us, Luke, but what I still don't know is what the problem is between Austria-Hungary and Serbia, because that's what seems to have ignited the unrest and pulled in Germany.'

'There was an alliance between Austria-Hungary and Germany,' Luke repeated patiently. He realized it was hard for them to take it in. It had taken him many evenings poring over newspapers and several conversations with Matthew Connolly to begin to understand and, even now, he was finding it difficult to explain the intricacies of the international politics to his friends. 'Oh, and there's one other thing. We have a long-standing pact with Belgium that if they're ever attacked, we will go to their aid.'

The other two stared at him.

'And we'd stand by our promise, wouldn't we?' Ron said hoarsely.

'Yes,' Luke said solemnly, 'we would.'

'Would our lads have to go if we got pulled in?' Ron asked.

There was silence for a moment before Luke said heavily, 'It's likely, Ron. I can't lie to you. Of course the regular forces would go first but, if it got serious, they might bring in conscription.'

There was an even longer silence. Only Jack, with no son, was not directly affected, but this was short-lived as Luke said, 'Of course, with all this suffragette business, I reckon you'll get women and girls volunteering to do some sort of war work. They'll take it as an opportunity to prove themselves, if you ask me.'

Now, they were all worried.

Twenty-three

'So,' Queenie asked, linking her arm through Harry's as they walked in the park. 'Where are you taking me on Bank Holiday Monday? It's only a couple of weeks away. The seaside?'

'I wasn't thinking of doing that. How would we get there?'

'Isn't there a trip from somewhere around here? I've never seen the sea.'

Harry laughed. 'Neither have I. I'll ask around, if you like?'

Queenie hugged his arm. 'Oh do. I'd love to go.'

Despite enquiries, Harry couldn't find an organized trip, so they settled for a picnic in the park.

'We'll ask Molly and Ben to come,' Queenie said.

'Won't she be busy with the suffragettes?' Harry said. 'I bet they'll have a march or something planned for that day. The crowds'll be out if it's nice weather.'

'Then she'll have to choose between us or them, won't she? At least we'll find out where her loyalties really lie.'

'You devious little minx,' Harry teased her, tapping her on her nose.

The idea spread and by the time Bank Holiday Monday came – a warm August day – the picnic had extended to include not only Harry, Queenie, Ben and Molly, but also William and the three sets of parents too.

'I hope you don't mind,' Harriet said as she set down the basket of food she'd brought as her contribution, 'but I've asked Mrs Mayberry and young Tom to join us. Being a widow, these holidays are the most difficult for her.'

'Of course we don't mind,' Mabel said generously. 'The more the merrier. We don't want anyone being on their own on a festive day, now do we? Molly – spread the blankets out on the ground. William – bring that hamper over here. Oh, what a lovely spread we're going to have with everyone chipping in.'

Molly spread out the rugs beneath the shade of some trees while the menfolk in the party carried the hampers and baskets and set them down round the edge of the tablecloth which Ethel had brought. The men soon went to sit down to watch their womenfolk set out the plates of food.

'I hope we're not late,' Alice said as she and Tom joined them. 'I've brought some homemade ginger beer.'

'That sounds delicious. Perfect for a hot day.' Mabel smiled at her.

'Can I do anything to help?'

Soon food was being passed around as the spread before them was eyed enviously by other visitors to the park.

'I wish we'd thought of that,' they heard one young woman say. It might have been expected that, as the afternoon wore on, the youngsters would form their own little group apart from the older members, but that didn't happen. The families all sat together, teased each other and laughed at silly jokes. Even Tom, who on occasion felt himself an outsider, was enveloped into the families.

'Now, what about a game of cricket?' Harry said. 'I've brought the stumps and a bat. Ben, have you remembered the ball?'

Soon, the menfolk were happily engaged in a game of cricket a short distance away while the women stayed in the shade.

'It was so kind of you to invite us to join you,' Alice Mayberry said. 'I worry about Tom sometimes. He doesn't seem to have a lot of friends.'

Queenie and Molly exchanged a look but said nothing. They'd always found him a bit of a nuisance, a hanger-on around Harry and Ben. Queenie was not about to change her view, but Molly felt a flash of sympathy for him. She hadn't known much about Tom's home life before today, but now, listening to the conversation passing between the older women, she gleaned that his life was perhaps not as easy as she might have imagined. He worked at The Brush alongside the menfolk of the Spencer family and, because his mother had been a widow for some years, it seemed he was the main breadwinner, even though Alice took in washing to supplement the household income.

'He's a good lad,' his mother was saying. 'He even helps me about the house, although I expect he wouldn't want his mates to know that. Housework's beneath a man, isn't it?'

'No, I don't believe it should be,' Mabel said. 'That's partly what the suffragists are fighting for. More equality all around, not just to have the vote.'

'I can't say I agree with you there, Mabel,' Ethel said. 'It's a woman's place to care for her husband and family. The men go out and do a hard day's work. They're the breadwinners. Why should they be expected to do housework when they get home?'

'I agree with you to a point, Ethel,' Mabel said. 'If that's the way a married couple want to work – as a team – then that's fine. But I've known women who've had to drag themselves out of bed just after giving birth because their husband felt it was beneath him – or not his job – to get himself and the older kids something to eat. I'm very lucky in that Ron will lend a hand when it's necessary.'

'But you've got Molly now.'

'Indeed, I have,' Mabel said and smiled at her daughter. 'And she's a treasure. Never too tired to help out, even when she's had a long day at work. I can't say the same for William, though. He never lifts a finger about the house, although he does give me part of his wage for his keep.'

'Nor does Queenie, if I'm honest,' Ethel said. 'But I know that's my fault. I've always said if they go out to work, then looking after them and the house is my job.'

Mabel laughed. 'She'll have to learn if she marries your Harry, won't she, Harriet?'

Harriet grimaced comically. ''Fraid so, because Harry thinks all that's beneath him. I suppose that's my fault too.'

'Not really,' Ethel said. 'It's how we've all been brought up. A woman's place is in the home, isn't it?'

'I do my bit,' Queenie said defensively. 'And I give you part of my wages, don't I, Mam? And if – when – me and Harry get married, I'll be happy to stay at home and look after him.'

Molly dropped her head as the thought of Queenie and Harry being married stabbed at her like a knife.

'Looks like the game is over,' Harriet said. 'Let's get the food and drink out. They'll be hungry all over again if I know my lads.'

As if anxious to prove that she would be a good wife to Harry, Queenie got up and began to lay out the food from the hampers that had been moved into the shade. For once, Molly stayed sitting where she was.

They all agreed it had been a wonderful day, and it was to be one they would remember for ever because, the next day, the world, and all their lives, were to change.

Twenty-four

The men heard the news first. It spread like wildfire through their places of work.

'Our government has declared war on Germany.'

'Never! Whatever for?'

'Because the Kaiser has invaded Belgium.'

'What does he want that little country for?'

'He doesn't. They're saying that he's devised some plan to go through Belgium to invade France on a weaker front. He reckons he can be in Paris in nine days.'

'But why are we involved?'

'Because we've got a years-old promise to protect Belgium.'

'It's madness,' Jack muttered.

'But I thought all the trouble was between Austria-Hungary and Serbia, and that the assassination of that archduke triggered it all.'

'That's how it started, yes, but it's all these alliances that have brought other countries in too. Some reckon the Kaiser just wants an excuse to go to war.'

The three men and William met in the pub on the way home by chance. It was unusual. Saturday night was their night for a pint together but the news had disturbed everyone. Nothing was ever going to be the same again. They'd all felt the need to get together with other menfolk, even more than they actually needed a pint.

'There's one good thing that might come out of it,' William said as they sat down around a small table, their pints in front of them.

'Really?' Luke said. 'I can't think of anything good about it.'

'It might stop the suffragettes.'

'Or make 'em even more determined. They'll not like the fact that their menfolk are being sent to war by a government which they've had no part in choosing,' Luke said. 'And to be honest, I can see their point. Harriet will have to let her sons – her only children – go, if conscription comes in.'

They were all silent for several minutes while they thought what the consequences of this war might mean for all of them.

'Evidently,' Luke said, 'this all kicked off last week. I heard rumours about it, but I didn't want to spoil our day out on Monday.'

The other three nodded. 'It was a good day, wasn't it?' William murmured. 'Us all being together.' He paused and then added, 'So what happened last week, Mr Spencer?'

Luke drew in a deep breath. 'After the assassination, Austria-Hungary delivered a humiliating ultimatum to Serbia. I think they agreed to most of the terms, but not all. So then, expecting retaliation, Serbia mobilized quickly, followed by Austria-Hungary, and Russia partially mobilized. Three days later, Austria-Hungary declared war on Serbia. One or two countries declared neutrality, but the upshot of it all for us is that Germany invaded Belgium to outflank the French army, so, we're pulled into it. It's likely that the rest of the British Empire will follow suit.'

'What? All of them? Canada, Australia and . . .'

'I assume so.'

'So we're really in it now, are we?'

'Up to our necks.'

'I expect the newspapers will keep us informed of what's going on,' Jack ended.

Ron laughed drily. 'And the street grapevine. It's as good as any newspaper.'

'Well,' Luke said, getting up. 'I'd better get home. Harriet will be in a right state if she thinks there's going to be a war and the lads might have to go. See you Saturday, if not before.'

To Luke's surprise, Harriet seemed unnaturally calm. 'What will be, will be,' she said. 'I don't want them to go to war, of course I don't, but I wouldn't want to be the mother of sons who didn't answer the call of duty in their country's hour of need.'

'I can see now,' Luke said slowly, 'why you want more say in the choosing of the government which has to make such tough decisions.'

Harriet frowned thoughtfully. 'I don't suppose whatever government was in charge at a time like this would make a different decision.'

'No, I expect you're right, but even so . . .'

'There'll be a suffragette meeting soon, I expect, to discuss all this. I wonder what they'll decide . . .'

There was a great deal of chatter as the women

gathered in a school room for a hastily called meeting a few days after the declaration of war.

Betsy banged a gavel on the table and waited until the women had settled themselves into seats. Harriet, Alice Mayberry, Mabel and Molly sat together.

'I am sure I don't need to tell any of you about the news we all received recently,' Betsy began, 'but I do have some news about ourselves and our fight for Votes for Women.' She took a deep breath. 'Mrs Pankhurst, who, as you know is the leader of the WSPU, has decreed that we should suspend our militant actions for the duration of the war. That doesn't mean we can't still keep the pressure on by peaceful means and behind the scenes. Mrs Pankhurst herself plans to help the Government recruit women into war work. Now, I don't know about you ladies, but I am in full agreement with that and I plan to follow her example.'

'But what will women be able to do to help?'

'Many of our menfolk will join up and, if the conflict goes on, no doubt the Government will introduce conscription, although if they do, I fully expect certain occupations will be protected mainly because they will be valuable to the war effort,' Betsy explained. 'As regards to what women can do, firstly, nurses will be needed. I, for one, intend to offer my services in that area.'

'Begging your pardon, Miss Anstruther, but you're not married. You're free to go and do whatever you want. What can married women do to help?'

'There'll be all sorts of gaps left when men volunteer. In agriculture and certain industrial jobs linked to the war, such as the manufacture of munitions. That sort of thing.'

'And you think women might work in factories?'

'It's possible.'

'Or be sent to work on farms?'

Betsy nodded. 'I don't see why not.' She smiled. 'I think our capabilities are very underestimated, don't you?'

A hand went up. 'Am I right in thinking that you believe this might be a way for us to prove our worth? That in a time of crisis, women can step up to take the places of men who have gone to war?'

Betsy's smile widened. 'Exactly.'

There was murmuring among the audience which Betsy, for the moment, did nothing to silence. Now it was Harriet who put up her hand. 'Then I'm with you in that.'

'And so am I . . .' The phrase, now voiced by almost everyone there, rippled around the room.

'But what can we actually *do*?' the same voice that had first asked the question repeated. 'Wives and mothers can't leave home to do some of the things you've suggested, or even to do nursing.'

'Those who must stay at home can do a lot of fundraising. Our boys will want all sorts of extras that the army can't provide.'

'Cigarettes, chocolate, do you mean?'

'Yes, and, if the war continues into the winter, they'll need warm clothing. We can all knit and sew, can't we?'

Excited chatter now broke out among the women as they began to see in what ways they could help.

*

As they walked home together, Harriet said, 'I expect you've seen the news in the papers the other day that Lord Kitchener is calling for one hundred thousand volunteers to join the armed forces?'

'Yes, we have,' Mabel said, but was unsure how to continue. Harriet was the mother of two young men who were both old enough to enlist, as indeed was William.

Harriet gave a thin smile as she realized Mabel's dilemma. 'And yes, before you ask, both Harry and Ben are thinking about joining up.'

Molly bit her lip to stop herself crying out because the first name that had come to her mind was Harry's. It wouldn't do, she told herself sternly, for her to ask about him. After she'd schooled herself, she said softly, 'Both of them?'

She heard Harriet's sigh. 'Aye. I don't think one would go without the other. And we've heard that if they volunteer together, they'll be allowed to stay together.'

'That'd be good, wouldn't it?' Mabel said.

'In some ways, yes,' Harriet said, 'but if they were fighting side by side . . .' She stopped speaking as if, suddenly, she could say no more.

'Ah yes,' Mabel said softly. 'I see what you mean.'

'What?' Molly said. 'What do you mean, Mrs Spencer? I don't understand.'

But it was Mabel who said, 'They could both get hurt at the same time.'

Now Molly understood only too well.

Twenty-five

When Ron came home from work, he had sombre news. 'The younger fellas at the foundry are leaving in droves to enlist.'

For a moment, Mabel looked worried, then she took a deep breath. 'I suppose it's to be expected if the country's at war, especially with Lord Kitchener's announcement. Who's going to carry on the work though?'

'We do have some work in hand to complete and I expect some orders will still keep coming in, but it's unlikely to be normal.'

'Has William said anything about enlisting?'

'Not yet, but . . .'

'He'll get caught up in all the – excitement.'

Ron nodded. 'We'll have to prepare ourselves for that, yes.'

'So – are you likely to be laid off at some point?'

'I don't think so, at least not – yet,' Ron said slowly. 'Jack thinks – and he's a bit more in the know than the rest of us – that it's very likely we'll be involved in war work of some sort for the Government.'

'Making munitions, you mean?'

Ron shrugged. 'We don't know. I'm not sure the bosses themselves know yet. I'm guessing – and it is only a guess, mind you – that they have to get in touch with the right government department and make an application. There'd be a lot to organize. But Jack's promised I'll be the first to know what's happening.'

The news cast a gloom over the whole family and, although she said nothing, Mabel was fearful that the news would drive her son to volunteer along with several of his workmates. Everyone's future in their safe little world was suddenly very uncertain.

'The news from Belgium isn't good, is it?' Luke said. Since the war had started, the three older men and William met more frequently. Luke threw a newspaper on the table as he sat down. 'But there is a glowing report on how our chaps conducted themselves at Mons.'

'I thought we lost that battle. We retreated, didn't we?' Ron said.

'We did eventually, but the French officers were full of praise for our lads. They said they were calm, no nervousness or excitement. They fired with – and I quote – "methodical efficiency". And there was even sort of praise from a captured German officer. He said that they'd never expected to have to face anything like that.'

'Praise indeed,' Jack murmured as he read the piece.

'And the cavalry weren't forgotten either. They surprised their own officers, it says here, by their brave charge.'

'May I see, Uncle Jack?' William said. As he read the article, his eyes caught sight of another column on the same page. 'There's a piece here about Lord Kitchener calling on the empire for even more volunteers.'

'And underneath that,' Luke put in, 'there's a piece about a Loughborough man who'd been working as an engineer out there. He was on his way home when he witnessed some of the fighting. Evidently the church bells were rung and the villagers left. Rifle fire broke out and some woods were set on fire.' He chuckled grimly. 'I think the poor fellow beat a hasty retreat, as he didn't stay to see what happened.'

'I don't blame him,' Ron muttered.

'There's a piece here about another Loughborough man,' William continued reading, 'who'd lived in Belgium for some time but he came home to join the Leicestershire Regiment last week. Blimey, it says he's already on his way to Wigston Barracks. That didn't take long, did it?'

The four men were silent until William said, 'There's another article here that says the local rifle club are opening their range on a Saturday afternoon to anyone wishing to learn to shoot. I reckon I'll go along to that.'

'I showed that to Harry and Ben. They're going.'

'Right,' William said decisively as he folded the newspaper and handed it back to Luke. 'Tell them I'll see them there next Saturday afternoon.'

'Have you heard about officers from the Leicestershire Regiment coming to Coalville to select fifty recruits?' Harry said one evening as the two brothers went upstairs to bed.

Ben blinked. He hadn't been to Coalville often, even though it lay only a few miles south-west of Loughborough. 'Why there? Why not here?'

Harry shrugged. 'I haven't a clue, but that's what's happening.'

'And have they got them?'

'Seems like it, according to a mate of mine at work. He lives there and cycles into work here every day. His brother's joined, he said, and they're already being dubbed as the "Famous Fifty" or even the "Coalville Fifty". Of course, they won't be going overseas yet. There'll be all sorts of medical inspections and the like, to say nothing of training to be done first.' Harry looked at his brother solemnly. 'But it makes you think, doesn't it?'

'Yes,' Ben said quietly, understanding Harry's meaning. 'It does.'

'Are you coming with me to the market place tomorrow afternoon, Moll?' Queenie asked when she called at the Wyngates' house on her way home after an afternoon walk in the park with Harry.

Molly blinked. 'Whatever for? Tomorrow's Monday. I'll be at work.'

'No, you won't. Your factory's shutting early so that folks can go and see them off, and Mr Gilmore has given me the afternoon off so I can go too. Miss Parkinson's going an' all.'

'See who off? Queenie, what are you talking about?'

'There's a band of recruits from Shepshed and Loughborough leaving tomorrow afternoon on the train to go to enlist.'

'Really? I hadn't heard about it. But if the factory closes early, as you say, I'll definitely come.'

'I'll see you there, then.'

'Where shall I find you? Molly began, but Queenie had gone.

The following afternoon, Molly walked to the market place along with several of her workmates, who were all anxious to wave off the volunteers.

'My Alfie's going,' one of the girls said. 'I'm that proud of him.'

'My brother's going with him,' another one said. 'They're pals, aren't they? It's nice they're going together.'

'I can't see Queenie,' Molly murmured when they arrived.

'There're so many people here. Isn't it wonderful they're getting so much support?'

'*There* you are,' Molly said as, at last, she saw Queenie and pushed her way through the throng to stand beside her. 'I didn't realize there would be so many folk here.'

Queenie smiled. 'They're here to support their boys. But look over there. Isn't that one of your suffragette women, handing something to any young men in the crowd who are just watching? What is she doing?'

Molly's face was grim. 'She's handing out white feathers.'

'But – but why? What does it mean?'

'A white feather is a sign of cowardice, so if you give one to a fella who's the right age to serve his country but is not in uniform, you're telling him he ought to volunteer. It was in the papers. Something called the Order of the White Feather has been formed recently by some admiral and it seems that Mrs Pankhurst is in favour of it. She's encouraging her members to do the same.'

'So is that what you're going to do?' Queenie asked.

'No, I am not. I don't agree with it.'

Queenie raised her eyebrows and smirked. 'Disagreeing with your idol? Fancy that.'

'I don't agree with everything Mrs Pankhurst advocates,' Molly snapped. 'You know that.'

Molly watched the woman handing out feathers among the crowd and saw the stunned look on the faces of the young men receiving them. Several looked ashamed and turned away, pushing their way through the crowd, unable now to cheer their peers who were, in the eyes of the crowd, doing the honourable thing and going to war.

'I'll be that proud to see my Harry in uniform.'

Molly's breath caught in her throat. 'Is he – has he volunteered, then?'

'Not yet, but he will. He was talking yesterday about the Coalville Fifty. He said they're an inspiration.'

Molly said nothing, but she felt as if her heart was breaking. If Harry and Ben were to go and probably her own brother too, all caught up in a fever of patriotism . . .

As three o'clock approached, the crowd grew even bigger and a loud cheer went up as several motor cars carrying young men stopped outside the town hall.

'Why are they stopping there?' Molly asked Queenie. 'I thought they'd be going to the station.'

'They will, but maybe they've got to collect some paperwork – like train tickets,' Queenie said. 'I don't know.' She laughed. 'Maybe some big-wig wants to shake their hands and wish them well.'

Perhaps Queenie had been right since, after several minutes, the young men appeared carrying papers in their hands and then tucking them into their pockets. They lined up, four abreast, in the market place and began to march towards the railway station, singing 'It's a Long Way to Tipperary' as they went. Swept along by the throng, Molly and Queenie followed. The whole route was lined with cheering crowds.

'Where have they all come from?' Molly said. 'It's a working day.'

'Lots of places have closed for the afternoon,' Queenie shouted above the noise. 'They want to give their workmates a good send-off. Even some of the bosses are here.'

Molly began to turn away. 'I'm going home, Queenie. I can't bear to see them go.'

'Oh no, you're not. You're staying with me,' Queenie said firmly, putting her arm through Molly's and almost dragging her along to follow the line of marching young men. Suddenly, she bent down and picked up a Union Jack flag that someone had dropped. She thrust it into Molly's hand. 'Here, wave this. Let them know you're giving them your support. Let them know you're proud of them.'

'Of course I am, but . . .'

Her protests were futile. Carried along by Queenie's

enthusiasm and the crowd's patriotism, Molly had no choice. She could not escape.

When they reached the station, Queenie pushed her way through the crush, dragging Molly with her until they were allowed on the platform. There was scarcely room to move.

'Come on, Moll. Let's get as close as we can. Look, there's a nice-looking lad leaning out of the window. Give him a wave. And smile, Moll. They don't want their last sight to be a miserable face . . .'

But there were many women, young and old, on the platform weeping openly as they waved off their loved ones.

Queenie glanced around her with disdain. 'Anyone would think they're going off to war right now.'

'Well, aren't they?'

''Course not. They'll be going to training camps for several weeks. None of these volunteers will go abroad yet. Besides, they're only going to Wigston Barracks to enrol in Lord Kitchener's Army.'

Molly was thoughtful for a moment before saying slowly, 'Maybe you're right, but it's the first stage, isn't it? Once they've done that, they're in the army and there's no going back.' She nodded towards the distressed women. 'And that's what they're realizing.'

'Oh Molly, you're so naive. Don't you read the papers? My dad says it's all going to be over by Christmas. These lads will probably never even fire a shot in anger. They might not even get to France.'

'So why are you making such a big thing of waving them off?'

A Woman of Spirit

'It's a bit of fun, isn't it? A bit of excitement in our dull little lives.'

Molly glanced at the young men hanging out of the carriage windows, laughing and waving and cheering. A dark cloud floated overhead, blocking out the sun for a moment and Molly felt a sudden chill. She shivered as the train pulled away. The sound of the cheering faded and the figures became indistinct, almost like ghosts.

'Oh Mam,' Molly wept when at last she got back home, 'it was awful. To see all those lovely young men going off with such hope, such joy almost. It broke my heart.'

'Sit down, love. I'll make us a pot of tea. Look, Molly, you mustn't take it to heart so. All those young men you've cheered on their way today are going because they want to, not because they've been called up and have to go whether they want to or not.'

'There was a woman there giving out white feathers to young men not in uniform. Queenie said it was one of our suffragettes, but I didn't recognize her.'

Mabel frowned. 'Oh yes. I've heard about that. The chap that's started this Order of the White Feather organization seems to think that the womenfolk of this country ought to persuade their menfolk to go – that they should be ashamed of their husbands, fiancés and boyfriends who are not in uniform. Mind you, at the moment, they don't seem to need much telling. They say that the local recruitment centres can hardly cope with the numbers volunteering.'

'Mam,' Molly said in a low voice. 'What about

William? Has he said anything? I recognized one or two of his workmates leaving on the train today.'

Mabel shook her head. 'Not yet, but he seems lost in thought a lot of the time now.'

'I don't want him to go, Mam, and I don't want the Spencer boys to go either.'

'I know, love. I know,' Mabel said softly. 'But there's not much we can do about it. As they keep telling us, we're only women, after all.'

Twenty-six

When Molly and the two menfolk in the Wyngate household had gone to work on the Wednesday morning and Mabel was readying herself to begin cleaning the bedrooms, there was a sharp knock on the back door. Opening it, she was surprised to see both Harriet Spencer and Alice Mayberry standing there. Mabel's welcoming smile faltered a little when she saw their expressions. It seemed that this was not a friendly social call.

'We've got a bone to pick with you, Mrs Wyngate,' Alice said, her mouth tight. 'And it's a juicy one.'

'Come in. I'll make tea—'

'We'll step inside but no, thank you, we won't take tea with you, if what they say your daughter's been doing is true?'

They both stepped across the threshold and into Mabel's kitchen.

'Molly? Whatever are you talking about?'

'Yesterday morning, our boys' – Harriet cleared her throat and glanced at Alice as if to include Tom – 'each received an envelope containing a white feather through our doors. It must have been done late on Monday night.'

'And if we are to believe the rumours,' Alice put in, 'then it was your Molly who delivered them.'

'We all know how good she is at putting leaflets and suchlike through folks' doors,' Harriet said. 'We've never minded about suffragette information; in fact, I've been all for that, but I have to agree with Alice that this is something different.'

Mabel's face turned white and she put out her hand to a chair to steady herself. Then she sat down heavily as her legs gave way. She stared up at the two women. 'Molly wouldn't do anything like that. Who – who's said it was her?'

Again the two women glanced at one another.

'Mrs Kirk, who lives on our street. She heard the rumour yesterday morning in town from her friend, Miss Parkinson,' Alice said.

'Miss Parkinson who works at Gilmore's shop. Where Queenie works?'

The two women looked at each other. 'I'm not sure, but I expect so,' Alice went on. 'Anyway, Molly was spotted at the station seeing the volunteers off on Monday and there was a woman there handing out white feathers to young men of fighting age in the crowd. Mrs Kirk reckons that's where Molly must have got the idea from and she thought it was just the sort of thing she'd do. After delivering all them leaflets about the suffragettes, she's got a taste for it.'

Mabel was still shaking her head in disbelief. 'I know Molly went there to see the lads off, but – but she came home in tears. She could hardly bear to watch them go, she said.'

'Did your William get one? A white feather?'

'No. At least, I don't think so.'

'No,' Alice said grimly. 'She wouldn't give one to her own brother, now would she?'

The colour was coming back to Mabel's cheeks now and she pulled herself up, though her legs still felt very shaky. 'You're wrong. I know you're wrong. Whoever did this, it wasn't Molly.'

'Well, you're going to defend your own daughter, aren't you, Mrs Wyngate?' Harriet said. She paused and bit her lip before adding, hesitantly, 'I don't want to believe it of Molly, but Mrs Kirk said that Miss Parkinson said she'd heard it from a reliable source, so . . .' Her voice faded away. It seemed to Mabel that Harriet was torn.

'Thank goodness the suffragette meetings have been postponed for the duration of the war,' Alice said. 'We don't need to meet with you anymore, Mrs Wyngate. And if Harriet'll take my advice, she'll tell Ben no more walking in the park with Molly on a Sunday or coming round to their house.'

As they stepped out of the back door again, Harriet paused briefly and added, a little sadly, 'It's a pity because I liked her. I enjoyed her visits, coming round to chat about the suffragettes. But you can tell her from me – and I'm sorry to say it – that if our lads volunteer now, we shall blame her. She'll have shamed them into going.'

Mabel closed the door behind them and leaned against it for a moment. She was still shaking and couldn't think straight. 'No, no,' she said aloud to her kitchen. 'I don't believe it. Not Molly. Not my Molly.'

*

For the first time in a long time, tea was not ready and waiting when the menfolk and Molly arrived home from work.

'You not feeling well, love?' Ron asked in concern. 'You look a bit flushed.'

'I – I've had a nasty shock today. I'll tell you about it later. Go and wash your hands. Tea'll be on the table in a minute.'

'I'll help you, Mam,' Molly said at once. 'You sit down.'

Mabel could hardly eat a thing and all her family couldn't help but notice. As Ron got up after his meal, he said, 'You sit down, Mabel, love. Molly, you clear away and then we'll all sit down and hear what has upset your mother so.'

When Molly had finished washing up in the scullery, she joined the rest of her family in front of the range.

'Now,' Ron said. 'What's this all about?'

Mabel explained about her visit from the two women that morning.

'Mam, I'd never do anything like that, I promise you.' Now Molly had tears running down her face.

Mabel reached out and clasped her daughter's hand. 'I know you wouldn't, love. I believe you, but it's all round our streets that it must be you because of you delivering suffragette leaflets.'

'I told you no good would come of you being involved with those women,' William muttered.

Molly jumped to her feet. 'I'll go round and see Mrs Spencer. Right now. I can't let them go on thinking it was me.'

'I'll come with you—' Mabel began, but Molly shook her head.

'No, Mam. This is something I must do on my own.'

As she walked through the September evening, she felt the first chill of autumn and drew her coat around her. She was shaking by the time she knocked on the Spencers' door, but this was not from the cold.

It was Harry who opened the door. He stood looking down at her for a long moment before saying harshly, 'And what might you want? I think you've done enough damage already, haven't you?'

'It wasn't me, Harry. I swear.'

His mouth – the mouth she loved so much, the mouth she had so often dreamt of kissing – twisted into a sneer. 'I don't think anyone is ever going to believe that, Molly. You're well-known for being practised in pushing unwanted stuff through folks' doors. It was only tolerated in this house because my mother happened to have the same interests and, much to her regret now, she actually encouraged you. But this . . . this is something very different.'

'Please can I see your mother?'

Harry shook his head. 'She won't want to see you or any of your family. You can tell your dad that he won't be welcome to meet up with us in the pub on a Saturday night either from now on. Oh, before you go, just tell me one thing. Did you give your brother a white feather?'

'I didn't give anyone a white feather,' Molly said. 'You've got to believe me, Harry. I would never do anything like that.'

'I don't believe you . . .' he hesitated before adding, 'although Ben's adamant you wouldn't do something like that and me mam's wavering. She really liked you, Molly, but the damage you've done to poor Mrs Mayberry is unforgiveable. If Tom volunteers, she's going to be devastated. And Queenie, your best friend, says she knows it was you. Just think, Molly, what you've done. You've turned your best friend against you. I hope you think it was worth it. I'll wish you goodnight. Please *don't* call again.' And with that he slammed the door in her face.

Molly hurried home, eager to get back to her own family. She was certain her mother and father believed her, although she wasn't sure about William. As she passed by the Palmers' front door, her footsteps slowed. She hesitated. She so wanted to know if what Harry had said was true and yet . . . Just as she was about to turn away and carry on towards her own house, Queenie came to the front window, tapped on the glass and then beckoned.

Molly bit her lip, unsure what to do, but then she found herself walking down the jitty to the Palmers' back door.

'It's all around the town what you've done, Molly,' Queenie said at once when she opened the door, without even greeting her friend. 'And to Harry and Ben of all people.'

'Queenie, I didn't. How can you believe that of me?'

Queenie shrugged, but opened the door wider in a silent invitation for Molly to step inside.

'Are you sure you want me here?' Molly asked tightly. 'No one else seems to want to speak to me now.'

'Are you surprised?'

'I haven't done anything, Queenie. Why will no one believe me? And why do they think it was me anyway?'

'Because you're the most obvious person after all that leaflet delivering. And you saw that woman at the station handing them out. We both did.'

'But I didn't agree with what she was doing. You know that, Queenie. Why don't you stick up for me? You're my friend and you know I wouldn't do such a thing.'

At that moment, the door into the scullery where they were standing opened and Ethel came in. 'Oh hello, Molly. What are you both standing out here for? Come into the kitchen where it's warmer. Nights are pulling in now, aren't they?'

Molly was surprised. She hadn't expected this welcome from Ethel. She glanced at Queenie who, seeing the question in her eyes, said, 'Oh, Mam knows all about it. Actually, she thinks it was very brave of you and the right thing to do.'

'She – she does?'

'Indeed I do,' Ethel said. 'Come in, Molly, and tell us all about it.'

When they were seated in front of the range, Molly asked tentatively, 'Where's Uncle Jack?'

'He's next door with his mate, Fred.'

'Does – does he know?'

'Of course. It was him told us about the rumours

going round. Now, Molly, what are you looking so down in the mouth for? You were right in doing what you did. We can't have fit young men avoiding answering their country's call in its hour of need.'

'But I didn't do it.'

'Didn't you?' Ethel shrugged. 'Well, whoever did, I agree with them. If I'd thought of it, I might have done it myself.'

Molly was open-mouthed at what she was hearing. But she couldn't help feeling relieved that there was at least one person on her side, even though she hadn't actually done what she'd been accused of. Yet again, this had come from nowhere.

'You come round here any time you want, love,' Ethel said to her, 'and hold your head up high in the street. You've nothing to be ashamed of.'

It was quite late when Molly went home to find all her family had already gone to bed. She locked the back door and crept up the stairs, undressing in the dark and slipping into bed. But sleep evaded her. All she could think of was that she would be blamed if the man she loved went to war.

Harry had been wrong about one thing: his father and Jack were not willing to ostracize their friend, Ron. When he tentatively entered the bar on the Saturday evening, Luke, who had been watching the door, beckoned him over to their usual corner. As Ron approached, Jack stood up and held out his hand with a smile. 'We know there's been a bit of bother among our womenfolk, Ron, but we're not going to let it come between us.'

'Our Molly didn't do what they're saying,' Ron said as he sat down. 'I hope you believe me, because I believe her.'

Jack gave a wry laugh. 'Aye well, whatever. She's always sure of a heroine's welcome at our house anyway. Ethel thinks it's a marvellous idea. She says she would have done it if she'd known about it. She's now reading up all about the fellow who started what they're calling The White Feather Brigade, or The Order of the White Feather, summat like that. It was some military fellow down in Folkestone who started it by organizing a group of women to hand out white feathers to men who looked like they were the right age but who were not in uniform.' He sighed. 'It caught on in a big way and the idea's spreading through the country, especially now the newspapers have got hold of it. But just between us and these four walls, I'm honest enough to admit that Ethel might feel very differently if she had a son.'

'I think what made Harriet angry was the accusation that our boys are cowards. They're not and I think, even before they got the feathers, they were thinking about volunteering. She knows they'll have to go eventually, one way or another, but she didn't want them shamed into going.'

'There's certainly a lot of the youngsters signing up around here. There's several gone from our works already.' Jack sighed.

Ron said, 'I just wish I could find out who did put the feathers through your letterbox, Luke, because I know it wasn't Molly.'

Luke was thoughtful for a moment before saying

slowly, 'Actually, Ron, I do believe you. And her. It's not the sort of thing Molly would do. Oh, I know she delivered suffragette leaflets, but that's entirely different. I'll try to talk to Harriet, but I know I won't be able to win Alice Mayberry round. Her Tom got one an' all and he's her only lad. Her only child. She's brought him up on her own and I know it's been a struggle. Still is, I imagine.' He shook his head sadly. 'We're all facing a very difficult time.'

The other two men were silent; they couldn't think of anything to say.

Twenty-seven

'You're early tonight,' Harriet remarked as Luke came in through the back door. To his surprise, both Harry and Ben were still sitting by the range.

He glanced at his sons. 'I thought you'd both be out. It's Saturday night. You always go out on a Saturday night.'

The brothers glanced at each other. 'Didn't feel like it, Dad,' Harry said. 'Not after what's happened.'

'Not even to see Queenie?'

Harry shrugged listlessly as if, right at this moment, he couldn't work up the enthusiasm to do anything.

'I've been talking to Jack and Ron . . .'

Harriet raised her eyebrows. 'Oh, so you're still consorting with her father, are you?'

Luke felt his wife's disapproval. This was going to be more difficult than he'd thought.

'Even if Molly has handed out feathers, it's not Ron's fault, is it?' he said reasonably.

Harriet glared at him but said nothing.

'No, Dad, it isn't,' Ben said quietly. 'So, had he got anything to say?'

'We chatted about it, yes. Of course we did. He's adamant that Molly didn't do it.'

'Well, Queenie's adamant she did,' Harry said.

'Is she now?' Luke murmured. 'How does she know that?'

'They were at the station together the other day and saw a woman handing out feathers. Queenie reckons that's what gave Molly the idea.'

'Ron says Molly has given him her word that she's not guilty and he believes her.'

They were all quiet for several moments before Ben said slowly, 'Well, I do find it hard to believe it was Molly. I got to know her quite well when we were chaperoning you and Queenie . . .' He even managed a thin smile towards his brother. 'And I don't think it's the sort of thing she would do.'

'She damaged that pillar box, didn't she?' Harry said. There was a surprising note of grudging admiration in his tone as he added, 'There's a lot more to Molly Wyngate than anyone thinks.'

'That was entirely different,' Ben retorted. 'Even Mam supported her in that, didn't you? Besides, she denied that, an' all.'

'Aye, good at denying things, isn't she?' Harry muttered.

'The pillar box was quite different,' Harriet said. 'It was just a protest. It wasn't going to result in anyone getting hurt, was it? This is something else.'

There was a long silence again until Harry levered himself out of his chair. 'Well, I'm off to me bed, but I'll tell you one thing: if I do decide to go, it won't be because a silly young girl has given me a white feather. I'll go because I think it's the right thing to do to serve my King and country.'

*

A Woman of Spirit

Molly had dreaded going to work each day. She believed that, if word spread about what she was supposed to have done, she would be ostracized at best or, at worst, attacked. But to her surprise, one morning during the following week, she was greeted at the gates of the hosiery factory by a group of women clapping and cheering her when she arrived.

'Good for you, girl,' Peggy White said, linking her arm through Molly's and walking beside her into work. The others fell in behind them. 'We're all going to do it now.'

'Oh please, Peggy, don't. I didn't do what's being said. I didn't give white feathers to anyone.'

'Now, now, you're not to be modest about it.' Peggy grinned. 'You've made us all think. None of us want to be seen with a young man of the right age who's not in uniform, now do we?'

At once, the picture of Harry in uniform came to Molly's mind. Yes, I do, she wanted to shout. I don't want to see Harry in uniform. I don't want him to go. But she said nothing and allowed herself to be swept into the factory on a tide of feminine patriotism.

It was a moment she would relive many times and shudder at the memory of her own cowardice in that instant.

Caught up in a fevered wave of patriotism, volunteers flooded the recruiting centres every day. The largest number of recruits signing up was recorded on 3 September 1914, and even over the days that followed, up and down the country, young men still flocked to join up.

In Loughborough, four young men went to the recruiting centre together: the Spencer brothers, Tom Mayberry and William Wyngate. In turn, they signed the attestation form for Kitchener volunteers, promising their fidelity and allegiance to the King for three years' service, unless the war ended sooner, and received the King's shilling. As if by mutual silent consent, not one of them spoke about what might, or might not, have brought them to this moment. Back home, the reception from each of their families was different.

Harriet, solemn-faced, hugged her sons and told them how proud she was of them. 'I knew you'd go at some point. I knew you wouldn't wait for conscription to come in, as it surely will if this war goes on for very long.'

'We thought that this way, Mam,' Harry said, 'we can stay together. We've been promised that. There were a lot of the lads from work there too.'

'There was talk about what they're calling "pals' battalions" being formed,' Ben put in. 'It started down in London in August and the idea is spreading.'

'They're formed of young men who are already friends – or even relatives – who either work together . . .' Harry began.

'Or play sport together,' Ben added.

'Or just come from the same neighbourhood,' Harry went on. 'And we've been told that we should be able to stay together. And with Tom and William.'

Harriet raised her eyebrows. 'William? William Wyngate? Well, well, she did give her own brother one, then.'

'Mam . . .' Ben began, but Harriet held up her hand. 'Don't say it, Ben. I won't refer to it any more. Time we moved on. She's not the only one handing them out. You'd have been given one sooner or later, I've no doubt. I've heard that a lot of my friends from the suffragette movement are now doing the same thing.'

'And the girls from the hosiery factory where Molly works are too, even to their own boyfriends. They say they don't want to be seen out with a young man who isn't in uniform. A lot of them are treating Molly like a heroine, so Queenie's heard, though not from Molly herself,' Harry said. There was still a note of bitterness in his tone. He was not so ready to forgive. 'Thank goodness my Queenie's got more sense.'

Tom Mayberry's mother was beside herself in torment. 'What am I to do without you, Tom? Haven't I devoted my life to you? What'll I do if I lose you?'

'You'll get some of my army pay, I'll make sure of that . . .'

'Oh Tom, it's not about the money. It's about my son. My only son, my only child' – her voice rose in anguish – 'you're everything to me. Everything. You're only going because of that wretched girl . . .'

'No, Mam, I'm not,' he said gently. He put his arms around her as he struggled to find the words to explain things to her. Alice's being widowed when Tom had been very young had brought them even closer than most mothers and sons. Perhaps, he thought, that was why he had never been able to make friends; his thoughts were always for his mother and making sure she was all right and as happy as she could be. He knew among some of his peers he had the name of being a 'mummy's boy'. And as for girlfriends, well, he hadn't seriously thought about that yet. He knew he wasn't the handsomest boy in the area – not with the Spencer brothers living just across the road. But now he was quite thankful he hadn't got a girl, certainly not one who might hand him a white feather. It was bad enough that one had been put through his door. On the night that it had happened, he had been getting ready for bed and drawing the curtains of his bedroom window when he had seen a shadowy figure hurrying along the street. Intrigued to see a girl out on her own this late at night, he had watched. First she'd gone to the Spencers' house and pushed something through their door. Then she had crossed the road towards his home and had done the same thing. As she had turned away, the hood of her cape had fallen back and he could see, in the glow of the street lamp, just who was making a delivery this late at night. Tom had shrugged. He'd leave it until the following morning. He'd had a busy day at work and was almost dropping asleep, but in the morning it was his mother who picked up the envelope and opened it. How he wished he had gone down the night before to retrieve it before she had found it. He'd been shocked. He would never have thought she could do such a thing, and especially delivering one to the Spencer brothers. That surprised him more than anything. But he decided to say nothing; he didn't want to be the one to cause trouble among the families who were such good friends now. He doubted they'd believe him anyway.

'Listen, Mam, I promise you my volunteering has nothing to do with white feathers. If anything, it's to do with Lord Kitchener's appeal. We've got to stand up to these invaders. At present our regular army isn't big enough to withstand Germany's might. Something had to be done, and Kitchener has done it. Appeal is just the right word because he's "appealed" to our patriotism and our sense of duty. If it goes on for some time, he's going to bring conscription in. You know that, don't you? It's common sense and if there's anyone in this world with a mountain of common sense, it's you. And there's another thing, me and the lads found out at the recruitment centre that those of us who join up together will be able to stay together, train together and go abroad together. So, that'll be good, won't it? I'll be with friends.' Mentally, he crossed his fingers, hoping that what he was telling his mother was true.

'So who else was there when you – you signed up?'

'Harry and Ben, William and several lads from work too. They've said we'll all go together.'

Alice sniffed and dried her eyes. 'Well, that's something, I suppose. So, are both Harriet's lads going?'

Tom let his arms fall from around her and moved away a little. 'Yes.'

'That's hard,' Alice said softly. Then she drew in a deep breath. 'There are going to be anxious mothers all over the country. We must support one another. I'll be there for Harriet as I am sure she'll be there for me.'

Tom squeezed her arm. 'That's the spirit, Mam.'

Alice was putting on a brave face. Inside she was in turmoil, but she knew she was not the only one.

'Ben! Whatever are you doing here?' Molly said when she opened the back door to his knock.

'I've come to say goodbye. We're off tomorrow.'

'Yes, I know. William's going too.'

'Will you be coming to the station to see us off?'

'I – think so.'

'Can I come in for a minute?'

'Oh – oh yes, of course. Sorry.'

As they moved into the kitchen both Mabel and Ron looked up in surprise.

'Hello, Ben,' Mabel said. 'Sit down. I'll get you a cuppa.'

'Don't go to any trouble, Mrs Wyngate. I'm not staying long, but I wanted to come round to see Molly before we go. I wanted to tell her that I don't believe the stories about her giving us white feathers and, even if she did, well, it's not so very terrible. Most of us would have volunteered anyway. To be honest, it was hearing about the Coalville Fifty that prompted me and Harry to join up.'

'That's good of you, Ben,' Mabel said, glancing at her daughter. 'Molly's adamant that she didn't do it and we believe her. But she's having a bit of a tough time because of all the gossip, aren't you, love? Some woman spat at her in the street yesterday.'

'Feelings are running high because so many are going from around here,' Ron put in. 'They're either for her or against her.'

'I didn't do it, Ben,' Molly said quietly. 'I promise you.'

Ben looked into her eyes and, in that moment, he knew she was telling the truth. But he knew also that he wouldn't be able to convince his brother and, knowing what he did about Molly's feelings for Harry, his brother's censure would be bringing her more pain than anything else.

Twenty-eight

When the next trainload of recruits left to go to training camp, the Spencer brothers, Tom and William were among their number. Members of their families were there to see them off, and Mabel and Molly were there too, but they kept their distance from the others. They were heartened to see, however, that William was warmly welcomed by his fellow recruits. There was a lot of laughter and back-slapping as they piled into the carriages and hung out of the windows to wave.

As she watched Harry enfold Queenie into his arms and bend to give her a loving kiss, Molly felt her heart would break. She had no right to wish him farewell, no right to ask for a photograph of him in uniform. She could not even ask to write to him, just as a friend.

Ben and the others pulled Harry into the carriage at the very last minute and, as he turned to look back, his glance caught and held Molly's gaze. He was stony-faced, with not the glimmer of a smile. He did not even raise his hand to wave goodbye.

As the train disappeared down the track and folk began to leave the platform, Alice caught sight of Mabel and Molly. Reminded afresh of what she believed had caused her son to volunteer, Alice walked towards them.

'Well, you've got what you wanted now, miss,

haven't you? They've gone and God alone knows if we'll ever see any of them again. I hope you're satisfied.' She gestured with her head towards a woman at the exit who was unashamedly handing out white feathers to young men not in uniform. 'Why don't you go and join her?' Alice said bitterly. 'Help send a few more young men to their deaths?'

Molly turned white, but at that moment, Harriet appeared and linked her arm through Alice's. 'Come on, love. Leave her be. She's not the only one.'

'But she's the worst in my eyes. They were her *friends*. How can you do that to your friends?'

'Mrs Mayberry—' Molly began, but Harriet pulled Alice away and Molly and her mother were left staring after them.

'Come on, Molly, love, let's go home.'

That evening there was a knock on the back door of the Wyngates' home. The door was opened and a cheery voice called, 'It's only me.'

Mabel and Molly glanced at once another.

'Queenie?' Molly murmured and then raised her voice. 'Come in.'

'I thought I'd pop round and see how you are. We must stick together now our boyfriends have left. Are you up for a walk in the park on Sunday? Only no flirting with any soldiers, Molly Wyngate.' Queenie wagged her finger at her friend. 'You've got a boyfriend who'll soon be in uniform and you must be utterly faithful to him.'

'He's not—' Molly began to protest but Queenie laughed.

'You can't fool me, Moll. It was always me an' Harry, and you and Ben, now wasn't it? He's a nice lad, Moll. You should hang on to him. And just think, one day we could be sisters-in-law.'

Molly did not dare to glance at her mother, the only other person in the room who knew where her true feelings lay. Instead, she smiled and forced herself to say, 'Yes, of course. That'd be nice.'

She had mixed feelings. She'd missed Queenie's easy friendship, their girly talks, but she hadn't liked the way Queenie had almost deserted her in favour of Harry. But, she reminded herself, her mother had warned her that that might happen. And if she was really honest with herself, if she had become Harry's girlfriend, wouldn't she have done just the same thing? Yes, she answered herself. I would have done.

There were other things too, though. It was hardly the actions of a true friend to believe that Molly had damaged a pillar box and had delivered white feathers. Molly pulled in a deep breath as she came a decision. She would remain friends with Queenie, but now she couldn't help being wary.

Ben was the only one to write directly to Molly. Even her own brother only wrote to their mother and father. He didn't even add her name to *Dear Mam and Dad . . .* and never once asked how she was.

When we left we first went to the Wigston Barracks and then before long on to Aldershot for training, Ben wrote. *I have to admit it's harder than we thought it would be. There are about twice as many here as there is accommodation for, so some of us have to sleep on the floor and meal times are a mad scramble! Still, it's all an experience and the fact that the four of us are together makes it bearable. We're now doing proper training, learning to march in lines and columns and 'left wheel' and 'right turn.' You'd laugh to see us. So many don't seem to know their right from their left. We haven't got khaki uniforms yet. We're dressed in old full-dress uniforms. Colourful, it has to be said, but not quite right! I'm sure we've all grown already and young Tom is filling out in all the right places. He's one of our group now and turning out to be quite a nice chap once you get to know him properly. I don't think he'll have any trouble finding a girlfriend next time he comes home in his smart uniform. I do hope you'll want to write to me. We're still good mates, you and me. Never forget that . . .*

Tears welled in her eyes at his kind words. She blinked them back furiously as she carried on reading.

It's lovely to have letters from home. I know we're not abroad yet, but sometimes it feels like it. And worst of all, the rumour is that we won't get home for Christmas.

The first Christmas of the war was always going to be difficult for everyone. So many young men throughout the whole country had left and with the news of the war's progress not hopeful, everyone was feeling uneasy.

During the months leading up to the festivities, there had been changes at the bellfoundry, although Jack and Ron still had employment. 'There're not many of us left now after all those who are eligible have volunteered but, fortunately for us, we're still needed. We've still got a bit of work,' Ron told his wife. 'And Jack says the bosses are in talks with the powers that be for us to get involved in war production, probably manufacturing shell casings.'

Mabel's mouth dropped open. 'But – but that's dangerous, isn't it? All that explosive stuff.'

Ron shook his head. 'No, Mabel, love. I said shell *casings*. They'll be taken elsewhere to be filled with' – he paused and then added – 'with whatever it is they put in 'em.'

'Oh. Oh, I see.'

Mabel said no more. She had to close her mind to lots of things these days. It was bad enough that William and his pals were going to be in danger every day once they were sent abroad, but now her husband was going to be involved in making the very equipment that would cause such devastation on both sides. Even enemy soldiers had mothers somewhere, she thought sadly. What a terrible waste this war was going to be for everyone.

'Look, Mabel,' Ethel said, when she arrived at the Wyngates' back door two days before Christmas Eve. 'Me an' Jack have been talking. We'd like the three of you to spend Christmas Day with us. You'll be missing William, and Molly will be on her own. And now that Harry's gone, Queenie could do with Molly's company. She's feeling him going badly.'

Mabel forbore to say that she didn't like her daughter being picked up and dropped just whenever it suited Queenie. But she had to admit that Molly herself had accepted Queenie back and they were once again spending a lot of their spare time together.

'I'll talk to Ron,' Mabel promised. 'See how he feels about it. I must admit we do miss William. He was always the one to liven up the day.' She sighed pensively. 'I liked it when they were little. They'd always play games together on Christmas afternoon while me and Ron had a nap by the front-room fire.'

Ethel laughed. 'Aye, us an' all. By the way,' she went on, 'there're no hard feelings between us about that feather business. For what it's worth, I agree with Molly. Young fellas, who are fit and able, ought to be in uniform. And I'm not the only one who thinks that.'

'But she didn't—' Mabel began and Ethel smiled. 'Yes, yes, I know what you're going to say, but we don't mind either way. That's what I'm trying to tell you. Let our two families just carry on as we always have. We don't need to come into contact with either the Spencers or Mrs Mayberry or anyone else, for that matter. Not for the time being anyway. It seems to me, Mabel, that the suffragettes and their cronies were all in favour of handing out white feathers, but it's suddenly a bit different when it's their own sons involved, isn't it?'

Despite the circumstances, the Palmers and the

Wyngates enjoyed their Christmas Day together. The two mothers had pooled the food they had prepared and, despite the hardships, they managed to put on a good spread.

But it was difficult to keep away from the topic of the war. It seemed to overshadow everything. 'I expect we might get some sort of food rationing if the war goes on very long,' Mabel said despondently.

'Well, they were wrong about it all being over by Christmas, weren't they?' Ethel said as she cleared away the dishes after tea.

'Queenie, I expect you've heard from Harry?' Mabel asked. 'Do you know where they are? We don't hear much from William. He was never much of a letter writer, but I did think he might write to us once he was away from home.'

Molly held her breath waiting for Queenie's answer.

'Luckily for me,' the girl smiled, 'Harry seems to quite like writing letters. He writes to me every week without fail, though his mother says she doesn't hear much from him. I think Ben writes to her fairly regularly so she hears news about them both.' She shrugged. 'I suppose there's no sense in them both writing more or less the same news, is there? But, no, I have no idea where they are. I wonder if they're not allowed to say.'

Molly said nothing. She knew exactly where they were from Ben.

'That's understandable,' Jack murmured, agreeing with Queenie's remark.

The friendship between the two fathers, who still met regularly on a Saturday night, had never wavered and, although they didn't say much to their respective spouses, Luke Spencer still joined them in the local pub each week. But Ethel was a little sharper than perhaps either of the men had given her credit for.

'I expect you two still meet up with Mr Spencer on a Saturday night?' she said casually.

Jack and Ron glanced a little guiltily at each other, prompting Ethel to say, 'Aye, I thought so.' She shrugged. 'Not that we mind, but I would like to think you'd tell us all if you hear any news from him about the lads.'

'Of course, Ethel,' Jack said at once. 'We wouldn't keep anything like that from you.'

As the two families parted company late in the evening, Mabel said, 'Thank you, Ethel. It's been a good day. You must come to us for New Year's Eve, if you'd like to.'

'That'd be nice, Mabel. Thanks.'

'You up for a walk in the park tomorrow afternoon?' Queenie asked Molly. Then she laughed. 'Only if it's not raining, mind you. I don't want to get my new coat soaked.'

'Yeah, all right.' Molly smiled even though she guessed it might be difficult for her. Queenie, as she always did, would talk about Harry non-stop, little realizing how Molly would feel.

'I'll call for you, then,' Queenie promised.

Although the day was cold, it was clear skies and the two girls found that several others had had the same idea.

'Look, over there,' Queenie said suddenly. 'There's

three young fellas not in uniform. Aren't you going to give them a feather?'

'No, I am not.' Molly looked across at the young men who were obviously with their wives or girlfriends. There were other women in the park in small groups but with no men in attendance.

'There's a lot of women here without men,' Queenie said. 'Just like us. I bet their fellas must have joined up too. Well, if you're not going to do anything, then I will.' She pulled three white feathers out of her pocket and marched towards the group.

'No, Queenie. Stop. Please don't.' She tried to grab her arm but Queenie twisted free.

'I'm only doing what you did,' Queenie smirked and then raised her voice. 'Hey, you . . .'

The three young men and the women with them turned. Now Molly hung back. She groaned as she saw Queenie holding out the feathers to them.

'Aren't you ashamed of yourselves?' she heard Queenie say. 'Fit and healthy young men like you not in uniform. And as for you' – she turned on the girls – 'you should be embarrassed to be seen out with them.' Haven't you heard the song?' Queenie began to sing. *'Oh! we don't want to lose you but we think you ought to go, For your King and your Country both need you so . . .'*

Biting her lip, Molly watched from a short distance away. She drew in a horrified gasp as one of the young men held up his arm to show that he had no hand, only a bandaged stump.

'Mons,' he said shortly. 'Sorry to disappoint you, but I can't go back. I can't fire a rifle now. In fact,

I can't even hold one properly. And as for these two, they're wounded but not so seriously. When they're fit enough, they'll have to go back and face the horror. And believe me, me duck, it's carnage. So, keep your white feathers for others, eh? There's a good girl.'

Queenie's face turned white as her gaze fixed on the young man's injured arm. She recoiled visibly, turned away, picked up her skirt and ran.

Molly knew her own face was fiery red and tears threatened, but she was brave enough to stand and look the wounded young man in the eyes. 'I'm so, so sorry,' she said shakily.

He shrugged. 'It's not your fault, me duck. I saw you trying to stop her coming over to us. But just tell your friend that there are more and more wounded coming back home now – some of 'em for good. And once they're here, they can't wait to get rid of the uniform. Believe me, none of us want any reminders.' Again he held up his arm. 'This is enough.'

Molly nodded and whispered again, 'I'm sorry.' Then she too turned away.

When she caught up with her, Queenie said defensively, 'How was I to know? They should still be in uniform even if they are wounded.'

They hardly spoke to each other as they walked home.

'See you tomorrow,' Queenie said as they parted outside the Wyngates' home. Molly watched her friend walk the rest of the way to her own house, swinging her hips as if she hadn't a care in the world. She'd soon recovered from the shock. But Molly hadn't. A sob escaped her lips as she headed down the jitty and almost fell through the back door.

'Oh Mam – Mam,' she said, burying her face against Mabel's shoulder.

'Molly, love. Whatever's the matter? Has something happened? Has there – has there been bad news?' Even though their boys were still in this country, Mabel knew that sometimes accidents happened in training.

Between hiccups, Molly told her what had occurred in the park. 'This poor man. He'd lost his hand, at Mons, he said, but Queenie hadn't noticed and she – she handed him a white feather.'

Mabel sighed. 'Aye well, that's the risk you run if you're going to hand them out willy-nilly. Now, Molly,' she added more briskly, 'pull yourself together and help me get the tea ready. Just tell Queenie straight that you didn't like what happened and that you won't go out with her any more if she's going to do that.'

'Yes, Mam, I will.'

Twenty-nine

'There's a letter from William,' Mabel greeted Molly when she returned from work one evening in January. 'They've had a visit from Lord Kitchener himself, so that perked them all up a bit, but he says the weather is appalling. They've had so much rain, he can't imagine what it must be like in the trenches if they've had similar sort of weather out there. They spend most of their time wet through and shivering. He says they've started long route marches. I expect most of them are in the rain.' Mabel frowned worriedly, always the concerned mother. 'We must send him some more warm underwear so he always has something dry to change into.'

Molly didn't disillusion her mother but she was rather afraid that there would never be enough spare dry clothing! The end of 1914 and the beginning of the New Year had been the worst they could remember for rain and it didn't look like it was stopping any time soon.

'Oh, I almost forgot. There's one for you, but I don't recognize the handwriting.'

As Molly reached up to the mantlepiece to pick up the letter, she asked, 'Did William say where they are?'

'No, just that they're still in training. But he's fine

and actually enjoying the camaraderie. He's still with the Spencer lads and Tom, but he says they've all made more friends and they're a great bunch. He says he hopes they get to stay together as they all look out for each other. That's nice, isn't it?'

Molly opened the letter addressed to her and gasped in surprise. 'It's from Tom.'

Mabel looked up. 'Tom Mayberry?'

Molly nodded as she began to read the letter.

> *Dear Molly,*
> *I hope you won't mind me writing to you, but I would really like someone to write to back home, especially when we get sent overseas. There's Mam, of course, and I write every week to her, but that's not like having someone of my own age to write to and to hear from. You're a kind girl and although I know I could never hope that you'd be my girlfriend, I just wondered if you'd be friends with me like you are with Ben. If I don't hear back, I'll know you don't want to. And don't worry if the answer is 'no', I'll understand.*
> *Yours hopefully,*
> *Tom.*

'What do you think, Mam?' Molly asked as she handed the letter to Mabel.

'Poor lad,' Mabel said slowly, when she'd finished reading it and had handed it back to Molly. 'He's always been a bit of a loner – an odd one out – hasn't he?'

'Yes, he was at school. He never seemed able to make friends. Not even with other boys, never mind the girls. To be honest, he was a bit – well – silly, though he has grown up a bit since then.' She sighed. 'He'll never be the best-looking lad in the street but then I should know what that feels like.'

'Now, Molly,' Mabel said, pretending severity. 'What have I told you about that?'

Mother and daughter smiled at each other.

'So, are you going to write to him? All I'd say is this – well, two things really. One – don't give the lad false hope that you feel anything romantically towards him, and two – don't tell Queenie.'

Molly blinked. 'Why not? Tell Queenie, I mean.'

Mabel wriggled her shoulders. 'I can't put my finger on it, love. It's just this feeling I've got about her. Somehow I don't trust her anymore.' She paused and then beneath her breath added, 'Not sure I ever did.' But Molly's attention had been drawn back to the letter in her hand.

'I'll think about writing to Tom. I can't see it would do any harm and I do feel sorry for him. I'd do more if I could. I'd go round and see his mam, but I know she wouldn't want to see me.'

Mabel frowned. 'That's the bit I don't understand. Tom must know how his mam feels about you and that white feather business, so why does he want to write to you?'

'I don't know, Mam. I really don't know. Perhaps – perhaps he doesn't feel so strongly about it as Harry does.' It hurt her even to say his name and to remember the look on his face as the train had pulled out of the station. It was a picture in her mind she could never erase however hard she tried.

'Well, if you do decide to write to him,' Mabel was saying, 'make it plain from the outset that it's just friendship you're offering, nothing more. Don't give the poor lad false hope.'

Molly took a week to decide that she would write to Tom. Her reason was a little selfish, she had to admit, although only to herself. That way, she would hear news of Harry. And Ben, too, of course. She hadn't expected to hear from Harry, but she was grateful that Ben wrote to her regularly.

As they met after work one day, Molly steeled herself to ask Queenie, 'Have you heard from Harry?'

'Oh yes. I hear every week. Lovely long letters full of . . .' she simpered and wriggled her shoulders, 'well, I'm sure you can guess.'

Forcing herself not to imagine what Harry wrote in his love letters, Molly said, 'Does he mention the others?'

'Not very often. He has too much he wants to say to me.'

That evening, Molly wrote her first letter to Tom.

As the weeks went by, Molly heard regularly from both Ben and Tom, though not every week.

In March, Ben told her that they were moving to Andover, where they were comfortably billeted with local families.

A Woman of Spirit

> *It's so nice to have a decent bed, even if it's only for a short while. Proper uniforms and equipment have started to arrive,* he wrote, *but it's all getting much more serious now with all sorts of exercises and manoeuvres. And don't talk to me about the route marches we have to go on . . .*

Soon afterwards, however, in April, Tom wrote to tell her that they were at Perham Down Camp on Salisbury Plain. Two months later, they both wrote with great excitement to say that the King had inspected them.

> *You can guess there was a lot of spit and polish before his arrival,* Tom wrote, *but it was great to see him in the flesh and to think that he actually cares about the Leicester Tigers, as our brigade is nicknamed.*

And Ben wrote, *I felt sorry for the poor chap. He looked as if he carried the weight of the world on his shoulders. It must be an awful responsibility to be King of a country – well, several countries actually – at war.*

Molly was reminded once again how Ben's kindness and thought for others always shone through, but his last line brought her fresh anxiety.
But the other thing is, if he's been to see us, it must mean we're ready to be sent overseas . . .

*

'Molly,' Mabel greeted her one evening when she returned from work. 'You'll never guess what. I've had a letter from Betsy Anstruther.'

'Really? What about? Is she organizing a suffragette meeting?'

'No, nothing like that. She's signed up as a Voluntary Aid Detachment nurse and she's likely to be sent to France to work in a field hospital. Isn't that brave of her? Oh, how I wish I could go with her.'

'Do you, Mam? Really?'

Mabel laughed drily. 'No, I can't do anything like that. Of course I can't. But just sometimes, I wish I could spread my wings and do something useful. You see, I felt we were making some sort of contribution to society when we had the suffragette meetings, the marches and the flag waving. We were trying to change things so that they'd be better for women, but now I feel I'm doing nothing.'

'You're doing a lot, Mam. You're looking after Dad and me so we can do our work. Dad's work is soon going to be very important to the war effort, from what he's been saying, and even though I sometimes think mine isn't, soldiers need socks, don't they? And lots of 'em, from what the boys are telling us.'

'Yes, you're right, of course. I'm just being silly, Molly. Take no notice of me. I wouldn't change my life with anyone else. But we're living in strange times, aren't we? Never knowing from one day to the next what the news will bring.'

Mother and daughter regarded each other solemnly.

'So,' Molly said at last, 'does she want you to write to her? She struck me as being rather a lonely woman.'

'You're right. She hasn't any close family, so I think the suffragette cause was her lifeline. Yes, I shall write to her. We go back a long way.'

'But she wasn't – well – our class, was she?'

Mabel smiled pensively. 'No, but she never made me feel inferior and this war has been a great leveller. All classes are in it together.'

'I think it sounds as if she needs a friend back home to write to.'

'I'd have thought she'd have had a lot of friends among her own kind.'

'Not necessarily, Mam. Maybe they don't understand about her involvement with the suffragettes or what she's doing now and she thinks you will.'

'Perhaps you're right, Molly, love. And yes,' she added more firmly, 'I will write to her. She'll be doing a grand thing, looking after our boys.'

Molly said nothing but silently she prayed that 'their boys' would never have need of Miss Anstruther's care.

It had taken a few months for the bellfoundry to receive its government contract to produce parts for howitzer shells. Rumours were rife that there would no longer be enough employees left to do the work after so many of the workforce had volunteered for active service. The foundry was expected to deliver two hundred casings each week, following specific instructions on the different operations necessary to complete the finished item to the standard required.

'They'll have to employ female labour,' was the general opinion among women of the town, many of whom were eager to be seen helping the war effort.

'Dad,' Molly said carefully one evening as they sat together after tea. 'Are there any jobs going at the foundry?'

Ron frowned and glanced up. 'Why do you ask?'

'Because I'd like to apply for a job there.' She held up her hand as Ron opened his mouth to reply. 'Don't say it. That I'm doing a good job where I am.'

Ron smiled. 'That's exactly what I was going to say.'

'But it doesn't feel like I'm helping with the war effort, not like it would if I was making shell casings.'

'You're best staying where you are, Molly, love. There's a good girl. Besides, they won't be employing girls at the foundry. I'd bet a week's pay on that.' He picked up his paper, signifying there was no more to be said on the matter.

Mabel bent her head over her darning. When Ron spoke like that, even she did not argue.

Thirty

In the summer of 1915, at about the same time that the foundry began producing munitions components, the families heard that their boys were to go abroad. Now it was likely that they would be involved in the fighting. Even though they had all known it would come, it was still something of a shock. Alice hurried round to see Harriet.

'Have you heard?' she said, bursting in through the back door of the Spencer home.

Harriet sighed. There was no need to ask what her friend meant. She knew only too well.

'Come in, Alice, and we'll have a little chat.'

'Do you think they'll get leave before they actually go?'

Harriet shook her head. 'No, I don't.'

Alice's eyes widened. 'Why ever not?'

'Because they're boy soldiers, most of whom have probably never been away from home before. They volunteered – oh, very bravely, I grant you, but they're not hardened veterans. The authorities will be afraid that if they let them home, several of them might not go back. Then they'd likely be hunted down and court martialled for desertion.' Harriet did not add that desertion was viewed as being one of the worst crimes for a soldier. If found guilty, the punishment could be death by firing squad.

'Oh my. Then – then they'd better not come home, had they?'

'No, Alice, love. They'd be better to stay with their mates.'

'At least they're all together.'

Harriet nodded. She didn't want to upset her friend but she was a little doubtful that, once they were overseas, the four would remain together. Anyway, she told herself, she didn't really know one way or the other, so it was best to say nothing.

'I'm going down to Folkestone,' Queenie said during the last days of July.

Molly gaped at her and then the proverbial penny dropped. 'Oh, to see Harry off,' she said flatly.

Queenie nodded, her eyes shining. 'Dad's given me the train fare and enough to stay overnight in a boarding house if I have to.'

'That's nice of him,' Molly said, trying hard to keep her voice steady. 'They must really approve of Harry now.'

'Oh, they do. They think he's wonderful.' She put her arms around herself in a self-hug. 'And so do I. Once the silly war's over, we'll get married. Look, why don't you come with me? You'd like to see your brother off, wouldn't you? And Ben?'

Molly grimaced. 'I can't afford it.' Besides, she thought to herself, Harry, and William for that matter, won't want to see me. Not after the white feather business. They must be blaming me more than ever now that they're actually being sent into the fighting.

'I don't know why.' Queenie's scathing glance raked Molly from head to toe. 'It's obvious you don't spend much on clothes. You'd look so much better if you took a bit of trouble with yourself.'

Molly literally bit down on her tongue to stop a retort.

'Look, I'll ask Miss Parkinson if she'd make you a summer dress,' Queenie went on. 'I don't think she'd charge you much, and there are some lovely cotton prints on the market stalls at the moment. I'll come with you to help you choose something, if you like.'

For a brief moment, Molly was tempted. Queenie was her friend, she reminded herself. She wasn't being horrible, she was trying to help her.

'I'll – I'll think about it,' Molly murmured and forced herself to smile. It was tempting, she admitted to herself, but her mam needed her contribution to the household, especially now William had gone. Part of his army pay was being sent home, but Molly knew it didn't amount to much. In the meantime, she needed to be the one to help her family. Queenie shrugged and went back to planning her trip.

When Queenie returned from seeing Harry off, her eyes were shining with happiness. 'He's asked me to marry him,' she told Molly. 'When he comes home on leave, he says we'll choose a ring, and then I'll really belong to him and everyone will know I'm his girl.'

In that instant, any tiny vestige of hope that Molly had left was gone.

'I'm pleased for you, Queenie.' She forced a laugh. 'You've certainly captured the handsomest boy around here.'

Queenie's eyes sparkled. 'I have, haven't I? But you must promise me you won't tell anyone. Not yet. Not until I've got a ring on my finger and it's official.'

'You're telling your mam and dad, aren't you?'

'Not yet. Harry wants to do it properly and ask my dad for his permission.'

'Of course,' Molly murmured.

Queenie was looking at her rather strangely. 'What?' Molly said.

'Look, there's something else I'd like to – to confide in you, but you must swear you won't tell a soul.'

Molly hesitated.

'Oh, go on, Moll. I need to tell someone or I'll burst, and you are my very best friend.'

'All right,' Molly agreed, but she was still a little reluctant. She couldn't think what it could be that was so very secret.

'You know Dad gave me the money to stay overnight somewhere? Well, I found this lovely little boarding house. It wasn't too expensive, but the best thing was that Harry got a twenty-four-hour pass and – he stayed the night with me.'

Molly stared at her in horror. 'Oh Queenie. What if your mam knew?'

'She won't.' Her voice hardened. 'No one will know, because you're not going to tell anyone, now are you?'

'No – no, of course I won't. I promise, but – what if he – what if you're—'

'Pregnant? I won't be. Harry said he'd be very careful, that he wouldn't hurt me and that he certainly wouldn't leave me in the family way.'

Now Molly's curiosity got the better of her. 'And did it – hurt?'

'Just a bit the first time.'

'The *first* time?'

'Oh yes,' Queenie said airily. 'We made love three times through the night.' She giggled. 'I didn't get much sleep.'

Molly was shocked. After all Ethel's warnings, Queenie had still disobeyed her mother and put herself at risk of bringing shame on herself and her family.

Thirty-one

One morning a letter addressed to Molly arrived.

'I think it's from Tom,' Mabel said, handing it to her. 'You've had a few from him recently, haven't you?'

Molly nodded as she opened the letter. 'I hadn't the heart to refuse, Mam, when he asked, but I did as you said and made sure he understood from the start that we're just friends.'

> *Dear Molly,*
> *Thank you so much for writing to me again. You can't possibly know how much it means. I'm not the odd one out anymore, who only gets letters from his mam. It's very kind of you and I promise I won't try to 'overstep the mark'. We'll just be real friends like you are with Ben. Although I've always wondered if there's a little more between you two than either of you are letting on. Sorry, I'm not trying to pry. But you would be so well-suited. He's a good lad.*
> *Well, we're abroad now. That's all I can tell you without inviting the censor's black pen, but the four of us are all fine and still*

together, which is good. I know this war is an awful thing to have happened and we're going to face some hard times, but it is nice to see a bit of the world. We've travelled through some lovely countryside and it's dreadful to think it may soon be spoiled. Why countries have to fight each other, I'll never know . . .

His letter went on to tell her about his life now – at least, as much as he dared. When she had finished reading it, she handed it to her mother to read.

'I have to say, he actually sounds happy,' Molly said. 'Happier than he was at home, if I'm honest.'

When Mabel had read it too, she nodded. 'You're right. He does, but when you think about it, he didn't have much of a life here, now did he? No man as a role model and, sadly, no friends to speak of.'

'What happened to his father?'

'Accident at work when Tom was about two. I doubt he even remembers his father.'

'It can't have been easy for his mother either.'

'No, I don't expect it was. I didn't know her then. I've only met her recently through Mrs Spencer and the suffragette movement. You know, Molly, I really miss those meetings.'

'Yes, so do I.'

A few days later, Molly received a similar letter from Ben, which filled in a few of the blanks in Tom's letter.

> *Well, we're finally here. We left*—here there was a thick black line through whatever he had written; as Tom had predicted the censor had been busy with his pen . . . *very late at night. We left home shores in complete darkness and silence. There was no one to see us off. No bands playing or folk cheering us on our way. The only sounds were the waves. We arrived in*—Harbour in France about two hours later. Again the name of the place had been obliterated. *Then we marched three miles to the rest camp. I expect our troop departures are being kept very hush-hush, but the lads are saying that the people of that coastal town are getting used to troop ships leaving. It's no longer exciting to them!*

Molly frowned. Surely, she thought, at least Queenie and possibly a few other girlfriends and perhaps wives too would have been there? That is what Queenie had gone all the way down to the south of England to do.

> *I have no idea where we're going next and I probably won't be able to say anyway. Keep thinking of us, Molly, won't you? I do miss you and our walks in the park . . .*

'Have you heard from Harry since they landed in France?' Molly asked Queenie carefully.
'No, I don't expect they'll be allowed to write yet.'

A Woman of Spirit

'It must have been exciting seeing them on their way. Were there a lot of people there?'

'Oh yes, hundreds. All cheering. There were lots of tears, too, of course. I couldn't help crying when I was waving him off. I watched the ship out of sight until it was a speck in the distance and then I had to catch the train home.'

Molly couldn't ask any more, or Queenie might smell a rat and start asking questions Molly didn't want to answer. But the way Queenie was telling it, it didn't sound as if the ship had left in the middle of the night as Ben had said. And he should know: he'd been on it.

'Oh, I'm going to miss Harry so much, Moll, but you'll help me, won't you?'

'Of course,' Molly said stoutly, pushing aside the memories of all the times she had been left on her own while Queenie was out with Harry. 'That's what friends are for.'

It was just as her mother had warned her would happen when one of them got a boyfriend, but now Queenie needed her again and, even though she was missing Harry just as much as Queenie, that must remain her secret.

During their first month in France, Molly heard news from Ben and Tom and, in the occasional letters to her parents, from William. Her brother never wrote to her personally, and the realization that he believed she had given out white feathers still hurt her. One day, she hoped, they would all find out the truth, but she had no idea how that might happen and therefore had no hope that it would. She never heard from Harry.

We seem to be moving about a lot, Tom wrote, *but we don't feel we're doing very much. We've been involved in a few skirmishes but most of the time we seem to be training – yet again! We're doing a course in visual signalling at the moment . . .*

'Dad,' Molly asked Ron when he returned from the pub one Saturday evening in early September, 'Have you any idea where the boys actually are at the moment?'

'No, they can't say in their letters, can they? But Luke reckons they'll be heading towards the front line any time now to learn the ways of trench warfare from the more experienced soldiers. Probably somewhere in Flanders.'

Towards the end of September, Molly ran almost all the way home, without stopping to wait for Queenie on the corner as usual.

'Mam, Mam!' she called, bursting in through the back door.

'Oh, whatever's the matter? Has there been bad news?'

'No, no. Just the opposite. You know there was a new principal appointed at the Technical Institute in town recently?'

'Yes, what about it?'

'He's setting up workshops for the training of munitions workers and they want women. They're calling it "training on production".'

'Whatever does that mean?'

'Well, we'll be learning how to make things like shells and that, but what we make would be good enough to be sent out.'

'Are you sure, if it's what trainees have made?'

'Oh, I expect everything will be properly inspected. Besides, that'd be part of the training in itself, wouldn't it? Learning how to inspect products.'

Mabel frowned. 'Why are you saying "we"?'

'Don't you see? I can go to train to work in munitions and then I'd feel I was *really* helping with the war effort.'

'But you are now. Don't you think the soldiers all need clothing and—'

'Yes, I know, but this way it's a direct help. They're crying out for munitions workers.'

'Now, Molly, you know what your dad said. He didn't even want you working on shell casings if that had been possible, so he's not going to give his permission for this, now is he? Besides, you might have to go away once you've been trained.'

'Maybe not, if there are munitions factories near here by that time. Besides, William's away and in a lot more danger than I'd be in.'

'I don't know about that. I think that this work can be dangerous too.'

'Oh please, Mam, try to understand.'

'You must talk to your dad.'

Molly waited in a state of high anxiety until Ron

came home. Almost before he was through the door she said, 'Dad, the new principal at the Technical Institute is starting classes in the New Year to teach people to make munitions, and they want women. Please say you'll let me enrol.'

'Yes, I'd heard about that. But let's have tea and then we'll talk about it.'

So, for an hour or so, Molly was forced to curb her impatience. When at last Ron was sitting near the range with his pipe he said, 'Now Molly, I told you before you're already doing a valuable job, so why . . . ?'

'It's just that I'd feel I was being more of a direct help.'

'What about after the war? You probably wouldn't have a job to go back to afterwards.'

Molly's face fell. She hadn't thought of that. 'I'd find something. I've heard that women are doing all sorts of jobs now to take the place of men who've gone to war.'

'But the men will want their jobs back when they come home,' Mabel put in.

Molly and her father exchanged a glance. They knew they were both thinking the same thing. How many will come home, and of those who do, how many will be fit enough to work again? But neither of them voiced these thoughts aloud because one of that number was their beloved son and brother.

'What's Queenie doing?' Mabel asked suddenly. 'Has she had anything to do with this?'

'No. I haven't even seen her since I heard about it at work today. I ran all the way home to tell you.'

She giggled. 'I bet she was wondering where I'd got to. It's a wonder she hasn't been round.'

Mabel sniffed. 'There's time yet. I just wondered if she'd put you up to it, that's all.'

'No, she hasn't,' Molly replied shortly, a little put out that her mother still thought she was so in thrall to Queenie that she couldn't make up her own mind about what to do.

'The thing is, Molly,' Ron said, 'if you signed up for this training, then you would be expected to go anywhere they sent you. Now, it's bad enough for us, having William leave home and expose himself to danger. We don't want that for you. Do you understand? So, let's hear no more about it. You will stay at the hosiery factory and do your duty for the war effort there.'

It wasn't often her father sounded stern or laid down the law as head of the household so firmly. Even Mabel said nothing. But before Molly could argue, there was the sound of the back door opening and Queenie's merry voice calling, 'It's only me.'

'Told you so,' Mabel muttered.

'Where did you get to tonight, Moll? I waited ages on the corner.'

'Oh, sorry. I wanted to get home to tell Mam something.'

Queenie frowned. 'Not in trouble at work, are you?'

'No, of course not,' Molly snapped, annoyed that Queenie had interrupted what was, to Molly, a serious and important discussion. 'I – I wanted to tell Mam something, that's all. About – about doing something to help with the war effort.'

'Actually, I was a bit late leaving work myself. Miss Parkinson is being kept very busy with ladies wanting clothes altered instead of buying new ones. She's teaching me dressmaking, so even I'm doing my bit for the war in my own way.' She smirked as she added, 'Besides, keeping a handsome soldier happy when he comes home on leave and writing to him every week to keep his spirits up takes a lot of my time.'

Mabel kept her eyes firmly fixed on the sock she was darning, but her mouth pursed. She was not sure she liked the sound of what Queenie was saying. What was the girl insinuating? She hadn't been entirely happy when she'd heard that Queenie was being allowed to travel all the way down south to wave Harry off. Perhaps she should have a quiet word with Ethel.

Queenie turned towards Molly. 'I expect you're writing to Ben, aren't you?'

'Now and again, but not every week.'

'Well, you ought to be. I reckon you could snare him if you play your cards right.'

'I don't want to "snare" him, as you put it,' Molly said sharply. 'He's a good friend, that's all.'

'So you keep saying,' Queenie said. 'If not him, then what about Tom? He's desperate to have a girlfriend. Why don't you write to him?'

Before Molly could answer, Mabel stood up, determined to interrupt the way the conversation was going. 'I was just going to make a mug of cocoa. Do you want some, Queenie?'

'That'd be nice, Aunty Mabel. Thank you.'

A Woman of Spirit

As if sensing what his wife was trying to do, even though not fully understanding why, Ron said, 'I expect you hear from Harry regularly, Queenie. Is he all right?'

Queenie laughed. 'He makes it sound as if they're having a ball. What does William say?'

'William doesn't write very often, but he sounds fine.'

When Mabel came back into the room, she artfully turned the conversation back to Queenie and her work at the drapery. It was the safest topic. There was nothing the girl liked more than to be the centre of attention.

When finally Queenie had left and Molly had gone upstairs to bed, Ron laid his paper aside and asked quietly, 'What are your thoughts on this idea of Molly's to apply to the Technical Institute?'

Mabel considered for a moment before saying carefully. 'Ron, you and I have hardly ever fallen out in all the years we've been married, have we?'

'No, that's true. So what are you saying? That you don't agree with me in this?'

'Not exactly. I can see your point, but I can also see Molly's. We both know that what she's doing at the hosiery factory is valuable work, but she doesn't see it that way. And there's another thing. I know she's not "of full age" yet, as they say, but she's nineteen, Ron. She's a grown woman. And experiencing what we're all going through now makes these youngsters grow up a lot quicker.'

Ron sighed deeply. 'Yes, you're right. I still tend to

think of her as my little girl.' He paused and then added quietly, 'So, you think I should let her do what she wants?'

'I think we should let things lie for the moment and see what happens.'

Thirty-two

The first time in the trenches was a shock for the four lads. They were surprised that they had been able to come all this way together, but they'd learned that the pals' battalions had become even more popular.

'I wonder what the Coalville Fifty are doing now,' Tom remarked. 'I wonder if they're still one unit.'

'I expect they will be. That was the whole point, wasn't it?' William said. 'I was rather sorry we couldn't be part of it.'

'We've almost got our own little gang from Loughborough and district though, haven't we?' Harry grinned. 'There are more than just us four and we're all sticking with each other.'

'And now we're really going to be in the thick of it,' Ben murmured. 'This is what we volunteered for. Are you ready for it, lads?'

'Yes,' came the chorus from the other three. 'Let's get at 'em.'

The evening before they were due to move up the line, Harry, who seemed to be a natural leader among their little group, said, 'Now, have you all written letters home, destroyed any personal papers and filled in the wills in your paybooks?'

The others nodded. 'Makes it a bit real, doesn't it?' Tom murmured. 'I've not told Mam what's happening. It doesn't seem fair.'

Harry nodded. 'You're right, Tom, but just make sure you've said all you want to say to her, just in case . . .'

'I have. I make sure I do in every letter I send.' But to Molly he was able to tell the truth. *We're moving tomorrow and I'll give you three guesses where.*

The following morning, after they'd been issued with iron rations of bully beef, biscuits and a supply of ammunition, they'd moved up to the reserve trench, then the support line and at last they were there – on the front line, with the enemy's trench only about two hundred yards or less away across what they learned was called no-man's-land.

'Keep your heads down below the parapet at all times,' they'd been warned, 'and no talking unless it's absolutely necessary. Sound carries; they can hear you and will probably lob a grenade over.'

Harry was again the one to take the lead. He took it upon himself to look out for his brother and their two friends.

'Have you noticed how the trenches zig-zag?' William said. 'I wonder why that is.'

'If one section gets shelled or even a sniper fires down it, it can only affect one section of about twenty-five yards,' the corporal explained when he overheard William's remark. He was in charge of the ten or so men who were to man the section where the two brothers and two friends had arrived. 'Can you imagine the havoc it would cause if all the trench was in one straight line? Now, let me explain a few things to you, this being your first time in the front line. It's not so bad, once you get used to it.' He gave a dry laugh. 'The boredom's the worst, if I'm honest, when you want something to happen – and then wish you hadn't! I will be your corporal on this section. Anderson's the name, and there's Lance Corporal Myers here too. You'll soon get used to the routine but here are the basics: you'll be here on the front line for three to four days before being rotated out of the lines, first back to the support trench, then the reserve and then for about eight days' rest, though it isn't much of a rest as you're still expected to do whatever's asked of you.'

The men all smiled weakly. This was the army, not a holiday.

'Stand to is just before dawn until full daylight,' Corporal Anderson went on. 'Dawn and dusk are the usual times the enemy will attack, so every man must be alert. At daylight, nine of you will be stood down, leaving one on sentry duty. Then it's time for the daily rum ration – always a welcome time. Then it's breakfast. Our rations at the moment aren't too bad but the tea's pretty foul. The water's brought up in petrol tins and you can't hide the taste. After that, it's ablutions and cleaning your weapons, but only half of you at any one time, for obvious reasons. Then we'll get visits from the platoon sergeant, followed by a little respite before your two hours of sentry duty.'

Our corporal and lance corporal seem a couple of decent blokes, Ben wrote home to Molly when they'd returned to the rest area after their first time in the front line. *I'm hoping this won't get crossed out by the censor. I can't tell you where we are, obviously. We had one bit of a skirmish but thankfully no one among our little group was killed or even hurt. The food is pretty good. We even get a bit of bacon at breakfast and, would you believe, jam! I expect they try to feed us as well as they can because it's quite a strenuous life, especially with all the training thrown in! But your parcels from home are still most welcome – especially cake and chocolate. We share them around. Everybody does. There's a lot of camaraderie and, in our section anyway, very few fall-outs. I expect we all realize we're fighting a dangerous enemy, not one another.*

When they had finished their time in the front line, the four Loughborough lads were relieved to be returning to the reserve trench unhurt, but they were so desperately tired. 'I could sleep for a week,' Tom muttered as they stumbled through the connecting trenches. Already they had seen some gruesome sights that they would never forget. Now they really understood what they had let themselves in for.

'I'm just thankful we're still in one piece,' Harry said, shepherding the other three in front of him. 'We weren't far from that lad who got caught by a sniper.'

Tom shuddered. 'That was horrible. I was standing quite near him. Got him right in the eye. He went down like a stone. There was nothing anyone could do.'

A Woman of Spirit

'At least it was quick for the poor sod,' Harry said. 'The worst I've seen so far was that poor devil who got it in the guts in the next section to us. He was in agony and begging his pals to shoot him. Now, that's bad.'

'Did they?'

'No, 'course not. They took him to the nearest first aid post, but he'll be lucky to survive.'

'Lucky or unlucky,' Tom muttered.

They were thankful to be back behind the front line. When they'd eaten they propped themselves against the walls of a dugout. It was a bit of a squash but the four of them wanted to stay together whenever they could.

As they were drifting off to sleep, their heads lolling forward, Harry murmured, 'I wonder how Molly would feel about posting her white feathers through our letterboxes, if she could see us now and what we've just witnessed?'

Tom was awake in an instant. 'What did you say, Harry?'

'Oh sorry, I was just thinking aloud, that's all. Go to sleep, Tom.'

'No, Harry. It's important. Tell me exactly what you just said.'

As Harry repeated his words, the other two were wide awake again when, a moment ago, they had thought they would sleep for days.

'It wasn't Molly,' Tom said. 'I promise you it wasn't Molly who did that.'

In the darkness, Harry said bitterly, ''Course it was. We all know it was.'

Tom took a deep breath. He knew he was risking his new-found friendship with the other three, but he was fond of Molly, and now she was being so kind to him in writing, he couldn't let her shoulder the blame for something that wasn't her fault. 'This is the first I've heard that you blame Molly. But I know it wasn't her because the night the delivery was made I was just getting ready for bed. My bedroom's at the front of the house and I was drawing the curtains when I saw this shadowy figure moving along the street and pushing something through people's doors . . .'

'Go on,' Ben prompted softly when Tom paused.

'It was a girl, I could see that, and I watched as she put something through your door and then crossed the street to mine. She was so close, just below my window, and the hood of her cloak fell back and in the moonlight I could see exactly who it was. And it wasn't Molly.'

'Who was it, then?' William demanded, a sense of relief creeping through him to think that his sister might, after all, be innocent.

'I don't want to tell you. I'm no telltale.'

'That's not the point. We need to know, else how are we to really believe you?' William said. 'Is it someone we know? Someone from our streets?'

Now, without lying, Tom could not answer. 'Look, I'm sorry I said anything, but I didn't want Molly blamed when it wasn't her. Oh, I know she's viewed as a heroine to some folks who agree with the white feather nonsense, but we don't, do we? Especially not now we've seen what a hell-hole this is. So, I'm not letting on. If you can't take my word, then – then I'll find somewhere else to bunk.'

'Don't be daft, Tom,' Ben said at once. 'You're one of us – we're mates – we stick together. I'm glad you told us, and if you don't want to say any more then we ought to respect that. There's just one more thing though, Tom. I think we all ought to write to our folks and tell them, because I don't want Molly to be blamed any longer. I know our mam has cut her and her mother off. I think your mam has too.'

'Has she? My mam?' Tom said. 'I didn't know that. To be honest . . .' He was thoughtful for a moment before saying slowly, 'We rarely spoke about it and when we did – I remember now – no names were mentioned. I wish I had known. I'd have put her right before now. I'll definitely let her know.'

'And I'll write to our mam,' Ben said. 'That all right with you, Harry?'

Harry's voice came out of the darkness and there was ill-concealed anger in his tone. 'Yeah, fine. Like Ben said, Tom, we'll respect your decision, but I wish I knew 'cos I wouldn't half give whoever it was a piece of my mind, 'specially for letting Molly take the blame, an' all.'

'To be honest with you all,' Ben said as he closed his eyes, 'I never believed it was Molly. I didn't think it was the sort of thing she'd do.'

As they all tried to sleep after Tom's revelation had given them such a shock, William said quietly, 'Thanks for telling us, Tom. I shall have to write a grovelling letter to my sister now, but I am glad to know it wasn't her.'

After a while, uncomfortable though they were, three of the exhausted soldiers fell asleep. Only Harry was left staring into the darkness and listening to the sound of gunfire in the distance. Although weary, sleep evaded him for an hour or so. Troubled thoughts raced around his mind. Who could possibly have delivered those white feathers and let poor Molly take the blame? He fell asleep at last, but it was with the uneasy feeling that it had been someone they all knew and that was why Tom didn't want to tell them.

Thirty-three

'Have I forgotten your birthday?' Mabel laughed when Molly arrived home from work.

'I wouldn't have thought so, Mam, seeing as you were there at the time. Why?'

'You've got four letters, which all arrived at once but with different handwriting. There's one from Ben and one from Tom – I can recognize his handwriting now – and there's one from William actually addressed just to you.'

'From William – to me?'

Mabel nodded. 'But I don't recognize the last one.'

Molly picked them up from the table and leafed through them. She held the final one between trembling fingers as she stared down at the unfamiliar handwriting.

'That last one must be from Harry,' her mother suggested. 'Oh, do open them, Molly, love. Not that I'm nosy . . .' Mabel chuckled again. 'But I do want to know.'

Molly opened the one she didn't recognize and looked at the signature at the end first.

'Yes – you're right. It is from Harry. I wonder why on earth . . . ?'

She sank down into her father's chair by the range as she began to read.

My dear Molly, – if only, she thought, but then read on – *I want to send you my sincere apologies for ever having thought that you, of all people, could hand out white feathers. I am so, so sorry. Tom has just told us that on the night they were delivered to us – and to him – he was looking out of his bedroom window and recognized the person pushing the envelopes through doors in our street, and he is adamant that it wasn't you. He refuses to tell us who it was, so I suppose we'll have to be content with just knowing that it wasn't you. Please forgive us, Molly. Ben and me are both writing to our mam because we think she's been rather unkind to you – and your mam too – because of it. It seems that Tom and his mam had never discussed it, so he was completely in the dark about everyone thinking it was you. He's sorry he didn't know because he could have put things right so much sooner. We weren't close friends with Tom then like we are now. We've got to know him a lot better during our time here and he's a good lad.*
Yours ever,
Harry.

Both Ben's letter and the one from William were in much the same vein. Tom's was a little different. He was apologizing because he had not heard while still at home what was going on. Although his mother had known he'd received a feather, they'd hardly ever discussed it, and so she had never told him that throughout their neighbourhood Molly was being blamed.

Molly handed over all the letters for her mother to read – there was nothing private in any of them.

'Well, well, well,' Mabel said when she'd finished reading them. She met Molly's gaze as she said softly, 'Have you any idea who it was?'

'I . . .' Molly began and then looked away, avoiding her mother's perceptive scrutiny. 'No.'

'Well, I think I can make a shrewd guess. So all I'd say is, you just be careful from now on who your friends are.'

Molly was silent for several moments, but Mabel saw a flush creeping up her neck and into her face. 'There's – there's something I haven't told you, Mam.' Her fingers twisted nervously in her lap.

'What is it, love? Come on, you can tell me.'

'I – I've disobeyed Dad. I applied to the Technical Institute and – and I've been accepted onto a course to start in January.'

'Ah,' Mabel said. 'Then you'd better tell your dad after he's had his tea.'

Miserably, Molly nodded. 'I'm sorry, Mam. But it's something I so want to do.'

Mabel stood up and turned to go to the scullery. 'Well, I'd best get the tea ready. He'll be here soon.' With her back to her daughter, Mabel allowed herself a small smile. It was going to be an interesting evening.

*

Molly hardly ate anything at tea time and as soon as her father had settled himself in his chair near the range, she stood in front of him.

'First of all, I've had letters from all the lads. Tom's told them that he knew it wasn't me who put white feathers through their letterboxes. They've written to apologize.'

'Oh, that's good news.' Ron smiled up at her. 'I never thought it was, but it's nice to have them finally believe you, isn't it?'

Molly nodded, but she continued to stand in front of him, still ill at ease.

'I'm sorry, Dad, but I disobeyed you. I applied for training at the Technical Institute to make munitions and I've been accepted to start there in January.'

'I see,' Ron said noncommittally as he packed his pipe, deliberately keeping his face straight.

'I'm sorry,' Molly said again, 'I shouldn't have . . .'

'No, you shouldn't have. But what's done is done and I would never encourage you to go back on your word.'

'Yes, Dad,' she said meekly and began to turn away.

'You know, Molly,' he said, and his tone was full of sadness. 'That's the first time I can ever remember you disobeying me about anything. But I have to realize you're growing up. It seems I've lost my little girl.'

Molly dropped to her knees beside him. 'Oh no, Daddy, don't say that. I'll always be your little girl – but – but this is something I've got to do. I've just got to do my bit to help and – and making socks just isn't enough anymore.'

He smiled at her wistfully and stroked her hair. 'Just take care of yourself, that's all I want. I don't want you in danger like . . .'

He didn't finish the sentence but they both knew he was referring to William.

'I promise, Dad,' Molly said huskily.

Four days later, a knock came at Mabel's back door about mid-morning. 'Now who can that be?' she muttered as she went to open it. 'Just when I'm about to start my ironing.'

'Get the kettle on, Mabel, love,' Harriet said as she stepped through the door without waiting for an invitation. 'Me and Alice have got something to say to you and it's not easy, so we could both do with a cuppa while we do it.'

When they were all seated round the table with a cup of tea in front of them, Harriet said, 'If we could have worn sackcloth and ashes this morning, Mabel, we would have done.'

'Our lads have written to us—' Alice said.

'All of them.'

'To tell us that we were wrong about Molly having given out those white feathers. It seems Tom saw whoever it was, but because we hardly ever discussed it, he never told me—' Alice went on but was interrupted again by Harriet.

'And so Alice never told him what was being said in the street about Molly.'

'Or he would have put a stop to it long before now.'

There was silence before Harriet added, 'We're so

sorry we thought that of Molly. I'd like to tell her myself. Tell her she's welcome to come round to see me if – if she wants to.' She smiled. 'I've missed our little chats. She's a very intelligent girl, your Molly.'

Mabel nodded and smiled. 'She'll come round to see you, I'm sure. She's not a vindictive girl, though I have to admit it upset her a great deal to be blamed. Your boys have all written to her – our William too – but they say Tom won't tell them who it was, even though he recognized the person. Did he tell you?' she added, looking straight at Alice, who shook her head.

'No, he won't tell me either.'

Harriet stood up. 'We'd better let you get on. I see you've a pile of ironing to do and I've got some waiting for me at home, though' – she paused and then pulled in a deep breath to steady her voice – 'not as much as usual, I'm sad to say. D'you know, it's not a job I like, but I'd face a mountain of it if it would bring them all home safely.'

As she saw them to the door, Mabel said, 'Oh, by the way, Molly's been accepted at the Technical Institute to train to make munitions.'

'I heard about that,' Alice said. 'Good for her. She's doing her bit, then.'

'Is Queenie going with her?' Harriet asked, interested in the girl who might one day be her daughter-in-law.

'No, I think Queenie is well settled in her job at the draper's. She told us that the woman who works there is training her to be a dressmaker.'

Harriet nodded. 'Aye well, it'll be useful, I suppose.'

*

Molly replied to the four letters individually. She knew she would continue to hear from Tom and from Ben and, perhaps now, occasionally from William. But she had not expected to hear from Harry again, so it was a nice surprise for her when another letter arrived from him. Just a friendly note telling her as much as he dared about their life and ending, *We are all so sorry we won't get home for Christmas, but we have been told that we might get quite a long leave – about ten days, we think – in the New Year and, best of all, that the four of us might be able to come home together. Fancy, it'll be 1916 then. I wonder what the year will bring . . .*

At the beginning of January, Molly presented herself at the Technical Institute. On her first morning, being unsure of her surroundings, she entered the building and joined a group of women and girls.

'You look like how I feel,' a merry voice spoke beside her. 'Lost.'

Molly turned to see a girl of about her own age, smiling at her. 'I'm Olive Mason,' the stranger said, holding out her hand. She was about the same height as Molly, but a little plumper. She had unruly red hair, bright green eyes and freckles across the bridge of her nose. When she smiled her whole face seemed to light up and two dimples appeared in her cheeks.

'Molly Wyngate,' Molly murmured. 'Pleased to meet you. Do you know what we're supposed to do?'

'Haven't a clue. Let's just follow the others . . .'

At that moment a woman appeared and ushered them into a large room. Standing in front of the group, she told them her name was Miss Hartley, and for the next hour she gave them details of what work they would be expected to do.

'Initial training takes two weeks, or perhaps a little longer in some cases. You will then be assigned to a factory where your newly acquired skills are needed.'

Someone's hand shot up. 'Will that be local, miss?'

'Not necessarily,' the woman said. 'You'll be sent wherever you're required.'

The woman who had asked the question looked crestfallen. 'I can't leave Loughborough. My husband's enlisted and I've my elderly parents – and his – to look out for.'

'Then, I'm sorry to say, perhaps this isn't for you,' Miss Hartley said, as murmuring among those present rippled through the room. 'You must be prepared to leave home.'

The murmuring increased until Miss Hartley rapped on the table in front of her to bring the room to order. 'I apologize if this fact was not made clear on the application form. This is rather new to all of us. I will revise it at once for the future.'

'I don't want to leave here,' Olive whispered. 'Do you?'

'Not really, but I suppose we'll have to go where we're sent.' Molly glanced around her. Several of the women had already risen and were leaving the room. Only six older women besides Molly and Olive were left.

'So.' Miss Hartley came out from behind the table and approached those still left. 'Are you all staying?'

The women glanced at one another and nodded. 'We're either single women or our husbands have enlisted,' one explained. 'And we've no children.'

'Or they're old enough to be left,' another put in.

Closer now, Molly recognized two of the women, who had both been suffragettes. Conscious that perhaps it would be wiser to remain silent about her former involvement with the cause, Molly said nothing, but as the group formed behind Miss Hartley one of the women, Iris Williams, winked at her. Obviously, she had recognized Molly but was also keeping quiet about her former activities. She had been one of the militant ones and had been the first to congratulate Molly when there'd been speculation that she'd damaged a pillar box.

For the rest of the day the remaining group of women, now only eight in number, were shown around the premises, visiting all the places of work – 'shops', as they were called. Molly and Olive stayed together.

'Will we have to work those big machines?' Molly whispered.

'I expect so. They're called lathes, I think,' Olive said. 'My dad works on one of those at The Brush.'

'Oh well, you'll be all right, then,' Molly chuckled. 'It'll be in your blood.'

At the end of the tour, Miss Hartley led them to the canteen, where they were given afternoon tea.

'The canteen is open to everyone,' she told them, 'from eleven in the morning until ten at night, though, of course, you are only allowed a certain number of breaks in your day. The workers here will be very well catered for,' she added with a note of pride in her voice.

As they left the building, Olive said, 'So are you going to sign up?'

'I think so,' Molly said, 'though I'll have to discuss it with my parents first, especially because of the leaving home bit when we've finished our training.'

'Yeah, me too. We've only just come to live here and I love the little house we've got. My dad got a job at The Brush.'

'Maybe he knows a friend of ours, then? Mr Spencer.'

'I'll ask him. Where does your dad work?'

'At the bellfoundry. My brother works there too. At least, he did until he volunteered. He's abroad now. My Uncle Jack works there as well. Well, he's not my real uncle, but his wife and my mam have been friends for years. Jack Palmer. He's a foreman there.'

'Is he Queenie Palmer's dad by any chance?'

'Yes, he is. Why? Do you know her?'

'No, but I've heard about her.' Strangely, Olive's tone had hardened and, intuitively, Molly knew to remain silent about her own friendship with Queenie. 'Oh yes,' Olive murmured, 'I've heard about Queenie Palmer all right.'

Thirty-four

'So, what do you think?' Molly asked her parents as they sat together after tea that evening. 'Shall I join the training scheme? I really want to do my bit to help the war effort.'

'But you say you'll have to leave home once you're trained,' Mabel fretted. 'You could be sent anywhere. You'll both be away then, and – and . . .'

Ron turned to look at his daughter. 'I admire you for wanting to help – to do your bit – but I can also understand your mam's concern, especially if you had to move a long way from home. So, I suggest you do the training and then see what happens, eh? You haven't signed anything yet, have you?'

'Not exactly, Dad, but I really don't want to drop out. Several of the other women have had to when they found out about having to go away. There's another girl there, about my age. Olive Mason. She's ever so friendly. I really like her. Maybe we'll get a placement together. Her family have just come to live here. Her dad has started a job at The Brush. Perhaps Mr Spencer knows him?'

'I'll ask him when we meet up at the pub.'

*

'They're coming home on leave,' Queenie told Molly excitedly only a day or so after Molly had started work at the Technical Institute. 'All four of them. They're getting about ten days. Isn't that wonderful?' Her eyes were shining. 'I do so hope Harry is going to ask me a very important question.'

Molly felt a wave of sadness flow through her. It wasn't because she had any false hope following the letters she'd received from Harry. It was because once he and Queenie were engaged, it would seem so final. Being his girlfriend was one thing; being his fiancée was quite another. With supreme effort, Molly managed to plaster a smile on her face and say bravely, 'I really hope he does. It'll be nice for you both to have something to look forward to when all this is over.'

'What about you and Ben?'

Molly forced a laugh. 'I keep telling you, we're just good friends. Nothing more. But you believe what you want to.'

'Oh, I will, you can be sure of that.'

Molly was thankful she hadn't told Queenie about the letters she'd been receiving from Tom. That would have started another round of matchmaking on Queenie's part, but she was concerned as to how Tom would act towards her when he came home, now that they too were becoming friends through their correspondence.

She needn't have worried. No one saw very much of Tom once they all arrived home. He spent his leave with his mother, trying to reassure her that the four of them looked after each other and that conditions weren't as bad as the press made out. At least, not all the time. Alice wasn't deceived, but she cherished Tom's thoughtfulness. She could see a vast change in her son. He had matured so much in the few months he'd been away and reminded her so much of the man his father had been. The rigorous training she guessed all the recruits had had to do had broadened his shoulders. He even seemed taller and he walked down the street with a new confidence. He was no longer the puny boy who couldn't seem to make friends and who had been the butt of unkind jokes. She was grateful that now he obviously had the friendship of the other three young men, and he talked of the camaraderie of a wider circle with whom he lived and fought. If only, she prayed in the darkness of the night, he – and his three close friends – would come back after the war whole and unharmed.

'I went to see Mabel – Mrs Wyngate – after I got your letter,' Alice told him. 'Me and Harriet went together and Molly's been round to see Harriet since.' She looked at him sharply. 'Who was it you saw, Tom?'

She'd always been able to get the truth out of her son – even when he'd done something wrong. But the young man sitting opposite her now was no longer the little boy who could be cajoled – or even threatened – into telling the truth.

Tom laughed. 'Sorry, Mam. I'm a big boy now. I'm not telling anyone, not even you. So stop trying to wheedle it out of me and tell me, would you like an outing to the big city while I'm home? My treat, of course.'

William, too, spent most of his time with his family, joining his father at the pub on the Saturday evening. He did not mention anything about the white feathers either to Molly or to his parents, but Molly felt there was a change in his attitude towards her. It was more like the old days when they'd been good friends as children. And the subject of the suffragettes didn't even come up. Their efforts had been postponed because of the war and that had been the bone of contention between brother and sister.

On the Wednesday evening during the first week the boys were home, Molly was surprised to see Tom waiting outside the Institute at six o'clock when she finished her day's work.

'Hello. What are you doing here?'

'I've come to meet you and walk home with you. I wanted to see you and, because I'm guessing Sunday will be taken up with meeting Ben in the park, I thought I'd be cheeky and meet you from work.' His face clouded. 'You – you don't mind, do you?'

'Of *course* not . . .' She linked her arm through his. 'It's great to see you.' She looked him up and down. 'You look very smart in your uniform. I'm sure you've grown.'

Tom laughed. 'Well, certainly outwards if not upwards. All the marching and the PT have certainly given me some muscles I didn't know I had. So how are you . . .?'

'Oh, hang on a minute, Tom. D'you mind waiting for my friend, Olive?'

'Of course not.' He paused and then, bending his head closer to Molly, whispered, 'Is she pretty?'

'Well, I think so, but you'll see for yourself in a minute. Here she comes.'

'Is this the boyfriend, then?' Olive laughed as she caught up with them. 'Trust you to catch yourself a nice-looking lad, Molly Wyngate.' She smiled and her cheeks dimpled. Holding out her hand she said, 'Pleased to meet you – er . . .?'

Molly saw that Tom was staring at her new-found friend as if he'd never seen a girl before. Even through the dusk of a January evening, she saw the colour rise in his face and heard him stutter, 'Er – hello. I'm Tom – and you're Olive, is that right?'

'It is indeed. What's she been telling you? Nothing good, I hope.'

They fell into step to walk home, with Tom between them. Gallantly, he held out his other arm for Olive to take. They chatted easily, but the further they walked, the more Tom's head was turned towards Olive, and soon Molly began to feel she was playing gooseberry yet again. 'You stay with Olive, Tom. She lives quite near here but I'll see you again before you go back, I hope.'

'Of course. I'll call round to see your mam and dad one evening, if that would be all right?'

'Of course it would. They'd love to see you. See you tomorrow, Olive.'

Molly lingered a moment as she watched them walk into the darkness, their heads close together.

'Well, well, well,' Molly murmured, a small smile playing on her mouth. 'Who'd have thought it? A nice girl like Olive almost falling at Tom Mayberry's feet.' But she was delighted. Tom had matured into a nice young man and he deserved a chance at happiness when the war was over.

Harry and Ben were enjoying their time at home, being spoiled by their mother. Harry, of course, was spending a lot of his time with Queenie, and Ben managed to spend a Sunday afternoon with Molly, but the rest of the time she was working.

'Are you enjoying the training?' he asked her.

'It's great as long as I don't stop to think that what we're learning to make will be used to kill young men. Young men just like you. I know they're the enemy and I know it's got to be done. We have to win this awful war.'

'You're right, Molly. We can't let countries overrun each other. We don't want to be under the rule of the Kaiser, do we?'

'No, we don't.'

Ben put his arm around her shoulders as they walked along the pathways in the park and gave her a quick squeeze. For a brief moment, they looked like the other courting couples in the park. 'I know that when I'm sent over the top, I'm going to kill young fellas just like me and Harry. I feel dreadful about it, but we're always being told it's us or them. And that's all we have to remember. It sounds an odd thing to say, but it's dangerous to think too much.'

Molly leaned her head against his shoulder. 'Oh Ben, do take care. I couldn't bear it if anything happened to you.'

Ben didn't answer, but he gave her shoulders another squeeze.

'There's my friend Olive from work,' Molly said

suddenly as she spotted a couple walking a little way ahead of them. 'Oh my, just look who's with her.'

'Who?' Ben asked.

'It's Tom, isn't it?'

'So it is. The crafty devil. How does he know her?'

'I introduced him to her on Wednesday night. He came to meet me from work.'

'Did he now? Our Tom is coming out of his shell a bit. It looks as if they're getting very friendly. Come on, let's catch them up.'

Molly gripped his arm. 'All right, but no teasing him, Ben. Please. This – this might be important to him.'

Ben looked down at her, his face serious. 'Don't worry, Molly. Those days are gone. We're good mates with him now. Really good mates. The four of us stick together. We've made friends, of course, among the other lads, but the four of us are tight-knit.' He paused and then added with a sigh, 'We used to be a bit cruel to him when we were nippers. Me an' Harry realize that now. And your William does too, I think. Tom was a right "mummy's boy". We used to shout that after him in the street, but, being kids, we didn't understand the impact. Tom was all poor Mrs Mayberry had left after she lost her husband. He was everything to her. Still is, I expect. I just hope, for her sake especially, nothing happens to him in this war. We do our best to keep him safe, but it might not always be possible.'

'Him and Harry used to get into fights when they were kids, didn't they?'

Now Ben smiled again. 'All the time, and my brother

usually won. But I don't reckon Harry would tackle him now.' He chuckled. 'Tom's developed a lot of muscle from somewhere.'

As they neared the other couple, Ben shouted, 'Eh up, Tom.'

Both Tom and Olive turned. For a moment Tom looked disconcerted, as if he'd been caught out, but when Olive greeted Molly, he relaxed.

Olive's smile widened as she added, 'And you must be Ben. She's always telling me there's nothing between you, and yet here you are walking in the park on a Sunday afternoon with your arm around her.' She chuckled. 'Pull the other one, Molly Wyngate.'

'We're just good friends, Olive,' Ben said and grinned.

'It looks like it.' Olive was still laughing, but her tone was laced with friendly sarcasm. Then she smiled up at Tom. 'If that's what friends do, then . . .' She put her arm round Tom's waist and hugged him close – 'that's what we are.'

The four of them laughed and fell into step to move on together. Ben's arm was still across Molly's shoulders and now Olive's arm was around Tom's waist. A little shyly, Tom put his arm across Olive's shoulders and, when she didn't object, he left it there.

The four of them spent the afternoon in the park together, just walking and talking and laughing, all thoughts of war banished for a few precious hours. Just as they were heading towards the entrance to go home, they heard a voice behind them.

'Moll, wait for us.'

At once, Ben's arm fell away from round her

shoulders, but Tom, also recognizing the voice, kept his arm firmly where it was. In fact, he pulled Olive a little closer.

Without turning round he whispered, 'It's Queenie Palmer. D'you know her?'

'No, but I've heard about her. She's walking out with Ben's brother, isn't she? And she's Molly's best friend, right?'

'Supposedly,' Tom murmured.

'What does that mean?'

'It's a long story. Maybe I'll tell you one day.'

He looked down into her upturned face and his words and his glance suggested that he would tell her his secrets if they became closer. Sensing his meaning, Olive smiled and nodded. 'I'll hold you to that,' she whispered as Queenie and Harry caught up with them.

Olive turned to face them, waiting for the introductions to be made. She scrutinized Queenie. She was indeed what everyone said about her. A very pretty girl. Beautiful, some might say, but at this moment Olive didn't like the twist on the girl's mouth. It was almost a sneer as Queenie said, 'Got yourself a girlfriend at long last, Tom Mayberry?' Then her gaze rested on Olive and swept her up and down. 'You must be desperate for a boyfriend.'

'Queenie,' Molly interrupted swiftly, her tone sharp. 'Olive is my friend from work. She's training at the Institute too.'

'Friend? Really? Oh well . . .' She shrugged. 'If that's what you want, Moll. I'll see you around. Come on, Harry darling. Let's leave them to it.'

Queenie put her arm through Harry's and turned away, pulling him with her.

Harry glanced back over his shoulder, but his expression was difficult to read. For the first time in her life, Molly was disappointed in him.

'And that, Olive,' Tom murmured, 'is the famous Queenie Palmer.'

Thirty-five

Harry and Queenie went into the town centre just before the end of their leave.

'I'm sure he's going to propose,' she'd said excitedly to Molly the previous evening. 'I think this trip into town is to buy a ring. What do you think I should choose? Diamonds? They're so classy, aren't they?'

'I didn't know army pay was that good.' Molly tried to keep her tone light. 'Or has he come into money?'

Queenie tossed her blonde hair. 'I think he's been saving up. Only the best for me, Harry says.'

Queenie did not visit Molly's home that evening. Molly was surprised. She had expected that Queenie wouldn't be able to wait to show off her sparkling ring and that she'd be round to their house within minutes of getting home from the shopping trip. But on the day when the families all went to the station to wave them off on the train, Queenie was there. Her employer, like many in the town, was sympathetic towards young men in uniform home on leave and had given her the afternoon off, even though Saturday was a normal working day for shop employees. Molly watched as Queenie clung possessively to Harry's arm and reached up to kiss him passionately on the mouth.

'I'd better go and prise those two apart,' William said laughingly, 'or we'll miss the train.'

He shook hands with his father, and kissed his mother and Molly. For a brief moment he was serious as he said, 'I've no idea when I might get leave again. I've had a great time with you all and I'll remember it always. I'll try to write more often, Mam, I promise.'

And then he was gone, hitching up his kit-bag and climbing into the carriage where Ben and Tom were already hanging out of the window. The whistle blew and the train started to move.

'Harry! *Harry!*' Ben shouted, leaning out of the open door. 'Come on, man. You'll be on a charge if you . . .' His voice was lost in a puther of smoke, but Queenie was still hanging on to Harry's arm, crying hysterically.

'Harry, Harry, don't go. Not yet.'

At the very last moment he managed to release himself from her limpet grip, grab his kit-bag and leap for the carriage door. He would have fallen back onto the platform if Ben and Tom hadn't grasped his arms and hauled him in.

Queenie was standing on the platform, tears streaming down her face. Molly, holding back her own tears as the train began to move a little faster, went to stand beside her friend and put her arms around her.

'He – he didn't propose,' Queenie wailed. 'He didn't buy me a ring.'

*

A Woman of Spirit

In the carriage, as the train picked up speed, leaving the families waving goodbye, the four young men found seats for themselves, sitting opposite one another. The brothers on one side, William and Tom on the other.

Feeling he needed to explain, Harry said, 'I think she was upset because she was hoping I was going to propose this leave and take her into town to buy a ring.'

'Presumably you didn't, then?' Tom said.

Harry shook his head. He stared into Tom's steady gaze. A look passed between them. No words were spoken, but it was as if there was a communication between them. Something that told Harry he was right to hold back a little. Instead it was Ben who said, 'Mebbe it's for the best, Harry. We don't know what's going to happen, do we? Let's face it, we've got a very uncertain future.'

'It'd be nice to have someone special waiting back at home for us, though, wouldn't it?' William said pensively, not knowing the unspoken suspicions that were going through the minds of the other three.

'We have,' Tom said, thinking not only of his mother, but of Molly too now. She was becoming very special to him, even though he knew it would never amount to anything romantic. She had made that quite clear. He wondered briefly if she had a secret boyfriend and her heart already belonged to another. But now there was Olive. Even during the short time since he had met her, he knew she was going to be very special to him too. Already they had promised to write to each other. 'We have our families. They're all special.'

'I know, but you know very well what I mean.'

'Yes, I do.' Tom grinned. 'But we're not all good-looking enough to get such a pretty girlfriend as Harry, now are we?'

William regarded the young man, who had become a close friend and knew he could now be honest with him. 'You've altered a lot, Tom, since we joined up. It's been the making of you. There'll be someone out there for you one day, I promise.'

I think there already is, Tom thought, but he said nothing aloud. It was early days.

The carriage fell silent as the four young men and their travelling companions, all soldiers returning to duty, were busy with their own thoughts.

'Let's get you home,' Ethel said, grasping her daughter's arm and pulling her along the platform as the train became a speck in the distance. 'Making such an exhibition of yourself. I'm surprised and disappointed in you, Queenie.'

'She's upset, Aunty Ethel.' Molly tried to be the peacemaker.

'I can see that,' Ethel said tartly. 'She's left the whole world in no doubt of that. But there are plenty of wives and sweethearts on this platform who have conducted themselves with a modicum of decorum.'

'Let go, Mam,' Queenie sniffled. 'You're hurting me.'

'I'll hurt you, young lady, if you shame me like that again in public. I've a good mind to stop you seeing Harry . . .'

Queenie let out another wail. 'No, no, *no*. Not that. Oh please, Mam . . .'

They were halfway home before Queenie's weeping subsided into sobs. As they reached their street and approached the Wyngates' house, Queenie pulled herself free. 'I'll go to Molly's. I need someone to talk to who understands.'

'And you think I don't,' Ethel shot back. She glared at Queenie. 'Have you got something you need to tell me?'

Queenie stared at her. 'I don't understand. What d'you mean?'

'Have you got yourself into trouble? Is that why you were clinging to him?'

Queenie's mouth dropped open, while Molly felt her own face burn, almost as if she herself were being accused. This is what she had been so afraid of, ever since Queenie had told her that she had spent the night with Harry just before he was sent abroad.

'No, Mam, I haven't. I'm not.'

'Do you swear?'

'Yes, yes, I do. It's – it's not possible.'

'Mm.' Ethel made a sound as if she didn't believe her daughter. 'Well, I suppose time will prove it one way or the other. But if you are, my girl, you'll be out of the house and on your way to the workhouse.'

Now both girls were shocked to the core as they stared at Ethel.

'You – you don't mean that, Aunty Ethel,' Molly stammered.

'Indeed I do. She's always known how I feel about her getting pregnant before she's married. I've never left her in any doubt about that. Right, you can go to Molly's for an hour, but then I want you back home. You can help me get the tea for once. I've been far too soft with you. I can see that now. I don't know, making such a spectacle of yourself . . .'

Ethel turned away and hurried down the street to her own home.

Mabel, who had witnessed everything at the station and on the walk home, said gently, 'Come on in, Queenie, love, and let's get you a cup of tea. I'm sure you need one because I know I do.'

A little later, in the privacy of Molly's bedroom, Queenie whispered, 'You didn't tell your mam anything about what I said happened when I went away to see Harry off, did you?'

'No, of course I didn't. But you told your mam out there' – Molly gestured towards the street where the conversation had taken place – 'that it was impossible that you could be pregnant. If you and Harry – um – made love, then it could be possible, couldn't it?' Her heart ached at the thought, but she had to ask. And now there was something else to worry about. Had anything happened between them during this leave? They'd spent a lot of time together.

A bright pink coloured Queenie's cheeks and she dropped her head. 'I told you, Harry knew what to do. He – he said he'd be careful.'

'And you trust him?'

Her head shot up. 'Oh yes. We're going to be married. I – I know he didn't buy me a ring this time but I – I think that's because with this war everything's so uncertain. I know he's thinking of me. He doesn't want to tie me down if – if . . .'

A Woman of Spirit

Molly wasn't sure she believed any of it. She'd heard that young men going to war wanted to know there was someone to come back to. The number of marriages that had been hastily arranged in the past few months before embarkation, or when they were home on a fairly long leave, had doubled. A girl she'd become friendly with at the Institute had told her that. In fact, she'd been one of the ones getting married in rather a hurry. Sarah – a vivacious girl with shining black curls – had laughed. 'Everyone – even my mam – thinks I'm in the family way, but I'm not. It's just that Dougie wanted to be married before he went. "I want to know you're here waiting for me," he said. And I love him so much I couldn't say no, Molly, now could I?'

Molly had been thoughtful for a moment before saying, 'No, of course you couldn't.' She'd put herself in Sarah's shoes and realized that if had been Harry asking her, Molly would have married him in a heartbeat, whatever anyone had thought.

Not long after the lads had returned to duty and were back in the reserve trenches waiting to be moved up to the front line, Harry wrote a long letter to Molly.

> *Dear Molly,* Harry wrote, *I hope you won't mind me writing to you . . .* Mind! If only he knew. For a moment she closed her eyes and held the letter to her breast, savouring the feel of it, the knowledge that his hands had touched the same piece of paper. Then, with a sigh, she read on: *You don't know how good*

it feels to be able to write to someone and tell them the truth of what life out here is like. I can't tell anyone else about this, not even my mam and dad. It would be cruel of me to write such things to them. Ben and I have agreed that all our letters home should be bright and cheerful. We're not exactly telling them lies – we wouldn't do that – we are just not telling them the whole truth. But you're such a strong young woman, Molly, I know you can take it, and I need to write it all down to someone back home. All that involvement with the suffragettes certainly brought you out of your shell and just look at you now! Doing your (very important) work for the war effort. Obviously, I can't tell you where we are and even though I'm going to be careful, the censor's pen might be very busy. We're waiting to be sent up the line and I suppose we all get a bit pensive at such a time and think of home even more.

 It's a strange life out here. Much of the time when we're not at the front but working in the support trenches – work that is very necessary, I know – life is pretty boring. But when we have to take our turn on the front line, it is suddenly very scary and anything but boring. But there are quiet times even there when we can catch a few minutes' kip. Someone is posted as a look-out but the rest of us can sit down, leaning against the rough rock face of the trench wall, or lie down –

that is, if the trench is not half full of water as it often is after rain.

Apart from the shooting and the shelling, I suppose the worst thing to deal with is lack of sleep. Believe me, you can actually fall asleep standing up! Then there's the cold and the constant damp that can cause trench foot. Keeping us company are rats as big as cats. They're filthy creatures, bold as brass and spreading filth and disease, and lice are our constant companions. Oh, I could go on and on, but I won't. I just wanted to explain to you that it's not just bullets and shells that bring death.

But there are lighter moments too. We have some real jokers among us and while their humour is a little 'dark' at times, they do make us laugh. And believe me, we need to laugh . . . Harry ended his long letter with the words, *It's so bitterly cold here just now. If the German bullets don't get us, the freezing weather will. Several chaps are quite ill, but we four are okay. Do you remember, Molly, reading about Captain Scott who got lost in the Antarctic in 1912, writing "Great God! This is an awful place" . . .? Well, it is here too.*

Molly read the letter twice, knowing even then that this would not be the last time she would read it. She would hide it away in her bedroom, somewhere where no one else – not even her mother – would find it.

She lingered over every word, cherishing each one of them, even the hard-to-read sections describing the soldiers' suffering.

She was grateful and honoured that he had felt able to write an honest and open letter to her, but one thing puzzled her. Nowhere had he even mentioned Queenie. Not once.

Thirty-six

At the very end of the first month of 1916, the unthinkable happened. At the outbreak of the war, Britain had not expected to be bombed and, although a few coastal towns and London had been targeted, no one had anticipated that Midlands towns would ever be hit. On the night of 31 January, some towns had been warned, but no one in Loughborough was prepared for a visit of death from the air.

Although it was a Monday evening and not one of their regular times for meeting up, the three men – Jack, Ron and Luke – met up in the pub after their tea.

'I just had to get out of the house,' Luke explained. 'Harriet's missing the boys terribly now they've gone back – worse than when they first went, if I'm honest. I know it's an awful thing to say, but I almost wish they hadn't come home on leave. Even though she was worried all the time, things were fairly settled then. But now . . .' He sighed heavily. 'Harriet has to keep busy when she's upset about summat. She's cleaning the house from top to bottom and won't even stop in the evening.'

'I know just what you mean,' Ron sympathized. 'Mabel's sitting with her darning as usual but keeps bursting into tears. Even Molly's gone out. She's gone round to her friend's.'

'She's not at ours,' Jack said.

Ron shook his head. 'No. She's gone round to Olive Mason's place. That's the girl she's made friends with at the Institute. They've only just come to live here. Molly says her dad works at your place, Luke. Have you bumped into him yet? Pete Mason?'

'Oh yes, I know him,' Luke said. 'He seems a decent chap. Good worker. He lives somewhere just off the Ashby Road, the end nearest the centre of town.'

'Molly and Queenie seem to have drifted apart lately,' Jack said. 'I'm sorry about that. I like your Molly, Ron. She's a sensible girl. She's good for our Queenie.' He sighed. 'But it's to be expected, I suppose, when one of them gets a boyfriend.'

'Molly seems very tired when she gets home from work now. This munitions training seems to be a lot harder than her job at the hosiery factory. I'm surprised she's gone out tonight, if I'm honest, but—'

At that moment, there was a terrific bang that seemed to shake the whole building.

'My God!' Jack exclaimed, leaping up and spilling his beer. 'What the Hell was that?'

'Sounded a bit close—' Ron began as another explosion sounded.

'Let's get out of here,' Luke said. 'It might be our works. If it is, I'd better go and see if I can help.'

The three men, along with several other drinkers, hurried out into the night.

'No, it's not far enough over to be The Brush,' Luke said. 'It's more towards the bellfoundry . . .'

'It's not as far as that. It's that direction, but closer,' Jack said. 'I'd guess somewhere near the street called The Rushes . . .'

'Oh my God,' Ron breathed. 'That's near where our Molly's gone.' At once he set off at a run, the other two close behind him. There was another explosion in the distance, but nothing was going to stop the three men running in search of Molly and her friend.

'Where is it the Masons live?' Jack panted.

'Orchard Street, I think. It's round the corner from The Rushes.'

As they arrived at the end of the street, they could see that firemen were already there where houses had been damaged. They moved forward, but, anxious though they were, they knew they mustn't impede the emergency services.

'Any idea of the number of their house?'

'No.'

'There's folks coming out of their houses now. Let's see if anyone can help us.'

'They're in shock, Ron,' Jack warned. 'Poor devils. Go easy.'

'I . . .' Ron began, terror now overcoming his usual empathy for the feelings of others, but then he felt Luke's hand on his arm. 'We'll find her, Ron, if it takes all night.'

An elderly couple were staggering towards them, covered in dust and clinging to one another.

'Here, let us help you . . .' Luke and Jack moved to either side of them to take their arms. Neighbours, furthest away from where the bomb had fallen, came forward.

'Bring 'em to ours,' a young woman said. 'We've not been hit, though I reckon every window in the house is smashed. Come on, love,' she added gently to the elderly woman.

'Do you know where the Masons live?' Ron asked.

'Don't know that name,' she said vaguely, her mind wholly occupied in helping the old couple.

'They've not been here long,' Ron persisted, anxiety gnawing at his insides.

Her attention was caught now and she said, 'Oh, you must mean Ruby and Pete and their girl. Olive, I think her name is.'

'That's them. Which house do they live at?'

'Down the far end. Beyond where the bomb fell in someone's backyard.'

'Thanks, Mrs . . .'

Ron was already running down towards the damaged houses.

'We'd better go after him,' Luke said, 'but I don't reckon he's going to get through. Not past all the rescuers.'

When they caught up with Ron, he was arguing with one of the firemen. 'I'm sorry, sir, but you cannot come through here.'

'But my daughter,' Ron choked. 'She's further down the street. I must get to her . . .'

'You'll have to go round the other way, but don't try to get down The Rushes,' the man said. 'There's been an explosion there too.'

'Oh my God,' Ron gasped.

Luke took hold of his arm. 'It's a fair way round but, come on, we'll give it a try.'

'We've got to find her.' Ron was desperate now. 'If owt's happened to her . . .'

'Come on, Ron. Keep strong. She's not in these two. Let's get going.'

It was a long way round to the opposite end of the street, so they ran as fast as they could but they had to pause now and again to catch their breath. Reaching the other end of the street, they saw several neighbours were already comforting each other and helping where aid was needed.

'We still don't know what number they live at,' Luke said. 'Let's ask.'

He moved forward.

'Excuse me, we're looking for Mr and Mrs Mason . . .'

The man looked around him. He was dazed himself but, after a moment, he pointed a shaking finger. 'That's them over there with the two girls.'

'*Two* girls,' Ron said brokenly. 'Oh thank God . . .'

Already he was running further up the road.

'Come on,' Luke said. With fresh energy now they were hopeful that Molly and her friend's family were all right, they ran after Ron. When they reached him, he was already clasping Molly to him. 'Oh my girl, my girl. Are you all right? Oh, you're bleeding. Where . . .?'

'Just a cut on my forehead, Dad. Don't fuss.'

'Don't fuss, you say? Molly, you could have been—'

'But I haven't been. Olive's all right too, and her mam and dad.'

Reassured a little, Ron turned to Olive and her parents. 'I'm sorry. I was just so worried.'

'Of course you were. It was the glass from the windows, Mr Wyngate,' Pete said. 'We're all covered in it.'

'Ron, please. And you're Pete, aren't you?'

'That's right. And this is my wife, Ruby.'

'Pleased to meet you, Ron,' Ruby said. 'Though I could have wished for better circumstances.'

'Look, you won't be able to sleep in your house tonight,' Ron said. 'You must come back to ours. I'm sure we can find you somewhere to sleep.'

'That's very kind of you, Ron,' Pete said, 'seeing as there's not a window left whole and I'm not too sure yet how safe the walls are. We'd be glad to accept your kind offer. Maybe they'll let me go in just to collect a few belongings. I need my work clothes for tomorrow.'

'Don't worry about that,' Luke said at once. 'Take at least tomorrow off, Pete, to get yourself sorted out. I'll square it with the bosses.'

'That's very good of you, Mr Spencer. I appreciate it.'

'The name's Luke,' he said as he took Pete's arm. 'Now what do you need to retrieve from the house if they'll let you through?'

'Can you bring my work clothes, Dad?' Olive said. 'I'll have to get to the Institute.'

'I'll see . . .'

'Tell you what,' Luke interrupted, looking directly at Pete. 'If Olive goes with Molly, why don't you come to our house? Our two lads are both in the army.' He cleared his throat before saying huskily, 'Their rooms aren't being used just now.'

'But will your wives mind? I mean—'

'No, they won't.' Both Ron and Luke spoke in unison, and then Luke added, 'They'll be happy to help, I can promise you that.'

'Ron, you should go. Luke and me'll help Pete collect some belongings and follow you with Olive,' Jack said, 'but you ought to get Molly home and get that wound looked at.'

'Yes, yes, of course, you're right. Come on, Molly, love.'

He put his arm around her and led her away from the noise, the smoke and the dreadful destruction. Holding tightly on to Molly and stepping carefully over the rubble, they made their way to the end of the street and then towards home.

This atmosphere, these sights and sounds, Ron thought, must be what our lads are facing every day, but he kept his thoughts to himself.

Mabel was standing at the door looking up and down the street, straining her eyes through the dark January night. She was worried that Ron hadn't come straight back from the pub when he'd heard the explosions, and even more worried as to where Molly might be. Relief flooded through her when she recognized their shapes looming through the shadows. She hurried towards them, her arms outstretched, thankful to see them both, but alarmed once more when she saw Molly holding a handkerchief to her forehead.

'She's all right, love. Just a cut on her forehead.'

'Let's get you inside. Is it over? Has it gone?'

'Has what gone?' Ron frowned.

'The Zeppelin. Did you see it? All I heard was a loud throbbing noise.'

'No, I didn't. We were too busy running to see if we could help. We thought it was The Brush that had been hit.'

'You ran *towards* the explosions?'

'Well – yes.'

'How stupid,' Mabel said and then laughed. 'But so brave. Now I know where William and Molly get their courage from. Right, Molly, sit down while I find something to bathe your forehead.'

'Ouch!' Molly winced a few moments later as Mabel administered her own brand of first aid. 'That stings, Mam.'

'Better to hurt for a minute than get an infection in it. There, that doesn't look too bad. It's not a deep cut, but it might leave a little scar. Luckily, it's up near your hairline. You can grow a curl to hide it.'

Molly pulled a face. 'I don't think it's actually going to mar my beauty, do you?'

'Now, now,' Mabel began, but Ron interrupted. 'Mabel, love. Olive's coming to spend the night here and her parents are going to Luke's. Their house isn't safe to go back into until it's been thoroughly checked. I don't think there'll be a window left whole. Olive can have William's room, can't she?'

'Of course. I keep it clean and aired all the time, just in case . . .' Her voice faded away. She knew in her heart of hearts that her son coming home on unexpected leave was impossible, but Mabel always had hope. She cleared her throat and carried on more strongly. 'Jack didn't offer, then?'

Ron shook his head. 'There wasn't any need really. Me and Luke had already made the arrangements.'

'But there'll be other folks in that street in need of help, won't there?'

'No doubt. To be honest, we were just thinking about Molly's friend and her parents.'

Mabel sniffed. 'I expect Jack would know Ethel wouldn't want her routine disrupted. Was there much damage?'

'I think at least two houses were badly damaged.'

Mabel gasped and her eyes widened. 'Was anyone killed?'

'We don't know yet. The firemen were still trying to rescue folk, but if they were in one of those houses . . .' His voice faded away but his meaning was obvious.

'We were so lucky, Mam,' Molly said quietly. 'It could so easily have been Olive's home.'

'I know and—' Mabel began, but at that moment, a knock came at the door.

'That'll be Olive,' Ron said and went to open it, a moment later ushering Olive and her father into the kitchen.

Mabel held out her hand to Pete. 'I'm pleased to meet you, but so sorry for the circumstances. Do sit down for a minute. Have you time for a cup of tea?'

'That's very kind, Mrs Wyngate, but I ought to get round to Mr Spencer's.'

'Of course, but let us know if there's anything else we can do to help you. Now, Olive, is there anything you need?'

'I could do with a wash at your sink, Mrs Wyngate, if it's not too much trouble.'

'Of course, love. Come into the scullery. Molly, you go upstairs and make sure everything's all right for Olive in William's room . . .'

Thirty-seven

As the Wyngates were making Olive welcome, the Spencers were doing exactly the same for her parents.

'I'm sorry it's only single beds, but Luke and Pete can move one of the beds into the other room, if you'd like?'

'No, no, don't go to all that trouble, Mrs Spencer,' Ruby said and added, with a smile, 'It'll be nice to have a peaceful night away from his snoring.'

'You're taking this remarkably well, Mrs Mason. I'm not sure I'd be quite so accepting if my house had been damaged.'

Ruby shrugged. 'We were lucky. It's only stuff, isn't it? We're all right, thank the good Lord. That's all I care about, though I'm not sure yet what's happened to our neighbours.'

'Were you – good friends?'

'I'd met them, but we haven't got to know anyone in the street well yet. We haven't lived there long.'

'Oh no, I was forgetting. Molly told us.'

Ruby sighed. 'We know how lucky we are that our Olive isn't a lad and fighting at the front. I can't imagine what you and Mr Spencer must be going through with both your lads – away.'

'It's not easy,' Harriet admitted, 'but I'm proud of

them that they volunteered. Now, let's get you both upstairs. You look shattered.'

'I must admit I feel a bit shaky now.'

'It's the shock. Luke, open the brandy and give Mr and Mrs Mason a little nip. I'm sure they could do with it.'

'That's so kind and, please, it's Ruby and Pete.'

'Then it's Harriet and Luke.'

'Are you both sure you're all right to report for work?' Mabel asked worriedly the following morning when Molly and Olive were up early to get ready.

'I think it's the best thing we could do, Mrs Wyngate,' Olive said with a wide smile. 'Keep busy and let everyone know that a few bombs from the Kaiser aren't going to frighten us.'

Mabel smiled at her. 'That's the spirit, love.' She rather liked this new friend of Molly's.

Arriving at the Institute, the two girls were treated like heroines and fussed over by their workmates and even by the staff.

'You just do what you feel you can today,' the works' superintendent, Mr Owen, said. 'And you, Molly, be careful not to get dust into that wound. Can both of you come to my office before you go home tonight? I want to talk to you.'

'What do you think he wants with us?' Olive whispered as they went to the workshop where they would be working for the day. 'Have we done something wrong?'

'I don't think so. Not from his tone of voice.'

They worked side by side for the rest of the day,

but they were both wondering what lay ahead. During their lunch break, Olive said, 'I've been thinking . . .'

'Careful,' Molly teased. 'Don't strain anything.'

'Cheeky! Seriously though, we've been here four weeks now – longer than anyone else. I expect he's got a place for each of us.'

Molly, unsmiling now, said, 'Yes, I realized that too. But that'll mean us leaving home, won't it? And – and I don't expect we'll be sent to the same place, will we?'

Olive shrugged. 'I doubt it, but we'll know soon enough.'

As work finished for the day the two girls, who were rather apprehensive as to what awaited them, knocked on the door of the staff room where all the superintendents of the various workshops congregated when they weren't teaching.

The door was flung open by Mr Owen. 'Come in, ladies, come in. We have the place to ourselves.' He smiled. 'The others are either still working or have made a quick dash for home. Can't say I blame them. Do sit down. Now, as you must both be aware, you have been here longer than some of the others and have trained in – let me see – two different workshops already.'

The two girls glanced at one another.

'Is that because we're rubbish, sir?' Olive laughed.

'Far from it. In fact, the opposite is true.' He regarded them over the top of his spectacles. 'You have both done so well in anything we have asked you to do that we thought we'd prolong your training to undertake several different operations. You both seem to show skills and aptitude for the work. We are also asking two other young women to do the same. It would give us wider scope when trying to place you somewhere, and we are also extending the length of some of the courses.' He paused as he cleared his throat and shuffled some papers. Then he rested his elbows on the desk and linked his fingers together. 'So, ladies, are you willing to stay on at the Institute for the next few months and learn a lot more?'

Molly and Olive glanced at each other. This was so different and so much better than they had been expecting. They had thought they were going to be sent away from home to work, and probably be separated too.

'Thank you, Mr Owen,' Olive said, and Molly added, 'We'd be delighted to do that.'

'Of course, it won't be indefinitely, but we do think it could last several months. In time, of course, we shall have to place you somewhere.'

They both nodded and Molly added, 'We understand, Mr Owen.'

As they left the building to walk home, they were giggling excitedly together.

'We'll probably have to go away eventually,' Molly said, bringing them back down to earth, 'but at least this has delayed it for a while. Mam will be so relieved. I bet yours will be too, won't she?'

Olive's face dropped. 'Once it's safe for us to go

back home, yes. I don't want to sound ungrateful, but we don't want to impose on you and the Spencers any more than we're forced to.'

'You're not at all. I'm enjoying having you stay, if I'm honest, though obviously I'm sorry for the reasons that have caused it.'

Olive linked her arm through Molly's. 'I'm so glad I've found you. I was so worried about making friends when we moved here.'

'I don't know why,' Molly said candidly. 'You're easy to like.'

'So are you.' Olive smiled at her.

They walked the rest of the way back to Molly's house, revelling in the knowledge that they didn't have to leave home for a while yet, and that their new-found friendship with each other was secure.

They were just finishing tea and Olive was about to leave to go round to the Spencers' to see her parents when a knock came at the back door and Queenie came in.

'It's only me . . .' she trilled. 'Oh, you're here,' she said as she saw Olive. Her glance raked the girl from head to toe. Olive had changed out of her dirty working clothes, just as Molly always did when she arrived home, but she was still dressed in a plain skirt and blouse.

Suddenly, Queenie's expression altered and she smiled brightly at Olive. Her tone was silky as she said, 'I was *so* sorry to hear what had happened to your home. It must be awful for you. You're lucky to have made friends with Moll and have her family to take you in.' Again her glance assessed Olive's appearance. 'Have you lost all your belongings, then? If I can help in any way, do let me know. I might have one or two dresses I don't wear anymore.' She cocked her head to one side as if calculating Olive's measurements. 'I could get Miss Parkinson at work to show me how to let them out.' She moved and linked her arm possessively through Molly's.

'It's nice that Moll has a new friend. We've been best friends since we could first walk, haven't we, *Aunty Mabel*?' She accentuated the name as if sending a message to the newcomer of her closeness to the Wyngate family and the privileges it brought her. 'But now, of course, I've got Harry; we don't see quite as much of each other as we used to, though while he's away and I'm so desperately worried about him, Moll's a huge comfort to me.'

'There's no reason why we can't be friends,' Molly said, feeling a pang of sympathy for Queenie. She knew how much she herself was secretly missing Harry. It must be even worse for Queenie, who believed herself to be his fiancée. 'The three of us.'

'That'd be nice,' Olive murmured, but she had seen a look in Queenie's eyes that perhaps Molly and her mother hadn't noticed. The look that said, Molly's my friend. Keep away. 'Anyway,' she went on, 'I'm just on my way round to see how Mam and Dad are, and if they've heard when we can go back home. I'll be back before ten, Mrs Wyngate.' She deliberately addressed her hostess formally, making it clear that she had not been granted the privilege of calling

Mabel an honorary 'aunty'. 'Nice to see you, Queenie,' she said, although even Olive couldn't force sincerity into her tone.

'Don't forget,' Queenie said smoothly as Olive moved towards the door, 'if I can help you in any way, don't be afraid to ask. Any friend of Moll's is a friend of mine.'

'So is everything all right round at the Wyngates?' Ruby asked her daughter.

Olive plastered a smile on her face. 'Fine. Mr and Mrs Wyngate are lovely and Molly and me are good friends.' She bit her tongue to stop herself saying anything about Queenie. After all, she was now in the home of the girl's fiancé, and the Spencers were being every bit as kind to her parents as the Wyngates were to her. She hurried on to tell them all about the offer she and Molly had received about continuing with further training at the Institute. 'It'll mean we don't have to leave home, at least not yet,' she said.

'Oh, that's wonderful news.' Ruby clapped her hands and Harriet smiled and nodded her agreement.

'Have you heard anything about the house, Dad?' Olive asked.

'I went round today. It's been inspected by the building authorities and they say that we've been very lucky. It's structurally sound and safe for us to go back home once the windows have all been replaced.' He pulled a face. 'There's not a whole one left anywhere.'

'In the meantime,' Ruby said, 'I'm allowed to go in and start clearing up the mess.'

'I'll come and help you,' Harriet offered. 'And I'm sure Alice won't mind lending a hand too.'

For a moment, Ruby looked puzzled.

'Mrs Mayberry across the road,' Harriet explained. 'You met her this morning when she popped in for elevenses.'

'Oh yes. Nice little woman.'

Harriet nodded. 'She's not had an easy life and now with her only son away . . .' She cleared her throat. 'She'll be glad of something to do.'

'Well, there'll be plenty of help needed in our street alone,' Ruby said. 'I don't reckon there'll be a house that's not been damaged in some way.'

'Right, then,' Harriet said, metaphorically donning her organizing hat. 'We'll ask around. I'm sure we could get a working party together. Mabel will want to help and there are one or two more down our street I could ask.'

'What about Queenie's mam?' Olive dared to ask.

Harriet sniffed. 'Oh, I don't think we'll bother Mrs Palmer.'

Olive smiled inwardly.

Molly decided to impart the news to her own parents while Olive was out.

'Olive and I have been offered the chance to stay on at the Institute and learn several more operations,' she began. 'It'll mean we don't have to leave home at the moment, although we'll probably still have to go away eventually when we're placed with a munitions factory somewhere.'

Mabel sighed. 'Do you know how long you'll still be here?'

Molly shook her head. 'Not really. Probably a few months, Mr Owen said. There are several workshops we haven't touched yet.'

'Well, that's something, I suppose,' Mabel said, trying to force a smile. 'It might all be over before you have to leave.'

Molly and her father exchanged a glance. That wasn't something they could see happening in the near future.

Thirty-eight

As soon as they heard about the bombing of Loughborough, William, Ben and Tom wrote home, impatient for more news. Molly was surprised, but delighted, to receive a letter from Harry addressed to her alone.

Mam's written to say they have house guests and that you were slightly injured. I do hope it's not serious. Please write back and tell me how you are and what actually happened that night. Mam was a bit vague . . .

Molly wrote back at once.

My injury is very slight. Little more than a scratch, but I can now say I am officially a war casualty!

She sealed the letter carefully and pressed her lips to it. If only, she thought, I could deliver a kiss in person, but that, she knew, was never going to be possible.

Two weeks after the night of the bombing, the Masons' house was deemed safe enough for them to return. Throughout the town, ten people in all had been killed in the raid, but no one who was known to the Wyngates, the Palmers or the Spencers. Several people had been injured and nearby houses also needed structural repairs before being declared habitable again.

'You have been so exceptionally kind,' Ruby said, hugging Harriet. 'I really don't know how to thank you.'

'It's been a pleasure to have you both, and the Wyngates have loved having Olive to stay. Do keep in touch, won't you?'

'Oh we will, I promise. And Olive and Molly will see each other all the time at work, won't they? It's worked out well for them, hasn't it?'

The two girls were enjoying the work they were now being given. Moving between the workshops every so often gave them new challenges, and new faces to meet and people to make friends with. They continued to be close friends with each other during working hours, spending their break times together. Olive lived much closer to the Institute than Molly, so they only walked together for a short distance before they parted company, and then Molly often waited on the corner for Queenie to join her from the centre of town.

'Deserted you now, has she?' Queenie asked. 'After your mam has fed her for two weeks. I bet she did all her washing for her, an' all, didn't she? Harry's mam said she was sick of the sight of Olive's mam and dad by the time they left. She says it's nice to have the place to themselves again. Well, I'm glad to see the back of her. I can't say I've taken to her. And she's fat. Being seen out with her doesn't do you any favours, Moll. Now, are you up for a walk in the park on Sunday afternoon if it's fine? There's often a lot of handsome soldiers home on leave.' Queenie winked. 'You might meet someone nice, or are you still carrying a torch for Ben?'

With a supreme effort, Molly managed to keep her voice level as she said, 'I'm not carrying a torch for anyone, Queenie.' She crossed her fingers behind her back at the lie. The torch she carried for Harry still burned as fiercely as ever.

The moment had passed for her to retaliate against Queenie's spiteful remarks about Olive, and Molly regretted it. She should have been braver and defended her new friend. She castigated herself as she went through the back door of her home.

'Mam,' she said later that evening as they washed up together in the scullery. 'Has Mrs Spencer said anything about having the Masons to stay?'

'As a matter of fact she has,' Mabel said as she dried a plate and placed it in the cupboard. 'She liked both of them and she really took to Ruby. I think she's hoping the friendship will continue, especially for Alice. And I know I'm always welcome to join them whenever I want to. They've made that quite plain. We make a good foursome, supporting each other through these difficult times.'

'So – she – er – didn't mind having them to stay, then?'

'Heavens, no. She said she enjoyed the companionship. It took her mind off worrying about her boys. Ruby helped her about the house and Pete was company for Luke in the evenings. Evidently, they had long chats together about the progress of the war.' Mabel chuckled. 'You know, men talk. Why do you ask?'

'Oh, I – er – just wondered. You know, two women in the same kitchen and all that.' Molly forced herself to speak casually, as if there was no more to it than a spontaneous enquiry.

'Evidently it worked for the short time they were there,' Mabel said. 'Maybe it wouldn't longer term, I have to admit, but you can adapt to anything if you know something's only temporary.'

Molly was now as sure as she could be that what Queenie had said to her was not true. Next time I see Mrs Spencer, Molly resolved, I'll ask her myself. But the truth was she didn't get much chance now to go round to see Harriet; Queenie came round to their house most evenings and, on those days when she didn't appear, the girl herself told Molly that she visited Mrs Spencer.

'I've got to keep in with my fiancé's mam, now haven't I?'

'Who's this new friend Molly's found herself?' Ethel said belligerently as she sat down in Mabel's kitchen for a morning cuppa.

'Oh, Olive, you mean? They're still training together at the Institute, learning how to operate different machinery.'

'Our Queenie's quite put out about this Olive. She thinks the girl's not the right sort for Molly. Rather brash and loud and very self-opinionated, Queenie says. She was staying here with you, wasn't she?'

'That was only because their house was one of

those caught in the bombing in the Zeppelin attack. Her parents stayed at the Spencers for a few nights.'

'Oh, I see.' Ethel sounded a little mollified. 'I just don't want my Queenie to feel pushed out. She and Molly have been friends all their lives.'

'She won't be, Ethel, but I have to say, Molly felt a bit deserted when Queenie began to spend so much time with Harry.' Mabel didn't want to quarrel with her old friend, but there were times when she had to stick up for her own daughter.

'That's different when it's a boyfriend though, isn't it? And Molly has Ben.'

'They're just friends.'

Ethel laughed. 'Pigs might fly, Mabel. That's what she's telling you, but Queenie says it's far more serious than either of them are letting on.'

Mabel feigned a shrug. 'I wouldn't mind if that *is* true. He's a nice lad.'

'As is Harry,' Ethel shot back.

'Yes, he is. I don't deny that. And William says they're all good friends with Tom now. So that's nice, isn't it? I always felt a little sorry for Tom when they were younger. He never seemed to fit in.'

Ethel gave a sniff that spoke volumes, but she said no more.

'Sit down, Mabel,' Harriet invited when Mabel called in on her way home from shopping. Since the bombing, the four women, who'd been brought together by the catastrophe, met up at Harriet's home after they'd done their shopping on a Friday afternoon. Ruby, Harriet, Mabel and, of course, they couldn't leave Alice out. Although Ruby lived much nearer to the town centre, she liked the three women with whom she'd become friends and was happy to make the effort to walk the distance between their homes.

For some reason none of them had thought to include Ethel in these gatherings.

'Kettle's on the boil and Alice will be across in a minute. Ruby can't make it today. I think she said she's got an appointment at the doctor's.'

Mabel frowned. 'Oh dear. Nothing serious, I hope.' Folk like them didn't visit a doctor's surgery very often. It was far too expensive. They resorted to well-tried and tested home remedies passed down from mother to daughter for generations.

Harriet pulled a face, but it was not one of censure against their new friend. 'To be honest, I think it's a bit of reaction to the shock of the bombing. When you think what might have happened . . .'

Mabel nodded. 'I can understand that. I still shudder when I realize how close Molly came to being really hurt or – or . . .'

'I know,' Harriet said sympathetically. 'Best not to dwell on it, eh? Now, how is Molly? I haven't seen her lately. Do tell her to call round if she'd like to.'

'I'm sure she'd love to see you but, for one thing, she's very busy at work now.'

'That's wonderful, Mabel. I was so pleased to hear they'd been asked to stay on there. Learning of any sort is never wasted. That's always been my motto anyway.'

'And the other reason is that Queenie is monopolizing the rest of her spare time now that Harry's not here.'

'Ah yes, I see.' There was silence between them until Harriet said slowly, 'You know, I really shouldn't say this and it's only between the two of us, Mabel. I wouldn't even say this to Alice and we've been friends for years, but I rather wish it was your Molly who was walking out with our Harry. For some reason, I can't seem to get the measure of Queenie Palmer, and I'm usually very good at summing people up.' She smiled. 'Luke would tell you that.'

For a moment, Mabel stared at Harriet. She was conflicted, wondering if she should break her promise to her daughter and tell his mother about Molly's true feelings for Harry. But her conscience won the day. A confidence was just that and should never be broken. Aloud, Mabel said, 'I won't say a word, Harriet.' There was a pause before she added, 'Does Queenie come round to see you?'

'Now and again, but not what I'd call often.'

'Are they – Harry and Queenie, I mean – are they engaged?'

Harriet sniffed. 'Not that I know of. And I think I would, don't you?' She searched Mabel's face as she asked bluntly, 'Is that what she's saying?'

'Not in so many words, but I think that was what all the fuss was about at the railway station when the boys left after their long leave. I think she'd expected him to propose and present her with a ring.'

'Yes, it was a long leave they were given. Usually it's only about four days or so, Ben told me.' She sighed. 'So, I expect it will be some time before they can get home again. Ah, now here's Alice,' she added as they heard the back door rattle.

Mabel delivered Harriet's message to Molly that she'd like to see her whenever she could spare the time.

'I'll go on Saturday night. Mr Spencer will be out at the pub then.'

'What about Queenie? You usually go out with her on Saturdays.'

'She's going into Leicester with her parents to the theatre.'

Mabel gaped at her. 'And she didn't ask you to go with them?'

Colour suffused Molly's face and she avoided meeting her mother's gaze. 'I – um – no, she didn't.'

Mabel's eyes narrowed. 'Is it because they think we can't afford the ticket or the fare to get there?'

Molly forced a laugh. 'No, I don't think so,' she was able to say quite truthfully, mentally crossing her fingers that her mother wouldn't probe any further and guess the real reason.

When Queenie had told Molly about the trip she'd said, 'Everyone dresses up to go to the theatre. Miss Parkinson has made my mam a new outfit and me a new dress.' Then she had looked Molly up and down. 'You could come with us, but . . . Have you a better dress than that?'

Molly had bristled but had managed to hold on to her temper. 'No, I haven't,' she said shortly. 'But I'm quite happy with the clothes I've got, thank you very much. Besides, I don't think the theatre-going lot are quite my kind of people.'

'Haven't you any ambition, Molly? Don't you want to better yourself?'

'And how would I do that by dressing up and going to the theatre? Especially when there's a war to win.'

'You'd be mixing with a better class of people, and I hardly think the war is going to be lost because a few of us have a night out.'

'Well, I'm sorry, I know you mean well, but I haven't money to spare for fancy new clothes. My mam needs all I can give her now William's away. Anyway, thanks for asking. Have a lovely time.'

On the Saturday night, Molly walked to the Spencers' home. As she had guessed, Mr Spencer was out and Harriet was on her own.

'Oh, Molly,' she said when she opened the door. 'How lovely to see you. Do come in. How have you been? Your mam was telling me all about your continued training at the Institute. You're doing so well. Have you told Ben yet? He'll be so pleased when he hears. Oh, hark at me, bombarding you with questions before you've even sat down and then hardly giving you a chance to reply. But I'm that glad to see you. I've missed you and our little chats. All that silly business about the feathers. I'm so sorry you were blamed. I should have known it wasn't you. Ben believed in you, didn't he?'

Molly smiled and nodded. 'Yes, he did. I just wish we knew who it was. That would prove it then, wouldn't it?'

'Tom knows but he won't say. He won't even tell his mother and you know how close they are.'

'I do, and he won't even tell Olive.'

'Olive? Olive Mason?'

Molly's smile widened. 'Oh, didn't you know? They met when the boys were home on leave. Through me, actually. Tom came to meet me out of work when we were at the Institute and Olive was with me. They went out a couple of times and they're writing to each other now. So Olive says,' she added quickly, anxious not to let anything slip that would imply that she and Tom were also writing to each other. Not even Olive knew that, although she thought her own mother, seeing all the letters arriving in Tom's handwriting, would know her friendship with him was continuing.

'I'm delighted to hear it, though Alice hasn't said anything.' Harriet lowered her voice and leaned closer to Molly, almost as if she thought Alice might hear their conversation from across the street. 'Do you think she knows?'

'I honestly don't know, Mrs Spencer, but Olive's a very nice girl. I'm sure Mrs Mayberry would approve. Do you hear anything from the Masons now they've gone back home?'

Harriet's face lit up briefly. 'Oh yes, hasn't your mother told you? We meet every week on a Friday afternoon after we've all done our shopping.' She nodded towards the house across the road. 'Mrs Mayberry, your mam and Mrs Mason come here for a cuppa and a chat.' She sighed. 'Of course the war and our worries about the lads dominate the conversation, which I suppose is a bit hard on Ruby, but she's a very caring woman and doesn't seem to mind us rattling on about our boys.'

'Well, she's had her own brush with the war and its hardships now, hasn't she? I expect she was very grateful to you for giving them a home while their own was repaired.'

'They were very lucky. Several of the houses that were affected are still not habitable. And of course, the loss of life was so very sad.'

'So,' Molly said carefully, 'you didn't mind having them to stay?'

'Not a bit. I think I've even got her interested in joining our suffragette meetings. That's if they start up again after the war.'

It didn't sound like Queenie's version of how the Spencers had viewed their unexpected guests at all.

Thirty-nine

As the winter moved into spring, Molly continued to receive letters from the boys, as they all referred to them. Even William now included her name in his letters, beginning, *Dear Mam, Dad and Molly,* and, to her delight, Harry wrote to her every three weeks or so. Both Ben and Tom wrote more frequently, but she couldn't help being thrilled when she recognized Harry's writing.

We're on the move, he wrote in April. *Only about fifteen miles south-west, but it's further away from the front. We can still hear the guns and the shelling, of course.* That was to be expected, Molly thought. She'd heard it said that the shelling in France could sometimes be heard on the south coast of England. *We've been formed into working parties to cut down trees and prepare support trenches in this area. It's hard work but at least we're not getting shot at just now.*

In May, Ben wrote to say that they were working on a new railway line but, yet again, he was not allowed to say where. It was so frustrating, Molly thought, not to know exactly where they were, but she could understand the reason for secrecy. If the enemy got to hear of a railway line being built, and where, they would undoubtedly make efforts to destroy it. But by the end of the month, she heard that all four had returned to the trenches.

Molly sighed. It was inevitable, she supposed, but it had been a respite for them all: for the lads from being in the front line, and for those back at home from the constant worry of their safety.

Tom was the first to be wounded at the end of May. It was not a serious injury and having spent a few days in a field hospital, he was deemed fit to return to light duties in the reserve trenches. It did, however, excuse him from the front line for a couple of weeks. The worst part about it for him was being separated from his friends and not knowing what was happening to them. When he was allowed to rejoin them, he had news.

'The gossip is that there's going to be a huge push very soon around the Somme.'

'I'm not surprised,' Harry said. 'We've been hearing that the French are having a dreadful time at Verdun, and one of the lads reckons an attack in a different place will be to try to pull the enemy's troops away from that area. I don't know if that's right. There's all sorts of speculation flying around.'

'Yes, there is,' Tom said. 'But it is true about Verdun. I met a French lad in the hospital and he was in a poor way. He'll never go back to the front.'

'Maybe he's one of the lucky ones.'

'You wouldn't think so if you'd seen him. He'd had a leg amputated.'

The four of them were silent as realization hit

home. Not one of them was impervious to injury or worse.

'Right, enough of this morbid talk,' Harry said suddenly. 'Tom's back with us, so tonight we celebrate.'

'Just so long as we remember that we'll have to be up at the crack of dawn,' William said. 'We're moving up to the front tomorrow. And I'd rather face enemy bullets than our sergeant if we're not all bright-eyed and bushy-tailed.'

'Harriet,' Alice said, coming into the Spencers' kitchen with a letter in her hand. 'I've had a letter from Tom. He wrote it a week or two ago. Looks like it's been held up in the post.'

'Aye, some of them are, love. Then four arrive at once. That's what happens with our lads, anyway. What does it say? Is he all right?'

'He is now but he was wounded in the leg. It wasn't very serious, he says, and he's being sent back to the trenches and hoping to link up again with the other three soon. Do you think he's telling me the truth about his wound?'

'I would think so, Alice. He might be making light of it, but he wouldn't have been sent back into the line if he wasn't fit enough. He'd be a danger to others, ne'er mind himself. Oh no, I think he's being honest with you.'

Solemn-faced, the two women glanced at each other. 'Just shows you, though, doesn't it, how easily they can be wounded and we don't know anything about it until days, even weeks, later?'

Harriet nodded. 'There's a woman in the next street whose lad was killed. Mind you, she was informed pretty quickly, so, for us, I think we've got to think "no news is good news".'

'You're right.'

The three men – Jack, Ron and Luke – still met every Saturday night in their local pub, and now Pete Mason often joined them. It was a distance for him to walk, but they were the only real friends he'd made since arriving in the town. The four men discussed the war in more detail than their womenfolk did. There were also several other regulars who were doing the same thing and they would all share news they'd heard from their relatives at the front. One or two brought national and local newspapers and left them in the pub for others to read. Between them all they were able to form a good idea of what was happening.

'I don't like the sound of this "big push" they're talking about,' Ron said one day in early July of 1916. 'I reckon our lads could be involved in it.'

'There's a long article in one of the papers here,' Luke said. 'Wait a minute, I'll find it.'

He rifled among the papers lying on the end of the bar. 'Here it is,' he said, bringing a copy of the *Weekly Dispatch* with him to their table. 'It's a write-up about an interview with Lord Derby, the Under-Secretary of State for War.'

'Isn't he the chap who started the idea of the pals' battalions in Liverpool right at the beginning of the war?'

'I think so, yes,' Ron said and began to read aloud

from the paper. 'It's a brutal piece,' he commented. 'He's saying straight out that the only way for us to win is to kill Huns. That's what he calls them.'

Luke nodded. 'They call us "Tommies", don't they?'

'It says that the British policy is "to wear down the enemy".'

'I see what you mean about it being brutal, because surely that means just killing as many of their soldiers as possible.'

'We're fighting on a twenty-mile front that's defended by masses of enemy troops, but it says that our volunteer soldiers are proving themselves "worthy of the most splendid British traditions".'

'That's nice,' Luke murmured.

'Is it?' Ron glanced up. 'Sounds very worrying to me.'

'Go on, Ron,' Jack said.

'He thinks that the battle won't be won by spurts of military activity but by steady, constant pressure and moving slowly forward.' Suddenly, he gave a cynical laugh. 'But he adds that he is a civilian.'

'Then why does he think he's got the knowledge to make such comments?' Pete asked.

'Exactly.' Ron read on and added, 'He does pay tribute to our medical organization.' He jabbed the paper with his fingers. 'He says that only twenty-four hours after being seriously wounded on the front, soldiers can be back in a London hospital receiving expert attention. Of course, he's making light of the numbers, saying that many are only slight wounds and that they're soon returned to the front, but they're still counted as "casualties".'

'Doesn't seem possible, does it?' Luke said. 'About being brought home so quickly, I mean, but it's wonderful if it's true.'

'Oh, and it says here that the new steel helmet is saving a lot of minor head injuries and presumably saving more serious ones too. I hope our lads have been issued with them. I'll make sure Mabel asks them next time she writes.'

Luke snorted in derision. 'He can't hide the dreadful number that were slaughtered on the first day of the Somme, now can he?'

It was bad enough for those at home hearing about the huge number of casualties suffered by the British and their allies on the very first day of this new offensive, but for those who were actually there, it was like hell had opened up before them.

The bombardment over the previous seven days leading up to the 1 July had not achieved its objective. The enemy trenches and dugouts were far deeper and better constructed and when, on the whistle, the lines of British soldiers went 'over the top', they were mown down like wheat before a farmer's scythe.

The daily news from the Somme brought the families even more distress. When more and more wounded and maimed arrived home, discharged from the army because of their injuries and never able to return to duty, they were appalled.

'Why aren't we hearing anything from our lads?' Harriet asked of no one in particular several times a day. Even the normally resolute and phlegmatic former suffragette was uncharacteristically distraught.

'It must be chaos out there,' Mabel said, when the

A Woman of Spirit

four friends met on the first Friday following the dreadful news of the major battle. She was trying to quell her own inner terror, as well as soothe her friend. 'I expect the mail is probably way down the list of priorities at the moment.'

'But have you seen the figures?' Harriet would not let the subject drop. 'Almost sixty thousand casualties on the first day alone and – and nearly twenty thousand of them dead.' Her voice rose in anguish. 'Every one of them some poor mother's son and for only three miles of ground. It's – it's obscene. That's what it is.'

Alice, sitting nearby, bit her lip until she drew blood. Here was Harriet – the acknowledged strong one – giving way. Ruby, although not quite as involved as the other three – she had no son out there – was moved to take Alice's hand in hers and rub it comfortingly. All she could think of to say was, 'If something had happened to one of them, you'd have heard.' Her words sounded inadequate, even to her own ears.

But Mabel picked up on it. 'She's right, Harriet. If any one of our four had been hurt on that first day, we'd have heard by now.'

Harriet pulled in a deep breath and tried to steady her beating heart. 'You're right, of course. I'm sorry. I shouldn't be saying all this to you . . .'

'Of course you should,' the other three chorused. 'That's what friends are for.'

Harriet gave a deep sigh as she tried to calm herself. 'But there's no one else who understands like you.'

'No, they don't. Even Ethel doesn't and we've been friends for years,' said Mabel.

'But she hasn't got a son out there, has she?' Alice said.

Mabel nodded towards Ruby. 'Neither has Ruby, but she understands, don't you, me duck?'

Ruby nodded. 'Yes, I think I do. I can imagine that if Olive had been a boy and he was out there right now, I know exactly how I'd be feeling.'

It was almost the end of July before the families received letters, and then several arrived at once. But they held a little bit of good news for a change.

> *We've been through an awful time,* William wrote to his family, *but the four of us have been very lucky. We've all come through unharmed but we lost several of our pals, although, contrary to what you might hear, we have made some ground. Now we hear that we are to march away from here for a while. I fully expect it will involve more training and that we will return to the front line in a few weeks. Oh, and by the way, Harry has been made a lance corporal. We thought he might get moved with the promotion, but luckily we can stay together. It won't make any difference – we've always done what Harry tells us anyway!*

'William's told us the lovely news,' Molly said, when Queenie came round that evening.

Queenie frowned. 'What news?'

'About Harry.'

Queenie's eyes narrowed. 'What about him?'

'About him being made a lance corporal. I thought you'd be that proud, you'd be singing it from the rooftops.' She bit her lip to stop herself adding, *I know I would.*

For a brief moment, Queenie's eyes flickered and Molly knew instinctively that the girl didn't know. But she recovered quickly and laughed, 'Oh that. Yes, it's nice, isn't it? But it's no more than I expected, really. Shame it's not all of them, but then I suppose Tom Mayberry isn't officer material, is he? Not even a junior one.' She put her head on one side and asked, 'What about your William? Hasn't he been promoted?'

'Not that he's said. It sounds as if they always followed Harry's lead.'

Queenie preened at the praise. 'Yes, I expect his superiors saw that in him. That he's a natural leader. Maybe, by the time all this is over, he'll have a really good position in the army.'

Mabel bent her head over her knitting.

'What are you making, Aunty Mabel?'

'Scarves for the lads, ready for the winter. We've formed a knitting and sewing group to send parcels out. They need all sorts. Scarves, socks, even balaclavas, I don't doubt.' She paused and then felt obliged to say, 'Perhaps your mam would like to join us.'

'Oh, I don't think so.' Queenie almost looked down her nose, as if their little scheme was far too unworthy of her mother's attention and time. 'She's far too busy.'

Mabel feigned innocence. 'Is she, Queenie? Has she

joined some sort of group already, then? She hasn't said.'

'I don't think so, but she has enough to do looking after Dad and me.'

'Well, she certainly keeps her home spotless, that's true.'

Mabel kept her eyes down. She didn't want Queenie to see the hint of mischief in them, but knowing her mother well, Molly detected the gentle dig. It was beneath Ethel Palmer's dignity to be helping with the war effort and yet, if she had only realized it, her neighbours would have thought far more of her for taking part in helping 'our boys' than being so fixated on having the cleanest front doorstep in the street. Not for the first time, Mabel wondered why the Palmers were still living in their terraced street. She guessed it was because Jack flatly refused to move from his roots.

When Queenie had left and Molly had closed the back door firmly behind her, she came back to sit with her mother near the range. She took up her own knitting again. 'Oh, I've dropped a stitch. Can you help me, Mam?'

'Give it here,' Mabel said, with a good-natured sigh. 'Not very skilled at this, are you, love? I hope you're better with your big machinery.'

'Oh I am. I like working on the big lathes the best.' Molly laughed. 'I just find knitting so fiddly, but I do want to do it. I'll get better.'

When Mabel had picked up the dropped stitch and done a row of her daughter's knitting to set her back on track, Molly said, 'Mam, I don't think Queenie knew about Harry's promotion, do you?'

'No, I'm sure she didn't. I was watching her carefully, but she wasn't going to let on, was she?' Mabel paused and then asked, 'Does she know Harry writes to you?'

'Heavens, no. She'd go berserk. And she doesn't know I write to Tom now, either. But I do tell her I write to Ben. That way, if I happen to forget myself and tell her something the others have told me, she'll think it's come from Ben. She still believes there's something between me and him.'

'And is there?'

'No, Mam, there isn't.'

There was silence between them as their needles clacked.

'Shame really,' Mabel murmured, more to herself than to Molly. 'He's such a nice lad.'

Molly and Queenie still met for a Sunday afternoon stroll in the park, and if there were any young men not in uniform, Molly tried to steer her friend away from them. But sometimes she failed. It seemed that, despite their previous unfortunate encounter in the park, Queenie was still determined to shame young men into joining up. One day in late September when the battle on the Somme had been raging for almost three months, there was a group of five young men in the park kicking a football between them. Not one was in uniform and none of them appeared to be wounded. Queenie marched up to them.

'Why are you not in uniform?' she said loudly.

They stopped their game and glanced at each other.

'We're miners,' one said. 'We're more valuable here.'

Queenie's lip curled disdainfully. 'My fiancé worked at the local engineering factory. I'm sure he was "valuable", but he went. He volunteered in the first month and now he's at the Somme.'

'Poor devil,' another young man muttered. 'I hope he survives.'

The tallest of the five, broad and strong, moved to stand in front of Queenie. 'I went in the first month too, but I was sent home because it was thought my civilian job was more useful. I'd have stayed out there if they'd let me. But, in the army, you have to do as you're told.' He looked her up and down. 'And what do you do, miss, if I might be so bold? Are you willing to take my place in the mine? Not that they'd take you, but you don't look as if you're one of the women who'd be willing to get their pretty hands mucky.'

Queenie tossed her curls. 'Haven't you heard about the Technical Institute here that trains people, women mainly, to make munitions? We do our bit.'

'So, are we still going to be handed a white feather?'

Suddenly, Queenie put her head on one side and smiled disarmingly at him. 'Not today. You've had a lucky escape. I can understand you are doing vital work here.'

As Queenie tucked her arm through Molly's and they turned away, the five young men laughed and one shouted, 'He's a lucky fella, your fiancé. I hope he comes back to you in one piece.'

Queenie glanced back over her shoulder and gave a saucy wink.

Molly was quiet as they walked home. Queenie had lied. She had implied she was doing important war work, rather than still serving well-to-do women in a drapery store and learning to be a dressmaker.

'You all right, love?' Mabel asked as mother and daughter washed up together in the scullery after tea. 'You're a bit quiet tonight. Queenie giving you problems again?'

'Not – really, but she approached a group of lads playing football in the park this afternoon and challenged them about why they weren't in uniform.'

'And?'

'One had actually enlisted at the start but he'd been sent home because he's a miner. They all are.'

Mabel nodded. 'Of course, it's a vital job. Where would we all be without coal, eh?'

'She was so shocked that time when she saw that poor man who'd lost his hand that she ran away. I thought she'd learned her lesson.' Molly sighed. 'But it seems not.'

Mabel lowered her voice so that Ron, sitting in the kitchen, wouldn't hear. 'Ethel was very worried about her for a while after the lads were home on leave. She watched her like a hawk to see if – well, you know. But time's gone on now and she's obviously all right. I think Ethel can breathe easier now.' She paused and then asked, 'D'you know if her and Harry get up to anything? You know what I mean.'

Molly felt the colour rise in her face. 'Please don't ask me, Mam. You know how strict you've always been on us not breaking confidences.'

Mabel sighed. 'Fair enough. But in a way you've told me what I wanted to know.'

'Don't say anything to Aunty Ethel. Please, Mam.'

'I won't let you down, Molly. Besides, there's no need to worry this time round. But I am concerned what might happen if they come home again on leave. I'd be put in a very awkward position.'

At the end of September, letters arrived to all the families from their boys, which had been written a couple of weeks earlier. This time there was disturbing news. Even the censor had not scored out their destination, presumably because it was common knowledge where the fighting was taking place.

We're back on the Somme . . .

Forty

Telegraph boys, nicknamed 'the angels of death', speeding into a street on their bicycles brought out anyone who saw them. Women stopped their work and children stopped playing to watch where they went. Which house was about to receive dreadful news?

On a cloudy dismal day, as she stood up from cleaning her front doorstep, Alice saw the boy first, pedalling down the middle of the street towards her. She watched him, her hand to her mouth. She could not speak, could not call out to any of her neighbours. Her gaze was fixed on his progress but she felt, rather than saw, a few neighbours emerging from their houses. Those whom the boy had already passed, moved after him. One of their number was going to need their support any minute now.

As he came nearer, he slowed and Alice's heart seemed to stop for a moment, and then began to hammer. She watched as he glanced at the paper in his hand and then looked about him, checking for the number of the house he wanted. He moved on slowly until he was level with her, but his eyes turned towards the house opposite her.

The Spencers' home.

'Oh no!' Alice whispered as the boy dismounted, wheeled his bicycle towards Harriet's front door and knocked.

Why couldn't he have gone on further down the street? Why couldn't he have knocked on someone else's door? There were other young men in the street who'd gone to war, most of them alongside Tom and Harry and Ben. She knew them all. They'd all played in the street together as youngsters, fought each other in boyish scuffles but had come together to fight a common foe. She didn't want any of them to be killed or seriously wounded, but certainly not Harry or Ben. Please, not Harry or Ben. They were like sons to her too.

Harriet had opened the door and the boy had put the telegram into her hand. Now he was scuttling away, mounting his bicycle and pedalling as fast as he could back up the street, not glancing at any of the women who were still walking slowly towards Harriet. Galvanized into movement, Alice hurried across the street to put her arms around her friend and take her back inside her home. She closed the door on their neighbours, even though she knew each and every one of them meant only to be kind and supportive.

'Come and sit down and we'll open it.'

Harriet was in a daze. 'You open it,' she said in barely a whisper. 'I – I can't.'

Alice opened it with trembling fingers and read it swiftly.

'It's Ben,' she choked. '"Killed in action", it says.'

Harriet let out a howl of grief and buried her face

in her hands. Alice put her arms about her friend and held her close, but she could find no words of comfort that wouldn't sound trite. After a few moments, Harriet stirred against Alice's shoulder.

'Luke,' she screamed. 'Fetch Luke.'

'Of course,' Alice said, standing up and making for the front door. Several women were still in the street, huddled together, not knowing what to do. As she approached them they turned to face her, their faces aghast.

'Could one of you fetch Luke home, please?'

'I'll get my Archie to fetch him,' one said. 'He's on nights and he's in bed, but he'll willingly get up to do that. You go back to her, Alice. Leave it with us.'

None of them asked which son it was. Their father should be told first and they respected that. But obviously something serious had happened to one of the Spencer boys. Gradually, they dispersed back to their own homes, but for all of them, the day was ruined.

It seemed an age before Luke arrived home, though it was less than half an hour. With tears streaming down her face, Harriet held out the telegram to him. Grim-faced, knowing already that something dreadful had befallen one of his sons, he took it and sat down suddenly, read it swiftly, moaned and dropped his face into his hands.

Silently, Alice moved into the scullery and made tea. She placed it on the kitchen table.

'I'll go now,' she said softly, 'but let me know if there's anything I can do.'

Luke couldn't speak but he nodded and squeezed Alice's hand in a gesture of heartfelt thanks.

In the street, there were only two women left talking together.

'Which one is it?' one asked. Alice didn't think there was any harm in telling her now.

'Ben. No details yet, just "killed in action".'

'They'll get a follow-up letter or Harry will write.'

Alice nodded, but left them to go to her home. She tried to settle to her housework, but her mind kept going to the sad couple across the road. Poor, poor Ben, was all she could think. She hoped that it had been quick and that he hadn't died in agony.

The day dragged and Alice kept going to the front window to see if there was any movement across the road. About mid-afternoon, as she was standing there looking out, she saw their front door open and Luke come out. He crossed the street towards her and Alice flew to her own front door to open it.

'Alice, love,' he began. She was shocked at the sight of him. He looked like he had aged ten years in the space of the few hours since they'd heard the news. His voice was husky and his eyes red-rimmed. 'Harriet would like the Palmers and the Wyngates to be told. And Ruby too, when you've got a minute. Do you think . . .?'

'Of course, I'll go at once. I'll make sure they all know.'

'There's nothing much you can tell them yet, but we'll keep them informed when we hear more. I must get back to Harriet . . .'

'Will it be all right for me to call in when I come back?'

'Of course, Alice. You're welcome any time.'

'I don't want to intrude.'

'You won't be. We could do with the company, if I'm honest.'

'Then I'll be there whenever you want me.'

Ten minutes later, Alice was on her way to the two houses two streets away with news she had never wanted to deliver.

'Hello, Alice. Come in, love. What brings you here . . .?' Mabel began with her usual welcoming smile, and then she noticed Alice's solemn face and the tears in her eyes. Her fingers fluttered to her mouth. 'Oh no. No!'

Mabel grasped Alice's hand and almost pulled her into the house.

'It's Ben,' Alice said quickly. '"Killed in action" was all the telegram said. 'They'll hear more by letter.'

'Or if one of the others writes home. Have you told Ethel?'

'No, I came here first. I know Molly was good friends with poor Ben.'

Mabel shook her head sadly. 'She'll be devastated. I never believed in friendships between boys and girls, but they really seemed to make it work. Just wait a minute, I'll get my coat and we'll go together.'

Ethel was shocked. 'Do you know if the others are all right?' she asked when the news had sunk in a little. 'Harry and your two boys?'

Alice and Mabel glanced at each other. 'Not really. There's been no news of them.'

'Perhaps one of them will write. Maybe they were there.'

'Not too close, hopefully.'

The three women looked at each other, fear in their eyes.

Ron arrived home before Molly.

'Do you know what's happened?' he asked the moment he came through the door. 'I've just heard that Luke was fetched home from work.'

'Ben's been killed in action.' There was no way Mabel could soften the blow, but she was so glad that Ron had arrived home first. He would be with her when she had to tell Molly.

'Oh no. That's dreadful. Poor lad. What – what about the other three? Any news of our William?'

Mabel shook her head and whispered, 'However am I going to tell our Molly?'

'We'll do it together.'

'She'll be devastated.'

'I know.' Ron paused, then asked, 'Does Ethel know? She'll have to tell Queenie.'

Mabel nodded. 'Alice came round and we told her together. She was shocked, naturally, but at least it wasn't Harry.'

Not yet, Ron almost said, but he held his tongue. Their own son was out there too, alongside the others. It could so easily have been the Wyngate household receiving a telegram.

As they had predicted, Molly was distraught. She began to cry and couldn't stop. Tea was forgotten by all three of them.

'He was one of the nicest lads I knew,' Molly wept. 'He was always so kind. A true friend. I really loved him.'

There was really nothing her parents could say to ease her pain. At last she raised her tear-streaked face. 'Is that all they know? No more details?'

'Not yet.'

'And the other three?'

'We don't know. We can only wait,' Mabel said gently.

'That's going to be agony.' Her tears flowed even faster.

Indeed, it was for all the families who waited for news.

The expected letter giving more details of Ben's death duly arrived. He was reported to have died instantly and suffered no pain.

'That's what all the letters to bereaved families say,' Luke said in private to his male friends, but he did not voice these thoughts to his wife. 'Perhaps we'll get to know more when we hear from the other lads.'

'Where did it happen?' Ron asked gently. 'Did they say?'

'Somewhere near a place called Gueudecourt. He'll be buried somewhere near there, I expect. I just wish we could hear something about Harry.'

But no one received a letter from the three young men who were left, not even Queenie. The constant questions were: *Where are they? Are they all right?*

At last, two letters came to the Wyngates, one from William to his parents and one from Tom addressed to Molly, but surprisingly their letters only posed more unanswered questions.

We are grief-stricken by Ben's death, William wrote, *but mercifully, it was quick. We can attest to that. It's what the authorities always say to the next-of-kin, but we know that this time it's true. A shell burst very close to him and he was killed instantly. Tom and I were further down the line and although we saw what happened, we weren't near enough to be injured. And, of course, by now, you will know what happened to Harry. Sorry this is short, but I have to go. We're on the move.*

Mabel shook the letter angrily. 'No, we don't know what happened to Harry, you silly boy,' she said aloud to the empty room. 'You should have said.' She stood in the middle of her kitchen, unsure what she should do. I'll open Molly's letter, she decided. She won't mind on this occasion. She's always telling us they're not private love letters. Maybe Tom's had the sense to tell her more.

But Tom did not even mention Harry, concentrating on how much he mourned Ben's loss and saying how much he knew Molly would miss him too.

'Oh, drat the boys,' Mabel muttered. 'I'll have to go down to Ethel's. Maybe Queenie has had a letter from Harry.'

Ethel opened her door tentatively, afraid of what further news there might be.

'I've had a letter from William,' Mabel said, waving it in front of Ethel's face. 'Him and Tom are all right, but he doesn't mention Harry.' She deliberately avoided mentioning Tom's letter to Molly. She knew Molly had not confided in Queenie that she was corresponding with him. 'I just wondered,' she went on, 'if Queenie's had a letter from Harry.'

Ethel shook her head. 'No, there's been nothing recently at all. Queenie's quite put out about it and, of course, after the news about Ben, she's even more worried.'

'Right, then, that settles it. I'm going round to Harriet's. I hope to God there's not more bad news.'

'I'd come with you, but I'm just cooking something for Jack's tea. Let me know what you hear, though, won't you?'

'Of course I will.' As she turned away she pursed her lips irritably. Surely Jack Palmer could wait for his tea just this once.

Mabel's heart was thumping madly as she knocked on Harriet's back door. It was opened quickly and Mabel saw the immediate relief in Harriet's eyes when she saw a neighbour standing there.

'Come in, Mabel.'

'Have you heard from Harry?' Mabel asked without preamble as she stepped inside.

Harriet frowned. 'No. Why?'

'Harriet, love, I don't want to worry you but I've had a letter from William that's a bit odd. Look . . .' She thrust the letter into Harriet's hands. 'You read it and see what you think.'

Harriet's eyes were wide with fear, but bravely she scanned William's letter twice before she looked up. 'It does sound a bit mysterious, doesn't it? But I – I don't think he's been killed because we would have heard that. Wouldn't we?' she added, sounding a bit unsure now.

'Of course you would, but I can't understand why Harry hasn't written to you himself, especially after losing his poor brother.'

'I know. Luke and I were only saying last night that it's a bit odd Harry hasn't written. Luke wondered if he's on his way home – you know, been given some compassionate leave to come and be with us for a few days.'

'Ah, now I hadn't thought of that. Luke could be right. Let's hope he is.'

But the days passed and there was still no news of Harry. Both Alice and Mabel wrote to their own sons, imploring them to let them know what had happened.

You seem to think we know something about Harry, Mabel wrote to William, *but we don't. All we know is that Ben has been killed in action. Harriet and Luke have had a formal letter now about where and when it happened and where he is buried and a very complimentary one from Ben's commanding officer, but nothing about Harry. Please write and tell us anything you know. We're all beside ourselves with worry.*

But before William had had time to reply to his mother, Harriet heard from Harry himself. His writing was almost illegible but the contents of the letter explained the reason.

A Woman of Spirit

I am in hospital in Aldershot, seriously wounded. They've had to amputate my left leg. Will write more when I feel better . . .

'I've come to see both you and Ethel,' Harriet said to Mabel when she appeared at her door. 'I'm not sure if he's written to Queenie. Will you come with me to their house, Mabel? He's – he's obviously in a bad way. His letters are usually much longer. Chatty, you'd say. And his writing's dreadful now. Not – not like him at all . . .'

Harriet dissolved into tears. Both her sons had met with disaster and even though Harry was still alive, she knew he was by no means out of danger, however upbeat he was trying to be.

'Of course. We'll go to see Ethel straight away,' Mabel said, patting her friend's shoulder. 'Queenie won't be home, but it's perhaps best if she's not . . .'

Ethel was shocked. 'Oh, the poor, poor boy. Are you and Luke going to see him?'

'I – I . . .' Harriet stuttered. 'I hadn't thought that far yet, Ethel, to be honest, but yes, I expect we will.' She paused and added, 'Queenie could come with us.'

For a brief moment, Ethel stared at her. 'Oh – er – yes. Right. I'll – um – tell her that.'

After they'd stayed with Ethel for about half an hour, Harriet and Mabel walked back to the Wyngate house.

'However am I going to tell Luke? He'll be devastated. One of his sons gone and the other maimed for life.'

'But at least Harry's still alive, bless him,' Mabel said. 'We'll all rally round and help him. And he's got Queenie to come home to. He's got a pretty girl waiting for him. Not everyone has.'

'Mm, I just wonder though . . .' Harriet began and then she fell silent.

'What?'

'Oh, nothing. I must get back home, but thank you so much for your support today and – and before – when we heard about Ben. It means more than I can put into words to have friends like you and Alice, and Ruby now. She's become a good friend too.'

Forty-one

'Molly, love, sit down. I've something to tell you,' Mabel said when her daughter arrived home.

Molly turned white but did as her mother suggested. 'It's – it's Harry, isn't it?'

Mabel nodded. 'He's been very badly injured. He's back in England in hospital, but they've had to amputate his left leg.'

Molly groaned. 'But he's alive,' she whispered with heartfelt thankfulness in her tone. 'He's still alive.'

'Yes, but he's obviously very, very poorly.'

'Yes, yes, of course, but there's hope. If he's still alive there's always hope.'

Mabel watched her daughter, her heart going out to her. Only Mabel knew about Molly's feelings for Harry. It was something they never spoke about, but Mabel knew. Strangely, Molly didn't weep this time, not like she had over Ben. But then, as the girl said herself, this time there was hope.

'Does – does Queenie know?'

'Ethel does, so she'll know as soon as she gets home.'

'We walked home together, so she'll know by now. I – I'd better go down . . .'

'I'd leave it a bit if I were you, love. Let her mam tell her on her own.'

At that same moment, Queenie was staring at her mother with horrified eyes. She stepped back, feeling for the arm of the chair behind her. She sat down suddenly as her legs gave way. Then she began to shake her head in denial. 'Oh no, no. I can't bear that. It'd have been better if he'd been killed outright – like Ben.'

'Queenie,' Ethel was appalled, 'how can you say such a thing? How can you even think it?'

'I can't marry a man with only one leg. I just can't. I won't.'

Ethel stared at her. 'My God,' she whispered, 'is that the sort of person I've brought you up to be? So selfish and self-centred? I'm ashamed of you, Queenie. It's probably thinking of you, knowing you're waiting for him, that's pulled him through.' Ethel thought for a few moments. 'You don't really feel like that, do you? It's just the shock. When you've calmed down and thought about it . . .'

Queenie shook her head vehemently. 'No, I won't. I don't even want to see him.'

'But you must . . .'

'There's no "must" about it, Mam. Like I said, it'd have been better if he'd been killed outright. I could have mourned him as a hero. Everyone would have felt sorry for me, but this . . . Oh no, no! I don't want a husband who's only half a man.'

'There are going to be a great many wives and

sweethearts who will have to face such injuries to their loved one.'

'Well, not me. Someone else can play nursemaid to him.'

Ethel looked down at her daughter helplessly. She couldn't believe what she was hearing. 'You'll feel differently when you see him. When he comes home.'

'I won't, because I won't see him.'

At that moment there was a tap at the back door.

'That'll be Molly. Mabel will have told her. Now, look, Queenie, don't say anything to her about not wanting to see Harry. D'you hear me?' Ethel's tone was suddenly very firm, so demanding that even Queenie had to take notice.

'All right. I won't say anything yet. I can see how it looks to others, but I mean it, Mam.'

'Shh. She's coming in,' Ethel hissed and then raised her voice. 'Come in, Molly, love. I expect your mam's told you. Isn't it awful?'

'Yes, it is,' Molly said, glancing at Queenie's white face. The girl was pursing her lips and Molly was sure that it was because Queenie was trying hard to hold back the tears. She sat beside her friend and took her hand. 'At least he's alive. He'll come back to you.'

Queenie pressed her lips together even harder as she nodded. But she did not speak. She glanced at her mother as if imploring her to let her tell the truth, at least to Molly, but Ethel held firm. She was sure it was just the initial shock that had caused Queenie to be so heartless.

'He's in a hospital, Mam said,' Molly went on,

blithely unaware of the turmoil in Queenie's mind. 'In Aldershot. Shall you go to see him? Mam said that Mrs Spencer said this morning that you can go with them.'

'I . . .' Queenie began but caught sight of her mother's frown. She swallowed hard and said, 'I'll see.'

'Do you want me to go with you to see them? Mr and Mrs Spencer, I mean.' It took every ounce of Molly's willpower to offer this little act of kindness when all she wanted to do was to run round to the Spencers' house and beg them to take her to see Harry. But she couldn't do that. She wasn't his girlfriend and no one other than her own mother knew about her feelings for him. All she could do was to act the concerned friend to them both. Once he was home, she could see him just as a friend. For the moment she must rein in her emotions, but it was far from easy.

Queenie shook her head and her words were stilted. 'No – they'll need time – on their – own.'

'She's in shock,' Ethel said. 'Give her time, Molly, love. She'll come round.'

Molly caught the glare that Queenie gave her mother and was puzzled by it. 'I'll – um – go, then,' she said. 'You know where I am if – if you need me, Queenie.'

Queenie merely nodded but did not speak again. Ethel went to the back door with Molly. 'She's in shock,' she whispered again. 'I'm sure of it. His injury will alter both their lives and Queenie just needs time to come to terms with it.'

'Of course,' Molly agreed but as she walked slowly home, she was deep in thought.

'How is she?' Mabel asked as Molly stepped through the back door.

Molly sighed. 'Strange, if I'm honest, Mam. Aunty Ethel says she's in a state of shock at the news, but—' She hesitated.

'What, love?'

'If it'd been me, I'd have rushed round to his parents and begged to go with them, because they're bound to go to see him.'

'Of course they will,' Mabel said gently knowing that this was still what Molly would like to do, but couldn't. 'If it was William, I'd be off on the next train.'

Molly nodded. 'Alongside me and Dad.' She sighed. 'There's nothing else I can do now. Queenie knows where I am.'

'Why don't you go round to see Harriet? Just as a friend. Like you did when poor Ben . . .'

Molly frowned. 'I'd like to. Would you come with me?'

'Of course. We'll go after your dad gets home and we've had tea. Maybe he'll come with us. After all, he's big pals with Luke.' At the mention of the word 'pals' they glanced at one another.

Ron indeed wanted to accompany them. He kept shaking his head and muttering, 'Terrible news. Such dreadful news. Why should one family have to bear so much?'

When Luke opened the front door to their knock, Ron said at once, 'We'll understand if you'd rather we didn't come in, but we just wanted to—'

'No, no, Ron. Come in. We're pleased to see you.'

'Are you sure . . .?'

''Course I'm sure. It's at times like these we need our friends.'

When they were all seated, Ron said again, 'We're so very sorry to hear about Harry.'

Luke sighed heavily. 'Aye well, coming on top of losing our Ben, it has hit us hard, I don't mind admitting.'

'Do – do you think they were together when it happened?' Ron asked tentatively.

'Yes, they were. Alice had a letter from Tom this morning and he said they were all in the trenches together, only him and your William were a little further down the same section. Ben and Harry were side by side . . .'

Luke passed a hand wearily across his face as he imagined his boys standing together, shoulder to shoulder, to face the enemy. Harriet put her hand on her husband's arm. 'But at least Harry will come back to us,' she said firmly. She glanced at Mabel, Ron and Molly. 'I heard this morning that there were three other lads from around here. They joined up together and stayed together. They were killed on the same day as Ben.'

Ron nodded. 'Yes, I heard something similar at work. Three brothers who worked at your place. They enlisted the same time as your lads. All three of them have been killed too. On the same day, I reckon.' He sighed heavily. 'These pals' battalions are all very fine in theory. A great idea that they should sign up together and train together – I agree with that – but it's not so good when they're in the front line together and die together. Whole streets – whole communities – are in mourning.'

Luke looked up at his friend. 'You know, Ron, you've got a point there. I hadn't looked at it like that before. But you're absolutely right.'

'That poor mother,' Harriet said. 'Losing her three boys all at once.'

'Aye,' Ron said heavily. 'Her only sons – in fact, her only children.'

'Oh, that's dreadful,' Harriet said, wiping away tears. 'At least Harry's life has been spared. He'll be coming home to us.'

It took three days and a lot of persuading before Queenie would agree to go to see Harry's mother. By this time, Molly was even more sure that Queenie was behaving very strangely for a loving fiancée.

'I know it's been a dreadful shock for you,' she forced herself to sympathize, picking up on what Ethel had said, although she still didn't know the whole truth. 'But I'm sure it would mean so much to Mrs Spencer if you were to visit her. And even more to Harry to know you were supporting his mam and dad. And when he comes home . . .'

This time there was no mistaking the shudder that ran through Queenie's body. Molly frowned. 'What? What is it, Queenie?'

They were just turning into the street where the Spencers lived when Queenie stopped suddenly. 'I can't, Moll. I can't go any further. I just can't see them.'

Molly put her arm through Queenie's. 'It'll be all right. The first time is the hardest, but they're making arrangements to go to see him and if you're going with them—'

'I'm not.'

Molly gaped at her. 'What? What d'you mean?'

'I'm not going to see him and I'm not going to their house now. I can't, Moll. It's best if I end things now.'

'End things? Whatever do you mean?'

'Are you stupid or what, Moll? End things with Harry.'

'But you're engaged to him. You're going to marry him.'

Queenie shook her head. 'No, I'm not. I thought he was going to propose. I thought we were going to buy a ring that time he came home on leave, but we didn't. He never even asked me. And he was – well – odd, when he came home. A bit – well – cold with me. Not a bit like he was before he went away.'

'Oh.' Molly was shocked. Queenie had told her a deliberate lie about being engaged. But she was even more horrified that Queenie was going to end the relationship because he'd been badly wounded; that she had no intention of standing by him. Of caring for him. She almost said the words she was thinking out loud. *If it was me, I'd be on the first train to see him, and as soon as he came home I'd be helping Mrs Spencer to nurse him, to care for him.* But she held her tongue. Slowly, almost as if she were ending their friendship too, Molly withdrew her arm from Queenie's.

'Then I will see if Mrs Spencer will allow me to go with them. I'm Harry's friend, just as I was Ben's.'

'Do what you like. You can have him for all I care.' Suddenly, Queenie's eyes narrowed. 'He's going to be a cripple, Moll. Just be careful what you're taking on.'

With a supreme effort, Molly managed to keep her tone light. She didn't want Queenie to guess her real feelings for Harry. 'I'm just going to see him – if they'll let me – as a friend. That's all. But if I do go and he asks about you as he's bound to, what do I say?'

Queenie shrugged as if she'd already forgotten all about Harry Spencer. 'Whatever you like. The truth, if you want. You're a great one for the truth, aren't you?'

'I can't tell him that.' Molly was appalled. 'If you really mean it, you're going to have to tell him yourself.'

'Oh, I mean it all right.'

'Then do your own dirty work,' Molly was stung to retort. It was the first time in the whole of their lives that Molly had answered Queenie back in that way. The first time ever that she'd stood up to her. 'I'm certainly not doing it for you.'

With that, Molly turned and walked quickly away in the direction of the Spencers' house, leaving Queenie staring after her with narrowed eyes. 'Now, I wonder . . .' she murmured.

Forty-two

Harriet answered Molly's knock at once. For a brief moment there was fear in her eyes, as if every time she opened the door now she expected there to be bad news. Relief flooded her face as she saw who it was.

'Oh Molly, love. Come in.'

'I just came round to see if you had had any more news of Harry. Ben and I were good friends, as you know,' she went on in a rush, the words tumbling out as if she couldn't wait to explain her visit in a way that Harriet would understand while not guessing the real truth. 'And I'm friends with Harry, too. Maybe not quite as close to him as I was to Ben, but I – I care about him.'

Harriet touched Molly's hand. 'I know you do and I know he's fond of you too. When he wrote to tell us the truth – well, as much as he knew – about that white feather business, he was full of praise for you, saying what a lovely-natured girl you are and that he was bitterly sorry he'd ever thought you could have done such a thing. And he's right. I only wish—' Harriet broke off and shrugged. 'Ah well, no sense in wishing for the moon. What about Queenie? She's not been round to see us since we heard the news.'

A Woman of Spirit

Molly glanced away, unable to meet the woman's gaze now, but she knew that Harriet was watching her closely. 'What is it, Molly, love? Because I can see something's troubling you.'

'I – I think Queenie's in shock. She – she's finding it very hard to accept that Harry has been injured so – so badly.'

'Is she now?' Harriet uttered, but her tone hardened. 'I see.'

Molly had the uncomfortable feeling that Harriet saw only too well and guessed there was far more behind Molly's words. She was far too perceptive; but then she was the young man's mother and that's what mothers were.

'I'm sure she'll come to see you – and him – when she's had time to – to come to terms with it. It's a huge shock for all of us, isn't it? But at least he's alive. He'll come back to us – to you.'

'Yes, he will,' Harriet said softly. 'Unlike poor Ben.'

Tears filled Molly's eyes, but whether they were for Ben or for Harry even she didn't know.

'Are you and Mr Spencer going to see him?'

'Yes, as soon as we can make arrangements.'

'Would you – take a letter to him from me?'

'Of course.' Harriet was silent for a moment and then, with her gaze still fixed on Molly, she said, 'Why don't you come with us?'

Molly's mouth dropped open. 'Me?'

'Yes, you.'

'Oh, Harry won't want to see me. It'll be Queenie he'll want to see.'

'But from what you've said Queenie doesn't want to see him – at least not yet. Not in the hospital.'

'Well . . .' Molly was sorely tempted. How very much she wanted to see him for herself, but she didn't want to be second best. She didn't want to see the disappointment in his eyes when she – and not Queenie – arrived at his bedside. But the longing was too much. Impulsively, she said, 'Yes, all right, I'll come with you.'

She was surprised to see the smile that spread over Harriet's face. 'You'll be able to get time off work?'

Molly nodded. 'I think so. It'll be on compassionate grounds, won't it? I know we're only friends but I'm sure in the circumstances they'd understand. I can only ask and see what they say. When were you hoping to go?'

'Early next week. And we'll pay for your fare. It'll be our treat.' Molly opened her mouth to protest, but Harriet held up her hand. 'We'll be pleased to have your company. We could do with a younger person to help us travelling.' She gave a small smile. 'Me and Luke have never done much. Never been further than a trip into Leicester or Nottingham. Apart from that time I went to London for Miss Davison's funeral, but then we had Miss Anstruther with us. She organized everything.'

'That's very kind of you. Is there – is there anything he needs? Anything we can take for him?'

'We'll be making up a parcel of clothes, food and maybe a book or two. He was never a great reader but perhaps now reading might help to pass the time;

it must be very tedious when you're stuck in a bed, and I should know.'

Molly did not speak but there was a question in her eyes. Harriet, noticing it, smiled. 'I was a sickly child. Often missing school and spending days in bed. Luckily for me, my parents believed in education, even' – her smile widened briefly – 'for a girl. So, whenever I was ill my mother used to scrounge whatever books she could from her friends and neighbours. There was the library too, of course, but even the penny rate was a bit high for my parents sometimes. A penny could buy quite a bit of food off the market stalls when they were packing up at the end of the day.'

'I'll see what I can find to take him,' Molly promised. 'My mam's always believed in learning for both me and William. She was very fair in that, never making me feel left out or that education mattered more for William than it did for me. And she loves reading herself.'

Molly was already feeling excited about the trip to see Harry. She just hoped he wouldn't be too disappointed to see her and not Queenie.

She packed a parcel for him from her family, putting love in with every piece. Mabel gave her a scarf she'd just finished.

'I know he won't be going out much, but maybe the hospital wheel them outdoors and winter's only just around the corner. I've made a fruit cake you can take. It'll keep well and he can share it with the other patients. Oh, poor lad,' she moaned. 'I feel for him. I do hope he can overcome it. Have you told Queenie you're going to see him?'

Molly shook her head. 'I daren't.'

'You do realize, don't you, that this could end your friendship with her?' Mabel said and then looked Molly straight in the face. 'But who do you care the most about, Queenie – or Harry?'

'Harry,' Molly said without a moment's hesitation.

Mabel smiled pensively. 'There you are, then,' she said. 'I think you've got your answer. But I do think you should tell her that the Spencers have asked you to go with them.'

Molly said nothing, but knew her mother was right.

Molly missed the letters from Ben but she still heard regularly from Tom and, of course, shared those from William too. Just before the planned visit to Aldershot, another letter arrived from Tom. The first page was full of enquiries about Harry and reassuring her that he and William were fine and still together.

> *We've moved north now and guess what? William's been made a lance corporal. I expect he'll tell you himself so don't let on to your mam and dad until he does. It's great being best pals with an officer, even if it is a non-commissioned position. I get a lot of ribbing from the other lads, but it's mostly good-natured and I can handle that.*

I bet you can, Molly thought as she folded his letter and tucked it into the dressing-table drawer where she kept all the letters she'd received from the boys at the front. You had to stand enough teasing as a young boy. This war had made Tom grow into a young man and had given him a self-confidence he'd lacked before. And, she realized suddenly, she had changed too – not only through her association with the suffragettes, but also because of her insistence on doing war work. And best of all, Queenie no longer held sway over her. She pulled in a deep breath. She would go this very minute and tell her the truth – that she was going to visit Harry whether she, Queenie, liked it or not.

''Lo, Aunty Ethel. Is Queenie at home?'
'Yes, come in. We're in the kitchen near the range. It's turned cold tonight, hasn't it?'
''Lo, Uncle Jack. I just wanted a word with Queenie. I hope you don't mind.'
'Course not, love. You're always welcome. Pull up a chair near the fire.'
'It's all right, Dad,' Queenie said, getting up. 'We'll go up to my bedroom. Girly secrets, you know,' she added with a coy smile.
Jack cleared his throat as if embarrassed by the mere thought and disappeared behind his newspaper.
'Come on, Moll,' Queenie said, leading the way upstairs.
As soon as they were alone in Queenie's room, Molly asked, 'Have you heard from Harry?'
'No, but I expect he finds it very difficult to write.' Her tone hardened a little as she added, 'Have you heard something?'
'Not really, but I just wanted to be sure that you definitely don't want to visit him. His parents are

going next week and they've asked me to go with them if you don't want to. I think they want the company of a younger person on the trip. Mrs Spencer says they've never travelled far on their own and are a bit nervous. But if you want to go, Queenie, I'll willingly step aside.'

Queenie stared at her. 'You? Why should you go to see him?'

'I'm friends with him, just as I was with Ben.'

Queenie's lip curled. 'Oh, nothing like you were with Ben, Moll. We all know what really went on between you two.'

Molly sighed and shook her head. 'I just don't understand why no one will believe that we were just friends. Very good friends, but only friends and nothing more.'

'Well, you should know why no one believes you. You're a liar, we all know that.'

Molly's mouth dropped open and she stared at Queenie, who ticked the points off on her fingers. 'It was you who damaged the pillar box, wasn't it? Twice, if I remember correctly. I wouldn't be surprised if you didn't have something to do with that fire that was started deliberately at Red House. And it was definitely you who put those white feathers through the letterboxes and caused Harry and the others to volunteer. You hadn't even the courage to hand them out face to face with young fellas not in uniform, like I did. And now you're making yourself out to be something special by working in munitions. Oh, you've got a lot to answer for, Molly Wyngate, and don't think I don't know what you're up to.' She stood up and thrust her face close to Molly's. 'You want Harry for yourself now that Ben's gone, don't you? Well, you won't manage it. I'm his *fiancée* and he'll never even give you the time of day while I'm around . . .'

'You're wrong, Queenie. I would never do anything like that.'

'Oh yes, you would. You've ditched me in favour of that ugly cow, Olive Mason, and now I know just what you're up to with Harry. Sucking up to his parents so that they take you with them to see him. You don't deceive me. I've known you too long.'

'You're so wrong, Queenie, about all of it. Why are you saying all these horrible things to me? I thought we were friends. Best friends.'

'Not any more, Moll.'

Tears were streaming down her face as Molly stumbled to the door and downstairs. She rushed through the kitchen without even speaking to Ethel or Jack. She was sobbing as she felt her way down the jitty and turned towards her home.

'Mam, oh Mam . . .' she wailed as she threw herself into Mabel's arms.

'Oh, my dear girl, is there more bad news? Here, sit down.'

Molly fell into a chair and cried even harder. 'Queenie's fallen out with me. She – she said some horrible things.'

Little by little, between sobs, Molly poured out all that Queenie had said to her.

'Molly, love,' Mabel said quietly, 'she's not worth your tears. I've had my suspicions about her for some time. She began to alter when she started walking out with Harry but even before that, she showed signs of' – Mabel paused, searching for the right word – 'it wasn't exactly bullying, but it was controlling. She was always the one in charge, now wasn't she? You did whatever she wanted, even' – she added with a sigh – 'when it came to which brother you were friends with. She decided she wanted Harry, so that was it. You tagged along on the sidelines when we both know that really you would have liked to walk out with him yourself. I didn't interfere because you seemed – well, if not happy, then prepared to go along with it, but don't think I didn't notice.'

Molly sniffed miserably. 'But we were best friends. I thought we'd be friends for ever like – like you and Aunty Ethel. Oh,' she exclaimed and her eyes widened, 'oh Mam, is this going to ruin your friendship with Aunty Ethel?'

'Don't worry, love. Our friendship has altered over the years too. She's grown away from me. She's always had grand ideas and she's fostered them in Queenie. She's spoilt her. That girl is selfish and self-centred. I pity the man who marries her because she puts on an act when she's working on getting her own way and then, when she's got what she wants, she alters. I pity poor Harry if he does marry her.'

'But will she marry him now?' Molly murmured. 'She's refusing to go and see him and I'm so afraid that she won't want to care for him properly when he comes home.' Molly shook her head. 'I just don't understand her. One minute she's telling me she's going to finish it with him, the next that he's her fiancé. I just don't know where I am with her. And now this . . .'

Mabel said nothing.

Forty-three

'Oh Molly, I'm so glad you've come with us,' Harriet said as they settled into their seats on the train. 'I don't know what we'd have done without you making all the arrangements. I wouldn't know where to start, would you, Luke?'

Luke smiled at Molly. 'No, I wouldn't, and it's good to have you with us, Molly, love. Harry will be glad to see you.'

'It should be Queenie sitting here, though,' Molly said quietly. 'I think he's going to be so disappointed it's not her.'

'We'll see,' Luke said, but the smile never left his face.

When they reached the hospital and found the right ward, there were still ten minutes until visiting time started. The sister in charge of the ward said, 'Only two at a time to each bed, I'm afraid, or we get far too many visitors in the ward at once. And please keep the noise to a minimum. There are still some very sick patients on this ward.'

'We're here to see Harry Spencer?' Luke said. 'Can you tell us how he is?'

The sister's stern face suddenly relaxed as she smiled. 'He's doing nicely now. He was, of course, very ill at first, as I think you must realize, but he's a bit of a lad, isn't he? Flirts with all the nurses . . .' She glanced at Molly. 'Oh, I'm sorry, are you his girlfriend?'

Molly shook her head. 'No, just a good friend.'

The sister glanced at her watch. 'You can go in. Just say "hello" and then one of you must come out and you can take it in turns. He's in the bed at the far end.' She chuckled. 'I think the nurses have their favourites and he's been given a lovely position near the window, especially as he can't walk yet.'

'Will he ever walk again, Sister?' Luke asked.

'Oh my goodness, yes. He's got a lot of willpower, your son. Never fear, he'll do a lot better than most.'

Harry was leaning back against his pillow, his eyes closed. His skin was grey and he looked much thinner. Harriet gasped. He didn't look as if he was 'doing nicely', as the sister had said. Not to his mother's eyes. As the three of them stood around the bed, he must have become aware of their presence. His eyes opened and then he blinked once or twice.

'Am I seeing things?'

'No, son, we're really here,' Luke said.

'Mam . . .' he whispered hoarsely as Harriet bent to kiss his cheek. Harry clasped her hand. 'Sorry I can't get up.' He turned his head and caught sight of Molly standing quietly at the end of the bed. 'Oh Molly, you're here too. How lovely.'

She searched his face for the faintest sign of disappointment, but there was nothing. His smile was genuine as he held out his hand towards her. After a moment's hesitation, she took it. 'I'm sorry,' she began, 'that it's me and not—'

'Don't. Don't say it. I'm so very glad to see you.' His face clouded as he glanced around at the three of them. 'How – how are you all coping with the news about poor Ben?'

'I think "coping" is the right word,' Luke said. 'We're just so very thankful that you're still with us. It would really have been unbearable to lose both of you.'

'I was right next to him, Dad, and there was nothing I could do. I feel so guilty . . .'

'Then you mustn't,' Harriet said firmly. 'Like your dad says, we've still got you. And I'll give thanks for that every day for the rest of my life.'

'But I'm never going to be the man I was, am I?'

The words burst from Molly's lips before she could stop them. 'But you're still the Harry we all love.' She felt him squeeze her hand. 'A head wound that might have taken the real you would have been so much harder to bear. What's a leg in comparison?' She forced a cheeky grin. 'You've got another one and they're doing wonders with prosthetic limbs now. I've been reading about it and besides, the place where I'm still training – the Technical Institute – they're going to have longer courses to train wounded soldiers who can't go back to the front. So, don't think you're going to live in idleness, because you're not.'

'Oh Molly, you're so strong. How I've missed your common sense. Don't ever change, will you?'

A nurse came down the ward. 'Sorry, only two visitors to a bed.'

'Oh sorry, we forgot,' Molly said hurriedly. 'I'll go out and come back for the last half an hour, if that'd be all right.'

She gave Harry's hand a quick squeeze and reluctantly pulled herself free. As she passed down the ward, the nurse stopped her. 'I'm sorry to have to turn you out for a while, but Sister is very strict on the rules. Look, there's a lad over there halfway down the ward who doesn't get any visitors. Go and have a word with him. I'll introduce you, if you like.'

'All right,' Molly said and followed her towards the young man sitting up in bed and watching the door into the ward hopefully.

'Toby, this is Molly. She's come to see Harry, but his parents are here too and you know the rules. Would you like to chat to her while she waits her turn?'

He turned to look at her and his face lit up. Molly smiled back. The young soldier reminded her poignantly of Ben, with short curly hair and kind eyes.

'That'd be great, pet,' he said in an accent she didn't recognize. 'Ah'm from Newcastle, see, and my mam can't get here easy. She's on her own now, like. I'm hoping they'll send me closer to home as soon as they can.' He smiled timidly. 'I keep watching the door, hoping to see her walk through it, even though I know it's not likely.'

'It's nice to meet you, Toby,' she said as she sat down. 'What happened to you, then?'

For the next half an hour they chatted and soon Toby's laughter was ringing through the ward. When the nurse returned to say that Luke was leaving the ward so that Molly might have the remainder of the visiting time with Harry, she said, 'You must be good for him. I've never heard Toby laugh like that before.'

'She's a bonnie lass, nurse,' he said, with a grin. 'I wish she was my girl and not old Harry's. I'll have to have words with him.'

'It's been nice talking to you,' Molly said, laughing as she got up. 'I hope you soon feel a lot better and can get nearer home.'

'Well, there's one good thing. I won't be going back to the front. When I do get home, it'll be for good. Thanks again for talking to me. You're a kind lass as well as a bonnie one.'

Molly smiled weakly. It was the first time she could remember anyone describing her as 'bonnie'. But it was a nice feeling, even if she didn't quite believe it. Perhaps the poor lad's eyesight had been affected.

'So, what did young Toby have to say?' Harry asked as she sat down beside him.

'Oh, just about his home and his mam. Doesn't sound as if he's got a dad.'

'He hasn't. He's a bit like poor old Tom. He's all his mother's got.'

'Then I'm glad he's going home to her.'

'So, tell me all about the work you're doing now. I'm very proud of you, Molly.'

Harriet sat on the other side of the bed, listening quietly while, for the remainder of the time, Molly told him all about her training and the various machines she was learning how to operate.

'My word,' Harry said, 'you'll be able to get a job at The Brush soon.'

When it came time for them to leave, Molly realized that not once had Harry mentioned Queenie. And nor had she.

Knowing that the trip to see Harry would be emotional and tiring, Molly had arranged with Mr Owen to take an extra day off. When she arrived downstairs about mid-morning she found Mabel standing in the middle of the kitchen with an unopened letter in her hand, just staring at it.

'Molly,' she said, 'I've got this letter and I don't recognize the handwriting. I don't know who it's from.'

'Well, open it and find out.'

'I – I daren't. It might be bad news.'

'Give it here.'

Molly tore open the letter and read it quickly.

'What is it? Is – is it bad news?'

'Yes and no. It's from a girl – a nurse – called Louise Dodds. She's nursing William, who has had a bullet wound to his right hand so she's writing for him.'

'Oh no!' Mabel breathed, her eyes wide and staring. 'He's been injured.'

'Yes, Mam, but she assures us it's nothing serious. He's in a hospital behind the lines but' – Molly pulled a face – 'as soon as he's well enough, he will have to go back to the front.'

Mother and daughter stared at each other, a turmoil of emotions running through them. At last Mabel said, 'Yes, of course. Where is he? Can we go and see him?'

Molly shook her head. 'He's not in England. The hospital is in France.'

Mabel groaned. 'Oh, this wretched war. When will it be over?'

Molly wrote back to the nurse thanking her for her kindness and asking if she would be good enough to keep them informed of William's progress. Louise wrote once more to say that William had recovered and had been discharged and was on his way back to the front.

Molly didn't know whether to be happy that he hadn't been severely injured and had already recovered, or terrified because he was returning to the war zone.

It was several weeks before Harriet heard that Harry was to be sent to a local hospital.

'He's been very lucky. There have been several beds allocated for military use in Loughborough Hospital and he's been given one,' she told Molly. 'It'll be so much easier to go to see him, but I have no idea when we'll actually be able to have him home.'

Although she said nothing to Harriet, Molly was determined to persuade Queenie to visit him. Molly was nothing if not fair-minded. She wanted to do what was right for Harry and even though Queenie hadn't been mentioned when she'd visited him in hospital, she was convinced he must want to see his girlfriend. Perhaps talking about her had been too painful, so he had avoided the subject altogether. She had seen little of Queenie over recent weeks. They no longer met up to walk home together after work, partly because their hours no longer coincided, but Molly had the uncomfortable feeling that Queenie didn't want to meet up with her. She had to accept that their spat was serious and terminal to their friendship.

After work one evening she walked down to the Palmers' house.

'Is Queenie in, Aunty Ethel?' she asked when the door was opened in answer to her knock.

'Er, no. She's – um – out with a friend.'

'It's just that Mrs Spencer has heard that Harry is to be brought to the Loughborough Hospital and I thought it would be so much easier for Queenie to visit him.'

'Er – oh – yes, I suppose it would. Look, Molly, you'd better know the truth. Queenie won't be seeing Harry anymore. She doesn't want to marry a cripple and I agree with her.'

'I see,' Molly said tightly. 'Has she told Harry?'

'Yes, she's written to him.'

'When? When did she write?'

'After you got back from seeing him.'

'Not before we went?'

'Oh no. It was definitely after.'

Molly nodded. 'Well, that's that, then. There's no more to be said really, is there?'

'No, Molly, there isn't.'

As Ethel began to close the door, Molly said, 'Mam sent her regards. She hasn't seen you lately.'

Ethel stared at her for a moment before saying, 'No, I know. It's – difficult now. But tell her – tell her I'm still her friend. I'll always be her friend.'

Forty-four

Molly returned home in a brooding mood. She couldn't understand the meaning behind Ethel's final words and even Mabel couldn't think what she'd meant.

'I haven't seen much of her recently, I have to admit. I suppose our friendship has sort of followed you and Queenie's and you two aren't close anymore, are you?'

Molly sighed. 'It began to fade when Queenie started walking out with Harry. Just like you warned me it would.'

'And then it seemed to get worse when you were accused of posting white feathers through young men's letterboxes.'

Molly nodded. 'Yes, I was hurt at the time that Queenie didn't believe me – that she didn't stick up for me. Anyway, that's all over now, thank goodness. And the boys seem to believe Tom that it wasn't me, which is really all I care about.'

Mabel was thoughtful. 'Tom knows the truth, doesn't he? But he's refused to tell them who he saw.'

For a long moment, Molly stared at her mother. 'Oh Mam,' she whispered, 'how stupid am I?'

Mabel frowned. 'What d'you mean?'

Molly thought for a moment before saying slowly,

A Woman of Spirit

'Just after the incident about the pillar box, Queenie told me she'd had to throw away one of her skirts because she'd got a stain on it that wouldn't wash out.'

'Yes, I remember that because I thought it such a waste. Go on.'

'Could it – could it have been – ink?'

Mabel nodded slowly, her expression grim. 'It could indeed.'

'And – and . . .' Molly was even more hesitant. 'If she could do that and let me take the blame, then she could have been the one delivering those white feathers. I mean, I saw her handing them out in the park. But would she *really* do something like that and then let me – who's supposed to be her best friend – take the blame?'

Mabel sniffed derisively. 'I wouldn't put anything past that young woman. You were such good friends as children, but she's changed as you've got older. Queenie's very selfish and just look at what she's doing now. She's ending her romance with Harry because he's been wounded in a war that she probably encouraged him to enlist for.'

In a small voice Molly said, 'She said something dreadful when I went to see her after we'd first heard about his injury.'

'What?'

'That – that it would have been better if he'd been killed like Ben and then everyone would have felt sorry for her.'

'You see – you see. It's all about *her*. Not a thought for poor Harry and how he'll have to live out the rest of his life. No intention of being at his side to love and care for him.'

There was silence between them before Molly said slowly, 'I wonder now if Harry has had an inkling all along. Was that why he didn't propose when he came home on leave? Why he didn't buy her a ring? And when we went to see him in hospital, he never mentioned her. Not once. I thought that it was because she hadn't gone to see him and he was upset and trying to hide it. But now – I wonder.'

'Didn't he mention her at *all*?'

'No, although he wanted to know about everyone else we know.'

'But he didn't know then that she was ending their relationship, did he?'

'No. Aunty Ethel said she wrote to him just after we'd been to see him. So, no, he didn't know when we were there.'

'Well, if we're right – but I don't suppose we'll ever find out the truth – I think the lad has had a lucky escape.'

'Harry's going to be brought to Loughborough Hospital in about a week's time. He's written to tell me,' Harriet said when Mabel answered her knock. 'Please will you tell Molly? He's asking for her to go to see him, if she will.'

'Come in a minute, Harriet, if you've time.'

Harriet smiled. 'Oh, I've time, Mabel, if it's to do with my boy. She will go, won't she?'

'Of course she'll go. She's very fond of Harry.'

'I hope so. He's going to need all the friends he

can get, especially now that little madam has thrown him over.'

'Is he very cut up about it?'

Harriet frowned. 'D'you know, strangely he's not. I thought he'd be devastated because they were inseparable at one time. Me and Luke really thought there was going to be a wedding. We were surprised when they didn't announce their engagement when he came home on leave that time.' She pulled a face. 'I think Queenie was too, judging by her display of hysterics at the railway station.'

'Look, Harriet, maybe I shouldn't be telling you this, so I'm asking you to keep this to yourself.'

'Of course, I will, Mabel. Go on.'

For the next half an hour, Mabel told her all that she and Molly had suspected about the desecration of the pillar box and then about the delivery of the white feathers, ending, 'Tom knows who it was who delivered those feathers but he won't say and, although I respect him for that, it leads me to believe that the reason for his silence is because it's someone we all know.'

'It would explain a lot of things,' Harriet said slowly. 'Especially if Harry thought it was Queenie.'

The two women looked at each other as Mabel said softly, 'It would, wouldn't it?'

'But I respect your confidence, Mabel. I won't say a word to anyone, not even to Luke.'

'I'd be grateful. I haven't said anything to Ron about our suspicions.'

'Best keep it between ourselves, then, particularly when we really haven't any proof.'

'Queenie and Molly aren't as friendly as they used to be. In fact, they've had a big fall-out and that has rather put a distance between me and Ethel too. Oh, we've had our differences of opinion – always have had – but the friendship was strong. At least, I thought it was.'

Harriet squeezed her arm. 'Well, you've got me and Alice. And Ruby too, now. You can pop round to see us any time you want. We'll always be pleased to see you.' She didn't add, although she was thinking it, that she had never taken to Ethel in the same way she liked Mabel. She thought Ethel believed herself a bit above her neighbours. 'And now I must go. We're hoping Harry will be home soon and we're turning the front parlour into a downstairs room for him. It'll be like a bed-sitting room where he can have friends visit.'

It was the custom in many such households that the front parlour was only used on Sundays and special occasions like Christmas. 'High days and holidays,' Mabel always called it. But now there was a good reason for the room to be used all the time.

'I do hope Molly will visit him,' Harriet said as she left.

'Oh, she will.' Mabel beamed. 'I can promise you that. You'll likely get sick of seeing her on your doorstep.'

'No,' Harriet said seriously, 'I never would.'

Letters still arrived from William and Tom and it seemed as if they were both making the effort to write more frequently now that there were only the two of them.

We're still together, Tom wrote to Molly. *I thought we might get separated when William was in hospital, but he's back here now, thank goodness. The weather's getting colder so please tell your mam to keep knitting. Her socks are a godsend. We've heard we're to undergo yet more training, but at least we'll be away from the front line for a while. By the way, I don't know if Olive has told you but we're still writing to each other. She's a lovely girl and it's so nice to have someone waiting for you back home when all this is over . . .*

Olive had told her and asked a little nervously if Molly minded.

'Mind?' Molly had said, linking her arm through her friend's as they walked to the corner where they went their separate ways. 'Of course I don't. I'm delighted for you both.'

'But he was your friend, I . . .'

'Olive,' Molly said firmly, 'why can no one understand that boys and girls can be true friends? It's ridiculous that you only have to speak to a boy and everyone gets the idea you're walking out with them. Tom and I are good friends and I hope we always will be. Just like you and me are, I hope.'

'Oh yes, definitely,' Olive said with a big grin on her face.

A week later, Queenie arrived at the Wyngates' home.

'I'm not coming in,' she said, when Molly opened the door.

'I wasn't going to ask you,' Molly said. She folded her arms across her chest and stood like many women did when they were about to have a barney with a neighbour. 'What d'you want?'

'I've just come to tell you that I've been to see Harry in hospital now he's so much closer and we've made up. He understood why I hadn't been to see him because I was so terribly upset. We've sorted everything out and we're back together, so there's no need for you to go to see him anymore. He has me.'

Molly felt tears prickle the back of her eyes and the lump in her throat felt as if it would choke her.

With a supreme effort, Molly managed to say, 'I'm pleased to hear it. I only want what's best for both of you.'

And with that, Molly shut the door before Queenie had time to say any more. She leaned against it and allowed the tears to fall. After a few moments on her own, she pulled in a deep breath, wiped her eyes and went back into the kitchen.

'Who was that at the door?' Mabel asked warily. Visitors to front doors in their street were rare and usually heralded officialdom in some form.

'Queenie.'

'Queenie? Whatever did she want?'

'To tell me that Harry's arrived at the local hospital and that they are back together. She – she said there's no need for me to go and see him anymore. What she really meant was "Stay away. He's mine".'

Molly was suddenly reminded of what Queenie had said years earlier when they'd first started to meet up with the two brothers. 'Harry's mine, so keep your hands off,' and from that moment on Queenie had monopolized him.

Mabel gave one of her famous snorts of derision. 'Don't take any notice of that little madam. Harriet says he wants to see you, so you go.'

'That was before they'd made up. It might be different now.'

Mabel shrugged. 'You'd better do what you think best, then. What about you and her? Are you friends again too?'

Molly pulled a face. 'I didn't give her the chance to get that far. Besides, if she's anything like she was before when they were – they were courting, I won't be seeing much of her anyway.'

'That's true,' Mabel said.

Molly was still frowning in thought. 'I am surprised, though. About them getting back together, I mean.'

Mabel was quiet for a few moments before saying slowly, 'So why has Queenie changed her mind?' She paused, sighed and then said, 'Let's just leave it for now and see what happens, eh? Time can often resolve things better than we can.'

Molly put her arms around her mother. 'You're so wise, Mam. I hope I'm like you one day.'

'Harry's home now,' Ruby told Mabel when she called round to see her at the beginning of December. 'He's going to have a temporary prosthetic leg because they have to wait for the stump to heal properly and any swelling to go down before they can fit a permanent one. No one knows exactly how long that's going to be. I expect it varies from patient to patient. Harriet's going to be busy, but the front room was all ready for him.'

'I'll call round to see her and ask if there's anything I can do to help.'

'I've already offered and she says she's sure there will be, but she's had that many offers of help from all her neighbours in the street, she's overwhelmed. I think, more than anything, she wants to know that there'll be plenty of visitors for Harry.'

'I'm sure there will be. He was always popular among his own age group and everyone likes the family as a whole. Oh, he'll not go short of visitors.'

'Molly, aren't you going to see Harry?' Mabel asked one evening after tea when Ron had gone out to meet his pals at the pub.

Molly hesitated. 'I'd like to, but Queenie warned me off. I don't want to bump into her.'

'You could go round on a Saturday afternoon. She wouldn't be there then as the shops are still open. She works until about six, doesn't she?'

'I could,' Molly said doubtfully. She was sure that Harry wouldn't be bothered about her visits, not now that he had his fiancée visiting him and no doubt a lot of his pals, at least those who were not still overseas. Sadly, there were several fewer than there had once been when they were all youngsters together.

'Well, I'm going to go round myself and find out exactly what's been happening. You've got a face like a wet week most of the time. Even Ruby said the other day that Olive's quite worried about you.'

Molly smiled. 'Olive's a good friend, Mam. She's

open and honest. A bit too blunt sometimes perhaps, but at least you know where you stand with her.'

'I prefer folk like that,' Mabel said. 'Right, I'm off round to Harriet's. You coming?'

Molly was tempted but shook her head. 'No, Mam. She might be there.'

Mabel didn't have to ask who her daughter meant.

Forty-five

'Where is she? Where's Molly? Why hasn't she been to see me? Is she ill?'

'My word, Harry,' Mabel said as Harriet led her into their front room. 'That's a barrage of questions.'

'Sorry, Mrs Wyngate, but I've been so worried about her. I thought she'd come to see me as soon as I got home. I know coming to the hospital was difficult because the visiting hours didn't fit in with her working hours, but . . .'

'Sit down, Mabel,' Harriet said. 'Harry, let her catch her breath and have a cuppa before you bombard her with questions. Mind you, Mabel, I've been concerned about her myself. You told me she'd never be off our doorstep once he came home, yet we haven't seen hide nor hair of her. I'd've come round to yours to find out, but . . .' she smiled and nodded her head towards her son. 'I've been a bit busy getting him settled and sorting out a routine for us all.'

'I can understand that,' Mabel murmured and sipped her tea. 'Do you need any help, Harriet, because I hope you know you only have to ask?'

'That's very kind, but I have to say, what with Alice and Ruby and one or two others down our street, we're not short of willing hands.'

'Everyone's being so kind,' Harry said quietly. 'It's very humbling, to tell you the truth. But please tell me about Molly. Is something wrong?'

'Nothing physically. She's fine, but she's a bit upset. Her and Queenie have had a big fall-out and Queenie told her to stay away from you now that you and she are back together.'

Harry stared at her and she heard Harriet give a little gasp.

'Back together? She told Molly that?'

'Yes. You're engaged now, aren't you?'

Harry pulled himself up in the bed. 'No, we are not,' he roared, making Mabel jump so suddenly that her cup rattled in its saucer. 'I've not seen her ever since I was injured, nor do I want to. Not now.'

'But she wrote to you, didn't she? When you were in hospital in Aldershot and broke off your – erm – romance, but made up with you when you got back to Loughborough hospital. That's what she told Molly.'

Harry was staring straight at Mabel and shaking his head very slowly. 'Yes, she did write to me then, just once, but I've not seen or heard from her since. And we're certainly not back together. So, will you please tell Molly that I want to see her more than anything? I want to be there for her about Ben. She must be heartbroken to lose him.'

'Yes, she is. They were good friends.'

'Friends? It was a lot more than that, wasn't it? Queenie said they were walking out together. She said that Molly was talking about them getting married once the war was over.'

Now it was Mabel who shook her head. 'No, it was you and Queenie who were going to do that.'

Harry was quiet for a moment before saying slowly, 'Maybe once upon a time, I might have thought about it. When we first got friendly – the four of us – we had some good times. Walking in the park on a Sunday afternoon. Listening to the band. Going to the fair and theatre. At that time, Queenie was bright and bubbly and fun to be with but' – he paused and then went on slowly – 'I suppose it was after Molly got involved with the suffragettes . . . Oh, I don't know. I'm not very good at this analysis stuff. Perhaps you ladies can work it out, but Queenie changed.'

Mabel nodded. 'I know what you mean. Molly first got involved with the suffragist movement because she was being left on her own so much when Queenie was out with you. But that was natural,' she hastened on, not wanting Harry to think he was to blame.

'But Queenie said the opposite,' he said slowly. 'That between seeing Ben – and she implied that they were walking out together – and the suffragette meetings, Molly hadn't time for her any more. From that very first time we went walking in the park, she said, let's leave them to it. Molly's got a "thing" for Ben.'

Mabel stared at the young man. How blind men could be sometimes, she thought, but it was not her place to tell him where Molly's true feelings lay. That must come from the girl herself when – and if – the time was right.

'I have to talk to her. Please, Mrs Wyngate, ask her to come and see me.'

'Now, take it easy, son,' Harriet said, 'Don't go blundering in with your size nines.'

Harry laughed ruefully and called upon his black sense of humour. 'Size nine, Mam. Just the one now.'

'He wants to see you, Molly. There's no doubt about that.'

'But Queenie said—'

'Never you mind what she said. You go and talk to Harry face to face. He's told me some things today—' She stopped short.

'What things, Mam?'

But Mabel shook her head. 'You should hear it from Harry himself.' She pressed her lips together as if to stop them saying things of their own accord.

'Okay. I'll go now. Right this minute.'

Molly's heart was thumping as Harriet showed her into the room. His single bed had been placed near the window so that he could look out on to the street and wave to passers-by. Molly's arms were full of gifts to welcome him home. She paused on the threshold as she watched his face for his reaction. He looked pale and tired, she thought, but her heart lifted when he sat up beaming at her.

'I didn't know it was my birthday and it's not quite Christmas yet. Come in, Molly. It's good to see you. Thank you for coming.'

'I've brought you some chocolates and a few books. My dad loves reading and he's lending you these. He said he thought you'd like them better than my mam's slushy romances.'

'That's very kind, but please don't bring me too many chocolates because I'll eat far too many.'

'That's what I'd hoped you'd do.'

'Ah, but you see, I must be careful not to put on too much weight. I'm hopefully going to get an artificial leg eventually and the doc said they'll want my stump to stay the same size.'

'Oh, I'm sorry. I didn't realize . . .'

'No, of course you didn't. Trouble is,' his grin broadened, 'I love chocolate and would eat them all. I shall certainly enjoy these before I have to have a fitting.'

'I don't think you need to worry, Harry,' his mother said, who was straightening his bedclothes and plumping his pillows. 'You look like you have lost a lot of weight to me. It wouldn't hurt you to put a bit back on. You'll need to build up your strength for when you start hopping about.'

Molly drew in a breath. She was amazed how open – almost blunt – they were both being about his injury. But then, she supposed, it was the best way to deal with it. Confront the facts head on.

'Army grub, Mam. It's be great to be back to home cooking.'

Harriet turned to Molly. 'He's already able to get about on two crutches. It was great to see him come into the house on his own two feet.'

Harry guffawed. 'One foot and a crutch, Mam. Let's be honest here.'

'I've got a bit of news, although maybe you already know,' Molly said.

Immediately, they both looked alarmed and stared

at her. Realizing that 'news' these days often meant something dreadful had happened, she said hastily, 'Oh, it's good news. We've had a letter from William to say that he and Tom have got leave together and it's a long enough time for them to get all the way home.'

She didn't say that she'd also heard the news from Tom in his regular fortnightly letter to her. That they were writing to each other was still a secret from anyone other than her own parents.

Harry punched his right fist into the palm of his left hand. 'Oh, now that *is* good news, Molly. When will they be here?'

'By the weekend, I think.'

'Please ask William to come and see me, won't you?'

Molly giggled. Already her heart was lighter than it had been since she'd heard he'd been wounded. Seeing how he was dealing with the personal tragedy with such courage had given her real hope for him. Harry would be all right. With his family and friends around him he would build a life for himself. And, of course, now he had his fiancée back too. It would not be the life he had planned, but it would still be worth living. 'I don't think you'd be able to keep him away.'

'I wouldn't want to, Molly. Nor you. I hope you'll come round whenever you can, although I do realize you're doing a very important job now.'

'Of course I will, if you really want to see me.'

'Yes, of course I do.' He stared at her for some moments before saying softly, 'You are looking a bit tired though. Are you working too hard?'

'No more than anyone else.'

'Are the other girls there nice?' Harriet asked. 'Have you made any friends? I know about Olive, of course. She's still working with you, isn't she?'

'They're all great, and yes, Olive and me are still good friends.'

Suddenly, the spectre of Queenie seemed to be in the room. Harriet heaved herself up while saying, 'If you'll excuse me, I must get your dad's tea started. You stay as long as you want, Molly, love.'

When she'd left the room, Harry cleared his throat. 'Why haven't you been to see me since I came home, Molly? You promised you would. Mam said you'd threatened you'd never be off the doorstep. I'd've liked that. So, what happened?'

'Queenie,' she said simply.

Harry frowned. 'What has she got to do with you coming to see me?'

'Well, you're back together, aren't you? Engaged, she said, and – and—'

She stopped when she saw Harry's frown. 'I haven't seen Queenie since I was home on leave that time. She used to write to me but I've not heard from her since I was wounded, except that one letter to say it was all over between us. So, we're not back together and certainly not engaged.' He paused and then asked harshly, 'Is that what she's been saying?'

Numbly, Molly nodded and whispered, 'She – she told me to keep away.'

'Did she now?' Harry said softly, his gaze never leaving Molly's face. 'And will you?'

'Not if you want me to visit you, I won't.'

'I want you to come and see me as often as you can spare the time.'

'All right.' She paused and then added, 'I tried to persuade her to come to see you in Aldershot and then when you got to Loughborough, but she said she'd written to you and ended things between you.' She forbore to say what Ethel had said; that would have been too cruel. She would never tell anyone that other than her own mother. 'But recently she said she'd been to see you in Loughborough Hospital, and that you understood why she couldn't face coming to see you before, and that everything was all right between you again and that – that you'd got engaged.'

'I never heard from her at all after I was wounded until that one letter. She never came to see me in the local hospital and she's not been round here since I've been home. To be honest I'm not that bothered about her. There are things—' He stopped suddenly. 'Well, never mind about that now. But just tell me I won't lose your friendship, Molly.'

Molly smiled genuinely. Oh, if only you knew, Harry, she thought but managed to say quite steadily, 'You won't. Queenie and I are not as close as we once were. Our lives have gone in different directions, ever since I joined the suffragettes, I suppose. At first, Queenie seemed keen too but then, when she started walking out with you, she lost interest in the movement.' She laughed. 'Understandable, really. She much preferred to be with you.'

'And now she's lost interest in me, but that's understandable too after what's happened to me.'

'No, it isn't,' Molly shot back hotly. 'If you truly

love someone, you don't desert them when they need you the most.'

Harry stared at her. 'Poor old Ben,' he said suddenly. 'I'm so sorry he didn't come back to you, Molly. Are you truly heartbroken?'

'Harry, I keep telling everyone that I loved Ben dearly, but as a friend or even a brother. The same way I love William, but we were not, and I don't think we ever would have been, romantically involved. Please believe me. I'm devastated we have lost him, but he was not the love of my life.'

'And is there someone who is "the love of your life"?'

Molly's heart seemed to turn over in her chest, but with a supreme effort she smiled and managed to say flippantly, 'Now, now, Harry Spencer, you're getting far too inquisitive.' She stood up. 'I must be going. I'm at work early tomorrow morning, but I'll come and see you again soon. I expect you've got the whole street queuing up to visit you. Especially the girls,' she added impishly. 'And you'll have William and Tom home at the weekend.'

'Folk are very kind. Mam says she's had a stream of visitors leaving little gifts for me ever since they knew I was coming home.'

'Yes, they are good. The neighbours have all been supporting one another. It's good to see how the community has become even closer since the war started.'

As she moved towards the door she wiggled her fingers in a wave.

'Now, just a minute, Molly Wyngate, you don't get

away that easily.' He tapped his cheek with his finger. 'I want a kiss right here.'

Molly felt the colour flooding her face, but she laughed and moved towards him. As she bent to peck his cheek, he gently held her chin so their faces were close together.

'You're a good 'un, Molly,' he whispered huskily. 'You will come again, won't you? As often as you can.'

'Of course I will. Now, you do as your mam tells you and get yourself stronger. I want to see you up and walking on your new leg. Promise?'

'I promise.'

Forty-six

The arrival home of William and Tom caused great excitement in their respective streets.

William showed off his injured hand to his family and pulled a face as he said, 'I know I should be thankful it wasn't more serious, but I could have done with a "blighty" wound that would have kept me out of the war. Mind you, I wouldn't have wanted one like poor old Harry, so I suppose I should be grateful.'

'There's no "poor old Harry" about it,' Molly said tartly. 'Don't you dare visit him with that attitude, William Wyngate, or you'll have me to deal with.'

William blinked and then raised his eyebrows, while Mabel and Ron hid their smiles as Molly went on. 'He's to have an artificial leg fitted soon and then you'll see. He'll be up on his own two feet.'

'I had a letter from him,' William said. 'He told me that he and Queenie are no longer walking out. Is that true?'

'Yes, it is. It seems she couldn't deal with his injury. She wouldn't go to the hospital to see him and she's not even been to their house since he came home. I don't see much of her now, to be honest. Our paths have gone in different directions. I'm doing war work and Queenie is working at the draper's.'

'But you can deal with seeing Harry like that, can't you?' William said softly, his gaze never leaving his sister's face. 'It sounds as if he's got a real champion in you.'

Molly avoided his scrutiny. She was afraid he would see far too much.

'Molly, I owe you an apology,' William said suddenly. 'Oh, not about white feathers this time. This is something else the war has taught me. I'm sorry I was so harsh about your interest in the suffragette movement.'

Now Molly looked at him in surprise, while Mabel and Ron exchanged a glance.

'You see,' William went on. 'I met this nurse called Louise . . .'

'Oh, the one who wrote to us?' Mabel interrupted.

William nodded. 'Yes. She was assigned to the ward I was on.' A slight tinge of red appeared in his cheeks. 'And – um – I have to admit, I rather fell for her.'

'Oh William, that's lovely,' Mabel said. 'Does she feel the same way about you?'

'I – think so.'

Molly frowned. 'But what has this got to do with me and the suffragettes?'

'Because . . .' William gave a self-deprecating smile. 'Louise is an ardent admirer. She supported Mrs Pankhurst faithfully until, at the start of the war, she did what her heroine advised her followers to do – find some way to help with the war effort. So Louise trained as a VAD nurse.' He held up his hand. 'And before any of you say anything, I am not blinded by my feelings for Louise, but she has altered my attitude towards women in general, which I now see was reprehensible. I thought them the weaker sex, less intelligent than men and far less capable of – well – anything. But if you could see what I have seen, you'd understand the reasons for my change of heart. The nurses – especially those in the field hospitals – are so courageous. They treat the most horrific injuries under actual gunfire and they never flinch. They work tirelessly, often long after their shift should have finished to care for the never-ending stream of wounded. And they're so knowledgeable . . .' Even now, William could not keep the note of surprise from his tone as he admitted that women were just as intelligent as men. His gaze caught and held his sister's. 'I was so prejudiced and bigoted, Molly, and I am truly sorry. Women deserve to be given the right to vote just as much as men. A woman's place should be exactly where she wants it to be. It should be her choice. There, now you've heard me say it.'

Molly smiled at him. 'I certainly have and I am very grateful for your honesty, William. It means a lot to me that you have had a change of heart.' Her smile widened impishly. 'Thank goodness for Louise and all her fellow nurses for more reasons than the obvious one of caring for you. Now,' she added, standing up. 'I'm just going round to see Harry. Are you up to coming with me?'

'Of course,' he said, standing up too. 'And I'll be sure to rib him as I always have done.'

'Good. Come on, then.'

*

Tom was already seated beside Harry when they arrived. He stood up at once and greeted Molly with a sly wink out of sight of the other two young men. Both he and Molly knew they had to be very careful what they said and how they acted if they still wanted to keep their correspondence with each other a secret.

Tom pretended to look closely at her. 'Are you all right, Molly? You look a bit – er – peaky?'

Molly laughed. 'I'm just tired, Tom. Work's quite hard, though it's good to be doing something useful, even though I don't like the end product.'

She glanced round at the three of them. It was good to see them together again, but it was sad that there was one missing.

Molly stayed about an hour, chatting and laughing with the three of them, happy to see that their attitude towards Harry was just what she wanted. They were teasing him like they always had and even making black-humour jokes about his injury. 'You've only got one leg for us to pull now,' Tom said.

'Well, I'll have to go,' Molly said. 'I'm at work early tomorrow and I have to get my beauty sleep.' She laughed. 'It's even more necessary now than before.'

'I'll walk out with you, Molly,' Tom said, getting up too. 'I must spend as much time with Mam as I can.' He grinned at his friends. 'I'm still a mummy's boy at heart.'

Harry and William looked a little shamefaced. 'We were horrible to you at times when we were young, Tom. I'm sorry,' Harry said.

Tom shrugged. 'To be fair, you had a point, but I think I've changed a bit.'

'You definitely have,' the other two said in unison and they all laughed.

Outside, Tom looked down at Molly. Quietly, he said, 'Well, now I know why you made it perfectly clear from the outset that there wouldn't be any romance between us.'

'What? What do you mean?'

'It's obvious. You're in love with Harry, aren't you?'

Colour flooded her face and Tom had his answer. 'Don't worry. Your secret's safe with me.'

'I'm sorry, Tom, if—' she began but he interrupted.

'Don't worry about me. I'm not nursing a broken heart, but I do like being good friends with you. Besides, as you probably know, I have Olive now.' They smiled at each other. 'We've been writing to each other. I told you, didn't I? You don't mind, do you?'

'Of course not. I'm delighted for you.' She chuckled. 'She asked me the very same thing. She's such a nice girl, Tom. She's probably my best friend now.'

'Really? What about Queenie?'

Molly sighed. 'It's a long story, Tom. Maybe I'll tell you one day. But now, I really must go.'

'Ta-ra for now, then. I'll see you again before we leave.'

'Just mind you come back safely, Tom,' she whispered and touched his arm. 'For Olive now, as well as your mam.'

The war was suddenly very real again.

*

A Woman of Spirit

The evening before William and Tom were due to travel back to France at the end of their leave, Tom crossed the road to see Harry. He found him in a sombre mood.

'I'm glad to be out of it, Tom, I have to admit, but I almost wish I was coming back with you. I feel I've deserted you and William.'

'Don't be daft. You've been lucky in a way. Oh, I know it's awful you've lost a leg, but at least you've got a future. You must be missing your brother.'

'I am.'

There was silence between them, until Harry blurted out, 'Tom, I want you to tell me something, if you will.'

Tom was suddenly wary as if he guessed what might be coming. 'Go on.'

'That white feather business. It's really important to me to know the truth. I know you said it wasn't Molly. Ben always believed it wasn't her, but—' He ran his tongue round his lips that were suddenly dry. 'If – if I say who I think it might have been and you don't deny it, then I'll know, but you won't have told me.'

Tom frowned. 'Well, I will in a way, won't I?'

Harry sighed. 'It's really important to me, Tom, and I swear I won't tell a soul. Was it – was it Queenie?'

The silence between them lengthened until Tom stood up. 'I really can't tell you, Harry,' he said in a low voice. 'Please don't ask me.'

After a moment he stuck out his hand to shake Harry's. 'I'd better be off. Mam is putting on a nice tea for my last night at home. And she's invited Olive round. You know – the girl I told you about.' Tom had confided in both William and Harry about his fledgling romance, but he'd still not told them about the letter-writing between him and Molly. He'd told Olive, but no one else. He held out his hand and looked down at Harry's upturned face. Their eyes met and there was understanding between them.

As he shook Tom's hand, Harry said seriously, 'Now, you take good care of yourself – and of William. Look out for each other, but don't stand next to one another when you're in the front-line trench. Just promise me that.'

'We'll be careful,' Tom promised him. He would dearly have loved to say more. He would have liked to ask Harry to watch out for Molly, but he knew the girl herself would not like it. He had promised to keep her secret and he would. He wondered, though, if, one day, Harry might see how she felt about him for himself.

Forty-seven

Christmas, 1916, was very different for everyone. There was hardly a household in the land where anxiety didn't spoil the festivities. It was hard to celebrate when there was little or nothing to be glad about. Already there were so many who would never come home and many more had returned maimed for life. How could anyone make merry?

The Wyngates and the Palmers didn't meet up at all this year. Mabel, Ron and Molly were invited to spend an evening with the Spencers, but of course everyone missed the young man who was no longer there. It was with some relief when the New Year dawned.

Early in January, Mr Owen called Molly and Olive to see him again.

'Here we go,' Olive muttered, as they opened the door and stepped into the room. 'We've been in all the workshops now. I expect he'll have found a placement for us.'

'Come in, ladies, come in. I have some news for you.' He shuffled some papers on his desk and regarded them over the top of his spectacles for a moment. 'We have received a request for two of our girls to make shell casings. They're desperate to find women already fully trained who can start work immediately. I understand they've been let down badly at short notice. But best of all for you both, it's here in Loughborough. At the bellfoundry. So, if you'd like to take up the positions, you can leave immediately and report for work there next Monday.' He shuffled his papers again. 'You will be met by – let me see – a Mr Palmer. Now, are you willing to accept?'

'Oh yes,' the girls chorused. 'Thank you, Mr Owen.'

Outside the room once more the two girls hugged each other. 'Won't our mams be pleased,' Olive said.

Molly giggled. 'They will, but I'm not sure about my dad. It's where he works, you know.'

Molly waited until they'd eaten, washed up the tea things and were sitting in front of the range. Ron was contentedly packing his pipe and Mabel had taken up her knitting.

'I've got something to tell you . . .' Molly began.

Before she could say any more, her mother groaned. 'Oh no. I've been dreading this day. You've been found a placement, haven't you? Where is it you're going? You said a girl was sent to Peterborough last week?'

'That's right, Mam, and before that, a couple went to Sheffield.'

'Is that where you're going?'

'No. Not nearly so far.'

'Where, then? Don't keep me in suspense, Molly, there's a dear.'

Ron had dropped his paper into his lap and was listening intently. There was not a flicker on his face indicating he might know something.

'Evidently,' Molly said slowly, 'they're in desperate need for two ready-trained turners . . .' She paused again for effect. 'At the bellfoundry.'

There was still no hint on Ron's face that he had known anything about it, but nevertheless, Molly asked, 'Did you have anything to do with this, Dad?'

'No, Molly, I didn't, I promise you.' Then he frowned. 'The only thing . . .'

'Go on,' Molly prompted.

'Well, I did happen to say to Jack that your mam was getting herself in a tizzy about the prospect of you having to go away from home, but I certainly never asked him to find you work.'

Molly chuckled. 'I believe you, Dad. Thousands wouldn't.'

Ron sat up in his chair. 'Now, look, Molly . . .'

'She's teasing you, Ron. Molly, just remember that we believed you about the pillar boxes and the white feathers, didn't we? So, you've got to believe your dad when he gives you his word he had nothing to do with it.'

'All right, then.' Molly paused and then added more seriously, 'But it won't make things awkward for you, will it, Dad? Me working there.'

'I don't think so.' Ron relaxed back into his chair. 'I'm in charge of stores – of goods in and out. I don't have much to do with the workers. That's Jack's area. Just one thing, though,' he added with a chuckle. 'I would suggest you don't call him Uncle Jack at work.'

*

The days and weeks passed and the three men – now four sometimes when Pete joined them – always met in the pub on a Saturday evening and still exchanged news about the war. Even Luke, who'd lost one son and had another maimed, still took a keen interest in the progress of events. He was very worried about the young men in the neighbourhood who were still out there, especially Tom and William. And although Harry's life would be drastically altered, at least he was alive. So many, including his younger son, were not. He wanted the whole sorry business over and done with.

'From what I can glean from Tom's letters – he's writing to Harry regularly now – they seem to be moving about a lot. They're doing long route marches but he says the weather is bitterly cold.'

'What do they need such a lot of training for? I thought they'd done all that before they even went out there.'

'I really have no idea. Perhaps Harry could tell us.'

'My guess would be that it keeps them fit and occupied when they're not in the front line,' Jack said.

'You could be right. I hadn't looked at it like that. They sometimes have to march long distances to where they're needed, so I suppose you're right about the need to be fit and healthy at all times.'

Molly visited Harry whenever she could. Little by little she began to stop feeling that it was Queenie he would rather see. She could see for herself that his face lit up when she entered the room, even when he was in what his mother called one of his "dark moods".

'You're good for him, Molly,' Harriet told her. 'He's been very down since the two lads went back. He still is. He misses the camaraderie, their banter, but you seem to be the only one here who can lift his spirits. I think it's because you don't pander to him and tiptoe around him. You give it to him straight and that's what he likes – and needs – if I'm honest.'

'Perhaps I'm a little too blunt at times.' Molly grimaced.

'No, no, you're not. You treat him as if he's perfectly normal and the loss of his leg is just a nuisance that has to be overcome. And he will overcome it, given time. He's got a fitting next week for an artificial leg. It's taken a while but his stump is almost fully healed.'

'That is good news. Am I supposed to know?'

'Of course. But even that doesn't seem to have buoyed him up today. Anyway, in you go and see him.'

Molly smiled as she entered his room, but there was no answering smile on Harry's face. He was sitting staring out of the window and didn't even look towards her.

'I hear you'll soon be able to take me dancing at the town hall,' Molly said as she moved to stand next to him. But still he did not look up or make a sound.

'Harry Spencer, are you going to talk to me or shall I just go home?'

'I'm no use to anyone,' he said flatly. 'I'll never be able to go dancing again.'

'Of course you will. Your mam says you're getting your leg next week. Aren't you pleased?'

'It won't work. It'd have been better if I'd—'

'Don't you dare go any further, Harry Spencer. I won't have it. You'll get your leg next week and you'll practise walking on it until you can move properly.'

'How would you know what'll be possible?'

'Because there's a chap who's just gone to train at the Institute. We still keep in touch with some of the people there. He lost his right leg and he's got an artificial one.'

Now Harry looked up. 'He's working? Actually working?'

'He certainly is from what I hear. Oh, I admit they've found him a sitting-down job.' It was better to be perfectly honest with him, Molly decided. 'Because to stand all day would put too much pressure on his stump. But that's the only concession they've made. He does a proper job and works the same hours as everyone else. So, let's have no more talk that you won't be able to do this or that.' She bent closer so that her eyes were level with his. 'You'll be able to do whatever you set your mind to, or I'll want to know the reason why.'

Slowly, a smile spread across his face. 'Oh Molly. What would I do without you?'

'You'd sit here wallowing in self-pity, I've no doubt. But I'm not going to let you. So, when you go next week about your leg, you'll listen carefully to what they tell you and you'll do exactly as they say.'

Now, he was actually laughing. 'Yes, miss. You're just like that teacher we had at school. All you need is a cane in your hand.'

'Oh, I know the one you mean. She used to cane the boys on their backsides and the girls on their hands. I couldn't write for two days one time after she'd given me three strokes.'

'You? Got the cane? I don't believe it. Whatever had you done?'

Molly wriggled her shoulders and glanced away. 'It – it was someone else, but I got the blame.'

Softly, he said, 'And that someone else didn't own up?'

Molly bit her lip and shook her head. She refused to say any more but Harry had a shrewd idea just who that 'someone else' might have been. Softly, he whispered, 'Seems like it became a habit.'

'What did you say?'

'Oh, nothing. Nothing that matters now.' He reached out and took her hand. 'So, do you think you'd be able to recommend me for training at the Institute?'

They were laughing together as Harriet came into the room carrying a tray of tea and biscuits.

'Now, that's better. See what I mean, Molly? You're the only one who seems to be able to drag him out of these dark moods he gets.'

Harry sighed deeply. 'I'm sorry, Mam. I know I'm being difficult. It's only when I remember the shelling, the gunfire, the terrible fear in the pit of my stomach when I was moving up to the front line, knowing exactly what I was going to have to face. And then losing Ben. I tried to look after him, Mam . . .'

'I know you did, son, but standing right next to him probably wasn't a good idea. We might have lost the both of you. I heard you telling Tom that he and William shouldn't stand together.'

'Yes,' Harry said. 'I did because we've learned that the hard way, haven't we?'

The fitting of Harry's artificial leg went remarkably well. With the advice of the doctors, nurses, his parents and with Molly's encouragement, which everyone agreed was little short of bullying, he was soon walking well.

'You don't need a stick, Harry,' Molly told him firmly as she walked beside him along the street for the first time.

'The doctors said . . .'

'Never mind what they said. Alfie at the Institute doesn't use a stick, so you're not going to either.' She glanced around. 'Now, just look at all the neighbours coming out to wish you well.'

Indeed, doors were opening and busy housewives were pausing in their daily routine to cheer Harry on his way.

'That's the spirit, Harry.'

'We're all so proud of you.'

'Good to see you standing tall again, Harry.'

'You're still the best-looking chap in the street. Keep going.'

Harry grinned and waved to them all. Each and every one of them had been to see him since he'd come home, but now they were so delighted to see him out and about again.

When they got back home, Harry's face was grey with fatigue, but he was triumphant. 'I couldn't have done it without you, Molly. You've made me feel whole again.' He smiled. 'Well, nearly.'

'You've done it yourself, Harry. All you needed was a gentle push.'

He burst into laughter. 'Not so gentle, sometimes.'

Molly smiled ruefully as she was forced to agree. 'Well, that's true, I suppose.'

He was gazing at her. 'I liked walking down the road with you at my side, Molly. I know I have no right to ask, not now, but – but would you be my girl? I'll quite understand if you say "no". I'm not the fella I once was and many will still call me a cripple.'

Molly was staring at him open-mouthed. They were the words she had longed to hear for so long yet, now, they had a hollow ring. Colour flooded her face. At last, she said, 'I think perhaps it's time for complete honesty between us. I've loved you, Harry Spencer, for as long as I can remember, certainly since I was about eleven and you used to pull my pigtails. I know I'm not beautiful – not even pretty – but I will not be second-best now to Queenie. I will always be your friend. I'll still come to see you and make sure you're doing what the doctors tell you, but no. My pride won't let me say "yes", even though with all my heart I wish I could.'

Molly turned and fled from the room before he should see her tears. She rushed past Harriet without a word and ran all the way home before she collapsed sobbing against her mother's shoulder.

Forty-eight

Molly dragged herself to work over the next two weeks, but she couldn't bring herself to go round to the Spencers' house. She lost weight and was tired all the time. Finally, her mother said, 'I shall get our doctor to you, if you don't improve soon. You're not right, Molly.'

But Molly's visitor on Sunday morning was Queenie.

'Can you come out for a walk, Moll?'

'I don't feel well. We'll just stay here, if you don't mind.'

Queenie eyed her. 'You do look a bit peaky. I'm glad I decided not to do war work if that's what it does to you. Anyway, can we go up to your room? I need to talk to you.'

'We're all right down here. Mam and Dad have gone to church.'

'Oh. Right.'

Queenie sat down in Ron's chair. 'So, I've heard you've been visiting Harry every spare moment you get?'

'He needs company and most of his mates have gone to war. But why should it bother you? It's over between you, isn't it?'

'No, it most certainly is not. So I don't want you visiting my fiancé anymore.'

Molly gaped at her as Queenie went on with a smug smile. 'I'm going to go round and see him and explain why I couldn't visit. I was so devastated and heartbroken at his injury, that I couldn't bear to see him hurt. He'll understand, I know he will. But I've heard that now he's up on his feet, he looks almost normal.' She put her head on one side and simpered. 'He's quite the hero, isn't he? There's to be a piece about him in the local newspaper and they might ask me to be pictured with him. You know, his loyal fiancée standing by him and all that.'

'Why don't you tell me the truth, Queenie,' Molly said, as the headache she'd had for two days worsened. 'First, you say you've finished with him, then that you're back together. But Harry tells a different story. He says he hasn't seen you at all. One of you is lying to me. So who is it?'

Queenie smiled. 'He's being kind to you, Moll. He feels sorry for you now he knows how you really feel about him. "I'll let her down lightly," he said.'

Molly felt sick. She was too tired to argue any more. Perhaps Queenie was telling the truth, because how did she know that Harry knew how Molly felt about him? She'd told him herself, hadn't she, in an unguarded moment, and he must have told Queenie. But why . . .? Molly put her hand to her head, feeling dizzy. She really couldn't take any more. She felt so ill. Tears welled in her eyes but she was determined that Queenie should not see her cry. She pressed her fingernails into the palm of her hand.

'Then I wish you both every happiness,' she managed to say surprisingly steadily.

Queenie didn't stay any longer and when she had gone, Molly dragged herself upstairs and got back into bed. And that was where Mabel found her an hour later, her head buried beneath the bedclothes and sobbing as if her heart would break.

Mabel gathered her into her arms and held her close, rocking her gently.

'I'm getting the doctor to call tomorrow and I won't take "no" for an answer.'

'It's not that, Mam. Queenie's been round while you were at church. She's adamant that they're back together and – and . . .' Her voice rose as she broke into fresh tears.

'Aw, love. I'm so sorry. But I'm going to insist you have the doctor visit. You've lost such a lot of weight. I'm really worried about you and your dad agrees.'

Too exhausted to argue any more, Molly nodded and sank back against the pillows.

The doctor called the following day. He was a middle-aged, friendly man with a kindly bedside manner.

'She's just worn out, Mrs Wyngate,' he told Mabel downstairs when he had examined Molly. 'But there's nothing seriously wrong that a couple weeks' bedrest, followed by plenty of fresh air and good food for a further two weeks, won't put right. The work she's doing is vital, I know, but I can't let it undermine my patients' health to this extent.' He looked sternly at Mabel. 'She's not to attempt to go back to work until I say so, Mrs Wyngate.'

'We'll do exactly as you advise, doctor. You have my word.'

Three days after the doctor's call, Harriet knocked on the back door.

'Mabel, Molly hasn't been round to see Harry recently. We thought she was busy at work, but now we hear she is ill and you've had the doctor.'

In the terraced streets, where money to pay for medical attention was tight, a house call by a doctor was a serious matter.

Mabel sighed but opened her door wider in invitation for Harriet to step inside. 'I expect Queenie's told you, has she?'

'No, she's not said anything. She's been round – came last week. Took her all this time to come near him. But Harry's seen right through her. He sent her away with a flea in her ear.'

Mabel gaped at her. 'You – you mean they're not back together?'

'Most definitely not. And I, for one, am extremely pleased.'

'She's been round here telling Molly that they're back together. That they're engaged and that Harry's to have his picture in the paper and her standing with him as his "loyal fiancée".'

Harriet snorted. 'The only bit that's true is that, yes, the local paper do want to do a piece about him. After so much loss and sadness, they want to have an uplifting story of Harry's bravery and how he's rebuilding his life after such an injury.'

'Molly's in bits.'

'Is she? Last time she came round, she flew past

me out of the house without saying cheerio, and Harry wouldn't tell me what had happened between them.' Harriet regarded Mabel closely. 'I can see you know something, but I wouldn't expect you to break your daughter's confidence. Look, I'll get Harry to come round. Would she see him?'

'She's quite ill in bed.'

'Oh my! Is it serious? Molly's not one to give up easily. I know that.'

'The doctor says not. She's just exhausted from the work she's been doing.'

'I'll tell Harry. I don't know what's gone on between them, but it's high time this was sorted out. I'm very fond of Molly, you know, Mabel.'

At last Molly fell into a deep, but troubled, sleep. She tossed and turned and only woke now and again to take a drink from the cup her mother held to her lips. Day passed into night and back into day again and she was barely aware of people coming into her bedroom, sitting by the bed for a while and then leaving.

On the morning of the third day, she awoke feeling better. She no longer had a fever and felt calmer. She became aware of someone sitting beside her bed and turned her head.

'Harry,' she whispered croakily. 'Am I dreaming?'

'No. It's really me.' He took her hand. 'But I think you have been having some nasty nightmares.'

'What are you doing here?'

'I'm here to make sure you get well.' He chuckled,

relieved to see her looking so much better. 'I'm here to do a bit of bullying myself now.'

'How did you get here?'

'I walked.'

'All that way?'

'It's not so far when the person you want to be with is at the other end of the journey.'

Her eyes filled with easy tears. 'Oh Harry. You shouldn't be here . . .'

'Your mam doesn't mind.'

'No, no, I don't mean that. Your fiancée won't like it.'

'My what? Who on earth could that be?'

'Queenie, of course.'

For a brief moment anger flashed in his eyes. 'And where did you get that foolish idea from?'

'From her. She came round the other day – oh, perhaps it's longer than that now. I don't know how long I've been – well – out of it. But she said you'd made it up and that you were engaged.'

'You really have been having nightmares.'

'No, no, I didn't dream it. I know I didn't. Ask Mam. She'll tell you.'

Softly, he said, 'She already has. Darling Molly, it's just not true. I hadn't seen Queenie since the time I was last home on leave and before I was wounded. And yes, she has been round to try to make up, but I sent her packing.'

'You – you did?'

'I most certainly did. I don't like schemers and liars.'

'What? What d'you mean?'

'I became suspicious of her quite some time back.'

'Suspicious of her – what about?'

'Putting white feathers through our letterboxes.'

'Why did you think that was Queenie?'

'Tom knew who it was. He'd seen the person that night putting envelopes through our doors.'

'I know, but he wouldn't tell us who it was, would he?'

'No, and that made me think it was someone we all knew and also someone that, to know their identity, might hurt one of us. That could really only be you or Queenie and he was adamant that it was not you.'

'But you haven't got proof, have you?'

'I've got as much as I need. Besides, there are other things. The fact that she picks you up and drops you as a friend whenever she feels like it. The fact that she hasn't undertaken any form of war work. She's content to stay in her nice little genteel job in a draper's shop safely out of harm's way. And, most of all, if I'm honest, she hasn't stood by me since my injury. She's not the girl I thought she was and – she's not the girl for me.'

'But do you still love her?' Molly whispered.

'No, Molly. What I felt for her was infatuation – a pretty face and a lively, fun-loving nature. But she's not the girl I want to marry and spend the rest of my life with. Not the girl I want to be the mother of my children. We're not out of this war yet. All sorts of things can happen. There's still a long way to go. So, we've got to grab our happiness where we can.'

He leaned forward and raised her hand to his lips. 'So, Molly Wyngate, from now on you can consider yourself my girl and, this time, I won't take "no" for an answer.'

Forty-nine

Molly recovered well and returned to her work. She was happier than she could ever remember being in her life, but she and Harry decided to take things slowly. He had made enquiries about enrolling on a course at the Technical Institute, but before he could start there, Pete Mason called one evening.

'The foreman asked me to come and see you, Harry. They're keen to interview you about re-employing you. They asked me to tell you as they thought it would come better from me than from your dad. No one wants you to feel it's favouritism. They're keen to help disabled soldiers if they can,' Pete told him, 'and you're remembered as a skilled worker. They want to help you.'

In May of 1917 Harry returned to his old place of work. The loss of his leg now became just a nuisance to be surmounted, but the nightmares of his time at the Front would take much longer to heal – if they ever would.

The war ground on through 1917. News came of the dreadful battle at Passchendaele. William and Tom both wrote home to tell their families of the awful conditions. How soldiers, horses and equipment were lost in the mud without even a shot being fired by the enemy. Their families' anxiety grew. It stayed with each and every one of them through their waking hours, like a leaden weight in the pit of their stomachs. Nights were hardly better when they woke at three in the morning with a start, wondering if the next day would bring bad news.

And it's the summer too, Tom wrote to Molly in exasperation, *you'd expect this sort of weather in winter, but not in August!*

There was always hope that the war would end soon, but by the beginning of 1918 it was still raging and the German General Ludendorff had planned a series of spring offensives.

'Well, I see this as a last-ditch effort,' Jack remarked.

'I think you're right, but they're still inflicting a lot of damage and loss of life. Why can't they realize they can never win?' Luke said. 'Not now that we have the Americans on our side.'

'They just don't like the taste of defeat.'

'So, because of their pride, we have to go on losing fine young men, on both sides.'

'That's about the size of it.'

'By the way,' Jack said. 'I've got a bit of news, but I think Ethel's going to see Mabel tonight to tell her and Molly. It's about Queenie.'

The other two exchanged a glance and then looked at their friend.

'Nothing wrong, I hope,' Luke said.

Jack shrugged. 'It depends how you look at it. I don't agree with it myself, but—' He took a deep breath and began to explain.

Queenie never visited the Wyngates now, but at the same time that Jack was sharing the news with his mates, her mother knocked on the back door of their home.

'Ethel,' Mabel said, deliberately making her tone welcoming. 'This is a nice surprise. Do come in.'

'I've come to tell you and Molly something. Is she in?'

'Er, no – not at the moment.'

'Round with Harry, I expect. It's all right . . .' Ethel put up her hand as if to stall any comment. 'I've not come to fall out with you over that. In fact,' she went on as she settled herself near the range, 'I was pleased when it was finally all over between him and our Queenie, if you want the truth. I thought she could do better for herself. I never thought he'd amount to much anyway, and how's he going to support a wife and family now? For a while after he came home I thought she might be rekindling the flame, so to speak, but I'm pleased she came to her senses and decided to end it once and for all.'

This wasn't the version that Mabel had heard but she kept quiet.

'No, what I've come to tell you,' Ethel went on without waiting for Mabel to make any comment, 'is that Queenie has found herself a lovely new job. It's in Griffin and Spalding in Nottingham, in the dress and silks department. It's a real step up from what she's been doing here. Mr Gilmore's shop was all very well for a start, but Queenie deserves better. She's ambitious and I want to see her do well. I'm sure one day she'll get married, but this war has changed everything, hasn't it? It's taken the cream of society's young men with their officers' way of leading from the front. All very admirable, I'm sure, but where does it leave our girls? Without suitable husbands, that's where.'

Mabel stared at her friend. She had always known that Ethel aspired to better herself and her family, but she had never thought that she was an out and out snob.

'That sounds nice,' was all the enthusiasm Mabel could muster. Here was her own daughter, making herself ill trying to help the war effort, and Queenie was carrying on with the life she wanted to build for herself without a thought for the greater good. 'So, will she travel every day?'

'Oh no, I shall find some nice lodgings for her and she'll come home on a Sunday to see us.'

'You'll miss her,' Mabel found the empathy within her to say. She knew how much she would have missed Molly if she'd gone away to work in a munitions factory, which they had all thought at one time might happen.

'Of course I will, but it'll be such an opportunity for her. She'll meet such a nice class of people.' Ethel leaned forward as if imparting a confidence. 'I've almost persuaded Jack to look for work in Nottingham. If he does, we shall move there and then she can live at home again.' On and on Ethel droned for half an hour until she looked up at the bracket clock on Mabel's mantelpiece. 'Well, I must go. Jack's tea won't cook itself.'

Mabel stood up to see her friend out. 'Has Queenie learned to cook if she's to live on her own – at least for a while?'

'Oh no. I shall find lodgings for her where it's all-in. There'll be plenty of time for her to learn all that when she finds herself a suitable young man and gets married.'

Ethel had already stepped across the threshold and was about to head home when she said, 'Oh, and how is Molly now? I heard she'd been ill a while back.'

'She's a lot better, thank you. She'd been working too hard.'

'Well, I'm surprised you ever let her do that training, Mabel. I wouldn't have let Queenie do something like that, even if she'd wanted to.'

As she closed the door behind her erstwhile friend, Mabel was shrewd enough to think, well, I don't think I'll be seeing much of you in the future. Not if Queenie's going up in the world and you're going to try to follow her to Nottingham, because, if I know you, poor Jack won't stand a chance of refusing. With women like Ethel, who needed to be a suffragette to get their own way, she thought wryly. She just hoped that the friendship between Molly and Olive would endure. She really liked the girl and her mother, Ruby. And Pete Mason, she'd heard, was still joining the other three menfolk regularly on Saturday evenings in the pub. She just hoped that Jack would continue to meet up with them, unless, of course, she thought wryly, Ethel put a stop to it or until they did move. She sighed as she thought back across the years of friendship she'd shared with Ethel. They'd been good friends, as had their daughters, but times changed. Girls grew up and mothers grew more ambitious for their offspring. At least, Ethel did. Mabel just wanted her daughter to be happy and her son home safely and unhurt.

Well, the first of her wishes looked like it was coming true. As for the second – if only this dreadful war would end and William came home, Mabel's life would be perfect. She didn't ask to 'go up in the world'. She just wanted all her family fit and well and together once again. In the meantime, the war staggered on through the spring.

'It's this fella Ludendorff. He seems hell-bent on last-ditch efforts . . .' In late March, Jack repeated his earlier prediction to his mates.

'He's had that many, he'll run out of ditches soon,' Luke quipped.

'I wish he would,' Ron said, with a heartfelt plea.

'I think it's because Russia's no longer in the war,' Luke said. 'He's been able to move all his troops from there to the Western front. More's the pity.'

'I think,' Pete put in, 'he's wanting to gain ground before the Americans get a real foothold.'

'I think you're right there, Pete.' Luke nodded his agreement. 'He must be fearful of their might once they get going.'

'Have you read about this huge offensive he's

launched along a forty-mile front? It says here,' Ron said, jabbing his finger at the paper he held, 'it's a bid for a decisive victory.'

'I'm surprised they name the places where they are,' Pete said. 'You wouldn't think they'd be allowed to do that, would you? The papers, I mean. Our boys get their letters heavily censored.'

'I suppose *where* the fighting is actually taking place can't be hidden,' Jack said. 'What they really don't want is the enemy to find out what's being planned. I suppose if the lads write home and tell us where they are and what they're doing, it might give the enemy a clue to what's coming up.'

The other three nodded agreement with his reasoning, though none of them were sure he was right.

'It's going to be an onslaught,' Ron said gloomily.

'I've got a bit of good news for a change,' Mabel greeted Molly when she arrived home one evening in April. 'I've had a letter from Miss Anstruther.'

'That's nice, Mam. Is she well?'

'Very, by the sound of it. She's still abroad nursing but she's written to tell me that something called the Representation of the People Act has been passed by Parliament.'

Molly frowned. 'What does that mean?'

'It means,' Mabel went on, a huge grin on her face, 'that women will get the vote. Well, some of them anyway, if they meet certain – what's the word . . .' She searched Betsy's letter again. 'Ah, yes, here it is. Certain criteria.'

'And what's that? I bet it won't apply to the likes of me.'

'It will in time, Molly, love. You'll have to be over thirty and married to a householder . . .'

'Are you sure, Mam?'

'It's what Betsy says. Here, read her letter for yourself. And she thinks that eventually it'll be granted to all women, no matter what their circumstances are. So, you see, Molly, love, you've helped to bring that about. I'm very proud of you.'

As she read the letter, Molly chuckled. 'I wonder what William is going to say to this.'

Mabel laughed too. 'He'll be fine about it. Thank goodness for Louise, that's all I can say.'

Between April and July the enemy launched more major offensives with some success, but each advance stretched their resources, as they struggled to replace equipment and weapons, to say nothing of the many men they had lost. Rumour was rife among the Allies that their enemy were sending seventeen-year-old conscripts – and possibly even younger boys – to the front.

It doesn't look as if we're going to get any more leave to be able to get home for a while. We've all got a feeling of anticipation but we don't know why. It's as if something is going to happen but we don't know what, William wrote to his family in the summer, and Tom wrote much the same thing to both Molly and Olive.

When Pete entered the pub on the second Saturday evening in August, the chatter seemed louder than ever. He glanced across to where his three friends always sat. Ron was on his feet waving a newspaper excitedly.

'The German army has collapsed. It's all here,' he shouted. 'There was a huge battle near Amiens on the eighth and a concerted effort by all the Allies – well, a lot of them, anyway . . .'

'From what I've read,' Jack butted in, 'it was an attack planned by the Australian and Canadian troops but with British support. It was, the papers say, "a stunning victory".'

'Ludendorff's called it "the black day of the German Army",' Luke said. 'Surely this must mean the end for them.'

Pete sat down and reached across for the paper to read the item for himself. 'It certainly sounds a possibility.' He glanced up at Ron, who, among them, was the only one to still have a boy at the front. 'Do you know where William and Tom are now?'

Although he hadn't intended it, his remark took the joy from Ron's face.

Of course, although the enemy were now on the defensive and being driven back, it took another three months before they were ready to capitulate. There was rejoicing in the streets up and down the country.

'The ironic thing is,' Pete said, 'the Canadians captured Mons just before the ceasefire.'

'The place where it all started, you mean?' Jack said.

Pete nodded and sighed. 'What a terrible waste of

life, just to end up more or less where we were at the beginning.'

Ron sat silently, twirling the glass of beer on the table in front of him.

They hadn't had a letter from William for six weeks and Molly had heard nothing from Tom either.

Fifty

'I just don't feel like celebrating,' Mabel said, on the day the war officially ended.

'There's dancing in the streets, and factories and shops are closing in towns and cities up and down the country,' Ron said. 'Look how early I'm home. Where's Molly?'

'Gone round to see Harry. She wants to sit quietly with him and his mam and dad. They're all thankful it's over – of course they are – but it can't bring poor Ben back, can it?'

'But you can't blame people for wanting to let their hair down a bit. There's cause for joy, too, Mabel. No more loss of life.'

'I know and I expect parties are happening in the town just like everywhere else.' She gestured with her head. 'There's a bit of a shindig going on down at the end of our street, but I can't bring myself to join in. All I feel is a great sadness.'

Ron eyed his wife shrewdly. 'It's because we haven't heard from William and Tom, isn't it? That's what's holding you back.'

Mabel nodded and tears threatened to fall. 'If only we could hear something, Ron. It's the not knowing that's so awful. We've had four long years of worry and I'm so tired of it. So very tired.'

Ron sat next to her and put his arm around her shoulders. 'Come on, old girl, buck up. You've been the strong one through all this. Don't give way now.'

Mabel rested her head on his shoulder, but there was a small smile on her mouth as she said, 'Not so much of the "old", thank you very much, Ron Wyngate.'

There was a long silence between them until Ron asked quietly, 'Are you missing Ethel? I know things are very different between you now. And with Molly and Queenie too. That friendship seems to have ended, but what about yours and Ethel's?'

'I think it's been dying for a number of years, if I'm honest. Ever since the girls grew up and Ethel started having fancy ambitions for her daughter. We want different things for our girls.'

'Now, I'm going to ask you summat, Mabel, love, but I'm not asking you to betray confidences. Was there ever anything between Molly and Ben?'

'Only friendship, like she's always said.'

'And you know that because . . .?'

Mabel was quiet for a moment. Keeping a confidence was so ingrained in her that even now, when it no longer mattered, she still hesitated to break it.

'Because Molly, bless her, always carried a torch for Harry.'

'Ah,' Ron said with a heartfelt sigh. 'Now it all makes sense. But Queenie, being the prettier one of the two, got her man, did she?'

Mabel let out one of her famous snorts of derision.

'Pretty, is she? Well, pretty is as pretty does, in my humble opinion. I've had my suspicions about her for years, but I couldn't prove anything. I still can't. But to my mind she's manipulative and devious. I think it was her that poured ink into the pillar box and later set fire to it and knowingly let the blame fall on Molly. I'm loathe to say it, but I'm sure she tells deliberate lies. All that nonsense about going down south to see the boys off. From what they told us, they left in the middle of the night with no cheering crowds. I also think it was her who delivered those white feathers, because I know it wasn't our Molly. I'd stake my life on it.'

'But – William didn't get a feather.'

'Exactly. Queenie's clever. She would think that by *not* giving William one, folks would more readily believe it was Molly who'd handed them out to the other lads, but wouldn't give one to her own brother.'

Ron was silent for some time before saying, 'Do you think Queenie knew that Molly – um – liked Harry?'

'Molly never told anyone apart from me that I know of, but maybe Queenie just wanted to be top dog and snare the best-looking lad in the neighbourhood, because you have to agree he was. Still is, for that matter.'

'He had a bit of a reputation at that time where the girls were concerned, didn't he?'

Mabel laughed. 'He did, but I think it was just that. A reputation. He walked out with one or two girls but, according to Harriet, there was no one serious until Queenie got her claws into him.'

'Did Harriet like Queenie?'

'No.' Mabel's reply was swift and decisive. 'She didn't.' Then she smiled as she added, softly, 'She's always liked our Molly.'

At that moment, they heard the back door open. 'Mam! Dad! Where are you?'

Mabel lifted her head and stared at Ron with wide eyes as she whispered, 'That's Molly. Oh no! Don't say . . .'

Ron patted her hand and stood up. 'In here, love,' he called, just as the door into the kitchen burst open and Molly almost fell into the room. Her face was wreathed in smiles, her eyes afire with joy.

'They're safe. They're both safe. William and Tom. They're not hurt in any way and they're coming home.'

'Oh Molly – Molly,' Mabel cried and now tears of relief flooded down her face. She stood up and enfolded the girl into her outstretched arms.

When they'd all calmed down a little, Molly explained, 'Olive came round to see Mrs Mayberry. She'd had a letter from Tom and wanted to be sure his mam had got one too. Then they both came across the road to tell us. He wrote to them last week. They were together – him and William – behind the lines and in comparative safety. By that time, everyone knew it was coming to an end anyway. They just didn't know exactly when.'

'Did Tom say when they might come home?'

'No. He says it'll take some time to get everyone back home, but he thinks that as they were two of the very first to go, maybe they'll be some of the first to be allowed to come home.'

'That sounds fair. Let's hope he's right,' Ron said.

'Oh Ron – Ron . . .' For a moment Mabel rested her face against his shoulder. She didn't often give way to tears, but these were of relief.

'There, there, love. It's all over now and we can all begin to look forward.' He smiled at Molly. 'When you go back to Harry's, be sure to tell Mrs Mayberry and Olive how delighted we are.'

It was good to know, Ron thought, that Olive now had a future with Tom too. If the war had done one good thing, it had seen him grow and mature into a fine young man. And his own son as well had been altered for the better, Ron believed. William had seen more of the world and had lost some of his bigoted ideas, and he too could now plan a future. Perhaps with the nurse called Louise. Molly's future was already settled with Harry. It wouldn't be an easy life, but it was what she wanted and both sets of parents would always be on hand. They would all feel the scars of this war for years to come and the grieving for those they'd lost would never truly end. But, now, for those who were left, there was at least hope.

At that moment, laughter and music from the street filtered in through the open door.

'Mrs Spencer has asked us all to go round to theirs. Mrs Mayberry is already there and Olive has gone to fetch her parents too. She said,' Molly added hesitantly, 'that Ben would be the first to want us all to celebrate. Do come, Mam.'

Mabel and Ron looked at each other. 'Whatever you want, love,' he said.

Mabel dried her tears and smiled. 'Yes, they're right. We should be with our friends on a day like this.'

As they went out, Molly glanced down the street. Beyond the Palmers' house, neighbours were gathering in the road. A table had been set up and the women were bringing out drinks and food for everyone to share. Someone was playing a mouth organ and a couple were already dancing. Laughter and singing echoed along the street. But there was no sign of the Palmers and their front door remained firmly closed.

'Do you want to join our neighbours, Mam, or . . .?'

'No, no, we'll go round to Harriet's.'

As the three of them began to walk up the street, Molly glanced wistfully towards Queenie's home. They'd had some good times together – a lot of them – but things had changed now.

As if reading her thoughts, Mabel put her arm through her daughter's and said, 'Don't you fret about her, love. They'll be leaving here soon, if Ethel gets her way.'

'Yes, Mam,' Molly said with a wide smile. Resolutely, she lifted her head and looked towards the future. She was ready to celebrate.

Acknowledgements

As always, this is a work of fiction, but I do a great deal of research to try to get the background details as accurate as possible. I am always very grateful to everyone who kindly shares their knowledge and expertise with me.

My sincere thanks to Kathy Phillips, Chairman, Loughborough Library Local Studies Volunteer Group and Sharon Gray, Treasurer, Loughborough Library Local Studies Volunteer Group for their interest and help.

Special thanks to Mel Gould, Chair of Trustees, Loughborough Carillon War Memorial Museum, who recommended that I should read *The Tigers, 6th, 7th, 8th & 9th (Service) Battalions of the Leicestershire Regiment* by Matthew Richardson (Pen & Sword Books Limited, Barnsley, LEO COOPER (2000)). This was an enormous help and a superb tribute to the men of those battalions.

My grateful thanks to Chris Pickford, Archivist, Loughborough Bellfoundry Trust, for his very helpful answers to my specific questions and recommending the book *Master of My Art, The Taylor Bellfoundries*

1784-1987 by Trevor S. Jennings (John Taylor and Company (Bellfounders) Ltd., 1987).

Thank you to Gary Harden, a guide at Taylor's Bellfoundry, who took me on a very interesting and helpful tour.

Other sources have included:

Fifty Good Men and True by Michael Kendrick (Michael Kendrick, 2005).

Loughborough Markets and Fairs 1221-2021 Researched and presented by Loughborough Library Local Studies Volunteer Group. Edited by Kathy Phillips. A Loughborough Library Local Studies Volunteer Group Publication (2022)

Suffragettes in Loughborough by Mike Shuker. (Mike Shuker for Leicestershire Labour History Society)

My love and grateful thanks to Helen Lawton and Pauline Griggs for reading and commenting on the early draft, and as always to my wonderful agent, Darley Anderson and his team, and to my lovely editor, Maddie Thornham, and all the fabulous team at Pan Macmillan.

No Greater Love
By Margaret Dickinson

Home is where the heart is . . .

Derbyshire, 1904. After a family tragedy and a broken engagement, Lady Elizabeth Ingham seeks employment by training to be a nanny. Known only as Lizzie, she secures a post at Alstone-in-the-Dale Manor caring for a four-year-old boy, Charlie.

When Lizzie arrives at the manor, she is appalled at Charlie's condition. He does not speak, but screams and kicks. The family and staff are at their wits' end and no one expects Lizzie to stay long.

But with patience and love, Lizzie soon brings a change and the attitude of the staff towards her alters. As Charlie gradually improves, Lizzie begins to feel at home at the manor, and new love enters her life when she meets the master of the house's brother.

But as the First World War looms and young men from the village begin to enlist, can Lizzie's new-found happiness withstand the hardships of war?

A Mother's Sorrow

By Margaret Dickinson

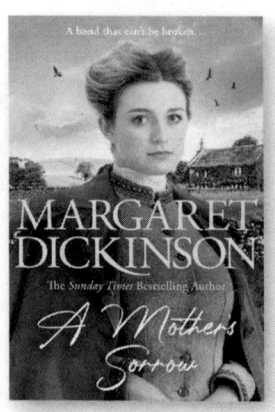

*Three young women. Two families united.
A bond that can't be broken . . .*

Sheffield, 1892. Patrick Halliday rules his family with a rod of iron. He's hard on both his wife and his elder daughter, Flora, but he spoils his youngest, Mary Ellen, because she reminds him of his beloved mother.

When Mary Ellen, aged seventeen, finds that she is pregnant, Patrick throws her out of the family home, and Flora goes with her. After wandering the Derbyshire countryside for miles, they find shelter on a farm, working for their keep.

When Flora must return to her job as a buffer girl in Sheffield's cutlery trade, she is reunited with her friend, Evelyn Bonsor. As both young women find love and fall pregnant, the Halliday and Bonsor families are united, despite the many trials that cross their paths.

Then comes the Great War. Through hardship and tragedy, these two families must stick together to weather the storm . . .

The Poacher's Daughter

By Margaret Dickinson

'I'm going to live in that house, Dad.
One day, I'll be mistress of Thornsby Manor...'

1910, the Lincolnshire Wolds. Young Rosie Waterhouse lives with her father, Sam, well known as the local poacher, in a cottage on the Thornsby estate. The land is owned by William Ramsey, a harsh and heartless man who is determined his only son, Byron, should marry well and produce an heir.

Rosie is quick to learn the tricks of her father's trade and it's when she's poaching fish from the estate's stream that she meets Byron. As their friendship blossoms, they realize that they are destined to be together, but William will stop at nothing to ensure that they never meet again.

As the years pass and the threat of war becomes a reality, Sam is involved in a tragic incident that will affect both his and Rosie's lives more than they could ever have imagined. Life will never be the same in Thornsby, but will Rosie find the happiness she yearns for?